WHAT
WE
NEVER
SAY

by

Paulette Stout

First Edition: 2022

Edited by Miranda Darrow.
Cover Design by Rena Violet
Interior Design by Rena Violet.

ISBN 978-1-7366371-4-2 (eBook Edition)
ISBN 978-1-7366371-5-9 (Paperback Edition)

Library of Congress Control Number: 2022906809

Published by Media Goddess Inc.,
241 Arlington Street #814, Acton, MA 01720

Visit **paulettestout.com** for author information.

YOUR FREE EBOOK IS WAITING

Meet the hero of *What We Never Say*—before our heroine does.

Kyle's photography career is on the rise in Los Angeles, but he can't take his mind of his ex. Her betrayal still stings, even three years and 3,000 miles away. How can he make a fresh start when so much was left unsaid?
Get a free copy of the prequel:

Love Only Better: All About Kyle

paulettestout.com/free

For those seeking love, acceptance, and healing.
Know you'll find it.

Phone pressed to her ear, Rebecca wove through the crowded New York sidewalk, desperate to find a newsstand. The cool September breeze chilled the light perspiration evaporating off her skin as she walked. A sweater would have been perfect, but there hadn't been time. Whatever prompted her best friend to force her out of the house to buy a magazine better be good. Barbara was flipping her lid, and that's saying a lot for a lawyer known for keeping her calm in court.

Rebecca maneuvered around a woman bending over her navy stroller to pop a squeaky pacifier back into her baby's mouth. Barbara wouldn't quell so easily. "Some things must be seen to be believed," she said. But what things? What was she talking about?

Before Barbara yanked her from her lazy Saturday afternoon, Rebecca was elbow deep in an epic pruning session on her crinkly houseplants. Kyle, her boyfriend, loafed on the couch engrossed in a Yankees game. Now, Rebecca found herself weaving through Manhattan sidewalks looking like a harried tourist.

"How long does it take to get to a newsstand?" Barbara said.

"I'm practically running. The two newsstands I remembered are bike lanes now."

When had she last held a magazine? Cracked the spine to enjoy the glossy pages inside? Not since college. Back then, she bought GQ to hang pictures of hot guys on the ceiling over her bed. She'd lay in bed for hours, getting lost in their chiseled features and dreamy expressions. Too bad they were the closest she got to the male species at the time.

The crosswalk light blinked "DON'T WALK" as she arrived at the corner. A herd of taxis accelerated up the avenue, darting around slower vehicles and causing near catastrophes. Rebecca's prize stood across the street: a green metal shed covered in lattice work. Colorful magazines hung from clips on every topic imaginable. Fashion. Motor sports. Health. News. Commentary. Sudoku puzzles. But like the New York Times, they were waiflike shadows of their former beefy selves. As a kid, schlepping the Sunday Times home for her dad required a forklift. No more. Digital ruled, which made this panic stroll into the print realm that much more ridiculous.

Rebecca rubbed away the chill settling into her idle arms. "Can't you just tell me? What's this obsession with me buying MOD?"

"You must hold the magazine in your hands, and you'll be glad I'm with you when you do."

The "WALK" light flashed and Rebecca trotted across, spotting the pink cover of MOD among the other fashion titles. This special issue ballooned to three times the size of Vogue, with "Our Favorites" stamped across the cover. Rebecca handed her credit card to the guy and started flipping through the glossy title.

"What page?"

"The spread isn't numbered, but look three pages past 187."

"Way to make it easy."

"Hey, complain to the publisher. I'm only a patron. How else am I supposed to see which color is coming next season?"

"Be like every other New Yorker and wear black."

Barbara sighed. "We need to address your wardrobe, but that's a conversation for another day."

"When I make lawyer money like you, we can talk about my wardrobe." Rebecca pocketed her credit card and stepped away to lean on a car and flip while the next shopper bought a roll of peppermint Mentos and the New York Daily News.

Un-numbered pages with ads made it hard to find her reference pages, but soon 187 flashed by and three pages later...

Rebecca gasped.

It couldn't be. Was it— No. No way. She looked up for confirmation that she hadn't shifted to an alternate reality, but the surly man waiting to pay for gum gave her a nasty look. Yeah, same reality. The thumbs on the woman behind him flew so fast on her smartphone, Rebecca wanted to yank the device away. How could she text at a time like this? Rebecca's world just flipped upside down.

She reached for the solidness of the car behind her. If not for that, she would have swooned.

"THIS is why I needed to be with you," Barbara said from the phone cradled in her neck.

"How is this even possible?" Rebecca asked.

"I don't know how he got in MOD, but the story must be juicy as hell."

There he was. Kyle. Her Kyle. Her boyfriend who wore nothing but T-shirts and jeans, wrapped in a bulky cream sweater with chunky tan buttons. Instead of his trademark Fruit of the Loom, he wore a pricey outfit by designer Calvin Klein.

In the two-page spread, Kyle leaned against a barkless branch with the sharpest, longest thorns Rebecca had ever seen. Scary sharp. Had he gotten cut doing the pictures? What was she saying? Kyle's face splashed across the world's top fashion magazine looking like someone who belonged on a dorm room ceiling. His glossy dark hair, blue eyes, and tan skin silhouetted against a cloudless, blue sky. But none of it made any sense.

"What the hell is Kyle doing in *MOD*?"

"No clue, but go search for 'Kyle Dillon model' and prepare to be blown away."

Rebecca jammed the magazine under her arm and palmed her phone to search. Sure enough, Kyle's photo results page filled every tile. No random pics mixed in to test whether you were paying attention. All Kyle. Every one.

Magazine pictures.

Runway pictures.

Red carpet in a tux.

This was nuts.

"You still there?" Barbara asked.

"Barely," Rebecca answered. "How could he not have told me? This is so big. He must have modeled for what? Years?"

"He better have a good reason to keep something this big a secret," Barbara said.

Rebecca reopened the magazine. The picture dated from 11 years prior. Yet it ranked as a favorite. Kyle rated good enough for someone to put it in a roundup of favorite shots. Yet, he'd never mentioned being a model in the eight months they'd been dating and the three months they'd lived together.

But why?

Rebecca hung up and headed back to the apartment. What would she say to Kyle? What did it say about their relationship that he hadn't yet told her? The two of them bubbled along without incident since he moved in, all smiles and good times. But they obviously weren't as close as she had assumed.

"Ouch!" Rebecca yelled as she walked into a parking meter.

She looked around, but no one noticed. And why would they? She could lie dead in the middle of the street and distracted New Yorkers would step around her. They'd probably tell her to die somewhere more convenient next time. Lucky for them, confusion wasn't fatal. Though, in her case it might be.

Basketballs careened off the backboard of the courts in front of their apartment, sneaker squeaks echoing off the surrounding buildings. Her eyes found their third-floor apartment window. Inside, Kyle sat watching sports. Meanwhile, his face splashed across the pages of *MOD*.

She took a seat on a park bench.

In the eight months they'd been together, they'd been through a lot. When first together, Rebecca had secrets of her own. Shedding enough shame to come clean took time—but she did. Kyle now knew everything there was to know about 29-year-old Rebecca Sloane. Her warts, her crazy parents out on Long Island, her history of less than stellar bedroom performance. And he loved her anyway. Why didn't he trust her enough to share his past life?

So he modeled.

Big deal.

Actually, it was a hella big deal, but why the secrecy? Every time Rebecca tried to talk about Kyle's college years, he'd change the subject.

"There's nothing to tell," he'd say.

"My life is boring compared to most people."

"I'm going to hit the bathroom."

"Pass the salt."

He'd been a master evader. But the time for diversions was over. Barbara rightly said some things must be seen for yourself. Now that she had, there was no unseeing.

She stood up, exhaled the tension knotting her chest, and headed towards her lobby door.

2

The apartment door slammed, jarring Kyle out of his TV-induced stupor.

"You went out?" Kyle lowered his legs off the coffee table and sat up.

"Yeah."

He patted the sofa next to him for Rebecca to sit. "This pitcher's duel is amazing. We should get tickets and go before the season ends. Or maybe your dad can spot us a pair of his season tickets? It might even get your mom off his case for never going in person." He reached for his beer, wiping the bottle's dewy condensation on his jeans before taking a long swig.

Rebecca picked up the remote and shut off the TV.

"Hey! What did you do that for?" Kyle reached for the remote, but a magazine slammed down on top of it. A magazine open to a spread. His spread.

Kyle flipped the magazine closed, fanning the cloying smell of perfume ads in his face. His stomach churned. No amount of faux fragrance would mask the boatload of shit about to hit the fan.

"Why didn't you tell me? What reason could you have to keep this from me all this time?" Rebecca said.

Her dreamy pools of brown steeled in a way he'd never seen them. Like she'd stepped into a cage match and was waiting for a competitor to throttle.

Kyle opened his mouth to speak, but no words came. They got stuck somewhere between his bone-dry mouth and overactive brain, unable to compose a coherent thought. He'd only himself to blame. His past was bound to come seeping into their present sooner or later. It was a mistake to pretend it wouldn't. Infinite opportunities to tell her came and went. But none of that mattered now. Someone forced his hand. Or a specific someone, rather.

Rebecca's jaw flexed. "Well?"

"I'm so sorry. I just—I don't talk about it. To anyone."

"So your whole family knows, and Vivian? No one thought to mention it?"

"They wanted me to tell you myself, but even they don't know everything. Not really."

"I'm sorry, but this makes no sense. Why is this such a big secret?"

Kyle hung his head. Would he fit under the table?

"Please, look at me," she said.

"Must I?"

"Yes."

Thinking of his modeling days made his insides churn with a mix of anger, fear, and revulsion. The people, the fakery, the broken promises and shattered dreams. How could he make her understand?

Kyle's legs gave out as he rose, sending Rebecca lurching to steady him.

Recovering under her watchful gaze, he made his way to the kitchen where he turned on the faucet to splash his face.

Rebecca followed, standing at a distance in the doorway. "Whatever it is, you can tell me. I won't tell anyone, but you have to let me in."

Water dripped down his chin onto his shirt, the blue fabric

darkening into wet spots. Those marks would fade in an hour. He'd been waiting for his modeling scars to evaporate for eleven years.

He dried his face on a paper towel and tossed it in the trash before meeting her gaze.

"This summer, I shared the most intimate and painful secrets I had with you," she said. "I cried. You accepted me, faults and all. Why won't you trust me enough to do the same?"

He sighed. "I trust you. Of course I trust you."

"No. You don't. If you did, I wouldn't have learned about your past career from a magazine."

Silence hung as her eyes implored him on. She loved him. He knew that. So why was this so hard? Once he started talking, it all might all come tumbling out. The whole nasty pile of garbage. She would never look at him the same way once she knew.

"Ky? C'mon."

"Give me a minute," he said.

Kyle bent into the chill of the fridge, the cool air prickling his damp skin to attention. Awakening him from his long slumber. He could do this, but liquid courage was in order. Grabbing a brown bottle, he twisted off the bottle cap and downed three-quarters of the Sam Adams with long gulps before grabbing another. The fridge door swung shut and he returned to the sofa where Rebecca sat twirling her hair.

"I guess we should call this our confession couch?" he joked.

Rebecca pulsed an eyebrow. "Your turn this time."

Kyle nodded, downing the last of his first beer.

She reached over to rub his shoulder. "I'll try to be as understanding as you were with my bedroom challenges."

"*Past* bedroom challenges," Kyle said with a crooked smile.

When they first met, Rebecca harbored so much shame for her inability to climax in bed that she kept him at arm's length for months. But with help, and love, she worked it through, gaining so much confidence and empowerment that it overflowed into all areas of her life. He could use a dose of that positive mojo right about now.

"If I can admit that," Rebecca said, "you can share whatever you think is so terrible."

Their eyes met, but he looked away.

She crawled over, nudging into the crook of his arm. "It's just me."

I can do this.

So why can't I breathe?

"I don't want you to think less of me," he said.

"I would never. I love you. Just start at the beginning."

Kyle's heart was racing more than before his first show in Milan. That day, he nearly blacked out, or did technically, black out. After the show, he had no memory of walking down the runway, doing two wardrobe changes, and filing around for the end of show revue.

Here it goes...

"I was working as an apprentice to a photographer senior year in high school. One day on an industrial photo shoot, someone on the set worked for a modeling agency. She took candid pictures of me and circulated them to her modeling contacts. Apparently, scouting for male models was fierce."

Kyle paused, but her sweet smile urged him on.

"There was a flurry of interest in me. Four agents approached for representation. Four! I couldn't believe it. My dad checked them out, and all were legit. We took some pictures, and they came out great, so I signed with an agency."

"That's amazing! You must have been thrilled."

"I was. It wasn't anything I ever wanted, then suddenly, suddenly I wanted it more than anything. My parents were pissed, but I deferred college for a few years until I left modeling. That freed me to do all sorts of jobs, but once I got booked as an underwear model, that sort of stuck. Bookings rolled in, so that was my job: I modeled professionally."

Rebecca wore a broad smile, shaking her head in disbelief. "That's incredible. To think that I've been living with a model for all this time! This is crazy!"

Kyle's heart plummeted through the floor. Those words. Hearing those words come out of her mouth justified his instincts to keep this part of him hidden. "That's why I didn't tell you."

"What? What did I say?"

"You didn't even realize. But now that you know, I'm no longer 'Kyle your boyfriend.' I'm the 'male model'; an object. A thing."

Worry swept her face. "I'm so sorry, I didn't mean—"

"It's not your fault, but that's why I don't tell people. No one looks at me the same way once they find out. Especially that I did underwear? Christ. It's impossible not to look at me like a piece of meat and imagine me practically naked."

"Well, I don't need to imagine," she said with mischief in her eyes.

"Yeah, for you it's okay. But for everyone else? My clients? I can't have everyone knowing. There are colleagues in the industry who know, but the worst I get sometimes is a pair of underwear stuffed in my camera bag."

"No way?"

"Yes, way. Richie will do it, but not too many others."

She huffed a laugh before refocusing. "So what was it like? Was it fantastic?"

Kyle stood and walked to the window. Scenes from his past playing in his mind. "Sometimes, yes. It was an unreal dream. To be traveling around the world. Seeing places and meeting famous people… powerful people…"

He grabbed his head with both hands, turning away.

It always came back to it. To her. She was inextricably woven into his modeling experience. He couldn't talk about it without her hovering over him like a dark shadow he couldn't shake.

"Kyle? What's the matter?"

"I've never said this out loud. Not to anyone."

"Said what? Please, just tell me."

He squeezed his eyes shut, pulse throbbing. "I thought she had good intentions, but I was too young and stupid to know better."

"Who?"

"Someone powerful took an interest in me. I thought it was genuine. I thought she saw something good in me and wanted to help my career. One word from her and designers snapped to attention. They began calling to book me for runway shows and magazine shoots around the world. My family was super excited, and so was I…"

"It sounds like there's a but coming," Rebecca said.

"After a while, she wanted—expected—favors." As soon as Kyle spoke the words, he was back there. Back in her apartment. On the brown leather sofa with the animal print throw blanket that smelled like the imported coconut oil she rubbed on him before…

Then her voice was in his head, exiting through his mouth. "She said— Didn't I like her? Didn't I appreciate everything she'd done to get me ahead? Didn't I find her attractive? Didn't I feel lucky to have all the doors she'd opened for me? Did I want them all to close?"

Rebecca stood up and crossed the room to embrace Kyle from behind, but he flinched at her touch, stepping away.

"I didn't want the doors to close. Not by a long shot. So I gave in. I let her have me. It made her so happy, but I rotted inside. I'd rush home after and wash so hard I'd have red marks for days. I'd tell myself what we did was okay. I should be flattered. Right? I'm a guy. Why didn't I feel flattered?"

Rebecca's tears garbled her voice. "I'm so sorry. I'm so, so sorry." She turned him to face her, grabbing his shoulders. "This is not your fault. Do you hear me? It isn't."

"I let it go on for months. I let her help me get jobs. I'd get on set and they'd slather me with that same fucking coconut oil, and I'd want to throw up—but I had to look pretty. Sexy. Then, I'd get dressed and go with her to events. Everyone thought we were together. But we never were, Rebecca, I promise. Not really. I never wanted it, I swear. But once it started, I didn't know how to get out. She threatened to say I raped her if I told anyone."

"Oh, sweetie." She wrapped him in her arms, his head resting against hers.

He'd held it in for so long, having it out circulating in the air in the room filled it with a dark energy. Ghosts of his past packing the room, but they were out now. He'd told someone and didn't implode. Even better, he stood wrapped in the arms of a woman who loved him. Still.

Kyle inhaled Rebecca in. A mix of spice and floral shampoo as unique to her as much as the dark curls tickling his nose. He hugged her tight.

"I didn't know what to do."

"How did you get away?"

"It's fuzzy, but somehow that night I got drunk and took some pills. Her driver dropped me half-dead at an emergency room. I never heard from her again."

Rebecca said nothing. What could she say to a bombshell like that? But with soothing strokes to his back, she communicated more through touch than words could ever express. Her arms squeezed tight, willing her strength into him.

Salty tears ran into his mouth. Then, it was as if his whole body began crying, not just his eyes. It came from deep recesses, from the roots of his hair, from his muscles, from his fingertips, shuddering his body as sobs escaped. A decade of pain crumbling the fortress of stone he'd erected to keep it all in. Keep it contained. To forge ahead as if nothing happened.

As if it was okay.

But it wasn't.

It wasn't okay.

The touching.

The oils.

The total control.

Emotion crashed through Kyle in waves, as memories surfaced, then receded as an ocean of tears washed the tension away. Cleansing his shame. It kept coming and coming. Now that he'd started, he couldn't stop himself.

Rebecca held fast, stroking his head, saying he'd be okay.

Kyle wanted to believe her. He wanted to believe he could get past it all. To feel normal again. To feel as he did before it ever happened. To regain that lightness, that freedom of spirit that the cameras captured. But could he? Could he do it? Maybe. Maybe he could. The time had come for him to try.

3

Rebecca's sneakers pounded the asphalt the next morning as she ran. The half-mile loop surrounding the fountain and grassy green was a central gathering place at their apartment complex. Picnickers, sunbathers, and the daily yoga contingent vied for prime space in the shade on summer days. But this morning, all her thoughts gravitated to Kyle.

Her rational side wanted to pursue the abuser and bring her to justice. Yet her heart wanted to yank the abuser to the ground by her hair and smack her with a baseball bat. Or a stiletto. Or whatever coffee-table book the woman had lying around. She deserved to experience the same pain she'd inflicted on Kyle.

Rebecca pumped her arms in time with her stride. As she exhaled, the sensation of holding Kyle's heaving body came flooding back. His anguish ripped through her, raw and unfiltered. She shivered at the memory. The strain of holding the secret in for so long must have been unbearable. Now, she needed to jettison that toxic energy into the universe, never to return. And so did he. As much as she loved and supported him, Kyle needed a professional.

So he could heal.

So he could recover.

Kyle recognized it himself. Hopefully, his contact would know someone good he could speak to. Someone who had treated other victims…

Victim.

In a million guesses, she never would have labeled Kyle a victim. He was tall, strong, confident, and rode around on his black motorcycle like he was untouchable. Yet, her Adonis was human. And like all humans, he was very much touchable—including without his consent.

Rebecca passed a playground where a mom stood rapt while her little one fearlessly swung from the monkey bars. The woman would advance to assist her child before catching herself and drawing back to pocket her hands in a silent pantomime of active unease. Rebecca knew the feeling.

Lingering beneath the surface, there'd always been a persistent unease about Kyle. A nagging fog. Something just out of focus Rebecca was unable to identify or touch. She could never have predicted the cause would be so traumatic. If only Rebecca could reach back through time and throttle his abuser before it all started. The best she could do now was ensure he got the help he needed to recover. So he could be happy and whole. The road ahead would be difficult, yet it was a journey Kyle must take. After hiding it for so long, it remained to be seen whether he could successfully confront his demons. For his sake, and their future, she certainly hoped so.

Kyle watched the coffeemaker drip the pot full, head light, heart full. This must be what peace feels like. All those monks in the mountains of Nepal did know a few things about life. Feeling right in your skin. It was the first morning in forever he wasn't on edge, struggling to keep his inner thoughts inner.

But that was over now. Words had power and he no longer had to watch his, ever fearful he'd let something slip. No more pretending. No more fear Rebecca would find out and reject him. They were thankfully past that point and onto a new, closer chapter that looked bright.

The coffeemaker hissed its last puff of steam. Kyle filled an artesian mug, the clay's grainy surface carved into a broad smile with "Say cheese" painted across the teeth. It was a gift from his mentor and photography master, Marco.

Thoughts of Marco always led back to Jane. You can't lead photography at a juggernaut like MOD for 30 plus years and not become synonymous with the infamous woman who made it a household name. Kyle ignored her periodic texts and calls for years, especially recently. An issue like "Our Favorites" smelled like a desperate attempt to get his attention. But she'd be disappointed. Kyle had no plan to take Jane's bait, now or ever.

Stop it. Stop thinking about what she did.

But how?

Rebecca was right. He needed help. But it had to be someone with experience treating other models. Struggles in the limelight were beyond the comprehension of most, doctors included. If anyone would know the right person, it'd be Marco.

He checked the time, knowing regardless of the hour, Marco would likely be awake. An artist with a prolific career like his didn't sleep much. He answered almost immediately.

"Ah, my friend! It's been too long,"

"It has. It has indeed."

"I wondered when I'd be hearing from you. You saw the issue?"

"One picture."

"She insisted, but even if she didn't, I wouldn't think of publishing a favorites issue without your face gracing the pages. Stunning. You always were."

"You're too kind," Kyle said.

"And you, my friend, are missed. What are you up to?"

They caught up on Kyle's food photography business, his brief escape to California after his even-briefer engagement, and his return to New York to care for his Aunt Bessie. All of which led him to Rebecca.

"She sounds lovely. When will I meet her?" Marco asked.

"Soon, I promise. But, actually, I have a favor to ask."

"Anything."

How should he put it? "When models encounter... unwanted attention, and need to talk to someone, is there anyone good you can recommend?"

"Mmmm. Might I ask, is this for you?"

Kyle swallowed hard. Rebecca knew, but did that mean he must bare his soul to anyone who asked? Marco? His family? Where did the confessions stop? He'd only just admitted it to himself, out loud. Luckily, Marco's wisdom prevailed.

"Pardon, please. It's not my place to ask. Yes, I know someone good. Someone discrete who has worked with many of those in this circumstance."

Kyle exhaled the breath he was holding. "Thank you. Can you text me the information?"

"I will. And remember: some secrets are poison. Best to lance and flush out, so healing can begin, yes?" Marco said.

Truer words were never spoken.

Sun streamed through the panoramic windows behind Jane's desk. She brought her white coffee mug to her lips. She loved white. It was clean. Pure. Crisp. A blank slate to do with what she wished. Just how she liked it. Just as she liked the people who worked for her.

Less thinking.

More doing.

She thought enough for everyone. Why waste time with the vapid musings of those less experienced, less accomplished. She could think of nothing more tiresome. When she was younger and less experienced, she'd listen to their ramblings. Now, she knew the truth. Those moments were wasted, time she would never again recover.

Now, instead of standing mute waiting for the idiocy to stop, she merely silenced it with a tired glance and a wrist wave.

Her time was too precious.

Her eyelids drooped to savor the office silence. There. Perfect. Sundays were the only times she could truly think unencumbered. Some of her most dynamic ideas happened in these trancelike moments. She needed more of them. Sometimes in the evenings, when she was nearly alone, she wished to whisk off the remaining stragglers to have some peace.

Instead, eager climbers would invade, asking tedious questions, offering suggestions to better their station. If only the thousands employed at MOD would just bow their heads and work. Cease tossing objections and roadblocks that only thwarted her vision.

Like the "Our Favorites" issue. No one expected it'd be a triumph. They were skeptics, every one. But it would be one of their most lucrative issues in years. Early receipts were off the charts.

MOD owned all the images.

No models to compensate.

No designers to haggle with like peddlers in an open market.

Genius, really.

The Valis Publishing board sent her an outrageous arrangement of exotic flowers, their card saying they planned to emulate her idea across their entire portfolio of 79 magazine titles.

So much intellectual property in house. Free.

Why hadn't the idea dawned on them before?

Because they are followers. Every one.

Jane bristled, swiping her mobile browser open to the latest blog she'd begun reading. The person who wrote it was no follower. Discussing women's intimacy in such an open and honest way was a topic she wished she thought of herself. Even the name of the blog was clever: Bedroom Diary.

Jane activated her voice dialing. "Call Viraj."

"Calling Viraj Gupta," the phone parroted.

The phone rang too many times before it was answered.

"I thought we agreed no calls on Sunday before noon?" Viraj said. "We need boundaries."

"Yes, yes, I apologize. Have you read the Bedroom Diary blog posts I sent?"

"I have."

"I'd like to reach out. Give her a bigger platform."

"If it's a 'her' at all," Viraj joked.

"Of course it's a woman. No man could write about this topic in such a raw and authentic way. Plus, no one else would admit to not having orgasms and share their struggle so openly."

"She's got a nice little following growing. What are you thinking?" Viraj asked.

Jane paced to the window to take in Manhattan's skyline. The woman could be anywhere in the world. But, she could also be under her nose, in one of these very buildings.

"Please investigate for me. Find out who owns the domain and offer to bring their content in house at MOD."

"Anything else?" Viraj asked.

There was, but nothing she could admit to her protege. One didn't share personal struggles with a subordinate. Especially something like her inability to forget...

"You still there?" Viraj asked.

"Yes. That's all. Enjoy your Sunday." Jane dropped the call, already distracted by her next thought.

Office quiet echoed in her ears, so loud it almost hurt. Or the implications of it did. No people, no sounds. No sounds, no work. Meanwhile, it was nearly Monday morning in Australia. Why was the office always so quiet on Sundays? Where were their priorities? Why was she the only one here?

The pink cover of the latest magazine beckoned from her desk, dangerous energy pulsing around where it lay. Lifting her mug to her lips, the coffee's bitter tang offended. The yearning always arrived in quiet moments like these. Stirring deep within, then amplifying until a nagging restlessness left her nerves frayed. But hope was worse. Like a hot fireplace poker, it prodded her toward her phone to call or text, only to suffer the sting of indifference. Never an answer. Not once in all the years of her trying. But this time would be different.

Opening the "Our Favorites" issue where it lay, she flipped the pages she knew by heart without looking. Burberry. Chanel. Salvatore Ferragamo. She skipped ahead to where the binding creased open from her frequent visits. Blue sky. Cream sweater. That face. The face that haunted her sleepless nights. The one that got away.

She slapped it closed. Of the millions of decisions she'd made in her life, his left Jane on the losing end. Her mind a whirl of possibilities as she fiddled with the silver cuff circling her wrist. Yes. It was time to tip that nagging equation in her favor. The only question was how.

4

First thing Monday was a lousy time for meetings. Whoever scheduled it had a less chaotic life than Rebecca. A dedicated worker, her hectic days ran late. So she didn't begrudge herself a few extra morning moments to get things going, grab a coffee, and now, shrug off her worry about Kyle. But all that took time and left her running late. Her boss, Darcy, was likely behind the nine-o'clock scheduling. Yet another way for Darcy to stick a finger in Rebecca's eye and make her start her presentation at a disadvantage.

Rebecca swept through the open door to Harry's office as he was finishing a call. He waved her into a guest chair next to where Darcy sat waiting. Her pin-straight posture willed Rebecca to straighten hers in response.

As MediaNow's owner, Harry deserved every bit of the fierce respect the ad industry showered on him. But a more caring teddy bear never walked the earth. That made it doubly silly for Darcy to act so formal around him.

There Darcy sat, profile glued forward like a soldier awaiting orders. Abandoning her trademark ponytail for a blunt cut at the shoulders was a distinct improvement. But that only gave free rein to the dandruff dusting the shoulders of her navy blouse like a winter storm. If only Rebecca could brush it off; two quick swipes should do it. Wouldn't that be a test for her newfound confidence? That is, unless Harry got there first.

"Sorry, sorry," Harry said, hanging up. "Every time I try to sneak a call in between meetings, it runs longer than expected. Apologies."

"No worries," Rebecca dove into her report. "The orientation program is going well. We did a brief survey of tier-one managers and they've noticed an improvement in work quality, task completion timeliness, and manager satisfaction since the pretest scores."

"I've heard competency is still lagging," Darcy darted a sideways glance at Rebecca.

"Yes, well, we've only just begun and now we know where to focus our efforts to continue making gains," Rebecca said.

"I've definitely seen fewer confused faces wandering about." Harry winked at Rebecca.

She smiled. "We didn't measure that but, good to know. We'll add that to the next survey."

"How would we word that question?" Harry continued. "On a scale of one to ten, have you seen more or less confused faces wandering around the office?"

Darcy folded her arms. "This is hardly a topic for jokes."

"Every topic is a topic for jokes," Harry replied. "Lighten up, Darcy. We're just having a little fun."

"Well, if we're done having fun, there's the matter of Rebecca's own competence to discuss."

Blood shot to Rebecca's face. "What are you talking about?"

"These side projects are taking her away from her core responsibilities."

"Can you share examples of how?" Harry said.

"Yes, I'd be interested to know as well," Rebecca said, slow blinking Darcy's stare.

"Well, there are assignments I've had to give to Evvy, as Rebecca wasn't available."

"If you'd come to me and asked, I could have taken them on."

"Excellent point," Harry said. "But we need to ensure that the work not only gets done, but that it's properly assigned to the right level worker. Maximize the talent we have. If we have managers and directors doing junior work, that doesn't really maximize our resources, does it?"

"Well... I'm..." Darcy sputtered

"Rebecca, since the onboarding training is bubbling along, I'd like you to work with HR on the manager training program. This exact point is critical for us to include. They already have it started, but I'd love for you to get involved as a team liaison. Does that work for you?"

Darcy narrowed her gaze at Rebecca.

It was clear how she felt about it. And she had a point.

Taking on a second side project, along with her usual responsibilities, might be a stretch. But how could she admit that in front of Harry? And Darcy? Admitting that would make Darcy's century—and reinforce her point about Rebecca's workload. She'd sit smirking at her desk in that glass fishbowl of an office, making faces as Rebecca passed by. The thought of it made bile gurgle up her throat.

"I see she's hesitant, Harry, but I'd be willing to—"

"I'll do it," Rebecca said.

"Splendid! I'll make the connections via email." Rebecca and Darcy rose to leave.

Once clear of Harry's door, Darcy pounced. "Always the hero, huh? Keep taking on more. We'll see how well you do."

She turned to walk toward her fishbowl.

Old Rebecca would be cowering right about now. But things had changed. Juggling it all would take effort, but Harry believed in her. And for once, Rebecca believed in herself too.

Kyle rummaged through his food styling kit looking for cotton balls. Where were they? He removed the motor oil and slid his hand around the bottom of his black canvas bag of tricks. At least, that's what his Aunt Bessie called the crazy mish-mash of supplies he used to transform ordinary household objects into delectable treats. Or so they looked on camera.

As the photographer, he wasn't technically in charge of food styling, but it never hurt to be prepared. He'd lost track of the number of times his kit rescued photo shoots from dissolving into disaster when a critical supply went missing. But that only worked if his bag was properly stocked.

Grabbing his keys, he was about to pop over to Aunt Bessie's apartment across the hall to raid her beauty supplies when his jeans pocket vibrated. His mother's face lit up the phone screen.

"Hey, I can't talk right now. Everything okay?" he said.

"Yes, just confirming dinner on Saturday. Are you sure it's not too much trouble to cook? We're happy to make a reservation."

"No, we have it covered."

"Okay."

"Can you do me a favor, though?" Kyle cradled his phone in his neck to free his hands. "Encourage my dear sister to be on her best behavior. She's been cranky as hell lately."

"It's the stress of the wedding. She doesn't mean anything by it."

"I get that, but before that it was the stress of her move to Texas, then the stress of her job, then the stress of her—"

"You've made your point. I'll talk to her."

"Thanks. I want Libby and Rebecca to get along, and she's not making it easy."

"It's to be expected, don't you think?" his mom said.

"I don't follow."

"You know how fond she is of Vivian. I think she harbored hopes you two would reconcile."

"Yeah, well, she's got to get over it. If Libby loves Vivian so much, she can marry her instead of Evan."

His mother shifted the conversation to her charity work up in Boston, but Kyle's mind drifted to his sister. He knew her better than anyone. Libby's "cooking up trouble vibes" were resonating clear across the country. She was coming to New York to scout wedding dresses, but something told him he needed to be ready.

Kyle hadn't yet decided how to tell his parents the dark truth behind his modeling career, but Friday dinner wasn't the time. No sense tanking what should be a celebratory mood. Besides, there was no rush. Kyle had yet to connect with the doctor Marco texted over. As long as his family missed Jane's showboating photo spread, he could avoid the topic all together.

All Kyle needed was for Rebecca to hold true to her promise and keep his secret under wraps. She would, as long as Kyle kept the conversation flowing in another direction. As much as he loved her, Rebecca was the worst liar he knew. Her emotions flashed across her face as clearly as if posted on the jumbotron screen in Times Square. If Kyle could stay quiet for eleven years, she could hold it together for one evening. And for both their sakes, she'd have to.

5

That evening, the bar was in transition between happy hour and the dinner crush when Rebecca dragged herself through the frosted glass doors. She stopped short to avoid colliding with a waitress carrying a tray of delicious smelling beefy burgers and golden onion rings still glistening from the fryer. Culinary heaven. Rebecca's stomach rumbled its approval. But between the boisterous chatter, clinking glasses, and blaring TVs, she hadn't even heard it herself.

Animated patrons surrounded Vivian, Kyle's ex-fiancée and current best friend, who sat alone at a high-top table nursing a beer. If it wasn't for Vivian's odd role in bringing Kyle and Rebecca together, Rebecca would never have embraced a relationship with the quirky videographer. As it was, she'd since become the human equivalent of a comfortable pair of shoes.

With a heart-shaped face and pin-straight blond hair perennially pulled into a ponytail, Vivian was all business. Well, all business and sarcasm.

"Ooof. Such a sad face," Vivian teased as Rebecca approached, her arm slinked across the back of her chair.

"Busy day." Rebecca hiked up onto a long-legged wooden chair.

"You need a drink." Vivian called over to the bartender, "Felix, we need a… What do you want?"

"I'll have a glass of pinot grigio," Rebecca said.

"Pinot grigio and a tequila shot," Vivian said.

"For me?"

"It'll add hair to your chest."

"Do I look like I need more hair?" Rebecca fisted a handful of her brown curls.

Vivian spat a breathy raspberry. "So what happened today?"

A glass of chilled wine arrived behind the white cocktail napkin placed in front of her. The thought of gossiping with Vivian would have been unthinkable three months ago. But she had quickly become a confidant after everything the trio endured. Though how much Rebecca could or should share with someone once engaged to Kyle was still an unknown.

Rebecca stole a fruity sip before answering. "It's nothing. My boss is just being her usual bitchy self. I have it handled."

Vivian lifted her beer mug for a long drink. "Any idea when Kyle's gracing us with his presence?"

"He said he was running late."

"I hear his family is coming to town," Vivian said.

"Yeah. His parents are driving down from Boston and Libby is flying in from Houston to go dress shopping. I wouldn't be overly concerned if it wasn't for—"

"Wasn't for what?" Vivian asked.

"I've only met the Dillons a few times. Any tidbits you can share would help."

Vivian screwed up her face thinking. "Overall, his parents are pretty normal. But they do meddle in annoying ways that can cause drama."

"Is that where Libby gets it? I hear she's a handful."

"She absolutely can be, but Libby's mush underneath. Don't take her bull and you'll be fine." Vivian flicked her head toward the door. "Here's our boy now."

Rebecca spun to see Kyle gliding in. Gorgeous as always. Dark wavy hair, olive skin that glowed from the fire burning behind his blue eyes. His perfect strut held new meaning following the revelation about his modeling. No wonder he was so irresistible when they first met. That night in their building's elevator, Kyle's smile lit up Rebecca's insides with electric tingles of happiness—and all before uttering a word. Now that smile greeted her every morning.

It still blew Kyle's mind to see Rebecca and Vivian chatting away like old friends. It was the stuff of odd swinger movies, but had become the natural state of things in their world. He almost felt weird for not being bothered. Had Rebecca objected, he would have distanced himself from Vivian. But there didn't seem to be any need.

"Sorry I'm late. Lost track of time," Kyle said.

"I know the feeling." Vivian twisted away from the table to hail the waitress at the precise moment Kyle bent to kiss Rebecca.

Smart girl.

"So what'd I miss?" he said, taking a seat between them.

"Not much. Though I've told her all your dark secrets."

Kyle flashed Rebecca a knowing glance, to which she imperceptibly nodded in reply. As much as he loved his childhood friend, he no longer shared every secret with Vivian. She lost that right when she blew up their engagement, not that he'd been able to stay mad at her for very long.

Kyle took a draft from a frosty glass the waitress put before him. "Libby's being cagey about the wedding planning. Any idea what's up?"

"Actually, yes," Vivian said. "She's asked me to be maid of honor."

What was his sister up to? Picking Vivian for maid of honor made zero sense. Plus, it insulted the one gal who'd stubbornly stuck by Libby's side since childhood. Way to reward the only person patient enough to overlook Libby's caustic exterior and focus on the sweetheart beneath.

"If Mel had any sense, she'd flip Libby a much overdue bird and tell her to stuff it."

"I thought she'd ask Melody too," Vivian said.

"Who's Melody?" Rebecca asked.

"She's Libby's best friend and has been since, what? We were in sixth grade?" Vivian asked.

"At least. Might have even been kindergarten. I can't remember," Kyle said.

"So what reasoning did she give you?" Rebecca asked Vivian.

"She said I was like the sister she never had. Plus, she'd known me the longest. Technically, she's right, but maid of honor? Christ, I've got to be the least girlie-girl of anyone she knows."

"Melody would have killed to be maid of honor," Kyle said.

"Right? It doesn't make any sense. Can you imagine me in some pink princess gown with huge sleeves? It's going to be a disaster," Vivian said, searching the golden depths of her beer for answers.

"I've never met Libby, but she must have had a reason," Rebecca said.

Kyle met Vivian's eyes. He knew the reason, so did she. But it wasn't going to work. He loved Rebecca. Vivian loved Vivian. Libby's childish wish for them to reunite was ridiculous. Somehow, he had to get Libby aside to tell her to knock it off. His relationship with Rebecca was too new to inject doubt into it. Especially where none belonged.

With Kyle off in bed, Rebecca cozied into the sofa to compose the latest installment for her personal blog, *Bedroom Diary*. Reader comments steadily flowed in and she hated to keep them waiting for fresh content. The conversation about Libby's chilly exterior reminded Rebecca of a douchey celebrity who called his ex frigid.

Why did men think that was? Did they never look in the mirror for one second and wonder *why* their women were underwhelmed after sex? And if they didn't know, it was up to the women to make sure they did.

Rebecca's fingers flew across the keyboard, words pinging around her brain so rapidly that she barely registered the notification chime of her Bedroom Diary email. She typically shut it off when writing. Probably another "urgent" notice about her website's domain registration renewal that was months away. She had half a mind to write to their marketing team and paste the Merriam-Webster definition of "urgent" into the body of an email.

But knowing a message sat awaiting attention diverted the flow of her writing. The tech overlords trained her well. She clicked open her email to view the message from someone named Viraj Gupta.

Dear Bedroom Diary,

We at MOD magazine have been following your column with interest and wanted to congratulate you on your growing success. We're reaching out to open a dialog about bringing your content to the pages of MOD. My contact information is below, and I look forward to hearing from you to discuss in more detail.

Warm Regards,

Viraj Gupta

Senior Editor, Features

MOD *Magazine*

MOD? Wants me to write for them?

"Holy shit!" Rebecca said aloud, before rereading the message multiple times.

She opened her browser and found an issue of MOD online to view the masthead. Sure enough, there was a Viraj Gupta listed there.

"This is for real. Oh my God, oh my God," Rebecca stood up, looking around the empty room as if there were a hidden audience waiting to cheer her news. But she was alone and Kyle was sleeping.

What did "bring her content to the pages of MOD" mean, exactly? Did they want to take it over? And if so, would she lose control of her words? Or was it something more limited that could funnel more readers her way? Readers she'd worked months to earn.

Since her bedroom drought ended, she felt compelled to share her journey to bliss with the women of the world. What started as a few posts on Medium became her own blog, the following of which grew steadily with each post. Never did she think it would get noticed by editors at MOD, or anything close to MOD.

Rebecca wrapped a curl around her finger, but enlightenment came quickly. She reached for her phone. Her girlfriend Leslie answered immediately.

"You're up late. What's up?" Leslie said.

"Guess whose blog got noticed by MOD?" Rebecca said.

"Shit, for real? I've written for them before, you know."

"Thought you might have. Any advice about how to handle?"

"Just play it cool. Let them talk first, and be sure you understand the scope of what they're asking for before committing to anything. Learn the deadlines, the money—"

"Money! Hell, I'd do it for free!"

Leslie sighed. "No. Don't go into a negotiation saying you'll work for free. You negotiate for a living. Is that what you'd do for your advertising clients?"

"No, of course not! Darcy would fire me."

"Well, you're the client this time. Put your tough-girl negotiating hat on when you connect with them. Keep me posted if you have any questions about the offer. I'm sure Barbara can lend her legal-eagle eye to any contracts, too."

"That's a great idea, yes. I'll do that. Okay, I'll play it cool and see what they say."

"Good luck!" Leslie said.

Rebecca wrote and erased five responses before settling on a cool, brief one. She checked it for spelling and tone and sent it from her Bedroom Diary email. She nearly used her personal email and signed her name, but that would have given her identity away to a complete stranger with unknown intentions. Leslie said they were reputable, but she'd have to be careful.

While Bedroom Diary was her passion, her day job paid the bills. No telling what Darcy and Harry would have to say about her side pursuit into the realm of women's pleasure. Nothing good, for sure. Hiding her identity did sometimes make her feel like a fraud. But this offer from MOD was the first sign she was on a path to making it pay off.

6

This was a mistake.

Kyle promised to "talk to someone," but meeting face to face with Dr. Joel Kaplan the next week made his skin crawl more than he'd thought possible. Kyle sat, knee bouncing uncontrollably while a reel of experiences he'd rather forget flickered across his mind.

Dr. Kaplan's consult room was straight off a movie set. Mahogany shelves crammed with psych books lined every wall. Framed degrees and leather furniture projected esteem. Strategically placed photos of family trips and professional junkets balanced all that with the right dose of humanity. Group portraits showing him at conferences, including with a few choice celebrities, were likely meant to impress. Beyond the environment, their absurdly predictable exchange likely replayed daily with every patient walking through his door:

Tell me about yourself.

How did you feel about that?

Tell me more.

It wasn't your fault.

What a bullshit line. Of course it was my fault. I let it happen.

My body let it happen.

The doctor's words reverberated around Kyle's insides, ringing false.

The door Dr. Kaplan stepped through to take an emergency call was wide open. Now was his chance to escape. This session was a joke, as he knew it'd be.

Kyle stood to zip the jacket he hadn't bothered removing and retrieved his motorcycle helmet from the vacant captain's chair next to him. Just standing made Kyle feel better. More in command. More like a man. But before he'd taken two steps, Dr. Kaplan returned.

"Going so soon?" Dr. Kaplan said.

"Yeah, I know you fit me in on short notice, but this... this..." Kyle scanned the staged room. "This isn't for me."

"Really?" the good doctor said, walking past Kyle and leaving his escape route unattended.

The door was right there. All Kyle had to do was walk through and he'd be free of this madness. He'd been forced onto enough couches, casting and otherwise. He didn't need any more. The faint ping of the elevator in the corridor beyond Dr. Kaplan's office drifted into their counseling space. He could see the suite's exit door. Calling. So why couldn't he move?

Leather squeaked as Dr. Kaplan sat down in a different spot. This time, an armchair. "I would never force a patient to stay, but you did call me looking to work through your trauma. That was a good instinct. Whether with me or someone else, those unresolved emotions need to be addressed."

Trauma. Hearing it said aloud, by a stranger—and about him—sent the room spinning.

Dr. Kaplan gestured to the empty armchair. Two seats, side-by-side. He shifted their location to a spot where they would sit, not as patient and doctor across a desk, but as fellow humans.

Same chair.

Same height.

Talking man to man.

Maybe the doctor had a few tricks yet? Tricks that could help Kyle cope. Besides, what would he tell Rebecca if he walked out? That he'd lost his nerve? No, he couldn't tell her he'd failed to face his demons yet again. She believed in him. It felt good to not be alone in this mess. He couldn't give up on himself before she did.

Kyle dropped into the chair, balancing his helmet on one thigh. The other resumed bouncing.

"What made you want to leave?" Dr. Kaplan asked.

"All your questions. Your—no offense—false platitudes about everything not being my fault..."

"So, you think you caused the abuse?"

"Yes. No. I don't know. Yeah, kinda. I kinda did. Maybe the first time not, but what about after? I could have walked away any time, but I didn't. I mean, I'm a guy..."

"What does being a guy have to do with what happened?"

Kyle laughed. "C'mon."

"No, seriously. What?"

"We're supposed to defend ourselves. I'm physically bigger than her. I could have stopped her. She just—she didn't start right away. I thought she believed in me. And then I was afraid to disappoint her."

"That makes sense," Dr. Kaplan said. "She groomed you. Controlled you in emotional ways..."

"Yes."

"Reeled you in slowly, then had you hooked."

"Exactly."

"Tell me, Kyle. You mentioned your strength and size advantage over her. But how were you supposed to physically overpower the emotional control she had over you? How were you supposed to wrestle your way out of the power she held over your career? Punch at air?"

In all the years following the harassment, not once had it occurred to Kyle that his physical size and maleness provided zero protection for his situation. Punching at air? Using brute force to escape an emotional situation? It definitely sounded absurd when framed that way.

"Plus," Dr. Kaplan continued. "You mentioned she was an extremely powerful woman, 20 years your senior. She was older and wiser than you were at the time. You were too young to understand that the situation wasn't about sex at all."

"Seemed that way to me." Kyle chuckled, his gaze drifting to the empty sofa. Suddenly, he was there. In her apartment. She pinned him against the arm of her couch. Telling him it was okay. Asking whether he found her attractive. His smile inverted.

"But that's where you're wrong," Dr. Kaplan drew him back. "In cases like yours, sex is a weapon of control. A means. The real thrill for her was in the power. Sexual harassment and assault are more often about the abuser exercising power over the abused."

"Abused. Next, you'll call me a victim," Kyle said.

"No, I'd never call you a victim. I'd call you a survivor."

Kyle's head snapped up.

A survivor.

It was as if a lightbulb flashed, illuminating Kyle's life in a way he'd never seen before. But in a way that felt real. Felt like it fit.

A survivor, not a victim.

The two sat in silence letting Kyle's unspoken words hover between them.

A survivor, not a victim.

Kyle took in Dr. Kaplan as he sat. Too anxious when he arrived, if asked, Kyle wouldn't have been able to pick his doctor out of a lineup. Now, he finally took the man in. With a lean face and dark hair parted on the side, his chunky black glasses framed empathetic eyes. His green sweater covered a blue and white pinstripe oxford that clung to his lean frame. With his jeans, he looked barely older than Kyle. But he was probably a decade older, having practiced for over ten years.

Still, Kyle expected a grizzled practitioner ala Sigmund Freud. Someone wearing a tie and jacket, at least that's how Kyle would style him were he in charge of casting. But then, this wasn't pretend. This was real. Dr. Kaplan was a real person with real ideas of his own. He chose to wear a sweater. Maybe it was time for Kyle to make different choices of his own.

I'm a survivor, not a victim.

Kyle put his helmet on the floor and removed his jacket. It was time to stop running.

7

Rebecca paused her food prep to watch Kyle chop veggies across the kitchen. His sniffing and eye wiping appeared to be from the pile of onions in front of him. He'd been impenetrable since he got home from his first therapy appointment two days before. It seemed to go well, but Kyle said precious little else. If only he'd give a hint about what happened. It was his private space to heal, so she dared not pry. But she was invested in his success. Absent a post-session recap, his family's Saturday dinner visit would be a well-timed distraction.

She returned to her assigned task, forming mashed falafel paste into tablespoon-sized balls. Between the garlic in the falafel, hummus, and cucumber salad they were preparing for Kyle's family, the meal could wipe out an entire coven of vampires.

"I hope they like garlic," Rebecca said.

"In our family, garlic is at the bottom of the food pyramid," Kyle said, chopping tomatoes, then using the blade of the chef's knife to scoop them into a glass bowl.

Rebecca placed another green orb onto the wax paper next to its mates, forming neat rows. "We've got quite a green army over here. Are you sure this isn't too much?"

"Nah, you'd be surprised how fast they go. This meal is a crowd-pleaser. We shouldn't have any complaints tonight."

"Or bloodsucking creatures of the night."

Kyle smirked.

"You mean Libby?" Rebecca asked. She knew little about Kyle's sister, but what she knew spelled trouble.

"You'll see."

"She can't be THAT bad," Rebecca said.

"I love her but, she's an acquired taste..."

"I won't be able to taste anything after all this garlic," she said, smelling her fingers before moving across their galley kitchen to squirt dish soap on her hands. But stacks of food processor bowls, prep dishes, and cutting boards blocked faucet access. The equipment materialized when Kyle moved in. The kitchen must be happy to have someone using it for something besides reheating takeout.

Kyle focused on his work, shoulders tense.

"You okay?" She reached over to rub his back

"Yeah. Why do you ask?"

"You're wound as tight as a drum."

"It's not what you think. But, let's not mention my appointment, okay?"

"Okay. But if it's not that, what's the matter?"

Kyle paused his chopping, setting the wide knife flat on the cutting board. "Nothing with my family is ever as easy as it should be. There's always some manufactured drama. But there's also nothing for you to be worried about."

WHAT WE NEVER SAY

Rebecca forced a closed-mouth smile. Kyle kissed her forehead, then handed her bowls of chopped lettuce and cucumber salad with feta cheese to take to the table.

It looked lovely. Set for five, bowls of glistening red, green, and leafy veggies reflected the candlelight from strategic spots around the table. Pretty as one of Kyle's food magazine pictures.

She wiped her hands on her jeans. "I'll be right back," she hollered, walking to the bathroom.

Gazing in the mirror, she fluffed her hair. Her late-day shiny complexion screamed for attention. Oily skin was the admission ticket to looking young as she aged. Her mother's side all had it. She'd be glad of it one day, but for now, she dusted translucent powder on her face to tone it down. Oily and nervous was no way to head into dinner. Rebecca shook out her limbs to release the tension.

Her white and black houndstooth shirt clung to her frame, looking fussy and foreign. The jagged pattern intersected at strategic angles, making it impossible to tell if it was black on white or white on black. Was it too loud? Why was she wearing something so bold? Transfixed, she didn't notice Kyle behind her until his soft lips nibbled her neck.

"You look beautiful. You always do," he said.

"Mmmmm." Her body responded instinctively to his touch.

He always knew just the right spot to get her purring.

"We have a few minutes, you know," Kyle said.

"Sweetie, I can't meet your family with just-effed hair."

Kyle stood behind her, his hands making their way around her hips and towards her inner thighs, pulling her into him.

A twitch of pleasure shot up her spine, sending her back arching reflexively. Her body said yes, but the ticking clock said otherwise. She spun to face him.

"You'll have to wait until after garlic-fest." She planted a loud smooch on his lips before wiggling away.

"You'll regret it. I'll eat extra hummus…" he yelled as she retreated to the bedroom.

"You can't scare me," she said, stretching her shirt neck to fit over her makeup-ed face, replacing it with a discarded shirt from earlier still lying on the bed. A solid black one with rouching around the waist.

Her body eased. Better. What was she thinking? Houndstooth?

The doorbell chime pinged. A half hour early.

"You see?" Rebecca yelled to Kyle as he paused by their bedroom door. "You would have had me naked and flustered when your parents arrived."

"There are worse things in the world…"

She smacked his shoulder. "Please, please behave. I want to make a good impression."

"Don't I always?"

"No, actually. You're naughty as hell."

The bell chimed again.

"Shit."

"Becca, relax."

"They'll think we were having sex," Rebecca said, jogging to the door.

"You know, not everyone is as obsessed with sex as you are," he said, following at a leisurely pace.

Rebecca swung the door open wide, plastering a smile so wide she felt her ears stretch. "Hello! Welcome! Neighbor let you in?"

"Yes, we still have our New York ways. Nice to see you, Rebecca," Kyle's mother, Sharon, entered and gave Rebecca a kiss on the cheek.

She wore a plum sweater set and black slacks that set off her blond frosted hair cut short enough that her beaded ruby earrings dangled freely.

Rebecca popped up on her toes to kiss Kyle's dad, Michael, whose height tallied just shy of Kyle's six-two frame. Wearing a crisp white shirt and trousers, he passed by in a blur of cologne and testosterone. "Rebecca…"

Guess he's not a kisser.

"You made it," Kyle said to his dad, diverting Rebecca's attention as they embraced. Distinguished with his salt-and-pepper hair and solid frame, Kyle would be his spitting image one day.

When Rebecca turned back, Libby crossed the threshold. With glossy, dark hair and blue eyes, Elizabeth Dillon was the female version of Kyle, yet more captivating, if that was even possible. Witnessing her raven beauty up close stole Rebecca's words.

"Hi. I'm Libby. Nice to meet you—at last."

"Yes. Same. Come in." Rebecca stood aside. "I have to say, pictures don't do you justice."

"That's sweet of you to say. Thank you."

So far, so good.

The sounds of back slapping and kisses circulated behind her as she locked the door.

"What a lovely apartment," Sharon said. "Have you lived here long?"

"I grew up here. My parents moved out to Long Island a few years ago."

"How lucky for you. An apartment in Manhattan," Libby said.

"I guess it is. It's all I've ever known, so I never think about it."

"We used to live in Queens, out in Forest Hills?" Sharon said.

"I had summer camp friends in Forest Hills. Spent a lot of weekends there on sleepovers," Rebecca said.

"Speaking of summer, where's Bessie? Isn't she joining us?" Sharon asked, taking a seat on the sofa.

"Nah, I couldn't get her to come. She wanted us to visit first. Maybe she'll let us drag her across the hall for dessert," Kyle said.

Rebecca took drink orders and returned with stemware for wine.

"We got this at a vineyard on Cape Cod. You must come up sometime. It's a great place to unwind," Michael said, uncorking the bottle they brought.

"Do you have a house out there?" Rebecca asked.

"No, we rent when we go. Makes more sense for us," Michael said.

"It's another world out there. You feel you've flown to a beach town far away instead of being only a few miles from Boston," Sharon said.

Libby stood apart by the window. Rebecca held a glass aloft. "Wine?"

"Not yet. Trying to pace myself."

"Elizabeth has a strange notion of starving herself into a smaller wedding dress," Sharon said to Rebecca.

"Mom! That's so rude."

"Well, come over here and sit. We're visiting."

Libby huffed over and dropped into their leather armchair like a rag doll. The movement transformed her from an adult into a petulant adolescent. Rebecca blinked the thought away. Last thing she needed was for Libby to read negative judgment vibes on her face.

"I can get you some seltzer and lime if you prefer?" Rebecca said.

"That'd be great. Ky," Libby whined to her brother. "Be a dear and get me a seltzer?"

She then pivoted back to Rebecca. "He can get it."

Rebecca's eyebrows shot up. Acquired taste is right. A bad one.

"So Rebecca, tell me again what you do in advertising." Michael dug into the cheese and crackers on the coffee table.

"I'm a media buyer/planner. It's the part of the business where we negotiate and buy the space where all the beautiful creative goes. TV, radio, online banners, billboards, magazines..."

"Ahh. Makes sense. I never really thought about the process behind how the ads get to where we see them," Michael said.

"Do you enjoy the work?" Sharon asked.

Interesting question. Rebecca hadn't reassessed her job prospects in a while. Darcy's sourpuss flashed to mind, but she blinked the image away.

"Most days, yes. It's a whirlwind. But I'm not sure it's my forever passion."

Michael chuckled. "Elizabeth works in marketing too, but is more focused on the wedding right now, I'd wager."

Libby perked up, clasping her hands. "Speaking of the wedding. I've booked a date for everyone to come down to shop for bridesmaid gowns. It's so exciting."

"That sounds like fun." Rebecca took a sip of wine as she sat next to Sharon on the sofa.

"Oh, it will be. There is so much stress with the planning that it's good to have fun, girlie moments to enjoy."

"Does Melody know about Vivian being the maid of honor?" Sharon asked.

"Yes, I told her. She totally understood. You made too big a deal out of it," Libby sank back onto the leather chair, checking out the arms.

"It just seemed out of the blue; I thought it would hurt her feelings."

"She was fine, but Leah said she won't be able to do it. I was pretty shocked. It leaves me with a mismatched number of bridesmaids to groomsmen."

Kyle slinked his arm across the sofa behind Rebecca. "That's a first-world problem if I ever heard one."

Libby shot him a nasty look.

"We'll have to come up with someone, and fast. The dresses need to be ordered," Sharon said.

"It's an important decision. I want to make the right choice," Libby said.

"Who's left to ask?" Michael said.

"Dad, stop. I'll figure it out…" Libby said.

"Will you?"

"Yes. I'll think of someone."

"I've an idea. Why not have Rebecca step in?" Michael said.

Libby and Rebecca eyeballed each other warily.

"We just met two seconds ago," Libby said. "No offense."

"None taken," Rebecca said.

"That's a wonderful idea." Sharon said. "With Vivian in the party, how would that look not to include Rebecca? Wouldn't that be odd?"

"No, really, it's fine," Rebecca said.

"You see? She doesn't even want to do it. We wouldn't want to make Rebecca uncomfortable, would we?" Libby said through a strained smile.

Rebecca looked to Kyle for support, but he leaned toward the coffee table to scoop a generous mound of gooey Brie onto his cracker while his dad had the knife occupied. Awesome. She needed backup, but the Dillon men had their faces buried in cheese.

"I appreciate the gesture, but I'm sure Libby would prefer someone else."

Please, someone, stop this madness.

"Nonsense," Michael barked. "Who wouldn't want to be in a wedding?"

"I've never been in a wedding, so I couldn't say…"

Rebecca nudged Kyle to get his attention. "Do something," she mouthed, to which he nodded.

"Mom, why don't you come help me in the kitchen?" Kyle said.

"Yes, of course. Show me what I can do," Kyle and Sharon wandered off.

"Can you point me to…" Michael said.

"Down the hall. Last door," Rebecca said.

"Thanks," Michael said.

The room's energy shifted once the two women were alone. Libby sat, staring away, the foot of her crossed leg wiggling like a fish at the end of a line. Rebecca knew the feeling. It must totally suck to have your parents perpetually meddle and treat you like a teenager. As rude as Libby acted, Rebecca couldn't help feeling sorry about the situation.

"Libby, there's no need. Please don't feel obligated."

Libby stood up, jaw clenched. "Oh, I don't."

Rebecca stood, walking to face her, "Good. I don't feel obligated either."

Libby's face flashed a moment of regret. Or was it respect?

How could this woman have come from the same parents as Kyle? To be so rude to Rebecca in her own home took stones the size of Nebraska. She'd rather stand naked in Times Square than play handmaiden to such a spoiled princess.

Rebecca walked past without uttering another word.

Kyle slid a stack of dirty dinner dishes onto the counter. What in God's name were his parents thinking? Forcing Rebecca into the wedding would be a disaster.

He returned to the living room, where Rebecca and his mom chatted together while his dad tapped his phone. Libby sat apart at the table, grinding her teeth. She hadn't said a word since their parents dropped the bombshell. Nor had she touched a morsel of one of her favorite dinners.

His parents were so consumed by vacation talk, they never once commented on their daughter. The one who sat behind an empty plate for the entire meal. Rebecca tried to make the best of a tense situation but wore a smile that never reached her eyes.

Ever dependable, the Dillon clan never failed to bulldoze their way through situations they could easily walk around. This time, though, they'd outdone themselves.

Libby pocketed her phone and stood up. "I'm going to meet some friends. Thanks for dinner."

"Wait, Lib—" Sharon said.

"Mom, let her go," Kyle said.

Libby slipped on her shoes and escaped out the door without another word. The heavy door slam jolted the assembly back to attention.

"I don't understand what came over her. She was in such a good mood on the way over from the hotel."

"Rebecca, please excuse Elizabeth. She can be moody at times," Michael said.

Rebecca's eyes had bugged clear out of her head. She mouthed to Kyle, "Bedroom. Now."

"We'll be right back," Kyle said to his parents as they walked down the hall to the bedroom, closing the door.

"What the hell!" Rebecca whisper-screamed, "I met her and five minutes later I'm in her wedding? She hates my guts. She didn't even try to hide it, I—"

"Come here," Kyle wrapped Rebecca in his arms, her heartbeat pounding against his chest as he nestled his chin on her head.

"This is ridiculous," she said. "I can't be in her wedding. Please, you've got to fix this."

"I'll talk to them. Hang in here. I'll take them over to Bessie's and have a chat."

Kyle grabbed his key and left their apartment door ajar to head over to his great-aunt Bessie's apartment across the hall. Being near her was the reason he'd moved back to New York from California. But his mom's claims of Bessie's frail condition were grossly overblown, leaving the stout 87-year-old overjoyed when Kyle moved across the hall to live with Rebecca. Bessie loved her independence and the freedom to come and go as she wished.

The door swung open into a dark apartment, but Kyle easily navigated to the entry table. He pulled the metal chain that set his aunt's dragonfly Tiffany lamp aglow. A puddle of color splashed across the mahogany table and onto the parquet floor.

"Maybe she forgot you were coming." Moving past upholstered armchairs and doilied tables, Kyle made his way down the shadowy hallway. But no stirring sounds came from behind his aunt's closed bedroom door.

He rejoined his parents, who had turned on enough table lamps for his mom to admire Bessie's display of family photos.

"I never get enough of Bessie's wedding pictures. That's me there. I was a bridesmaid." His mom pointed at her child self, loaded with curls and wearing a frilly white dress.

Several of the table's yellowed images would soon fade beyond recognition if not preserved. A rainy-day project, perhaps, when Kyle had some downtime.

"Let's go. We can stop by tomorrow." His dad put his hand on the small of his mom's back to leave.

"Hold on. We need to talk." Kyle guided the trio away from the hall so their voices wouldn't disturb his slumbering aunt.

"What about?"

"What about? You two can't be serious about forcing Rebecca into the wedding."

"I don't see what the issue is," Michael interjected. "She was short a bridesmaid, and Rebecca is handy. Problem solved."

"That's not how it works. Christ, they just met."

"If you're serious about Rebecca, it'd be an excellent opportunity for the two of them to get to know each other," his mom said.

"This is a huge overreach by you two."

"Is it?" his dad said.

"Yes. Let Libby choose whom she wants."

His mom sighed. "What you don't understand is that she has no one else. That girl, Leah, the one who said no—she's someone from her new office who had no idea why Libby asked her. They've only gone to lunch a few times."

"Shit, really?" Kyle said.

"Yes. She literally has no one else to ask. No friends. No other family. She's in a bind, whether she wants to admit it to herself or not."

"That's why she asked Vivian," Kyle whispered.

"It's impossible for people to get past that armor she throws up. No friends, no bridesmaids," his mom said. "But she has this unrealistic vision of a wedding with a big bridal party."

Kyle replayed their dinner scene with a new lens, an imaginary projection flickering on Bessie's apartment wall. His family put up with Libby's emotional antics because they loved the real person underneath. Acquaintances didn't have a stockpile of thoughtful gestures and sunshine smiles to counterbalance her prickly exterior. They had choices. And apparently, they chose not to be friends with Libby. Kyle had to remember to be more present for his sister, as much as she let him.

A hand rested on Kyle's shoulder, his mom's. "Elizabeth will come around. The suggestion surprised her, but she'll see it makes perfect sense. It'll save her some embarrassment, hmm?"

His dad opened a crystal decanter of amber liquid and gave it a smell. "Good stuff."

He poured himself a glass.

"Make Rebecca understand, will you?" his mom said. "There will be a lot of events for the wedding party. It not only helps Libby to have Rebecca there, it will make Rebecca feel welcome. Feel included."

Kyle came into the conversation loaded for bear, presuming his parents were clueless meddlers who'd gone too far. Their insights about Libby shined light on the situation in a way he hadn't considered. But saddling Rebecca with Libby's bratty bullshit was not the answer.

"I appreciate you want Rebecca to feel included. I do. But forcing those two together will only make Libby resent Rebecca. It'll sabotage their relationship right from the start. It's a horrible idea."

"Libby needs to be a team player," Michael said, speaking into his glass.

"She is. A team of one," Kyle said.

"Don't worry," Sharon said. "I'll talk to Libby tomorrow back at the hotel. I'll make her understand. Leave it to me."

Leave it to me.

That was the exact phrase his mom used to mop up the messes of their lives. From childhood squabbles to cranky teachers. Overbearing coaches and even the early challenges of his modeling career. Back then, just getting pictures, call backs, and learning the minimum necessary information to break into modeling had been too much for teen Kyle to manage alone.

Leave it to me.

Why had Kyle stopped leaning on his mom? On his parents? Every day, he prayed his parents would catch something was off with him. Notice the sunken circles under his eyes and his agitated state that fluctuated between anger, bliss, and pits of shame so deep he could barely find a way out. Sure, they lived in the same apartment. But with different schedules, his parents morphed into detached roommates. How could he pivot from that to admitting his utter stupidity for getting himself into an impossible situation? Nineteen-year-old Kyle would never. He thought he knew everything until he realized how little he actually understood. By then, it was too hard to admit he needed help. Still…

"Shall we go back? Rebecca will wonder what happened to us."

They retreated towards the door. But he couldn't, not yet.

"Mom, I—"

"Hmm?" The two of them stood blinking, waiting to be enlightened. He had their undivided attention, but he hadn't always. How could they not have seen the warning signs? Didn't they think something was off with him spending so much time with someone older? Did they never wonder why?

Kyle crossed to the wet bar to fill a crystal glass of his own. "Back when I was modeling, did you ever worry about me? About my safety?"

"Your safety?" Concern clouded his mom's face.

"Why drag this up now?" his father asked.

"I was just wondering."

"Something happened." His mom stepped forward. Torn between the husband behind her and the son before, she hovered in between.

Kyle sighed. "There's an issue out now with one of my old pictures in it. It's stirred up memories for me."

"Hope you got residuals…" his dad said.

Always about the money… "That's not how it works. But about my question?"

"Of course we worried about you. How could we not?" his mom answered. "That's why we went with you to every appointment and were in the waiting room for every shoot until you turned 18. After that, families weren't allowed."

"What about when I traveled alone?"

"This is absurd. Kyle—"

"No, Michael, it's okay," his mom stilled his father with a gentle hand to his chest.

"Kyle, we were there as much as you let us be. But you told us to stop coming, that you weren't a baby. Don't you remember?"

No. He didn't remember at all. But it certainly sounded like something his cocky younger self would have spouted to his parents. They were likely his last words before tossing on his helmet to ride off into a boatload of trouble. But admitting that now meant letting go of his lingering fantasy. The one where his parents were partially to blame for what happened. Where their neglect left him vulnerable. Where they ignored the warning lights flashing on his life vest as he drifted, lost, among an ocean of strangers. Instead, the fault lay squarely with him. He asked to be left alone, and they respected his wishes. If only they hadn't listened so well.

"My mistake." Kyle downed his glass and left it on the tray. He'd swing by and take care of it tomorrow. "Ready?"

"Sure…" his mom muttered, confused, as she stepped through the apartment door Kyle held open for them. Once through, he closed it, turning the key until he felt the dead bolt engage. If only he could lock away his past as easily.

8

Rebecca exhaled in time to the beats of her stride, arms pumping tension from the night before out of her body as she ran. Going into dinner, she expected a lovely evening, maybe punctuated by a cranky bride. Rebecca would see the perfect family in action: mom, dad, brother, sister. Just like the TV shows she watched in the afternoons as a kid while her parents scraped together a living. But Hurricane Dillon was something else entirely.

How could Kyle's parents be so oblivious to the madness of their idea? And to the imposition on their daughter? And her? It was so ridiculously obvious, it made Rebecca wonder why they were doing it. She must be missing a clue. A puzzle piece that made this sadistic game understandable, but she'd yet to find it.

Meanwhile, Libby was off stewing. How were they supposed to build a friendship after this? She'd resent Rebecca forever. Plus, it was a perfect recipe for mean girl antics on steroids. The rest of the wedding party would probably gang up on her, trying to drive her away, never realizing nothing would make her happier. But that would only disappoint Kyle's parents. They seemed to like her and support their relationship. Would that change if she backed out, regardless of how politely?

Rebecca approached the fountain at the center of her apartment complex, mist blowing in the early morning breeze. The cool tingles sparked her exposed skin to attention as she ran through. An instant of coolness. Rejuvenating her soul as fountains always did. On scorching days, she longed to finish runs by diving straight in for a frosty swim. The chlorine. The slippery pavement. How many times had her mother hauled her out of that fountain as a child? Too many to count. Why were children so much braver than adults sometimes? She missed that pure joy of acting on impulse, throwing caution out the window, and just doing. If only.

Head forward, she quickened her pace. Muscles flexing, breathing in time with her strides, the tension eased. But as soon as her mind emptied, work flooded in.

The side projects with Harry loaded her down, but gave her a chance to improve her self-confidence. On her recent 360 evaluation, Rebecca got stellar marks from all the evaluators. Except one. She gave herself the lowest marks by far, prompting Harry to put a "cut it out" mandate into her development plan. Confidence was still a new dress, but she was forcing herself to wear it. Even though the zipper pinched sometimes.

Self-assured Rebecca would tell the Dillons, "No effing way I'm going to be in Libby's wedding." So why didn't she? Instead, she sat like a mute lump while rebellious dialog careened inside her skull.

If Rebecca wanted out, she simply needed to speak up. She ran past the yoga gal again. Once more through the mist. Maybe it would stimulate an answer.

Kyle:
We need to talk.

Libby:
…

Kyle paced the living room waiting for Libby's pulsing dots to materialize into an answer. Must he always run interference with his sister? With his parents? Peacemaking the crises they manufactured out of thin air? Their vortex of chaos was so foreign to how he navigated life, he once wondered if he were adopted. But reflecting on how he'd managed his own modeling affairs, his genetics were likely dead ringers for theirs.

He paused in front of the foyer mirror, only to have his sister's face stare back. Yeah, not adopted. Their physical resemblance was undeniable. But that's where the similarities ended. He and Libby couldn't be more different. But if she kept up her nonsense, maybe he'd go find a new sister. And family. Or build a normal one of his own with Rebecca.

Kyle:
Pickup or I'll get Mom to go bang on your hotel door.

Her call was immediate.
"Didn't you do enough damage last night?" Libby said.

"Don't you think this princess act is getting old?"

"You obviously put them up to it."

"Don't dump this shit on my doorstep. We didn't even know you had an opening in the wedding party until you mentioned it."

Libby grunted her submission. "No matter. It's a nightmare. My wedding is a nightmare."

"Rebecca is not a nightmare."

"I don't want a complete stranger tagging along with my inner circle."

Kyle ignored the hanging fastball his sister tossed his way. From what his parents said, her "inner circle" was a duo at best—Vivian and the best friend she tossed aside in favor of his ex. But no sense throwing that in her face. Not yet, at least.

"You honestly think I want your wedding party to be a reality show of my girlfriends?"

He could hear her breathing, pondering an answer.

"Talk to them, Libs. See if they'll change their minds. If not, I expect you to be a lot nicer to Rebecca than you were last night."

"What do you mean?" Libby said over the distinct scratching sounds of nail filing.

"You were a bridezilla, and that's being kind."

"I flew up from Texas to meet your dumb girlfriend, and—"

"Whoa, show some respect. Would you like it if I talked about Evan the way you're talking about Rebecca?"

"No."

"And stop lying. I know you and Mom are here to shop for dresses."

"Ky, I…"

"What do you have against Rebecca, anyway?"

"I have nothing against her. I don't even know her." Sheets rustled as she rolled over.

"I don't expect you to be best friends, but being human would be a huge improvement. Can you manage that?"

"What's that supposed to mean?"

"Come on."

"No, what?"

"You make no effort to hide whatever feeling is streaking through that brain of yours. Out your mouth it comes. Regardless of how mean, immature, or selfish. You're better than that."

Libby huffed exasperation.

"You'd go far in life if you'd stop torching bridges everywhere you go."

"Oh, that's rich coming from you. How did giving up modeling help you?"

Libby was dangerously close to crossing a line. Despite Kyle ending his modeling career with a spectacular fall from grace, Libby still glorified the profession. He had no idea why.

"Ky, you could have been the biggest thing going when you were modeling, but you walked away. You lost everything."

"I gained everything. You could not be more off base."

"Stay out of my business. It's my wedding, and you'll not tell me how to behave."

"Complain all you want, but not to Rebecca. And that's not a request."

Kyle was muttering to himself in the kitchen when Rebecca entered, sweaty but exhilarated. He could use an infusion of positive energy right about now.

"Sister troubles?" Rebecca asked, nudging Kyle aside to get a glass out of the cupboard.

"Why is Libby so ridiculously stubborn?"

"You tell me."

"I can't explain it. Something changed during high school for her, and this petulant side came out with a fury."

Rebecca grabbed a paper towel and dabbed her face.

"I only know her from last night, but having a stranger as a bridesmaid has to suck."

"You're not a stranger," Kyle said.

"I am to her."

"So you don't want to do it?"

"I won't lie. I'd rather not. How would you feel were you in my place?"

Kyle leaned an arm on the counter in front of a partially cut melon. "It sucks. I'll give you that. But my parents are so excited to include you."

"Yeah, they made that obvious. But if I gracefully declined, they'd have to understand. Right?"

Kyle shook his head without speaking. Learning about Libby's social challenges the night before certainly shifted his thinking.

"What? You think they'd take it badly?" Rebecca said.

"If you're open to it, they think it'd be best for both of us if you agreed to join the wedding party."

"You're not serious?"

"I am."

"I thought you were on my side? This is lunacy!" Rebecca hipped her hands, her displeasure apparent.

"I am. I've thought it through and need you to trust me."

Rebecca screwed up her mouth, folding her arms. As much as it pained him to dump Rebecca in the land of Libby Dillon, he'd be around to help. With a sherpa and a map, she'd be fine. But she still had to buy-in.

Rebecca poked a finger in Kyle's chest. "You are SO going to owe me!"

"Is that a yes? You'll do it?!"

She sighed.

"Thank you, really. I'll keep on top of Libby. Let me know if our bride-to-be steps out of line."

"We had words last night. She will not make this easy," Rebecca said.

"I already spoke to her about that. I won't stand for her bitchy bullshit, bride or no."

"I get it. She's upset. As cranky as she was, I can't help feeling bad for her."

Rebecca approached for a hug, but Kyle recoiled. "Rain check? You're a little ripe, no?"

"What's a little ripeness between friends?" Rebecca pecked his cheek before stealing a chunk of melon. "I'll hold you to that hug, mister!"

She headed down the hall for a shower. Too bad forcing Rebecca into the wedding stank worse than a sweaty locker room after a ball game. Only time would tell if the gesture would pay off.

9

Rebecca awaited Barbara and Leslie for the impromptu, girls-only brunch she organized. She snagged a sunny window table at their go-to brunch place, a lazy neighborhood restaurant with a chill vibe. They served perfectly domed poached eggs with golden hollandaise and yummy mimosas. With only two ingredients, mimosas were a drink you'd think would be impossible to mess up, yet too many restaurants rose to the occasion.

The white tablecloth brushed her legs as she crossed them to pivot towards the window. Pedestrians sauntered by at a Sunday pace, chatting via Bluetooth earbuds while sipping towering cups of coffee. Others scurried home with copies of the New York Times folded under their arms. Sure, folks could get it online. But it was hard to break lifelong rituals like sprawling between the formerly massive sections of the Gray Lady for a lazy afternoon. Soon her words would be racked alongside it at newsstands.

A fork clanked on the floor, drawing Rebecca's attention across the aisle. The culprit: a toddler in a table-mounted booster seat. His dad bent over to retrieve the cutlery from among the mountain of food bits on the floor. Apparently, eggs and toast were no-goes, but the bacon made it down the hatch with a happy body wiggle. Carnivore instincts start early.

Next to the family was a table with two white-haired seniors tapping on their phones. Each ignored the other and had barely touched their overloaded plates. Hell, at this rate, Rebecca could probably nibble at their bacon without either noticing. If the girls didn't arrive soon...

"We're here, we're here," Barbara said. "Sorry to keep you waiting." Barbara leaned over to swap kisses. "Cross-town traffic was ridiculous. We ditched our cab and walked."

Leslie took an empty seat with her back to the window. Her usual spot. "Street fair. We should definitely walk back afterwards."

"More socks?" Rebecca teased.

"Don't knock it." She lifted her leg to model today's selection: a black sock with rusty fall leaves blowing in the wind.

"Anything to get my mind off my disaster of a dinner with Kyle's family last night."

Two heads popped over their menus.

"What happened?" Leslie asked.

"Guess who's in the wedding party for Kyle's sister?"

"You're joking," Barbara said.

"Wish I were."

"But I thought you were meeting her for the first time?" Leslie said.

"That tidbit didn't stop his parents from shoving me in."

Barbara spun to wave for the server. "Princess must have loved that."

"I'll say. It wasn't the reaction her parents wanted, but

we'll see if she calms down."

Tabling their menus, each ordered their usual meals and drinks.

"So what's this news that couldn't wait?" Leslie said.

"Well, you know how my blog has been picking up steam? Getting more attention?"

"Yes, and?" Barbara said.

"I spoke to MOD magazine and they want to collaborate on an article. Bring my words to a wider audience! Isn't that nuts?"

Barbara wrapped her in a shoulder hug. "Becca, that's amazing. Congratulations!"

"To our second budding journalist." Leslie raised her glass.

The three clinked and sipped. Rebecca did a happy wiggle—à la the toddler. She darted a quick glance back, but the munching child had migrated to his sippy cup.

Drinks all around.

"So what else do you know?" Barbara asked.

"Not too much. I'm waiting for more details and should get the paperwork within a few days. We'll see, but it feels real."

"Question," Leslie asked. "Are they hiring Rebecca Sloane or Bedroom Diary? Did they say anything about using your real name?"

Rebecca's stomach dropped. The last several months had been an amazing relief after a lifetime wandering in a sexual desert. Speaking openly to women about such an intimate topic energized her in ways she never imagined. However, the thought of rehashing it all using her own name was a non-starter.

"Yeah, no. Not going to happen under my name."

"You sure?"

"Of course! Can you imagine what a field day Darcy

and Harry would have, knowing I blog about orgasms at night? Darcy would probably find some stupid clause in the employee manual and get me fired."

Barbara swirled her Bloody Mary with her celery stick. "As your legal counsel, I'm sure you're on sound footing."

"Rebecca, think of how helpful this will be for all the women who didn't have the benefit of seeing an intimacy coach like Heidi Quinn. You have a lot of wisdom to share."

"More than I used to, at least."

Leslie ticked them off. "Between the medical study you were in and Heidi Quinn's coaching, who's better to speak to this orgasm quandary than you? You'll be able to tell the human side of the struggle."

"Ladies will eat it up," Barbara said.

"Damn right they will," Leslie said.

Her pals were almost more excited than she was, especially Leslie. As a journalist, she had tons of experience writing for magazines like MOD. She might need to lean on her friend, yet, given that Rebecca had zero experience writing for international magazines.

"Do you ever sit back and appreciate how far you've come?" Leslie asked.

"It's not like it's been that long…" Rebecca said.

Leslie leaned in, both elbows on the table. "You have to admit, your whole personal outlook changed after your bedroom breakthrough. You went from feeling broken and not worthy of love, to being empowered and in control of your destiny. Things with Kyle are great…"

"Wedding not withstanding…" Barbara said. Rebecca answered by a seesawing her head in pseudo agreement.

"Other women will so benefit from that same confidence boost. I have to admit, I'm almost jealous I'm not working on it."

"That's not a bad idea," Barbara said. "Leslie has a lot of

writing experience. Rebecca, you have the life experience. You could be an unstoppable duo."

"You know, you're right. I don't know what I'm doing, anyway. Are you really up for it?" Rebecca asked.

"Am I ever! I totally would love to help."

"Great, you're in! We'll do it together."

"Amazing! Thank you. I promise you won't regret it," Leslie hoisted a toast.

"To an amazing joint venture. May you inspire juicy orgasms the world over!"

"To juicy orgasms!" Rebecca said.

The three clinked, chuckling at the man at the next table, who flushed red after overhearing their toast.

"Be sure you both behave. I won't jump in to break up cat fights about differing artistic visions," Barbara said.

"I'd never!" Rebecca said.

"Wouldn't you?"

"No, Leslie's hair is far too thin to get a good hold. She'd have an overwhelming advantage!" Rebecca tossed her mane of curls.

The food arrived and they redirected their attentions. As they ate, Rebecca warmed to the collaboration idea. The thought of helping other women on a grand scale warmed her insides as much as her oozy poached eggs. And having Leslie help would be her hollandaise. Dipping a corner of crusty toast in her golden well of egg, she shoved it in her waiting mouth. Urgency surged through her, as if gobbling her Sunday breakfast would get the logistics settled faster. There was so much to say and women hungered for answers. And they'd waited long enough.

Kyle wrinkled his nose as the beer bottle hit his lips. The bitterness a perfect metaphor for his Sunday. A jumbled mess of conflicting ideas warred for supremacy in his mind. The sun was shining. It was a gorgeous day, by any measure. He should have been out on a ride, exploring country roads with the wind in his face. But there he sat. Inside. Alone. Hiding from life instead of experiencing it.

It'd be otherwise if the offending issue of MOD would quit staring at him from the coffee table. More than once, Kyle dangled it over the hungry mouth of the garbage chute, only to pull back at the last moment. Throwing it away felt like wasting a valuable clue. Yet his paper self offered no answers about what Jane was up to. Vain as it sounded, it was impossible to view the entire "Our Favorites" issue as anything but an excuse to get his attention. The image of Kyle held significance. It mesmerized Jane so much, she had it blown up eight feet high and papered it onto the hallway leading to her MOD office. The merciless ribbing Kyle took at the time did nothing to persuade Jane to take it down. But why now? Why, after all this time, did she toss this grenade his way?

Jane did nothing without a reason, which meant she was up to something. Not knowing hollowed out a familiar pit in his gut. The same sour foreboding accompanied his every interaction with her. And with good reason. He'd end up on the losing end.

Jane thought she knew him, but Kyle knew Jane, too. A master of patience, she'd wait until Kyle was at his most vulnerable before swooping in to steal his soul with a purr and an unwanted caress. And a mocking laugh. Yes, always a laugh. And a head toss that jiggled her body down to the stupid cuff clinging for dear life on her bony wrist.

Kyle shivered, willing the mental image away.

He'd had enough of her for a lifetime.

Two lifetimes.

Was Jane a phantom hiding in every shadow? No. But she wielded the levers of power better than anyone he'd ever seen—and always to her own advantage. She was toying with him. Stalking from afar. No way she'd stop with one magazine spread. Familiar electricity hung in the air. She'd be back. She'd be back, and he needed to be ready.

A key in the door made his heart skip until Rebecca swept into view, wearing a mass of shopping bags and an enormous smile.

"The best shopping ever!" she pulsed her bagged hands for emphasis.

"Where'd you go?" he said, muting the cheering crowds of a golf tournament.

Golf?

When had that started?

"Street fair. Third Avenue. I almost wish we hadn't eaten. The food looked and smelled fantastic." She untangled her arms from the bags and bounced onto the sofa next to him.

"How was your day?" she asked.

Kyle took a long draft of beer.

She surveyed the empty beer bottles on the coffee table. "What's wrong? Have you been sitting here all day?"

"I'm fine." Kyle floored his legs. Whatever she had done all day, he needed some of that positive energy. His beer clinked on the glass coaster as he set it down.

"Show me what you got."

Bag after bag emerged, nested within each other like one of those wooden Russian dolls. From patterned socks and leggings to hoop earrings, Rebecca fizzed with excitement. Her positivity, a breath of fresh air.

He rose and crossed the room to her.

"I don't know what I'd do without you," he wrapped her in his arms.

Rebecca dropped her bags and hugged back, burying her head in his chest in that way that restored his brokenness. Severed shards of glass fused together, at least for a moment. But those moments were growing, linking and leaving fewer gaps, day by day.

"Ky," she said.

"Yeah?"

She chewed her lip, churning it against his chest.

"Let's hear it," Kyle squeezed her tight with both arms.

"It could be good, I think. That man I mentioned the other day, we spoke and they want me to write for them. For their magazine."

Kyle pulled back to see her face. "What magazine?"

"MOD."

"Christ, Rebecca? Are you serious?" He pushed away. Having her close choked his lungs dry.

"It's a great opportunity to promote my blog, don't you think?"

"Why MOD? Why does it have to be MOD?"

"What's the matter with MOD?"

"That's where she worked!"

"That's where who worked?"

"The woman, who—you know—harassed me…"

"Really? She still works there?"

"Ah, yeah. She does."

Rebecca pulled him back in, her bright eyes seeking his.

"I know this is a strange coincidence—"

"You think?"

"The woman who hurt you doesn't know who I am. And she doesn't know I'm Bedroom Diary. You understand that, don't you?"

Kyle sighed. She had a point, but it felt more wrong than anything.

"Just because these events coincide doesn't mean one caused the other."

"Causation? You've been hanging out with our resident lawyer too much."

"Sweetie, it's impossible to hang out with Barbara too much. Anyway, we could all do with more logic in our lives. Clear thinking?"

"Yeah, well, my clear thinking—my common sense—says run. Run and don't look back."

"I'm done running. If my experience with sex coaching has taught me anything, it's that I'm more powerful than I think. I'm ready for this challenge. Besides, Leslie is going to help me and I think it'll be an amazing opportunity to help thousands of women who are hurting like I was."

Her eternal optimism was admirable, but flashes of their summer drama flickered in his mind like a bad movie. Her insecurities and secrets almost doomed their relationship before it started.

"This is a freight train with broken brakes coming right at us. Can't you see that?"

"I think you're being a little dramatic. It's just an article. I've been blogging for months and you haven't said a word. Not one."

Rebecca dragged him over to the couch to sit. "Everyone already knows."

"Not at work. Not Harry and Darcy. My family. Your dad…"

"Stop, stop. We're not using my name. This is not a big deal."

"C'mon. Be realistic," Kyle said.

"I am being realistic. My name won't be public. Everything will publish under the pen name Bedroom Diary, so it'll be completely confidential."

"But for how long? She'll find out. Then it'll lead straight back to me. To us."

Kyle flushed exasperation from his body with a heavy sigh, but it flooded right back, filling him with dread like a nightmare after waking. Why can't she see what a horrible idea this is?

The reality of their impasse settled in. Like his exchanges with Jane, he sensed he'd end up on the losing end.

"I don't want to go back to living in a fishbowl," Kyle said.

"We won't. I promise."

"What's your MOD contact's name?" Kyle asked.

"Viraj Gupta. He's an editor. Know him?"

"No. How old?"

"Late twenties, but that's a guess," Rebecca said.

Too young to have been there then.

Rebecca swiveled on the sofa to face him. "Please understand, this is something I really need to do. Leslie is helping, and I hope to get a few of Heidi's other clients to participate."

"This is snowballing already..."

"Ky, I need you to support me in this. Just like I support you with your work, your life, this crazy wedding..."

She had a point. Rebecca had been amazing in supporting him after he broke the big secret, keeping it from their friend group while putting up with an ungodly amount of shit about Libby's wedding. His defenses melted. Rebecca knew it too, as a broad smile returned to her face.

"You've got to stop worrying so much. Relax," Rebecca crawled on his lap, straddling him with her curvy legs. "It'll be fine. I promise. There's nothing to worry about."

"But…"

"Shush." She silenced his lips with her finger. "No more talking."

Her soft lips pressed against his.

Kyle's body answered. Against his wishes. Betraying him, like it had so many times before. Just like…

"No. No…" Kyle slid her off so he could stand.

"What's the matter?" Rebecca asked.

Kyle hugged himself, his chest heaving. "I'm not a toy."

"Who said you were a toy?"

Rebecca sat wearing a stunned expression. "Sweetie, did I do something wrong?"

He wanted to speak. To tell her. It's not the what, it's the how. The when. The consent. But all he could do was press his lips together so hard it hurt. The pain distracted. It always had. It was the only thing that saved him from crumbling completely. From crying like the pathetic tool he was.

Rebecca righted herself on the couch. "Is this about the article?"

Kyle looked away, acid inching up his throat.

"Why are you being so stubborn? I have the opportunity to help women, and you can only see a train careening off the rails. I've never met anyone so hell-bent on seeing darkness. Where does that come from?"

"Experience," he said through clenched teeth.

He strode to the window and threw it open. Shutting his eyes, he focused on the sounds. Children squealing from the playground. Chirping birds. Murmured conversations from the park benches three-floors below. Leaves rustling in the breeze. Pure. Clean. Life. It washed a measure of angst away. When his eyes fluttered open, his gaze landed square on his motorcycle. Its glossy black paint and shiny chrome calling him home.

He walked to the front closet for his jacket.

"Where are you going?" Rebecca asked.

"For a ride."

"Can I come?"

"No," he said a little too forcefully. "I need to think."

"Can't you think with me there?"

Kyle's fingers closed around his wallet on the foyer table. His keys were next.

"Kyle, you can't run away every time we need to talk."

"I'm not running away, I jus…"

"—just need some air," Rebecca mimicked. "I know."

She stood in front as he hiked his jacket on, chewing her lip. "I'm sorry if before—you felt—if I triggered—anything. But please don't shut me out."

He kissed her forehead. "I'm doing the best I can."

The motorcycle between his legs rumbled to life. Rebecca was right about him running away. But he'd dwelled alone in the shadows for so long, the last thing he wanted was for her to get lost in the forest with him.

Jane scratched her initials on the magazine proof of the accessory spread, the tactile sensation imprinting her authority. Three dozen samples had arrived from top designers vying for the coveted space. For once, her team did a good job of narrowing the selections down. So good she signed off on their recommended "top five" to make it into the layout.

Anyone can get lucky.

She stretched her arms overhead, curving from one side to the other before shaking out her weary hands. Paperwork. Was there anything more tiresome? Even she had to remind herself of its importance. Its critical role in the production workflow.

After all, sound paperwork proved her right more times to count when her underlings got sloppy.

Flawless execution built the magazine into a world-renowned leader. Any mistake, no matter how minor, would reflect on her. Cast doubt on her ability to lead. Make industry watchers wonder if she still "had it." No, she'd not give them the opportunity to cast doubt in her direction, as they had on so many of her peers before they were unceremoniously ousted. Sundays off were an indulgence she couldn't afford.

The copper straw clinked her teeth as she took a long sip of her citrus-infused ice water, cool tartness jolting her senses alert.

Back to work.

She opened the folder Viraj left with the latest round of contracts. Thumbing through, each was only worthy of a cursory glance. Then one caught her eye: Bedroom Diary. Jane's finger traced the terms of the deal. A cover story, 2,000 words with sidebars, yada yada. Tracking down the page, Jane looked to confirm the real name of the writer. The domain registration for the website matched the legal name on the contract: Rebecca Sloane, with a New York address.

Jane typed Rebecca's name in the search query which launched her LinkedIn page. She worked at MediaNow as a media planner. It was a small shop, but they were certainly making a name for themselves. At least Rebecca would understand the business, lead times and sensitivities required when working with magazines. It'd make the process work that much smoother.

Jane searched Instagram to see if she had an account. @BeccaSloane22 looked promising. She had posts about sexual topics, books, travel photos, and...

Jane's eyes widened.

Her trembling hand clicked one picture to be sure, enlarging it to fill her 40-inch screen. There he was. Kyle Dillon. In an embrace with this woman, this Rebecca Sloane. Her eyes welled as if recovering a lost child feared dead. But he wasn't dead. He was alive, and well, and happy, and…

Her chest constricted. Tight. Squeezing every puff of air from her lungs until none remained, leaving her gasping like a fish out of water. Jane hiccupped small mouthfuls of air until a coughing fit left her throat on fire. Pull it together. Her shaky fingers stretched for her ice water, nearly tipping it over onto her paperwork before tossing the cup back so hard the metal straw tumbled out to the floor along with a mound of crushed ice.

Blouse drenched, body shocked to attention, chest heaving, Jane struggled for enough oxygen to think clearly. Blinking rapidly did nothing to remove the vision before her. She'd been searching in vain for years, yet there he was. The fates brought him back to her precisely when she needed him most.

An unfamiliar loneliness had begun invading Jane's solitary moments in a way that petrified. She had no one and never had. But for the first time, she felt it. The nagging isolation clung like a third-rate celebrity to fame, but she had not an inkling what to do about it. But maybe that was about to change. Breathing restored, she risked a look back at the screen.

Ahh. She traced his face with her finger.

Longing rose unbidden. She hadn't seen the real Kyle in ages. Old images, yes, but those were ten years out of date. He completely dropped off the map after quitting modeling. Beyond a few tiny profile pictures in photography trade magazines and a few panel speaking gigs, Kyle vanished from public view. Forever stuck in time amidst his many file photos. But there he was in all his glory, but even better. He'd filled out. No longer the boy she knew, Kyle was every inch a man.

Glowing olive skin.

Electric blue eyes.

Dark hair with just enough curl to tangle your fingers.

Persistent hint of a five-o'clock shadow, making him look like a delicious rogue.

Seeing him happy with someone new made Jane's skin crawl.

Jane scanned Rebecca's posts. It didn't take a seasoned eye to tell they were in the deep infatuation stage. Wide smiles, arms draped all over each other, awkward selfie poses, Rebecca sitting on the back of his motorcycle—

Was it?

Yes. The very bike Kyle would never take Jane on. His escape vehicle, at the ready like the Batmobile in an underground grotto. Jane enlarged the browser window to see him closer. She knew every inch of that face. His dimples, every flash of mischief in his stunning eyes. She'd spent too many hours lingering over his face, over his torso. She squeezed the leather arms of her chair, imaging his muscular frame under hers...

Closing her eyes, she took a cleansing breath, massaging her jaw muscles to relax the clench.

Who was Rebecca? Really?

Jane zoomed in to get a good look.

A curly haired brunette, Rebecca was Latina from the looks of it. Nothing special. Nothing worthy of MOD. Though, she had a wholesomeness to her that was mildly appealing.

The chair creaked as Jane leaned back, putting distance between her and the screen glowing with images of her replacement. The one he bedded in her stead. They were together while she ached alone, passionless since his last touch. As much as she tried, the men who came after all paled in comparison.

Her mind drifted to his lovemaking. His touch. How he smelled. How he trembled. How he wooed her and made her feel like a real woman. She'd never been able to forgive him for how they ended. For his weakness. They could have been great, but he couldn't handle it. The spotlight. Couldn't handle being on the arm of someone of Jane's caliber. He forced her hand. He'd be dead if not for her quick thinking. But did he ever say thank you? Did he ever reach out to apologize? How much political capital had she wasted to mop up the aftermath of his sudden absence? And for what? To be left out in the cold as he moved on?

Jane lifted the Bedroom Diary contract. How could she reward this woman, her replacement, with a golden ticket to be in MOD? To reach MOD's global audience? To make a name for herself?

A name.

A household name.

And the spoils that came with it.

Her nostrils flared, drawing in as much air as she could manage, steeling herself to initial Rebecca's contract.

10

Kyle's mind was as twisted as the noodles in the bowl in front of him. His latest client, an Asian-fusion restaurant called Wok, needed new images for its website. But instead of focusing on the bright veggies, starches, and proteins in the bowls before him, Dr. Kaplan's words hung in his ears.

Was Kyle interested in meeting another survivor?

The good doctor saw accelerated progress when men sat face to face with others sharing similar experiences. It provided proof positive that they weren't alone, a point they likely spent too much time debating in their one-on-one sessions over the last few weeks. Show-and-tell with another client farther along in his therapy was likely Dr. Kaplan's shortcut around Kyle's stubbornness.

Apparently, men like Kyle were reluctant to give themselves grace. Physically larger, they admonished themselves that they should have been able to stop it. And if Kyle was honest with himself, that exact thought careened around his brain so often it bored a canyon. Rationally, he knew he wasn't alone. If he were, the world wouldn't need people like Dr. Kaplan. But knowing he wasn't alone didn't help matters. He'd known every day for eleven years what happened to him likely happened to others. From the Boy Scouts, to the church, to youth leagues, boys were not immune. So how would sitting with another "survivor" help him? He barely wanted to be in therapy himself. Sitting with someone else would make the entire enterprise unbearable.

Kyle bent over a bowl to refocus on crafting the perfect meal. What he wouldn't kill to add a dash of motor oil to darken and thicken the sauce, but it had to be authentic. Patrons needed to see authentic meals, even if theirs wouldn't be composed with a tweezer. Their dish would taste the same. They'd come in, order, dine, and leave satisfied. Why couldn't his therapy be that easy? Rebecca said to keep an open mind, but how could he? The thought of a joint therapy session left him mildly nauseated, a career hazard for a food photographer.

Kyle shifted his key light and the bowl of noodles, red peppers, and snow peas transformed into a glistening beauty. He depressed his shutter to take the overhead shots the client requested before moving along to more artistic angles. Ones they would likely prefer. He poured hot water from a thermos into a bowl, dunked three cotton balls in, and popped them into the tiny portable microwave he brought with him. When the timer beeped, he removed them with chopsticks and tucked them under the noodles, leaving gaps for the vapor to escape.

Instant steam. On film, the icy noodles would look tempting and warm.

Trickery at its finest.

Maybe that's what Dr. Kaplan's group was?

Trickery.

An opportunity for Kyle to trick his brain into telling himself he wasn't such a screwup to let it all unfold and do nothing to stop it. An experimental placebo, of sorts. He'd walk in and see another hurting human. Another damaged soul chewed up and spat out by the fashion industry. Hell, it might even be someone Kyle recognized or knew personally. How weird would that be? They'd compare notes like prisoners.

What'cha in for?

Harassment.

Me too.

Was she pretty?

Not bad. You?

Nah. Maybe once, but not anymore.

You want it to happen?

No.

Did you stop her?

No. She was my boss. You?

She held my future in her hands. She threatened to cry rape. She threatened to ruin my life...

How would any of that help his psyche? Hearing that someone else got shafted and tossed aside as he did? Dr. Kaplan probably meant well, but would it help?

Kyle's form reflected off a glossy black enamel partition. Hinged in two-foot sections, it separated the kitchen's bus area from the main dining room. In the stillness, six Kyles moved as one, a ghostly form in the shadowy restaurant.

He hipped his hands in a protective show of force. The shadow followed.

Six Kyles.

Formidable.

Maybe if there were six of him, he wouldn't have fallen prey so easily. He would have had some help fending off her threats and advances. He would have been able to summon the strength to resist. But maybe that was the good doctor's point. Reinforcements were at the ready. It wasn't too late to get help. Instead of fighting demons on his own, he could enlist a partner to defeat them together.

Could two heads be better than one?

Probably.

They certainly couldn't be any worse.

Rebecca plugged her ear against the blaring traffic as the call to Brad rang. Stepping outside her office was the only way to get any privacy. She was NOT having this conversation within earshot of colleagues, or Darcy. Both because she was free-lancing on the side and because, well, orgasm talk didn't make for polite conversation. But maybe reaching a wider audience with her message would help change that.

"Heidi Quinn's office, Brad speaking. How can I help you?" the familiar voice said.

"Brad, it's Rebecca Sloane. How are you?"

There was a pause.

She could picture him pushing up the bridge of his tortoise-shell glasses with one finger as he searched the memory banks.

Rebecca sighed, "What? You forgot your annoying Muppet already?"

"Ah yes, the pushy one."

After Brad refused Rebecca an appointment with his reclusive sex-coach-of-a-boss, she showed up unannounced and hollered up at his closed second-story window from the street below. It was quite a scene, but she'd do it again in a heartbeat. It had been the only way to get Heidi's attention. But the humidity that day hadn't done her curly hair any favors, a fact Brad couldn't resist mentioning.

"What can we do for you, sweetheart? If you want a double-dip, I can refer you to some talented women picking up Heidi's work."

"Good segue. I do need a referral, but of a different sort. I had such a transformational experience with Heidi that I've been blogging about it."

"Really? How bold of you."

Rebecca wasn't sure how bold she was hiding her name, but accepted the compliment. She could count the number of active women's intimacy blogs on one finger—hers. Guess that was bold-ish. Certainly better than keeping quiet, which is what she'd been doing for 29 years.

"Yes, well, I have an opportunity to write a story for a wider magazine audience and wonder if you might connect me with a few other clients willing to talk about their experiences with Heidi."

Brad milked the silence. "There's no kissing and telling in what we do."

"I get that."

"Women who come here expect the utmost discretion."

"Totally. I'd expect nothing less."

"So why do you always call up here asking for the impossible?"

"Because the impossible is often possible if you look at it from another angle."

"Girlfriend, the only angle around here is sealed lips." Brad slammed a desk drawer shut as if to emphasize the point, but he wasn't getting off that easily.

"Yes, but I'm trying to do my part to advance Heidi's work. To help more women, but in my own way."

"Picking up the mantle?"

"Heidi can't do it alone. There are millions of women out there who have never heard of masturbation coaching. They have no idea what sex is really like. Someone's got to help them."

"That's noble, but we don't make it a practice to give out client names. Just like we wouldn't give out your name."

Brad was great at erecting roadblocks, but needed to work on his creative problem solving. At least, where Rebecca was concerned. Someone so maddeningly unhelpful had no business working for a beacon of empowerment like Heidi.

"You're really turning me down?" Rebecca asked.

"Yes, sunshine. No can do."

"How about this? Email a few ladies who might be open to talking. Share my contact information and they can reach out to me if they're interested. What's the harm in that?"

"Interesting… but no."

"Can I at least connect to Heidi? Send her a few questions I can include in the article?"

A quiet, thinking Brad was way better than a hard no Brad. Rebecca forced herself to wait while his pro-con calculations played out. Silence was a powerful negotiation tool when artfully deployed. She'd recently closed a deal for one of her clients while the rep negotiated against himself, mistaking her silence for dissent. It was a wonder to behold.

"It could work," he said at last.

"It could."

No doubt Brad was trying to think up an excuse to say no. He had tons of practice.

"Where is this article going to run?"

"MOD magazine."

"MOD magazine! Are you kidding?" Brad lost all composure. "How'd you score that?"

"Funny enough, they came to me. They found my blog and wanted to amplify the message."

"Girl, you were holding out. MOD has done multiple features on Heidi. They're very into orgasms over there."

"That's an understatement." Rebecca had her nose buried in MOD for years looking for sex tips, but they never covered her particular problem. Their advice focused on getting the man and pleasing him, but stopped short covering what she should be feeling or demanding from him. An oversight shared by most media, but one she and Leslie hoped to rectify.

"So you'll help me?"

"Against my better judgment. I'll see what I can do."

"That's amazing! Thank you!"

Rebecca finished her call and headed back upstairs to her desk. Speaking to Brad brought back a flood of old emotions from when she called him desperate for help. It reminded her of the article's true purpose: to help women.

The work day flew, though Rebecca spent more time batting article ideas away than doing actual work. Now she was hopelessly behind on her to-do list, with a meeting looming.

"Hey, do you have a minute?"

Rebecca spun her desk chair to find Evvy, a junior staffer whom she'd been unofficially mentoring in the ways of their media buying and planning industry.

"Can you look for an open spot on my calendar?" Rebecca asked.

"Um, okay. That media plan I'm working on is due, and I need your help. Someone suggested remnants, but I don't understand what those are."

"Rebecca!" Darcy blasted from her desk.

Rebecca shrugged, rising to gather her things.

Evvy smiled. Darcy was a major handful and everyone knew it.

"I promise I'll help. Find some time and we can talk then."

Balancing her pad and her laptop, Rebecca strode down the aisle of gray cubes to her boss's office. Unlike where Rebecca sat in a six-foot high cubicle maze, executives at MediaNow worked in glass terrariums: interior glass walls designed to let the exterior light pour through the glimmering windows.

Rebecca used to scurry around ten steps behind Darcy, wincing at every nasty stare. It took Rebecca's experience with Heidi to finally grow a spine and stop letting Darcy use her as a doormat. Rebecca got stellar reviews and Harry believed in her. Rebecca was finally believing in herself too, but Darcy obviously preferred the old Rebecca. Somehow, she'd have to get over her disappointment.

Rebecca squinted as the afternoon sun reflected off the sheen of Darcy's mahogany desk. Mornings were a better time for meetings with Darcy. Her personal hygiene was at its cleanest. By afternoon, she welcomed the window glare as it made it hard to see Darcy's questionable grooming habits, though it did nothing to dispel the sour smell.

"If we don't start on time, we can't finish on time," Darcy said, adjusting her glasses as she abandoned her computer to face forward. Rebecca slipped her laptop onto the edge of her desk.

Rebecca sharing the desk was a power move of her own. They were colleagues, not master and servant. The first time took Darcy by surprise, but the effect subtly elevated Darcy's respect level. Though she still had a way to go to qualify as anything approaching civil.

"How goes the manager training?" Darcy asked.

"Good, thank you. I'm investigating consultants and programs to consider. I'd also like to augment the in-person training with an interactive eLearning software to make training fun."

Pleasantries? What's she up to?

"I don't know if we need that," Darcy said.

"It's worth considering. Gamification is proven to enhance content retention," Rebecca said, taking a sip from her travel mug.

Darcy leaned back. "It appears that you have this well under control, which I presume means you can handle an accelerated timeline."

"I don't think that's a good…"

"Oh, don't underestimate yourself. You're a rock star," Darcy cooed, her voice dripping with sarcasm.

"I'm not underestimating. I'm being practical."

"Come now, surely, a high achiever like you can handle a faster turnaround time."

Of course she couldn't, and Darcy knew it. Rebecca reached for her own drink for a sip. Day work, orientation training, manager training, and less time to do it all? No effing way. She needed every minute she could get, and then some. But if she said no, Darcy would tell Harry she was overloaded. He'd withdraw her projects just when she was making headway. If Rebecca said yes, she'd barely have time to breathe.

Darcy broke the silence. "I'm sensing hesitation. I'd hate to disappoint the client."

"No. No need."

Darcy's eyes flared. She'd caught her prey, and they both knew it.

"Excellent. Well done then. Let's turn to other matters. Did you finish the planning for Hollis Hotels?"

Rebecca nodded and proceeded to guide them through the plan without even thinking. Her mind busy computing how she was going to manage everything on her plate. Every assignment was an honor. Harry handpicked her for each one. How could she let him down? But even more, she wanted them all. She KNEW she could do them and excel. Individually. Yes. All together? Not so much. And that's without factoring the work needed to write the article with Leslie. Their meeting at MOD to get the details ironed out was the next day.

But as her dad often said, you don't slam the door when opportunity knocks. Rebecca would just have to work triple hard to ensure Darcy's expectations of failure were wrong. Too bad it'd mean Rebecca's instincts were wrong too.

"You finished with that?" Kyle said, reaching for Rebecca's empty plate.

"Yeah."

Rebecca's blank face stared out the window over their dining table. Dreamy and unfocused, it was the same expression she'd worn since arriving home.

Kyle bent into her line of sight. "Anyone home?"

She blinked. "I'm sorry. This article thing, it's brought back a lot of feelings that I haven't felt in a while. Ones I never thought I'd feel again."

"No one's forcing you to moonlight as a journalist. They liked your blog, but Leslie knows the story. She's dying to write it. Why can't she draft it without you?"

Rebecca shook her head. "No, it's important for me to see this through. It's me they found, and it's my life story. How would that look if I backed out?"

"Happens all the time."

"Not to me. This is a big deal. More eyeballs will be on my words in one day than in months of blogs put together."

Kyle called to her from the kitchen. "Not everyone is going to like what you have to say."

"That's precisely why I have to do it." Rebecca appeared where he stood, washing plates.

"There could be unwanted attention. Are you ready for that?" he said.

"You know, for the first time, I don't care. I am who I am. If I've learned anything in this whole mess, that, let's face it, everyone in our circle already knows about, it's that shame is a toxic emotion. It's long past time for me to let it go."

Kyle huffed a smile. "That's brilliant advice. I wish I could."

"Hey, you can. You'll get there, too. I promise."

Rebecca slipped in between him and the sink, wet soap suds dripping down his forearms onto her shoulders.

"I highly recommend making peace with your demons and moving on. It's liberating."

"Is it?"

"Quite so." She squeezed his butt with both hands, sending a jolt of longing through him.

He moved to caress her now familiar form. Down the curve of her back, his hands ringed her small waist, before rounding her hips to find their home on her butt. The butt that drove him crazy, especially in the tight jeans she always wore.

"This ass of yours will make me forget a lot of things," he said with a squeeze.

She reached for his head, bringing his lips to hers, exploring his loose curls.

As they kissed, he slid his hands under the waist of her top, caressing her supple skin.

Warm.

Home.

"Time for the bedroom, young lady."

"What about the dishes?"

"They can wait."

Kyle lifted her and tossed her over his shoulder.

"Hey!" she yelled, giggling, her socked feet kicking in futility.

"Look what I found!" Kyle gnawed at the butt inches from his mouth.

"Oh my God! Quit it," she laughed as he carried her to the bedroom.

After, Rebecca gathered the sheets around her body as she rolled toward Kyle.

"So, Libby texted me today," Rebecca said.

"Really?"

"Yeah. She told me to keep Saturday open in a few weeks to go to Texas."

"A bridal pilgrimage?"

"Bridesmaid dress shopping."

"Huh," Kyle said. "I guess she gave in."

"You'll be on your own that weekend."

"Maybe I should come with you? Keep her in line," Kyle said, trailing his finger up the curve of her hip.

"If I'm really going to be in this wedding, I can't hide from the bride."

"Might be best."

Her shoulder smack stung. "Stop it. You're not helping by making her out to be a monster. I don't know what to believe."

"She's not a monster, but she's a handful. My advice is not to let her see you sweat. Be firm."

She rolled on her back with a sigh. "Ky, I need to be who I am. She's got to like me or not like me, but I won't pretend to be something I'm not."

"Don't pretend, just don't lead with your belly."

"My what?"

"It's an animal thing. Followers show their belly as a sign of submission and respect. Don't do that. Libby only respects strength."

She furrowed her brows. "Am I going shopping or to a cage match?"

"Be prepared, and you'll be fine."

"And you? Maybe you can meet a friend or do something fun?"

"I'll be fine. You don't need to coordinate my schedule."

"But…"

"What?"

"I worry you're alone too much. And with women all the time. Between me, Vivian, Libby, your mom. There's a lot of estrogen floating around your world. Do you have any guy friends from when you lived here?"

The local friends Kyle had were mostly from modeling, and he'd lost all of those when his career imploded. Who needs friends that scatter at the first sign of trouble? No one. But maybe his solitary existence was a defense mechanism. Friends meant questions. Questions meant sharing. There wasn't much he wanted to share with anyone, except the woman sharing his bed.

Kyle scooped Rebecca close with his arm until her head rested on his chest.

"Go. Have fun. I'll take care of myself."

Just like I always do.

11

Test flashes pierced the morning blueness as Kyle entered his mentor's photography studio at *MOD*. Racks of clothes, tables of accessories, and empty chairs awaited the models who would arrive in a few hours' time for hair and makeup. But Marco's team hadn't yet arrived. Which gave Kyle ample time for coffee and conversation with his old friend.

"Alone in the dark," Kyle hollered as he ambled across the room. "Double-espresso with agave nectar?"

Marco looked up from his work, his goatee and trademark ponytail glowing white against his tanned skin and black kurta shirt. The silver embroidery around the neckline framed his head like a portrait.

"Ah, my friend. You—and that coffee—are a sight for sore eyes."

Kyle set the hot cups down to embrace his friend. Rebecca was right. He needed some male energy in his life. And no one's energy was better than Marco's.

"Work is going well?"

"Well enough." Kyle's lips welcomed a few sips of black coffee.

"That's not what I hear. You are making waves. Don't deny it."

"I'm more in the ripple league now, and that's fine by me."

"Ahh," he dismissed with a flip of his wrist.

"Not everyone is meant for this," Kyle said.

Marco bent to his viewfinder. "It's not what you were meant for. It's what you hunger for in your soul. What you can't live without."

Rebecca flashed to mind. "Are we alone?"

"For now."

Kyle lowered his voice. "Is my friend holding any—grudges?"

Marco laughed. "You need not whisper this, my friend. Everyone knows. And yes. She is, but not grudges. Quite the opposite."

Kyle fingered his scratchy beard growth. "Still?"

"Quite so."

"There hasn't been anyone?"

"They come and go, as always. No one special. *That*, my friend, would have been news. Just like you were."

"Don't remind me." Kyle slouched into a black stylist chair.

Marco smirked, then resumed his work.

"I've been working with Dr. Kaplan, you know. A few sessions. He wants me to meet with another client of his."

"Then you should do it."

"I said I would, but am having second thoughts."

"And you will have third thoughts and fourth thoughts, and so on, and so on." Marco circled his wrists for emphasis. "But you should still go."

His mentor's eyes closed to savor his espresso. Wrinkles in his sunned skin mapped a life well lived, and likely, a recent photoshoot outdoors. So at peace in the morning stillness, Kyle dare not intrude. A moment later, his eyes popped open.

"So? You go?" he asked.

"What if it's someone I know? Or worse, someone who knows me?"

"Then you have a new brother. Someone to help share the load, and you can share his."

He wagged a pointed finger in Kyle's direction. "You are making excuses. You will give this session a try. Yes? I say this because you have already decided. I tell you nothing you don't already know yourself."

Kyle combed both hands through his hair. He was right. Kyle had decided to give it a try. Marco was supposed to give him a pass. Give him permission not to go. But Marco still lived in the fashion world. He saw the excesses every day. The overstepping, the blurring of lines between client and model, between model and publisher. Did he register the damage beneath? Had he suspected anything in Kyle's case? If he had, he kept those thoughts to himself.

Marco stroked his goatee. "If you don't want to tell me, I understand. But—I fear—I fear I've made a grave mistake when it came to you, my friend."

Kyle looked up from the floor, meeting his concerned eyes.

"I always presumed the two of you were—consensual. But, was it?"

A familiar flight instinct rose in Kyle's body, tensing every muscle, putting senses on high alert. The set. The conversation. How often had he talked to Marco about what to do? How to get out? Too many to count, but never did he speak the truth about why. And here Kyle was, back again.

About to answer the one question Marco had never asked, and he had never volunteered.

Kyle swallowed hard.

Marco waited patiently for a reply. A reply eleven years in the making.

Kyle hiked his chin. "No. It was not consensual."

Marco wiped his face, his other hand on his hip, a profound silence lingering between them. "I feared this."

"There was no way for you to know. I didn't tell anyone."

"You looked happy…"

Kyle shrugged.

"Forgive me, please, for my ignorance," Marco said.

"I didn't tell you. Your career would've been at risk if I had."

"But what of yours? You lost it," Marco said.

"I have the career I was destined to have. The one I was supposed to have in the first place," Kyle said.

Marco hung his head in thought before looking up with sorrow clouding his soft hazel eyes. "What is the phrase? 'Evil needs only for good men to do nothing'? Well, I did nothing. I should have intervened. If I had…"

"You've twisted it around. Please, don't have regrets. I don't want that hanging between us."

He sighed. "I will try, but my heart is heavy for you. For what you are left to confront all these years later. Such a terrible thing, what happened—you know, you did nothing wrong?"

"You sound like my therapist…"

Marco stepped closer to whisper. "Listen to me. She holds more power in this industry than anyone. Godlike in many respects. Someone as young as you had no chance under those circumstances."

He was right, of course. But as a man, he couldn't help feeling like he was at fault. Who gets upset about a woman forcing herself on them? Isn't that what guys fantasize about all the time? How many porno movies glorified this exact office scenario?

But when it happened against your will. Happened under threats of financial ruin and false assault charges. It was emasculating and as far from sexy as it got.

He hated himself for letting her get away with it.

Marco continued. "I'm sorry. I'm sorry for not realizing. Not helping you. It's good you have support now. The doctor, and you have Rebecca."

Rebecca. Hearing her name off his lips in this room made Kyle's senses leap to high alert.

"My girlfriend is working on a project for *MOD*. Jane doesn't know her real name or that we're together, and I'd like to keep it that way. Can you keep your ears open? Give me a heads-up if there's trouble?"

"Of course. But Jane has changed since you left. Much more suspicious and secretive than before. Be careful, both of you."

"Thanks," Kyle said. "We will."

A beam of sun pierced the window, landing across Kyle's face. He looked up to greet it.

Marco snapped a shot.

"Handsome as ever." He smiled.

Kyle embraced Marco with a thump to the back and headed out before his team arrived.

Be careful. Truer words were never spoken.

Valis Publishing dominated 25 floors of a gleaming office building in lower Manhattan. Ironically, it was only blocks away from where Rebecca purchased the blinged-out black socks hiding beneath her wide-legged trousers. Paired with patent leather alligator shoes, a white top, and black tailored jacket, it was the best she could manage to walk into the fashion epicenter of the universe.

The security officer ushered her through to the 19th floor. She was right on time. If all went well, she'd be done and at her desk before Darcy finished her morning executive meeting.

When the elevator doors opened, Leslie stood near the window wearing a crisp white blouse of her own and camel blazer atop pinstriped dark-wash jeans. Effortless style. Rebecca released the breath she was holding.

"Hey there," Rebecca stopped short of kissing Leslie lest she leave a crimson-lips emoji on her cheek. It was something her aunts invariably did when they visited from Puerto Rico. The thought of their lively spirit made her smile.

"What?" Leslie asked.

"Nothing. Just drawing on some latent Latina courage." Rebecca moved in closer to whisper, "I'm glad you're here. I feel a bit out of my depth."

"No worries. They likely want to make sure you're a real person, a real SME."

"SME?"

"Subject matter expert."

"Told you. Clueless," Rebecca sighed.

"Don't worry. You'll be better than great. Hell, you already did the hard part. You lived through it!" Leslie bumped shoulders.

The receptionist walked them to a modest-sized window office of the editor that contacted her, Viraj Gupta. Tall and lean with a solid build, Viraj's honey complexion perfectly set off his thick, black hair. With a dimpled chin and hazel eyes, he looked ripped from the pages of MOD. That, and eerily familiar.

"Welcome, have a seat. So nice to meet you in person. Shall I call you BD?" Viraj said, rising and extending his hand to Rebecca across the desk.

"That works, if you don't mind. I want to keep my identity as low profile as possible, given the circumstances," Rebecca said.

"Of course. Why, Ms. Allen. I'm surprised to see you here."

"It's been a while," Leslie said, shaking hands.

"You look well, as always. I've been eagerly anticipating meeting BD," Viraj said, drawing his chair in to rest his elbows on the desk.

"Thank you," Rebecca said, pressing her lips closed.

Hurling would be so inappropriate right now.

"So, let's get to it. We're looking for a story about 2,000 words. The editorial staff is excited about this one and plans to include it as one of our supporting cover lines."

"Wow. That's big, and unexpected," Rebecca gulped.

"Your doing?" Leslie asked.

"Not too many bodies were harmed..." Viraj smiled.

"Given the length, our hope is for you to include a few call-out suggestions and sidebars with attributed first-person accounts."

"Sure, whatever you want," Rebecca said.

If Brad didn't come through with a quote from Heidi, Rebecca would have to form a Plan B. But with no one left, the stomach of Plan B was already churning.

"Readers love mystery," Viraj said. "The Bedroom Diary byline makes it really appealing to everyone. So relatable."

"Thanks. Having a pen name was the best choice for me, given my day job. And to protect my privacy."

"Yes, well, the only place where your name appears is on the contract. Besides me, the only people who have seen it are in the approval chain, mostly in legal and finance."

Rebecca relaxed into her chair. That level of secrecy was encouraging. Whoever harassed Kyle likely wasn't from finance or accounting. Weight lifted, her attention kicked in to survey her surroundings for the first time.

Framed covers of MOD circled the room, each labeled with an associated milestone Viraj achieved. Gleaming awards stood proudly on a glass table in the corner attesting to Viraj's accomplishments. He looked young, but experienced hands would definitely steward her article.

"Between the print and digital editions, MOD has a massive international following," Viraj said. "You'll be able to impact women around the globe in a very positive way. We are excited to get started."

"We? Who's 'we'?" Rebecca asked.

"Myself, the entire editorial team, really," Viraj said, obviously not appreciating Rebecca's tone.

Leslie leaned over, speaking low through a forced smile. "You're being rude."

"I'm sorry. The 'we' comment made it sound like more people know about me than he was letting on."

"Not to worry. We'll hold true to our confidentiality commitments in the contract," Viraj said.

"I have a lot riding on this, and a lot to lose if it goes sideways."

Rebecca's gaze drifted to the Manhattan skyline behind Viraj. Clear and bright, it shone with the optimism she longed to have about the endeavor. Leslie was here. Viraj was doing his best to remain composed. Instead of channeling her inner Kyle, she should be thankful for the opportunity to reach so many women in a magazine like MOD. Just because the woman who harassed Kyle worked at MOD didn't mean she would have anything to do with her project. For both their sakes, Rebecca hoped not. She didn't need a catty hallway scene with some woman still holding a torch for Kyle. Or worse, a pitchfork.

The conversation flowed until all details and deadlines were established. Rebecca and Leslie left with clear, albeit ambitious, marching orders. Honking traffic and construction jackhammering assaulted their senses as they emerged from the Valis Publishing cone of silence.

Rebecca shaded her eyes from the morning sun. "Did it go okay? I couldn't tell."

"Besides your little paranoid moment, pretty well."

"I just got spooked for a minute. I know you're used to this, but it's a big deal for me."

"Totally understandable. But we're good now, right? It's exciting!" Leslie said.

"Of course, yes," Rebecca said, ignoring her nagging misgivings. "So what now?"

"Why don't you outline your story in the order you feel it makes sense? I'll research some larger societal issues and data points we can pop in."

"That sounds good."

Rebecca gave Leslie a goodbye squeeze, wheels likely turning in her friend's blond head as she joined the flow of pedestrians on the busy sidewalk.

Rebecca headed north. If all went well, she'd be back at her desk before Darcy noticed anything was amiss. Hopefully by then, she'd believe it herself.

12

Since the infamous family dinner weeks earlier, Rebecca avoided Libby like Darcy avoided soap. But if her future included being a bridesmaid, one of them had to make an effort. No sense having wedding drama hanging over her head all weekend. Rebecca's Friday walk home from work was as good a time as any to chat with Libby. If cranky bride emerged, she could always pretend the traffic was too loud and hang up. *Contingencies...*

When the crosswalk light turned red, Rebecca popped out her phone and dialed Libby, tapping the call icon before she lost her nerve.

The phone rang three times before stony silence replaced the tones. With the street noise, Rebecca wasn't sure she answered.

"Libby?"

"I'm here."

"Oh, hi."

"Hello."

"I thought it'd be good if we talked."

"Haven't we said it all?" Libby answered.

"Look, I don't want to be in your wedding any more than you want me there."

"Oh, I doubt that."

A truck rattled by, belching acrid smoke. Its bitterness a distinct improvement over their conversation.

"This wasn't my idea. We didn't know about the opening until you mentioned it."

Libby sighed, "I know. I know. It's my bizarrely cruel parents up to their twisted mind games. It's my fucking wedding. Must they be so controlling?"

Rebecca was the last person to comment on the dynamics of the Dillon clan, a family unlike any she'd encountered before. Rebecca's family was a loud, pushy bunch on both sides. Her dad's Jewish relatives were obvious, wielding sarcastic guilt like Obi-Wan to bend you to their will. Her mom's loud Puerto Rican bunch out-mouthed each other, in your face, without mincing words. People battled and the victor emerged triumphant. The Dillons left no room for debate. Somehow, that was far scarier.

"Have they always been this way?" Rebecca asked.

"Yes. It's why Ky and I loved summers so much. On adventures with Aunt Bessie, we ran free without a moment's thought to our parents and their rules. I wish I could do that now."

"You can, you absolutely can. Don't let this ruin what will be a special day for you and Evan. It's all about the two of you in the end, right?"

"It's the end I'm worried about..." Libby said in a whisper.

"The end? I don't follow," Rebecca said.

"The wedding night? Forget it. I have to go. I'll add you to our text thread so you keep up with what's going on."

"Sure. Okay."

"Bye."

Rebecca's phone screen went dark. They'd made a start. She got a glimpse of the woman hiding beneath Libby's bratty facade. Too bad the pain she sensed there felt awfully familiar.

Rebecca's cell vibrated.

Then vibrated again.

And again.

Her eyes fluttered open.

The streetlights cast shadows on the ceiling where the blinds weren't quite closed. In the darkness, she could hear Kyle's steady breathing.

Another vibration.

She reached for her illuminated screen, blinking until her eyes adjusted to the brightness. A chat thread whirled apace between several unrecognizable numbers, and two she did recognize: Vivian and Libby.

Like it or not, she was officially part of the bridal party.

She willed her mind to clear. Shopping. It was about shopping for bridesmaid gowns. Where. When. What style. What color. The frenetic energy a sharp contrast to her drowsy state.

With nothing to add, she hearted the last message and tapped on Do Not Disturb before stretching her arm out to deposit her phone on the night table. She rarely silenced her phone at night, but with a West Coast bridal crew, that habit might need to change. Yet another sign her life was no longer her own.

Sliding under the covers, she snuggled into the furnace that was Kyle until her head found its comfy spot on his chest. Even asleep, his arm wrapped around to draw her in.

Warm.

Safe.

Loved.

Rebecca's eyes drooped until sleep claimed her.

"How does Leslie do this?" Rebecca said to her laptop as the cursor blinked impatiently on the blank screen. The same blank screen that haunted her all weekend. With Monday's work looming the next day, Rebecca had to make headway on this article. She sent Kyle out on a ride to get the apartment to herself. But hours later, words were as hard to achieve as her climax before her orgasm coaching with Heidi.

She'd spent a lifetime regurgitating the same sad story to confidantes, doctors, coaches, and more than a few park pigeons. She'd been blogging for months, sending words into the ether expecting no one would find them. But they had. Later more came. And now MOD.

This would be the first time women's pleasure would be featured on a platform this huge. That significance flushed her mind blank and left her fingers hovering limp over the keyboard. Whatever she wrote had to be good. It wasn't her little blog this time. There, she often posted a semi-random stream of consciousness and fixed the missed typos and half thoughts later. The MOD team expected perfection. A cohesive story to provoke, enlighten, persuade, and dispel all the nasty myths women harbored about their bodies. Authenticity would be key. Open and honest, she'd have to tell her true story in a way MOD readers would appreciate. All 60 million of them. No pressure.

She adjusted her pillow against the headboard of their new bed, a long overdue purchase to accompany the rest of their bedroom set. Tangible evidence of their nesting. Their commitment was real and definitely worlds apart from her ex, Ethan. A douche-of-a-man who dumped her in a fit of bedroom rage. In that very room.

Is that where it began? The post-sex frustration when Rebecca realized the angel of sex passed over her yet again? Shame followed next, washing over the moment her partner's eyes flashed disappointment. They finished, she hadn't. But whose fault was it? Hers or theirs? Or was she rejecting them? Ethan always took her failure personally, but of course he would. He was the center of the universe.

Rebecca's finger found a ringlet of hair, winding as she thought.

Why was sex always about the man? Why did his needs and fulfillment come first? His sexual cycle ran hot and fast. Women needed more time, care, and nurturing to build up to the crazy experiences she now had with Kyle.

The friend in her panties pulsed approval. Just thinking of her stellar mate had a physical effect on her. A sensation foreign to countless women.

That's it.

While she wasn't a writing pro, she did live this story. Who better to tell it? Leslie would tidy up any loose bits and grammar nightmares. Plus, on more than one occasion, Harry mentioned she had writing talent. Somehow, he found her monthly reports entertaining. She put a lot of effort in to make the dry subject sound compelling. She could blossom with a topic this personal. This forbidden.

She cracked her neck. Just be me. Tell the story and be honest. She released a cleansing breath and let her fingers fly.

"You've been at it all week." Kyle entered the bedroom, turning on the light. "Don't you need to pack?"

Rebecca flexed the stiffness out of her back. "Almost done. I feel like I've written this 30 times, but I like where it's going now."

The red glowing numbers on her night table showed ten o'clock. "Crap. I didn't realize it was so late," Rebecca said.

"What time is your flight to Houston?"

"Seven thirty, which means I need to be at the airport by…"

Kyle scratched his chin. "Around six o'clock."

"And I need to get up at?"

"Realistically? Four a.m."

"Are you for real?"

"Even on a Saturday, it takes about 40 minutes to drive to LaGuardia."

When Rebecca booked the flight, 7:30 seemed reasonable. She totally forgot to back out the travel logistics. Not that she had a choice. Her limited vacation allowance at work made days off a premium. Shopping for bridesmaid dresses with Libby and her friends definitely did not qualify.

"I'm going to show up at the appointment looking like I'm dragging in from an all-night bender."

Kyle flopped onto the bed next to her with a bounce, bending an arm behind his head on his pillow. "Somehow, I don't think anyone would make that mistake."

"Am I that boring?"

"No, you're not a binge drinker, drug addict, or raving extrovert."

"True, but you can have fun without being drunk. Some of us are happy to just be out and dancing."

"I was apparently too drunk to notice." Kyle rolled over to tickle Rebecca, who went wiggling away.

"Hey," she laughed. "I need to pack."

She walked to the closet door and peered in. "Everything I like is black. Will that look weird? What does one wear bridal shopping?"

"I'd suggest something with minimal fasteners, laces, buckles, or snaps."

She swiveled to face him. "Coming from any other man, that'd sound weird. Looking back, what's the fastest clothing change you've ever done?"

"I've stripped down for you in about ten seconds," he pulsed his eyebrows.

"Stop teasing. For real. For those fashion shows. How fast?"

He sat up, scratching his head. "Never thought about it, but it had to be under a minute. Maybe 45 seconds?"

"You're shitting me. That quick?"

"Yeah. But you've got like two or three people helping."

"Wow, that's crazy. Did everyone have so much help?"

Kyle's smile disappeared. "Not everyone. No."

"So why did you?"

"Um, let's get you back to packing. I'd suggest you wear a slip-on dress. How about the yellow one?"

"I look like a banana in it."

"What are you talking about? Yellow sets off your hair and skin. Don't get me thinking about your skin if you want to sleep anytime soon."

"Really? Well, I'll just have to wear it more often then!" She sauntered over.

"Pack, young lady."

"Ugh." Rebecca dipped her floppy body in protest and rotated back to the closet. Rebecca picked shoes and coordinating clothing suitable for Houston's 80-degree weather then tossed them in a carry-on bag.

Though, considering the busy bridal weekend ahead with Libby, clothing would be the least of her troubles.

13

Rebecca caught her reflection in the bridal store's gleaming windows.

Yellow dress.

Frizzy hair.

Bulky New York coat and suitcase.

Yup. She looked like a homeless Muppet. She turned back to her car, but the Lyft had long since disappeared around the corner. The vortex of air swirling around the car's open windows ruined the last of her ringlets. Figures she'd get the one driver in Texas with no air-conditioning.

It was a complete horror story.

She reached into her purse for an emergency hair elastic, then pulled her offending locks into a bushy ponytail. Slightly better. Exhaling, she pulled the shop's glass door handle to go in.

The salesperson, Bunny, guided her through the store to a seating area surrounded by changing rooms and full-length mirrors. Four women stood chatting and drinking what looked like lemonade from a glass pitcher, sweating almost as much as Rebecca was. The conversation stopped as they saw her.

Do I look that awful?

Bunny came up behind her. "I'll take your things into a dressing room."

Vivian broke the ice. "You made it! Welcome to Texas!" Approaching for a kiss, something she never did, Vivian whispered in Rebecca's ear, "Libby's in rare form. Just roll with it."

Rebecca stiffened, locking eyes for a moment. Vivian shrugged, linking elbows to resume introductions.

"You know our bride, of course."

Libby shifted her weight to one leg and did a hard look away.

"This is Melody and Gloria, but everyone calls her Gigi. Everyone, this is Rebecca, fresh off the plane from New York."

"I'm not sure how 'fresh,' but yes. Hi. Glad to be here."

The women shared awkward closed mouth smiles. Melody, Libby's childhood friend, had long dark hair slicked into a ponytail that hung down the back of her blue polka-dot dress. Gigi's rosy cheeks blushed the shade of her spiky pink hair. Meanwhile, Libby's gaze transfixed on a mirrored corner.

This is going to be fun.

Bunny instructed them to fan out across the store to pick the bridesmaid gowns they liked best. Most dresses came in all colors, so it didn't matter which they tried on. Bunny instructed them to dress and model each for the bride to consider.

Rebecca meandered to a rack with black dresses in a matte fabric. The rough texture slipped between her fingers. Crepe? Silk? There were a few off-the-shoulder gowns in a slim profile that flared at the bottom mermaid style. Each dress had a different waist decoration: rouching, flower appliqués, ribbons, and more. Rebecca grabbed a plain one and headed to the dressing room. She passed Libby, who tapped on her smartphone, not giving the surrounding activities a moment's notice.

"Everyone ready?" Bunny said after the changing noises quieted. "On the count of three, step out in front of your changing room: One. Two. Three."

The four ladies stepped out, no two styles looking alike. Rebecca had never been bridal shopping, but this seemed an ingenious way to see where everyone's head was at without bickering. Or maybe that would come next.

Rebecca stood in her black gown next to Melody, who chose a teal sheath with a princess neckline and cap sleeves. Gigi looked like a sofa swallowed her, wearing a puffy knee-length dress covered in pink flowers, a pink satin ribbon around the waist, framed by enormous sleeves that ballooned to the elbows. Vivian was typical Vivian. Somewhere she'd found beige silk pencil pants paired with a fitted tank and a long-sleeved bolero jacket.

Libby gazed up for the first time, her face lighting up with a smile. It was the first time she'd ever seen Libby smile, and it was electric. Identical to her brother's.

"Holy shit! Could y'all be more different if you tried?" She rose to examine each option.

"Pants? Viv? Seriously? Do you know me at all?"

Vivian shrugged. "You said to pick what I liked, so I picked what I liked."

Libby stopped in front of Gigi's floral disaster. She crossed her arms and cocked her head to ponder.

Formulating a snarky remark?

"This is a definite maybe. Bunny, could we change the fabric on this one?"

"Of course." Bunny rushed over to finger the dress. "We can change out the fabric, the waist ribbon, and even add lace."

"That's good to know. I have a few ideas."

"I have a few ideas too," Vivian said.

"Viv, shut it, will you?"

"Not until I die."

Libby glared at her.

"You asked me here, remember?"

"Being extra snarky to get kicked out of the wedding party isn't going to work. I know you too."

No Vivian? Rebecca would die for sure. She reached up to stress-twist a curl, forgetting she tied them back. Useless, her arms flopped down to her sides.

Libby resumed her inspections. "Melody, I like! Twirl for me."

Melody did a sassy twirl and stopped.

"Bunny, this is in contention, too. It would need to match the wedding's color scheme, though."

"What's that?" Rebecca asked.

Libby looked up as if noticing Rebecca for the first time. "Pink. What else?"

Rebecca stood awaiting her up-close inspection, but she stayed in front of Melody.

"That's a no for you, Rebecca." Libby turned tail and headed back to the couch to drink.

Of course. Why would she give Rebecca the courtesy of an up-close hello? She'd only risen at 4:00 a.m. to fly to Texas for the honor of being ignored and humiliated.

Breathe, Rebecca. Breathe.

Bunny next asked Vivian and Rebecca to try on the two favorites. The group then went round robin, comparing those and other dresses until Libby picked her favorite: the sofa nightmare with a different fabric. Libby would come back another day to select the fabric and trims. She needed more time, and the next wedding party had already arrived. From the sounds of it, they were having a little too much fun in the salon.

Meanwhile, Bunny took their measurements and sent them on their way to lunch at a nearby restaurant. The ride over would give Rebecca precious time alone with Vivian.

"That was nightmarish," Vivian said, buckling in behind the wheel of her rental car.

"Please tell me what the deal is with her? Why so joyless? It felt like a military operation. Those gals after us were having a ball."

"Libby's… difficult. She's always had trouble making friends."

"Why?"

"I don't know. Maybe her parents spoiled her too much? The only reason we get along is because I've never taken her crap. Not even when we were kids."

"Who is Gigi? I thought she only had three bridesmaids in total?"

"Oh, she's the alternate."

"The alternate?"

"I think she's still hoping to be rid of you and wants to be ready for that eventuality."

Rebecca strangled the air. "This is crazy. Why am I even here? She doesn't want me here, and I don't want to be here."

"Her parents insisted. She knows better than to argue."

"I don't get it. They barely know me."

"My guess is, you're the sweet daughter they want Libby to be. I think they hope you'll rub off on her."

"They told her that?"

"They didn't have to. She knows who she is."

"Kyle's family was supposed to be the normal family I'd join one day. You know, to make up for my crazy dysfunctional one?"

"Every family is screwed up in its own way. Theirs included."

"Guess so."

What a waste. Libby had so much going for her and was physically stunning. Women would kill to have looks like hers, but she hid them behind a scowl. Her electric smile could power a city.

"Did she ever model? Like Kyle did?"

Vivian looked sideways for a moment, but refocused on the road. "Why do you ask?"

"She's attractive. It would make sense if she modeled, too."

"It's a sore subject, so don't mention it."

"It didn't go well?"

"No, and it's another reason for her one-sided feud with Kyle. He went on to Paris, while she sat by her phone."

"But she's so beautiful?"

"Modeling isn't only about beauty. It's about charisma. It's about what's on the inside and projecting that through the lens. She has an innate disquiet. An intense one. You can see it in her eyes. That's fine if it's controlled, but she couldn't. She looks perpetually mad and few clients want mad-looking models."

Now it made sense. Kyle stole the glory, the attention Libby wanted for herself. And that bitterness left her without enough friends to fill out a wedding party. Where would she be without Kyle's women—past and present?

There was a reason their bridal shopping was eerily quiet: the bride. Sympathy bubbled within her, despite Libby doing nothing to deserve it. Had she ever discussed her jealousies with Kyle? Not likely. From what she could tell, the Dillon family wasn't much into soul-baring confessions. Maybe Rebecca's family was less dysfunctional than she thought?

Continuing the dainty vibe of the day, Rebecca and Vivian joined the others in an atrium patio of a teahouse restaurant.

Libby sat, shoulders slumped, texting on her phone while Gigi and Melody whispered together. But Rebecca hadn't flown all this way to be abused by a cranky bride.

"Hey, Libby, can we talk for a moment?"

Libby startled at being addressed, but under withering stares from the others, she relented with a huff.

They stepped out of earshot near an unattended bar.

"We can't go on like this. I get you don't want me here or in your wedding, but we've got to make the best of it."

"Do we." Libby crossed her arms.

"Why would you choose to be hostile when you don't need to be?"

"This is wrong. It's. Just. Wrong. It's MY wedding. What business is it of theirs?"

"Are you having a wedding, yes? Will it be beautiful? Yes. Will you have your brother's girlfriend in pictures? Yes. Forget about me and don't let this ruin your once-in-a-lifetime experience."

Rebecca cracked a smile, breathing with satisfaction. Would this direct approach work with a girl committed to be miserable?

"Are you done?"

"Are you twelve?" Rebecca tossed before abandoning Libby to return to the table.

Her chair legs scratched the floor as she pulled it out to sit. A drink was definitely in order, and the dewy carafe of white wine on the table would do nicely.

Vivian poured her a glass. "Looks like you need this."

"Deserve is more like it." Rebecca downed the contents of her stemware, letting the fruity tang go to work on her nerves.

"Hey, Rebecca. We're just talking about the wedding night," Gigi said.

"Evan is super hot. The best-looking guy Libby's ever dated," Melody said.

"Has she dated lots of people?" Rebecca flung out her napkin to drape on her lap.

"Tons. Never for long, though. She always says they're bad in the sack and moves on!" Melody giggled.

"She must have unbearably high standards. But who wouldn't when you look like her," Gigi said.

Maybe so, but something wasn't adding up.

"Question for the table," Rebecca asked. "How high are your standards? Do you leave a guy who isn't as you like in bed, or would you help him along?"

Awkward glances replaced the revelry from the moment before.

"Any guy damn well better be able to top my vibrator," Vivian said. "I have a very close relationship with it, and will pull that sucker out if he can't do the job. Am I right, girls?"

A chorus of "preach" and "oh yeahs" rounded the table as they clinked their wine glasses.

"I'm not going to lie and say sex is toe curling with my man. It's just not," Gigi said. "He has his moments and they come around often enough to keep me happy."

"But when your toes aren't curling. Does he know? Do you say, 'honey, a little to the left please and slow the hell down?'" Rebecca asked.

"Yeah, no. Dangerous territory. How about you, Mel?"

"My last long-term boyfriend was amazing. He always took care of me first, which I loved. But after we broke up, the last few guys have been just 'meh.' I wasn't going for a second dip, so there wasn't much point in the tutorial, you know?"

"Makes sense. Thanks for being so open about it." Rebecca hoisted her glass. "To better sex!"

"To better sex!" they toasted.

"Did you just say what I thought you said?" Libby sat, eyes darting to the other tables.

"A little loose talk while we waited for our bride to return." Vivian handed her a menu.

"To a toe-curling wedding night!" Melody raised her glass.

The ladies clinked, laughing and drinking.

Libby blanched. "Oh my God, you guys have GOT to keep your voices down."

"To loud wedding night sex!" Gigi said.

"To loud wedding night sex!" Clinks abounded.

We finally sound like a wedding party.

"Libs, do we need to get you some nighties? We can go after lunch," Melody asked.

Libby took a swig and hid behind her menu. "No. I'm good."

Vivian lowered Libby's menu. "You need to chill out, baby girl."

"Ooh, couple's massage! That's so hot. You should add that to your honeymoon itinerary. With oil," Gigi said.

"Have you oiled Evan?" Melody asked. "He'd look so amazing all glistening, don't you think?"

"Can we get our minds off my groom?"

"Your glistening groom," Melody belted back her wine.

"As your friends, it's up to us to prepare you for your wedding night. You know." Gigi nudged Libby's shoulder.

"We've been dating for two years. I think I know what to do."

"A little extra planning never hurt. Have all your wedding-night supplies handy." Vivian polished off her wine and poured more from the carafe.

"Like you'd know about that," Libby snapped at Vivian.

They locked stares. Raising Vivian's broken engagement

with Kyle was a bad idea. Knowing Vivian as Rebecca now did, it was tantamount to poking a bear.

"Rebecca, has Kyle ever complained about having sex with me?" Vivian said from her stare down with Libby.

"Not that I recall." Rebecca swallowed a laugh. If it wasn't said as a jab at Libby, the thought of Kyle and Vivian having sex would have her crawling under the table.

"Eww. TMI, you guys! My brother?" Libby shuddered.

"You know, Libs, I'm not getting sexy vibes from you," Vivian said.

"What do you mean?"

"You need help. Doesn't she, ladies?"

"Yes, yes!" Melody clicked glasses with Gigi.

"That's settled. After lunch, we're getting you sex toys for the honeymoon!" Vivian turned to wave for the waiter.

"Oh my God, we must!" Melody clapped.

"Totally," Gigi said.

"Not a chance," Libby said.

"Sorry, you've been outvoted," Vivian said.

Laughs echoed as Rebecca watched Libby shrink into the back of her chair. Her expression wasn't one of an experienced bedroom vixen. A woman who tossed guys aside for not measuring up. That was a lie. The more time she spent with Libby, the more layers revealed themselves. If Rebecca could figure out why Libby was so miserable, maybe she could help the poor girl claim the happiness right at her fingertips.

As much as Rebecca hated to admit it, adding her to the wedding party might have been a good idea after all.

14

Kyle removed his motorcycle helmet after pulling over in a New Jersey state park. Riding had always been an antidote to the gloomy funks he'd wallow in. But Rebecca's sunshine had become an equally effective cleanse for his fog. With her in Texas, memories that'd been keeping him awake and restless outmatched even a trusty ride.

If only he hadn't stopped that day at MOD. Kept walking down the stairs without saying a word. How different would his life be?

Kyle remembered it like it was yesterday. He was walking down the glass stairs between the 23rd and 24th floors at MOD Magazine, coming from a wardrobe fitting. Overjoyed he would be a background model on a fashion spread—one of many—with no guarantees he wouldn't get cropped out entirely. But even that was the chance of a lifetime for an 18-year-old with barely any experience. An opening. He'd meet people and it could lead to bigger things. He had to make the most of it.

And there she was.

Coming right at him up the steps, stopping short before they collided.

Kyle was so completely in his head, dreams of a cover on his mind, that he completely forgot to tremble in her presence.

He was "on." His persona took over.

She waited for him to step aside, but he stood firm, replying with a flirtatious smile and eyebrow raise.

She narrowed her gaze. Kyle laughed.

"What's so funny?" the iconic editor-in-chief said.

"For a moment there, you were a woman, and I was a man. I completely forgot to be afraid of you."

"You'd be the first. The first in a long while." She averted her gaze towards the skyline outside the window.

"That has to be hard. Being feared."

"Not always. It's an asset in this business."

"What about in life?"

"Life? What's that?" She chuckled.

Kyle stepped closer. "Have dinner with me tonight."

"You must be joking. I don't think so."

"Why?"

"I have plans."

"Cancel them."

Her head snapped around. "Aren't you a spunky one?"

"You'll have to dine with me to find out."

She pulsed a bemused eyebrow before stepping around Kyle to continue up the stairs.

"I won't ask again," he called up to her retreating form.

She turned, a wisp of curiosity flashed across her face. "Fine. Meet me here at eight o'clock. I have meetings until then."

Kyle smiled. "See you at eight."

"This better be good," she said.

Kyle called after, "I could say the same to you."

She stopped her ascent, whirling on her heel. "You've got a brass set on you."

"Maybe. You'll need to find that out, too."

What had possessed him? It was just like how his dad closed deals. Challenging when others retreated. An unexpected tactic befitting Sun Tzu. To let Jane Stuart walk by and not say anything? Kyle would have kicked himself for the rest of his life. No one spoke to her that way. No one. Little did he know at the time that no one spoke to Jane Stuart at all.

After that day, Kyle's career went from the cutting room floor to headlining shoots of his own.

Why hadn't he let it stop there?

He'd asked himself the same question thousands of times, always forgetting how young and foolish he'd been back then. She showered him with kindness and attention, and he soaked up every drop, believing himself deserving. Beyond flattering him and taking an interest in his career, she never asked for anything.

At least, not at the beginning.

But by then, Jane had pushed him to the front of the line. Recommended him to designers, got him added to fashion shows. He owed her everything.

So what if she got a little handsy?

She was lonely.

He owed her something.

He was a guy.

He'd manage.

Until he couldn't.

Until he felt rotten inside.

Until he stopped sleeping.

And had to use pills to stay awake.

And dull the pain.

A group of teenagers strolled by where he leaned on his bike. Eying him and giggling. One had curls like Rebecca. The thought of the woman he loved made his insides flip. Despite everything they'd been through, he couldn't help feeling like he wasn't worthy of her love. Like she was in love with a fraud and would leave once she learned who he really was. He never wanted her puddles of brown to look at him with anything but desire.

It was bad enough she knew about his modeling and harassment, evidence he'd been unable to handle his own business. Now, he had to prove his worth by helping her do what he hadn't been able to do for himself: stay clear of Jane. It could be a coincidence that Rebecca's blog caught the eye of MOD. But if they were to make it through unscathed, he had to keep Rebecca away from Jane's prying eyes. It was the only way to prevent Jane from ruining his life for a second time.

And protect Rebecca from getting caught in the cross fire.

Kyle slipped on his helmet and buckled the chin strap.

Protection. How fitting. It was precisely what they both needed from Jane.

Rebecca rubbed Kyle's hand across the table of their favorite diner. After a dainty weekend full of pink dresses, lace and bows, a gritty New York diner with fast, semi-obnoxious service was the perfect end to their Sunday. But her dining partner didn't seem to be feeling it, or much of anything, since she arrived home from Houston hours before.

"Hey, you could have ignored me at home?" Rebecca said.

Kyle snapped to. "Sorry, a little lost in my head. How was the trip?"

"The girls were a fun group, as it turned out. They actually made me feel welcome."

"That's a relief. I figured Libby—"

"I said 'the girls.' Libby, as Vivian said, 'was in rare form.' Although having only met her twice, it's the only form I've seen." Rebecca sipped her soda before resuming.

"Oh, that's not true. I saw her crack a smile once and her entire face lit up. Too bad she can't do that more. It might help her. Might have helped her modeling, too."

"Who told you?"

"Vivian mentioned her career didn't work out."

"What the— Can't that woman keep her mouth shut about anything?"

Rebecca withdrew her hand.

"Don't talk about Vivian that way. And I'm glad she shared it with me. Despite everything we've been through, I can't help feeling like you're still holding out on me. Or at least trying to."

"Rebecca, you know it all. I promise."

"Do I?"

"Yes. Who's mistrusting whom now?" Kyle asked.

"I'm sorry, but can you blame me?"

Kyle's eyes widened. "Do you post pictures of us on social media?"

"That's what's worrying you? My lame social media accounts with zero followers?"

"Do you have pictures of me there? Of us together?"

"Sure. A few. Why?"

Kyle pinched the bridge of his nose and looked away.

"Hey, I'm sorry. Should I have asked first?"

"Yeah."

Rebecca took the phone out of her zipped jacket pocket and swiped open her Instagram account.

"There are a few of us on Instagram, and maybe a couple on Facebook. TikTok is way too intense for me. You have to be on there regularly. How do people find time for anything else?" Rebecca said, swiping and tapping.

Kyle craned across the table to watch her work, nearly colliding with the two burger platters the server slid across the table before dashing off. Crispy fries beckoned, so she stole one.

"Becca, please…" Kyle said.

"One fry? I'm starving." Rebecca chewed while tapping and deleting. What had gotten into him? He was so on edge. She tapped delete on the last picture. "See? All gone. There weren't that many."

She tabled the phone and picked up her cheeseburger. His paranoia was raging. Either something happened while she was gone that he wasn't sharing, or his impending group session on Tuesday had him spiraling.

Kyle inhaled, nodding in relief as he unlocked her phone to check.

"You're worrying me. What's the matter?"

"Nothing. I'm fine." He forced a smile as he shifted focus to his plate. "Back to the trip. Did you pick dresses?"

Typical. Something put him on edge, but he wasn't sharing. Maybe she'd get it out of him later. A distraction might calm whatever had him rattled.

"Yes, we picked dresses. The most butt ugly things on the planet. I swear she picked them on purpose to make us look terrible."

"That's a possibility."

"I was joking."

"I'm not. She's very insecure about her appearance."

Rebecca froze, the fry hovering at her mouth. "Oh, come

on. She's the most beautiful woman I've ever seen. How could she possibly be worried about that?"

Kyle shrugged.

"This makes zero sense. She's lovely, or would be if she wasn't so bratty all the time. What good is natural beauty if it's buried under so much anger and bitterness?"

That thought triggered Rebecca's memory of Libby in their post-lunch bedroom toy shopping. The girls had to practically carry Libby into the sex shop they found online over lunch. Once inside, the poor girl hid in a corner fingering feather boas as her pals ran around gathering unmentionables for her "gift basket."

Rebecca tried to ease the tension, saying how awkward she felt when first in one of those shops. But the gesture failed. Libby bumped Rebecca out of the way, stormed over to the group, and began pointing at items for the girls to retrieve. Lifting her chin in defiance capped her first-rate theater.

Of course.

It's all an act.

Libby's constant dumping of boyfriends was likely a defense mechanism. Hell, Rebecca had given Kyle the runaround for months. She knew false bravado when she saw it. Libby was inexperienced. If she'd been telling sexcapade stories to her girlfriends, it would be too humiliating to admit her naiveté now. Meanwhile, her raven beauty kindled desire everywhere she went. What's a girl to do with all that unwanted attention? You never know if someone really likes you for you, or if they're just trying to get in your pants.

Rebecca popped a peek at Kyle, who was munching away at his meal. Having spent the weekend with his sister, it was impossible to unsee the resemblance. They shared identical jet-black hair with an enviable natural gloss. Those electric blue Dillon eyes penetrated souls without permission. Then add velvety olive skin and swoon-worthy facial symmetry, and it was no wonder admirers hounded Kyle wherever he went. And if Kyle experienced unwanted attention, Libby must as well.

That's why she wasn't able to perform for the cameras. How do you spend your days looking into a lens trying to entice sexual attention when that's the last thing you want? When you're scared as hell at the sexual longing you provoke in others? Her suspicions weren't something Rebecca wanted to discuss with Kyle. Since he wasn't talking, she might as well capture her swirling thoughts on the page.

Kyle devoured his meal in record time. When Rebecca finished, she tossed down her napkin. "Mind heading back? I need to do some work."

"On a Sunday?"

"Yes. My article won't write itself."

Rebecca owed it to her future readers to do her best. To get her clouded thoughts straight and cohesive. For her sake, she hoped Libby would be one of them.

Later that night, a stream of consciousness exited Rebecca's fingers, painful memories replaying in rapid succession. She'd heard journaling was a powerful therapeutic, but the lightness invading her spirit the more she wrote was truly breathtaking.

She fooled herself into thinking everything was fine after fixing her bedroom troubles. But thinking ill of herself for that long left scars. Despite her progress since then, pockets of shame clung stubbornly to her insides, refusing her attempts to flush them out. If her experiences with Kyle and Libby taught her anything, it was that no one was immune from self-doubt. On paper, they had it made. But each was a complex bundle of contradictions. In many respects, their wounds seemed deeper and more profound than her own.

Kyle's life still had holes for her. Hopefully, ones he was now addressing with Dr. Kaplan. But it left Rebecca wondering what was bubbling behind his gorgeous eyes. If nothing else, he deserved her unwavering support, patience, and grace. He'd earned it after unconditionally supporting her bedroom journey. Never a judging word. Never an off glance, or hesitation betraying his true thoughts about her situation. If only he could creak the door open just a little to let her reciprocate. To support him. Maybe she could help his healing? She'd have to ask. Really ask and have him answer. But she had no such intimate connection with Libby.

As women, they could have so much in common, but artificial walls kept them apart. Each were human beings, with her own feelings, experiences, and struggles. Including with self-confidence. And yes, including in the bedroom.

Sex required confidence. The confidence to know yourself and trust that whatever aroused you was perfectly fine. No one else needed to agree with it. Regardless of how we got there, everyone deserved to feel those awesome sensations. To let go.

Feel.

Savor.

A stream of words flowed from her soul, harnessing an energy unlike anything she'd experienced. Creating with purpose, everything clicking as if preordained. It was good. Really good. She knew it. She felt it. And that feeling intoxicated. No wonder Leslie loved her writing profession.

Rebecca would definitely continue writing once the article was done. She had the itch. Words now pinged around her brain, waking her at night. Urgently seeking an outlet, they'd vibrate until she released them on the page. Then, and only then, could she return to her pillow. It hadn't always been that way, but she couldn't even remember before. Before the words came. Before she found her voice.

In prepping for the article, Rebecca read many savvy memes with quotations from famous writers. One said writers could only control what they create, not how people react to it. Truer words were never written.

Rebecca had no idea how the world would react to her story. She could only control the honesty and sensitivity she brought to the subject matter. And the outrage. Yeah, there was space for that too. That this article was even necessary. But whatever lay ahead, Rebecca was creating words that would undoubtedly land with impact. Only time would tell if she'd live to regret it.

15

The six empty chairs in Dr. Kaplan's Tuesday joint client session threw Kyle. Were others coming? If so, he forgot to mention it. Kyle and the one other survivor sat mute, likely pondering the same question: why had they allowed themselves to get into this mess in the first place?

The session started three minutes earlier, but Dr. Kaplan had yet to speak. Was sitting in silence a psychological game? Or did the good doctor enjoy watching them squirm?

Kyle's left leg bounced as if he were waiting for the starting gun of a race to blow. He'd love nothing better than to follow his feet out the door.

"Was that uncomfortable?" Dr. Kaplan said at last.

Neither man spoke, eyes glued on the doctor.

"Would it surprise you to learn each empty chair in this room represents a male survivor hurting in silence and never coming forward? Approximately one in eight men in the US—or 14 million men—have experienced unwanted sexual experiences in their lifetime. This includes being made to penetrate an intimate partner, sexual coercion, unwanted sexual contact, and other unwanted sexual experiences. The media doesn't care. No one believes you exist. But here you are."

Kyle swallowed hard. Nowhere had he heard this information. Not once. He'd checked for data a few times online, but every search result returned with cases of male perpetrators. It only reinforced his oddball status in society. The male survivor. There was no outrage. No hotlines for men. No PSAs on TV. Nothing. Only silence. The empty chairs loomed large. Heavy, wooden, vacant. He wished his chair was vacant as well.

Dr. Kaplan adjusted his glasses. "So let's begin with a few questions. Raise your hand if you know a woman who has been sexually assaulted or harassed."

Faces of harassed models filled his mind. Many whose names he never knew. Was Libby among them? He never asked, but wondered. All the unwanted touching, comments, and innocent flirtations turned on their heads when men refused to say no. He raised his hand, as did the other man.

"Okay, now raise your hand if you're aware of where women in crisis can get help."

Both raised their hands again.

"Good. Now raise your hands if, since your incident or incidents, you thought you were the only man ever to fall victim to a woman."

Each eyed the other, willing the other to raise his hand first. Finally, Kyle raised his in futility, with his fellow survivor immediately following.

"Good. Now raise your hand if you thought you must have wanted or enjoyed what happened to you because of your physiological response."

No way. The other guy would have to go first. Quid pro quo.

Kyle pursed his lips, crossing his arms across his chest. He'd wait this one out, but it didn't take long. The man lifted his arm. Kyle hesitated, watching the other man arch his eyes in surprise.

"Nah, I'm playing with you," Kyle joked, raising his hand. "Hell, I was so convinced, I'll raise both arms."

"No kidding," the man lifted both his arms as well.

"But can you explain that for me, please?" Kyle asked. "How can we get aroused and not want it? I can't get myself past that one."

"It's an uncontrolled physiological response."

"Come again?" Kyle said.

"Think of it this way," Dr. Kaplan said. "When you cut an onion, what happens to your eyes?"

Kyle's mind went to their recent family dinner. He'd stood sniffing tears back, hoping Rebecca wouldn't mistake them for real crying, having just come from therapy.

"We cry," he said.

"Right. Are we sad when we cry from onions?" the doctor asked.

"No."

"That's because it's a physiological response to stimulation—the onion vapors. Does it mean we're sad or upset? Of course not. It means our bodies responded because they're wired to."

"Okay. That makes sense," Kyle said. "So why don't I feel any better?"

"You need to give yourself some time," the other man said. "At the beginning, it can be hard to let go of all the bunk you've got rattling around your brain. At least, that's how it was for me."

Dr. Kaplan introduced Kyle to Greg, first names only. Both worked in fashion—Dr. Kaplan's niche, so that wasn't surprising—and both met their harassers in the workplace. Unlike Kyle, Greg was a staffer for a powerful woman who made his resistance impossible if he didn't want to lose his job.

Their stories were eerily similar.

Late teens to early 20s.

Groomed with interest and flattery.

Felt obligated.

Tried to explain it away because they were men.

Societal expectations make it hard for men to come forward, the doctor said. Taught to be self-reliant, stoic, and emotionless, how are men supposed to feel safe coming forward? Being vulnerable? Voicing victimhood? Who would believe them? Who would care?

The doctor gave voice to Kyle's thoughts, but in a clear and succinct way he'd been unable to manage himself. Kyle sniffed back salty tears, only to have them stream down his throat. He tried to swallow, but the lump made it impossible. Who would believe me? How many times did he ask himself that exact question? His answer was always the same: no one. No one would believe me. No one would believe he wasn't the aggressor. That he was forced into something he didn't want and had no control to stop unless he wanted to suffer the ruinous consequences. A TV police desk sergeant popped to mind. He'd tell Kyle to get out. Scoot along. There were people with real problems to help, and he wasn't one of them.

Fear of the scenario kept him quiet.

He stuffed his emotions down deep until sucking pills and whiskey seemed the only logical solution. Though, in truth, that last night with Jane was a blur. But what wasn't blurry was his cowardice. To think dying better than starting over? Back then, his life revolved around modeling. Without it, there was nothing worth living for. What else could fill the void and take the pain away? How was he supposed to restore the safety, love, and dignity stolen forever?

Hopeless, he made a dangerous choice. The implications unimaginable: He could have died before meeting Rebecca.

Tears streamed down his cheeks faster than he could wipe them away. He sniffed, using his sleeve until wetness rendered it useless. Kyle leaned forward to pop a tissue out of the box on the coffee table, only to have Greg's hand get there first.

"After you," Greg chuckled, yielding to Kyle then taking a tissue of his own.

"Aren't we a pair?" Greg said.

"A pair of brave souls? Yes, you are," Dr. Kaplan answered.

A pair.

Not alone.

Kyle scanned the empty chairs, cupping the arms of his. Solid. Strong. Unshakable. Gripping the wood, his spine stretched to its full height. If he didn't confront his past now, it'd be impossible to build a new future. Yes, for himself—and yes for Rebecca. But what about the others? The empty chairs represented real people. A kernel of outrage took root. Who would speak for them? Who would champion the wounded and forgotten?

As much as he hated to admit it, knowing other male survivors existed did matter. Sharing the burden lightened the load by a small measure. But the balance of his psyche blew to smithereens after considering a simple fact: more victims wandering the earth meant more unaccountable abusers like Jane.

Rebecca eyed the empty chair next to her as Harry closed his office door. His head shook with disapproval before a word crossed his lips. It had to be bad. Harry never closed his office door unless someone was getting fired. Suddenly, Darcy's absence loomed large. Harry must have not wanted her there to gloat about whatever had him in such a foul mood.

Instead of diving right in with a jovial lilt to his voice, he sat there staring at her, arms folded across his chest.

"I don't get it, Sloane. We give you every opportunity to soar. Give you free rein of choice assignments anyone else in this agency would kill to have, and you kick the legs out from under us."

What the hell did she do? It's one thing to call her in for a known violation, but she honestly didn't have a clue what he was talking about. What had she done?

"Harry, I—"

"Shut it. I'm not done. Did you or did you not ignore Evvy's requests for help?"

All the times Evvy stopped by for help popped to mind over the last several weeks. Rebecca told her to put time on the calendar but only realized now she hadn't.

"I meant to connect with her, but never did. I was going to—"

"Going to? Really? You've been arriving late, leaving early, missing meetings in the middle of the day, your nose buried so deep in your computer, people walk by to talk to you get completely ignored."

Laid out like that, it wasn't a stellar track record. Admittedly, she'd been working on the MOD article during the day, but she'd only missed one meeting, maybe two. In-person meetings at MOD were unavoidable during business hours, but she made up by working after hours. At least she thought so. On second thought, maybe she'd dropped the ball on that too.

Rebecca's gaze sagged to the floor, avoiding the storm cloud substituting for Harry's head. She'd never seen him this angry. She'd heard rumors, but never really believed it possible. Big mistake. Given his jovial demeanor, it was easy to forget he was the fierce man who fought the big guys to build a thriving media business on the biggest ad stage in the world—on his own terms. Terms Rebecca neglected to follow.

"Can you tell me what this is about?" she asked.

"If you had bothered to check your work email or hadn't strolled in at 10:00 a.m., you'd already know. Evvy, forced to do your work unsupervised, sent in a nonrefundable and unauthorized remnant ad buy to the New York Times for $300,000.00. For a client who had neither the means nor desire to have this ad placed."

Bitter acid burned up her throat. "Oh, no—you mean…"

"This agency is on the hook for $300,000.00 because you were too busy to attend to your own work."

How had she let her work get so offtrack? It was her fault. How many times had Evvy stopped by her desk to talk to her? She meant to get back to her, but now that was too late. But was it? There may be a crafty way out of this yet.

"Has it run?" Rebecca asked.

"No, not yet."

"Harry, let me try to fix this."

"You can't Sloane. It's done."

"It's never done. Give me a chance. Please."

He looked off into space. Harry was like a second dad to Rebecca, and she had proverbially totaled the car. And sent Grandma to the hospital. And lost the family dog. Their agency wasn't big enough to absorb a hit like this without heads rolling, and Rebecca was first up at the gallows. She couldn't let her mess spill onto others.

"A few hours. Give me a few hours." Rebecca rose to her feet.

"Unless you have voodoo magic up your sleeves, I don't see how, but go ahead." Harry waved his arms in dismissal.

"Thank you. Thank you."

Rebecca turned to leave.

"And Sloane, I can't save you if you fail. I have a partner and employees who could all suffer from this."

Rebecca opened the door and headed to her desk, mind whirling a million miles a minute. There were no ways around it. Rebecca screwed up and someone had to pay.

Yes, someone had to pay.

Maybe a different someone?

A remnant ad in the New York Times was still valuable real estate. Anyone worth their salt knew it, which is why Evvy probably thought it was a steal in the first place. If the Times wasn't playing ball, she could find another playmate. MediaNow had a wealth of clients. Someone might be willing. All she'd have to do was to strike a private deal and send their ad copy in place of the original.

It could work.

She might not have voodoo magic, but she just might have a good enough trick up her sleeve to save her hide.

16

When Kyle's cellphone rang, the unlikeliest of faces filled the screen. His muscles tensed. Did she learn about him and Rebecca?

He paced the living room, the phone radiating a ferocious energy crying for attention that both attracted and repulsed. But no good would come from answering.

Ringing persisted. He'd set the maximum rings before voicemail kicked in, but it was as if those rules didn't apply to her.

The phone went still.

He released the breath.

Maybe it was a butt dial? A mistake?

Calm the eff down.

He sank to the sofa, cradling his head. The phone lay still. It had to be a mistake, thank God. Kyle reached for the remote, but before he turned on the TV, Jane rang again.

Shit.

What did she want?

His knee bounced uncontrollably.

The phone rang and rang, setting his nerve endings ablaze. Not knowing would be worse than whatever awaited him on the other end of the phone. A conversation eleven years in the making.

"I'm assuming this call is a mistake," Kyle said. He walked down the hall to the bedroom. Rebecca would be home any minute, and he didn't need Jane hearing her voice. There was still a chance she hadn't learned their secret.

"You can imagine my surprise when your face showed up on Marco's reel."

Kyle searched his memory for the morning weeks before. Marco took a single shot. Harmless. But he would never risk deleting a photo. Jane saw everything. A break in the photo numbering sequence would cause an inquisition.

"Delete it," Kyle said.

"Delete perfection? It took my heart away, but then you always did."

Kyle sat on the bed. "Are we done?"

"Why the picture? Why now?" Jane asked.

Sloppy mistake?

"I have to admit, it was an ingenious way to get my attention."

"That picture has nothing to do with me."

"No?"

"None."

"What business did you have with Marco, then?"

"He's an old friend."

"I'm an old friend. You don't visit me."

"We were a lot of things, but friends was never one of them."

Jane sighed. "Oh darling, we were way more than friends. If you've forgotten, I'd be happy to refresh your memory."

Kyle checked the time. "A hard pass on that one."

"We had explosive chemistry. We could again."

The familiar clank of Jane's metal bangles rattling about her wrist penetrated the phone. A nervous habit. But what did she have to be nervous about?

"You have a lot of fucking nerve calling me up like nothing happened. Have you forgotten what you did to me?"

"What I did to you? My boy, if not for me you'd be dead. Pushing up daisies in some long-forgotten plot of ground."

She would remember events that way, wouldn't she? Her chauffeur's valiant body-dumping at the ER ignored all the pain she caused to drive him there.

"I gave you opportunities others would die for. Fame. World travel. Red carpet evenings. Is that 'what I did to you'? I only gave you what you craved."

That very day in the safety of Dr. Kaplan's office, Kyle shared his most private struggles and gained assurances that what happened wasn't his fault. But Jane made it impossible to see it any other way. In mere seconds, Jane reduced him from survivor to accomplice. The same label he'd given himself.

Kyle exhaled, defeated. "What do you want?"

Jane paused. A rarity. "You are a stone in my shoe. One I can't shake."

"Bullshit. We haven't spoken in years."

"You left. But memories of you are everywhere. Old issues. Society pages. References in my love bio. You are still with me, whether you like it or not."

Her rot stuck as well. Every time he looked in the mirror. Every time he lied about his past to avoid answering questions. Every time he got dressed in jeans and T-shirts, the only garments he never modeled professionally. Every fashion season when young men walked the runways. How many of them were suffering as he had? Jane's fallout was everywhere. She'd done her job well.

"This conversation is pointless. I'm hanging—"

"Meet me. Once. For old time's sake."

"You've gone mad."

"We're meant to be, you and I. It's perhaps why your engagement failed."

Figures she'd heard about that.

"My life is none of your business. I'm sorry, but you're twisting what happened into sick fantasy that isn't real."

Jane clucked her tongue. "What an awful thing to say. What we did between the sheets was real as hell. At least to me."

Of course. She's horny and has no one else.

"Don't call again," Kyle said.

"Come over."

Rebecca's key slid into the door.

Shit.

"It could be like old times."

He heard the bolt open.

"No, this time, you will hear me." Kyle balled his fists.

"Did I mean nothing to you?"

"I'm hanging up."

"Kyle, I'm home!" Rebecca called.

"Who's that?" Jane commanded.

"No one. I've got to go." He hung up, doubling over in relief seconds before Rebecca entered the bedroom.

"Sweetie, you okay?" Rebecca stopped short in their open bedroom door. Kyle bent at the waist, sweat stains saturating the armpits of his blue T-shirt.

Kyle remained doubled over, not answering.

"Were you working out?"

"No," he sat on the bed, looking away.

"It is freezing outside. How can you be sweating? And have the windows open?" Rebecca crossed the room and closed the window, rubbing her own still-chilled arms from her walk home.

Kyle sat, motionless. His shoulders slumped, skin dewy.

"You look awful. You feel okay?"

"Not really."

She touched his forehead. "Your skin is clammy. Why don't you get in bed?"

She pulled back the covers, and Kyle slid in without muttering a word. It was her side of the bed, but he stayed put, rolling on his side.

His powerful form, a shell of his usual self. Childlike. She bent over to kiss him and he grabbed her hand.

"You know I love you, right?"

"Of course, silly. You rest. I'll check on you in a little while."

Rebecca switched off the light and left the room, leaving the door open a crack. She still wore her work clothes, but didn't want to disturb him to change. Rebecca opened the entryway closet to slip on one of Kyle's zip-up sweaters.

She breathed deeply. Wearing him was a perpetual hug. Having him in her life was even better. She was lucky. Rebecca stroked the soft merino wool as she headed for the kitchen. She lifted the tea kettle, sloshing the residual water inside.

Probably enough.

She pushed the burner, and after a few clicks, a blue flame ignited. Rebecca selected a mug, plopped in a tagless Orange Spice tea bag, and leaned against the counter to await the whistle.

Kyle looked like she felt. It'd taken her the entire day and phone calls to every current MediaNow client who ran ads in the New York Times. All 300 of them. Most hung up, but she only needed one. The situation reminded her of the time she walked door-to-door for a local group advocating for safer street lighting. Who'd be against that, right? Yet door after door slammed in her face. She couldn't get a ride home until she filled her sheet—300 signatures. The last one signed at nine o'clock in the evening, but she finished. When she found her ad-space-love-match earlier, the relief exceeded her signature win by a gazillion.

The close call proved something. While the MOD project ignited her passion for helping women, MediaNow paid the bills. She'd lost sight of that in recent weeks. But with the article almost ready to publish, she'd be able to put the whole thing behind her and move on.

A chill rippled through her.

Or was it disappointment?

Silencing the kettle, she filled her cup, blowing the surface cool as she made her way to the living room. On the couch, she curled up and tossed a throw blanket over her legs. She'd check on Kyle in a bit, after he slept off whatever made him as pale as she likely looked in Harry's office.

Just then, Viraj's name vibrated Rebecca's phone to life on the coffee table. Should she let it go to voicemail? After the day she had, very likely. But ringing phones were like falling objects. Rebecca snatched it before her mind registered the command.

Vibrations continued unabated.

Ugh.

"Hi, Viraj, what's up?" Rebecca said.

Jane perched at attention while Viraj spoke to Rebecca on speaker mode.

"Ah, I thought you weren't picking up, but am so glad you did," Viraj said.

"It's a bit late for work calls, don't you think?"

Jane almost piped in that work never stops. That to get ahead takes commitment and sacrifice, two things Rebecca obviously lacked. But she heeded Viraj's stern glance and remained silent. Her protégé knew her so well.

"Yes, but we're a global organization with offices around the world. Australia and Asia are awake, and so must we be."

"I don't see what that has to do with me?" Rebecca said.

"Right, well, we have to begin promoting our issue, and are already getting letters in from readers. This is a precursor to what a smash hit we think this piece will be. We'd like you to answer the letters so we can publish them in a few days' time. I presume that's no trouble."

"How soon would you want them back?"

"I'll send them over and we can circle back about the details. But if you can begin reading, it will help prime the pump for what's coming," Viraj said, before mouthing "are you sure?" to Jane.

Of course she was. Perhaps she gave Viraj too much credit? Perhaps Jane was growing too fond of Viraj and overestimated his abilities? He had been with MOD for years, long after others moved on to seek mastheads at online ezines of their own. As expected, those typically flamed out within a year. Meanwhile, the experience Viraj got at Jane's side was priceless. He knew how much work and commitment it took to keep MOD on top.

Rebecca stubbornly resisted. "You know how committed I am to this project, but I don't recall anything in the contract about answering letters. We'll need to revisit that, especially since that will be an ongoing endeavor. Am I right?"

"Yes, I believe that's the plan," Viraj said.

"And I need to coordinate with my coauthor as well."

Jane checked her watch, then hand-signaled to wrap up the call. She had all she could take of this ninny for the moment. Viraj had done his job well.

"Certainly, yes," Viraj said.

"Are we good to discuss next steps after the article comes out?" Rebecca asked.

"Let me check with Jane and get back to you."

"Who's Jane?" Rebecca asked.

"Our editor-in-chief."

Viraj wrapped up and disconnected the call before Rebecca could, a power move he'd likely learned from Jane.

Viraj slipped on his coat. "I'm not sure what the point of that was. Why I had to come over to call her with you at this hour?"

"I had my reasons. Nightcap?" Jane said.

"No. None for me," he said, buttoning his jacket.

"Lighten up." Jane stood, her tunic billowing behind her as she walked across the room to her wet bar.

"It's late. Do you want me to walk you to your car?"

Jane clicked a secret latch to open a glass door, which folded down to a work surface. She removed a crystal decanter of scotch and filled a matching highball to the brim.

"Stay. I can give you a lift home later," Jane said.

"Thank you, but no. I'm heading out. You should too." Viraj stood apart, his muscular frame evident beneath his bulky jacket and scarf effortlessly wrapped around his neck. He looked so much like Kyle.

So handsome.

But his skittish shuffling would drive her mad.

"Out with it," Jane barked.

"You don't need to drink that."

"Are you my daddy now?"

She lifted the glass to her lips. Golden liquid, warm and smooth, made its way around her mouth, a taste she forced herself to acquire with not a little effort. She couldn't very well stand mute at executive functions drinking wine spritzers while her male peers debated the finer points of aging in oak barrels. Everything she did, even the glass in her hands, was a testament to the personal sacrifices she made for success.

Viraj's footsteps echoing down the corridor drew her back, the space where he stood as vacant as his commitment to their magazine. Pity. Viraj wasted such promise on weak sentimentality. Pretending he cared for Jane's welfare? Laughable. He no more cared for Jane than Jane cared for him, or anyone else in her employ. Theirs was a business transaction and nothing else. When he was gone, Jane would still be there. On top. Towering over their small, petty lives from afar, while they scurried around unaware. Viraj would be no different than the rest. No different than Kyle.

17

"Has she called you before?" Dr. Kaplan's blanched face asked Kyle at their session the next Tuesday. Greg's mouth slacked open, but he quickly recovered.

"Not in eleven years."

Greg crossed his legs, tight. "Mine called once, but I hung up and blocked her."

"Yeah, didn't think I needed to. It'd been so long."

"Gentlemen, we must not let these abusers play mind games and squirm themselves back into our lives," Dr. Kaplan said. "If she persists, you must go to the authorities."

"And say what exactly, Doc?" Greg said. "A woman from my past keeps calling? Make her stop? C'mon."

Greg dismissed the idea with a wave.

"You have as much right to be safe as any other person," Dr. Kaplan said.

Greg dug in. "Don't you understand? No one cares. No one. No one believes women behave this way. When they do, they call it empowered. But we have the right to say no. We're not fucking sex slaves."

"No pun intended?" Kyle asked.

Greg paused his verbal assault. "No, I think I meant that one."

"Just checking."

"Take a breath, will you?" Dr. Kaplan said to Greg. "The fact remains that when we're victimized, it matters. It matters greatly. But it's up to us to make others listen, to make others understand. That's how we can begin healing."

Kyle shook his head. Healing was so passive. Where was the accountability? Why didn't Dr. Kaplan ever talk about that? They spent so much time talking about what happened to them and how it wasn't their fault. But not once had they discussed who shouldered the blame.

"I get Greg's frustration," Kyle said. "We're babbling here while my harasser walks around unscathed."

"Mine too," Greg said.

Kyle breathed heavily. "See what I mean? Where's their accountability? How do we get justice?"

"Justice?" Greg's bark of laughter broke in. "There's no justice for us. Mine's right where she was all those years ago; didn't miss a beat."

"I know I'm here to set a good example, but I do wonder sometimes if this is pointless. Us talking." Greg rose to his feet, waving his arms. "How is this helping anything? I'm sorry, but I feel just as lousy as I did when we started, and her bony fingers are clamped into that dumb magazine of hers like one of her silver cuffs."

Running a magazine?

Silver cuff?

What are the odds?

"Take a breath. This is a process that takes time. You've made marvelous progress so far." Dr. Kaplan tried his best Jedi mind trick on Greg. But he didn't need to be a Jedi to see it wouldn't work. Dude was hot. And who could blame him? Living a tortured life sucked, especially while your assailant ran free.

Greg paced his anger off for a few minutes, then took a seat. "Sorry. I've been at this a lot longer than you have and it's hard work. The frustration gets to me sometimes. Believe it or not, I'm way better than before. My family thinks Dr. Kaplan is a miracle worker."

"That's good to know," Kyle said.

"Yeah, but after today, I think I'll proceed solo. No offense." Greg rubbed his palms together, avoiding eye contact.

"I get it. No worries," Kyle said.

Treatment wouldn't be a straight line from broken to healed. There'd be some bumps. As much as he hated to admit it, he secretly hoped after a session or two he'd be cured. No way that was realistic; Greg made that plain. But as long as the trend line moved in the right direction, the work would probably pay off. At least he hoped so.

On the way down in the elevator, Greg spoke first. "Sorry to lose my cool up there. I'm probably not the best influence for you anyway."

"Meeting you has helped. Thanks for giving it a try."

Greg nodded. "You'll have good and bad days."

"I'm hoping for more good than bad, but the good days are on an extended vacation."

"It can feel that way," Greg said. "Hey, we're not really supposed to talk outside of these sessions, but if you ever want to grab a beer, or box, or get pissed off with someone who's been there, call me."

He handed Kyle his card. "Take care."

He exited the lobby and into the open door of a waiting Town Car. The driver closed it and scampered around to the driver's seat.

Who is this guy?

Kyle looked at the business card in his hand. His last name was Bailey. As in Bailey Cameras. The same camera he used himself. The same cameras Marco used at MOD.

Greg must have interned or worked for Jane.

If Greg fell victim to Jane, there were likely others. Other young men whose lives she ruined.

More victims.

More survivors.

With how many more still to come?

Greg's earlier words rang true. Their abusers were still running around free and clear like nothing happened. It was long past time to direct energies into holding them accountable. Or in the case of Greg and Kyle, a very specific abuser with a silver cuff.

Rebecca shook off the February cold while following the maître d' the table where Leslie was already sitting. With the article going live the next day, it was all Rebecca could do to keep from fizzing clear out of her skin.

"I thought I'd be last." Rebecca sat and pulled her chair in.

"Barbara will be along. I told her to come a little later. Give us a chance to talk about tomorrow."

"What's to know?" Rebecca poured herself a glass from the open wine bottle on the table.

"You're such a rookie," she chuckled. "When a cover story launches, there's a lot of social media and press about the issue to drum up interest. I'll be doing a bunch of media interviews that MOD set up."

"That's amazing."

"Yeah, it's going to be crazy. I wish you could join in, but there's no way to do that and keep your identity hidden. Unless…"

Rebecca waved her off. "No way. I'm NOT changing my mind. I'm anonymous and am happy to keep it that way."

"Suit yourself. But I can't help feeling like I'm stealing your glory."

Rebecca reached across the table for Leslie's hand. "Steal away. I couldn't have done this without you. You took my scribbles and made them sing."

Leslie squeezed back. "Stop, I barely had to touch anything. Your passion for helping women really came through."

When Rebecca started the Bedroom Diary blog, she considered it little more than digital musings no one would ever see. The whole topic being taboo lit an inner fire she didn't know she had. Women needed fierce advocates like her semiretired coach, Heidi. No one else was doing it, at least when it came to the bedroom. It remained to be seen how much of a difference Rebecca's words would make. Hopefully more than none.

"Those interviewers are likely going to ask about who I am. Are you ready for that?" Rebecca asked.

"I've been doing mock interviews and have my answers down cold. I should be able to talk intelligently about it without slipping."

Rebecca paused mid-sip of water. "Should?"

"Will, I will be fine. Your identity is safe."

Rebecca swallowed her water. "Good. I'm glad you're doing this and I'm not."

"Doing what?" Barbara said, bending down to give them each a kiss before sitting.

"Interviews. Leslie is going to be a media superstar while I cower in the shadows."

"So much for being out and proud." Barbara tapped her empty wineglass and Leslie filled her up.

"I couldn't be prouder, but out? Not ready for that," Rebecca said.

"The proud came through. Everyone at MOD loves this article."

Rebecca screwed up her mouth in thought.

"What's the matter, dumplin'?" Barbara asked.

"I do hope there will be some healthy conversation. That was the whole point of writing it."

"There will," Leslie said. "The entire MOD team will be mobilized. I'll be on social as well."

"Good. I'm barely on social media, and if I answered the jig would be up in terms of hiding who I am."

"The comments will go to the MOD channels, so no worries about that," Leslie said.

"See? All settled," Barbara said.

Rebecca reached for a crusty roll the server deposited on the table in a black wire basket.

"I'm crossing fingers that you two will be a smashing success tomorrow."

Barbara raised her glass, and the trio clinked.

"But," Barbara continued, "if the flood comes, know I'm here for both of you. My ark always has room for two more."

"Adjoining rooms?" Leslie asked.

"Absolutely, I'll move the giraffes over." Barbara cracked a smile.

The three perused their menus and ordered, settling into chatter about celebrity miscues. It was a sobering reminder of the price of fame. Rebecca prayed her bill would never come due.

Rebecca splashed, humming in the shower as Kyle entered, steam clouding the room and mirror.

"Hey, stranger!" she said.

"How were the girls?"

"Great, it was fun. Leslie says the article's promotion is going to be huge. They have interviews set up for her."

"Just her, though, right?"

"Yes, I'm in the clear. No worries."

He sat on the closed toilet, his head foggy from too many hours drinking alone at a bar on an empty stomach.

After the session with Dr. Kaplan and Greg, Kyle's senses screamed on high alert. Over too many pints, he'd convinced himself Jane uncovered his connection to Rebecca. Though, the only proof was Jane's emboldened behavior and the foreboding ache in Kyle's bones.

"She knows," Kyle said.

"Who knows what? What are you talking about?"

"My abuser. I'm sure she knows about you."

"That's impossible." Rebecca slid the curtain aside and popped her head out. "I've been working directly with Viraj. I haven't once talked to anyone named… What is her name?"

"Jane Stuart, the editor-in-chief of MOD."

"Did you say Jane? Viraj mentioned someone named Jane last night when he called."

"Why didn't you tell me?!?"

"Sweetie, you were sleeping. You looked like death warmed over. Don't you remember?"

"That's because Jane called me last night."

"Hold on." Rebecca shut off the water. "Jane called you last night? What for?"

"For a booty call."

"You're joking." Rebecca toweled her confused face dry, then wrapped it around her body. "The crazy woman who harassed you called for sex?"

"Pretty much."

"She's shameless. After all this time! Did she say anything else?"

No sense dragging Rebecca through Jane's lewd talk and nonsensical reminiscing. Not unless she wanted another shower.

"No. That was all."

"Good. Man, I'll be glad when this thing is over. Oh, that reminds me. They now want me to answer reader letters, but I said I had to review the contract and talk to Leslie."

He loved Rebecca, but she obviously had no concept of how dangerous Jane could be. The sooner they escaped her clutches, the better. They were tempting fate as it was.

"Viraj found your blog, right? Does it say your name anywhere?"

"No. Nowhere. Not even in the footer."

"Can you load the site for me?"

Rebecca padded into the bedroom, tucking the towel into itself. She flipped open the laptop on their bed and launched the Firefox browser. One of the favorites tiles showed her website's favicon, so she clicked. But the page loaded MOD's homepage.

"Wait a minute. Something's wrong." Rebecca closed the browser, opened it again, and typed in the URL for her blog. The URL was right, but everything else screamed trouble.

"Why is my website redirecting to MOD? Instead of my blog loading, my URL is routing to the MOD website. This makes no sense."

Unfortunately, it made perfect sense. At least in the crazy

world of Jane Stuart. This proved without a doubt that Jane discovered Rebecca's identity.

"Who hosts your website?" Kyle asked. "Check the date on your domain registration," Kyle said.

Frantic, Rebecca sorted her inbox by sender. Scrolling down, she found a string from the domain registrar and clicked the most recent email.

"I'm an idiot," Rebecca said. "It expired last night at 9:38 p.m." She slapped her face. "I'm an idiot. How could I lose my domain in an instant? Shouldn't I get the right to buy it back before someone snatches my web address out from under me? What the hell am I supposed to do now?"

"Hold on." Kyle knelt at the edge of the bed and typed in the address for a website registrar. He then typed the Bedroom Diary URL. Sure enough, Valis Publishing now owned Rebecca's web domain.

"Valis Publishing? How the hell did this happen?"

"What were you doing last night at 9:38 p.m.?"

Rebecca sat in stunned silence. "I was home after that nightmare of a day, you were in bed, I made tea... No. No way."

Kyle shrugged. "What?"

"Viraj called last night. It seemed out of character for him to be calling so late. I asked why the late call. He mentioned some bunk about their offices being open in Australia."

Kyle pulsed an eyebrow. "That's Jane-speak. She justifies her 24/7/365 work habits by spouting off about it being daytime somewhere in the world."

"You think Viraj kept me on the phone purposely to distract me while my domain registration expired? That's irrational! I'm a nobody. This is some very twisted stuff here."

"Not for Jane."

"But how would Jane have known to search for me in the first place? That means she'd have to discover me as Bedroom Diary, then somehow connect me to you?"

"No clue, but the domain being stolen means Jane now has your name as the prior owner. She's onto you and can't be trusted."

Rebecca dropped her towel to slip on some leggings and sweats. "You warned me. You warned me right at the beginning to be suspicious. I should have listened. Now I have months of content and nowhere to put it. My content is homeless. And what's worse, my loyal fans will now get sucked into MOD presuming I'm gone. I'd cry, but I'm so pissed at myself, my tears would evaporate."

She flopped on the bed, covering her face with a pillow.

Unlike Kyle, Jane's chaos was all new to Rebecca. Had he never mentioned Jane's name? Not once? Apparently so. His personal Voldemort, Kyle rarely let Jane's name cross his lips. Now spoken, he half expected his nemesis to fly through the window to suck their souls.

Kyle tilted the pillow off Rebecca's face. His heart seized at the sight of her tears. "This isn't over."

Jane's strategic advantage was a head start. By now, she'd likely laid land mines for them to stumble into. But they could minimize the damage and maybe even regain the lead. While Jane believed her plotting to be undetected, they spotted her sticky fingerprints everywhere. Only time would tell if they were too late to stall whatever she was planning. Meanwhile, they might gain enough time to launch a counterattack of their own.

The thought of getting even with Jane jolted his body to life in a way he hadn't experienced since his modeling days. Blood racing, mind clear, heart full of hope.

No more sitting idle. That was a luxury Kyle could no longer afford with Rebecca, her work, and reputation at stake. Plus, countless other victims were out there needing protection. Kyle would stand and fight. For Rebecca, the others—and for himself. The only problem: where to start?

18

Rebecca scrolled through Leslie's texts that had been flying in for two hours. Poor girl was up and texting at 4:00 a.m. Rebecca's nightly do not disturb setting was certainly getting a workout.

She opened her mouth to speak, but Kyle's even breathing stopped her. She could sit and watch him sleep forever, her heart bursting with love for all they had together. But sentimental musing would have to wait. They had a big day ahead.

Leslie:
I'll be on the *MOD Today* podcast at 6 a.m. They're in Australia!

Leslie:
7:15 a.m. local time I'll be on *Women Empowering Women* in the UK? Holy smokes!

Leslie:
Just booked *Maya and Mercy* on *Sirius XM*.

Leslie:
Added to *Bedroom Bites* also on Sirius. Since I'll be there.

Leslie:
Will be on the *Maggie Cho Radio Show* in Houston this afternoon!

Leslie:
We're trending on Twitter! Go login. Do you even have a Twitter account?

Rebecca's heart thumped in her chest. This was really happening. Did she have a Twitter account? She must, but couldn't remember the login, it'd been so long.

The international *MOD* publicity team had been up working its pixie dust magic across the pond while the US slept. The rest of the world was wide awake and reading *MOD* online.

Somehow, it never occurred to Rebecca that her article would find readers outside New York. Silly as it sounded, her entire existence revolved around her hometown, mega city as it was. To think that eyes were reading her words clear across the globe sent chills rippling down her back.

What were they saying?

She sat up.

Kyle was right. She may not like what she reads. She talked all bold the night before, but now nausea took hold.

Leaning on the headboard, her eyes drooped closed.

All she could see was the blue and black night mode screen of Twitter flashing horrible messages.

Her eyes popped open.

She looked back at Kyle.

How can he sleep at a time like this?

Rebecca flipped up the covers and walked with her laptop to the living room. She'd last logged into Twitter from her computer. Maybe the cookies would recognize her and log her in.

Her laptop blinked to life, and she opened her browser to login to Twitter.

Please. Please. Please.

Bingo.

BeccaSloane.

She must have made the account during college, Becca being a nickname she acquired from her college pals, though Kyle had since adopted it as well.

Sure enough, down the right sidebar #MOD trended.

WomenRock44:
OMG! This article on orgasms is ridiculous. @maureen6 @amybNYC have you seen it? #MOD

Zany8s:
Why am I only learning all this sex info now? #MOD #SEX #Orgasms

YouKnowJack89:
What freak would write a story like this? #MOD

@roxypoxy411
Bravo! #MOD for publishing this! Climaxes for all!

@karatequeen999
Better go grab a Magic Wand before they sell out! #MOD

@kingmaker
Who's the author? Any guesses? #MOD

@katieanneLEM
So who do you think wrote this? #MOD

@DontLookNowLook
#BedroomDiary! We love you! #MOD

@timebender789
Don't be shy, Bedroom Diary! Come forward into our ample bosom! If you're cute, naked. #MOD

@oldcrankypuss11
This anonymous #BD thing is a crock. There is no Bedroom Diary. #MOD

@monica>136nclud
Bet there's no #BedroomDiary. It's some old hairy guy with bad acne #MOD

@therealmadgelives [Verified]
Let's play a game: comment with a picture of who you think #BedroomDiary is. Wrong pics only. Best post gets a follow. #MOD

Celebrities were guessing at her identity?
Rebecca darted back to her phone, and sure enough, texts were pouring in from Leslie.

Leslie:
The article buzz is amazing. Can't wait to see how it develops.

Leslie:
Just got off my first overseas interview. They asked about the article but got fixated on the coauthor identity thing.

Leslie:
#BedroomDiary is trending.

Leslie:
Got revised questions from one of my interviews today.
Added questions about the secret author.

Leslie:
Early article focus now shifting to author identity.

Leslie:
Viraj is elated with the buzz. Says buckle up. Wonder if
they're behind the shift in focus...

Rebecca:
Just catching up. Do you think they planned this?

Leslie:
Yes. Definitely. Shitty they didn't tell us tho.

Rebecca:
Hang in there. Sorry you have to do this alone.

Leslie:
Me too.

This was not how it was supposed to go. Instead of taking a well-deserved victory lap for her debut in a world-renowned magazine, her blog was stolen, her future uncertain,
and her mouth tasted like ash.

The story she'd hidden for months was now plastered
everywhere along her route to work: bus shelters, cab tops,
digital signage. Even her usual morning zoo music station
was talking about #MOD. But Rebecca's mind had a singular

focus: Jane. The mystery woman was a mystery no more. It was creepy as hell thinking this powerful woman would bother messing with the life of a nobody like her—and had been for months. Like Wile E. Coyote chasing the Road Runner, Rebecca half expected a piano to tumble out a window onto her head. Small blessings. At least now that she was indoors, she was safe from Jane. Though Darcy storming over didn't bode well.

"Rebecca, did you know about this *MOD* issue?"

Her blood drained. "What do you mean?"

"If they were going to do a big issue like this, we should have put the February issue on our client plans."

"Most of our clients don't want to run adjacent to sexual content."

"Oh. Right."

"However, we can call around and see if any are interested in a quick web buy?"

Please say no.

Darcy bit her lip. "No. No, you're likely right."

They shared an awkward beat of silence with neither moving.

"Coffee?" Rebecca lifted her mug.

"No. Thank you."

Rebecca turned tail and headed for the kitchen, only to find every woman in the agency gabbing about *MOD* by the coffee station. The voices of one trio rose above the others.

"Could you ever admit to it?"

"Never. Holy shit. Share a private story like that?"

"I, for one, always give clear directions, if you know what I mean. You have to. Men are clueless."

Rebecca faced the machine and slipped her mug in, pressing her usual triple size with extra milk. Grinding noises ensued.

"Well, since she's been through the wringer, I just might write in and ask a few questions."

"And who would you be asking? For all we know, it's some dude in his mom's basement."

"No way. That article wasn't written by a dude, and certainly not one in his basement."

"Who do you think it is, then?"

"Not a celebrity. They'd never."

"Yeah, likely not. Who then?"

"Could be anyone."

"Old or young?"

"Hard to say."

"Can't be too old or they'd fixed the issue sooner."

"True."

"Someone with balls, though."

"Or desperate enough."

"Maybe Rebecca wrote it?"

The women giggled.

"Hey, Rebecca," Ashley, one of the media buyers, called over.

"Hmm?" Rebecca answered, eyes glued on the last drops filling her mug. It always felt like a forever wait. Today, time warped to an eternity.

"Who do you think wrote the 'Bedroom Diary' article in *MOD*?" Ashley asked.

Drip. Drip. Drip.

Screw it.

Rebecca lifted her filled mug, the last drops disappearing through the slats of the collection tray. She turned to meet six mascaraed eyes blinking in anticipation.

Rebecca sipped her coffee, the hot liquid scalding her tongue.

Stall. Stall.

"Well?" Mona asked.

"You're right. Could be anyone," Rebecca answered.

"Genius. No shit. Who do you think it is?" Mona said.

"No clue." Rebecca walked away.

"Why do we talk to her?" Mona loud-whispered.

"We don't," Ashley replied.

Their laughs at her expense faded as she put some distance between herself and the kitchen.

Why do I work here again? Rebecca thought as she reached the safety of her cubicle.

Darcy was a tool.

The buyers were stuck in high school.

Newbies, like Evvy, were too junior to be confidantes.

Alone in a crowd.

She thought of Leslie. Of how satisfying it had been working with her and on behalf of women. Her gut churned. It'd take some time to internalize that her blog was gone. All her words. All those stories, helping women. Did she have it in her to start over? Thievery aside, working on the *MOD* article ignited something in her soul previously missing. The thrill of taking her cause to the world and having them take notice was indescribable. Words could move people and make a difference. But not just words: ideas. All of which now belonged to Jane. And as far as the world knew, it always had. Rebecca didn't even have…

No, no no no!

Rebecca whipped out her phone and opened Twitter. #MOD was still trending as was #BedroomDiary, with Tweets tagging @bedroomdiary: the official page of the column. Official, but not hers. Another Valis Publishing score.

How had she let it all slip through her fingers so easily? Overnight, literally, all her work was gone. Rebecca had only herself to blame. Meanwhile, she neglected her usual work, the one that paid the rent. She'd have to buckle down if she was to meet all the aggressive deadlines she'd volunteered for, then ignored. As much as she hated to admit, MediaNow was all she had left. Once that would have been enough, but suddenly, suddenly it rang hollow.

Barbara's face lit up her vibrating phone.

"Hey," Rebecca answered.

"This *MOD* thing is outrageous!"

"I know. I can't really talk about it here, though." Rebecca scanned the empty aisle behind her.

"Figured, but I'm bursting. Every woman at the firm is going nuts. All five of us."

Rebecca smiled. "All five?"

"They're not big on diversity and inclusion at my company."

Rebecca couldn't hold back, not from her best friend. She hustled over to an empty phone room, shutting the door just before tears soaked her cheeks. She let it all out, about Jane stealing her website domain name, her pen name, stopping short of telling about Kyle, but sharing enough about the bad blood with Jane for Barbara to understand the situation.

"Oh sweetie, I'm so sorry! I've heard publishing can be ruthless, but I had no idea the extent of it. Does Leslie know?"

"Not yet. She's consumed with those interviews today. I didn't want to upset her, and I certainly don't want Jane to find out we're onto her," Rebecca said.

"Right. That's a good idea. But did you mention something about letters?"

"I totally forgot. I need to check the language. They want me to answer reader letters. Knowing Jane, I probably signed my life away in that contract, missing some minor 'you're our slave forever' clause."

"If only you could find a skilled lawyer?" Barbara's frustration was evident.

"I know, I know. I meant to send it to you, but it slipped my mind."

"You're way too trusting…"

"Well, I'm cured of that now. What am I going to do?" Rebecca said.

"Why don't you all come over tonight. We'll put our heads together and figure out what recourse you have."

Back at her desk, Rebecca opened her planning calendar, doing her best to avoid reflecting on the conversations swirling about her words, as well as more than a few choice words she had for Jane.

19

K yle looked as green as Rebecca felt by the time they
arrived at the steps of the brownstone on the Upper
West Side where Barbara lived with her boyfriend, Joe.
On the way, she and Kyle agreed to avoid his painful history
with Jane when recounting the details. The wound was too
raw; the events pulsing as if fresh rather than a decade old.
But then, wounds like Kyle's may never fully heal, though he
was doing his best to try.

Barbara buzzed them in and they ascended the three
flights of the 1900s brownstone to their apartment door.
The chunky wooden rail was slick from a century of touches.
Everything else had been renovated, from the linen wallpaper and octagonal floor tile, to the art deco sconces lighting
their way to Barbara's open door.

Garlic-sesame goodness greeted them, sending Rebecca's
stomach growling for the first time all day.

"Hungry?" Joe said as his muscular frame stooped to unpack glossy black takeout containers of sushi, sashimi, and hot stir fry from the shopping bag on their coffee table. With a short afro, manicured beard, and dark penetrating eyes, Joe was truly a handsome man. Matching her old sales rep from Sports Illustrated with her best friend had been a love match from heaven.

Barbara wrapped Rebecca in a tight hug. "We'll make this right. There has to be a way."

Her friend squeezed so much confidence and determination into Rebecca, she almost believed it. Lord, did she want to find a path forward that ended this mess with everyone in one piece. Or as close to unscathed as they could manage.

Joe locked hands with Kyle, slapping backs in a synchronized routine they must teach in high school.

"Never a dull moment around these parts," Joe said.

"You don't know the half of it," Kyle answered.

"Any updates from Leslie?" Barbara said. "I texted three times but never got an answer."

"Same. She sent a few texts, but the last arrived hours ago." Rebecca draped her coat over Barbara's entryway chair and returned to sit on the sofa. "Poor girl, stuck doing all the interviews on her own. I was so distraught about the Jane mess, I lost track of launch day."

"Didn't you say she looked forward to the press?" Kyle asked.

"She did." Rebecca craned her neck towards the kitchen entrance. "But that's because she's passionate about the topic. By this afternoon, all anyone wanted to talk about was the secret identity of Bedroom Diary."

"Since we don't know when she'll get here, let's eat. I ordered her favorites and she can dig in when she arrives," Barbara said.

The four gathered around the coffee table, chopsticks snapping around translucent mounds of fish. Each diner dipped theirs in personal soy sauce saucers Barbara produced from her cupboard. Dabs of green wasabi tinged each bowl according to each person's tolerance for the hot mustard. For a moment, the world melted away. No Jane. No MOD. No stolen URL. Just a few friends eating takeout and drinking wine.

Joe's mouth lit on fire after Kyle snuck a huge mound of wasabi into his soy sauce when he wasn't looking, sending the table into a fit of giggles just as the apartment door opened.

Leslie stood, arms folded. "Isn't this jolly?"

"Leslie, oh my God! Are you okay?" Rebecca hopped up to hug her, but Leslie stepped back.

"Quite the celebration. Kind of forgot about someone, didn't you?"

"I texted. We weren't sure when to expect you."

"Leslie, come sit. You must be spent," Barbara said from her seat on the floor.

"Yes. Yes I am. I've been talking since 4:00 a.m. And seeing you all this way, after the day I had…" Tears welled in Leslie's eyes.

"Oh sweetie." Rebecca enveloped Leslie in her arms, squeezing as the sobs came.

"I'm sorry. I just felt so fucking alone today. And to arrive and see you all together…"

"You're here now. Sit, eat."

Barbara scampered to the kitchen, returning with a container. "Look. We ordered spicy tuna for you," Rebecca said.

"I love spicy tuna," Leslie pouted.

"We know, honey," Rebecca said, rubbing her back.

She hadn't the heart to break the Jane news to her in that moment. Best they let her eat first. Leslie looked like she needed it, and they definitely all needed her brain power if they were going to figure out a way out of their MOD fix.

Leslie sat, opening her container lid. "I can barely talk. I've been talking and talking. Holy shit. I'll never do a cover story again."

"Well, at least the article is published. Did they mention anything about the letters?" Rebecca said, pouring soy sauce into a clean bowl for her.

Leslie popped a slice into her mouth, speaking while she chewed. "They want both of us in the MOD office tomorrow at 9:00 a.m.," Leslie said, reaching across the table for a lonely piece of sashimi from the large app combo they devoured.

"What for?" Rebecca asked.

"They want to talk next steps."

Rebecca sought Kyle's attention, but he looked away, lips pressed so tight they turned white.

"The letters?"

"They didn't say, but Viraj said they had plans."

"NO!" Kyle yelled, standing with such force the armchair he was in tipped over backwards with a crash. Chest heaving, he eyeballed the chair, but left it on its back like a stranded turtle. He grabbed his head with both hands, pacing across the room to collect himself. The assembly froze in place, each looking at the other, but none daring to speak.

After what seemed like an eternity, they all resumed eating. Joe rose and headed to the bathroom, stopping next to Kyle.

"You okay?" He grasped Kyle's shoulder.

"Yeah, thanks. Sorry about that." Kyle returned to right the chair.

Rebecca rose to give Kyle a hug, earning a forehead kiss. "I don't want you anywhere near Jane."

"You talk about her like you know her," Leslie said.

"Yes, we have a history. One that I don't want to talk about, but Jane won't let it go."

The group looked from Rebecca to Kyle, but neither said another word on the topic.

Barbara redirected the conversation. "I looked at the contract you sent over. You're right, follow-up reader letters are part of the original scope."

"Shit, really? That's pretty devious," Leslie said. "I've signed tons of Valis contracts and I've never seen that clause before."

"If you want to get paid, you need to follow through."

The last thing Rebecca wanted from Jane was money. A twisted soul with no scruples. The faster she could get away from Jane, the better. But then it hit her. They knew about Jane, but she didn't know that yet. For all she knew, they were blissfully ignorant to her backhanded dealings. The best way to keep tabs on Jane might just be by staying close.

"Ky, you won't want to hear this, but I'm going to that meeting tomorrow."

"What? No—"

"Hear me out," Rebecca interrupted. "We don't know what Jane is up to. How are we going to find out if we reject her engraved invite to her war room? If I stay engaged with her, maybe we can find our way out of this mess faster and be done with her, once and for all."

"She's got a point," Barbara said.

"I'm in." Leslie popped the last of her sushi into her mouth and wiped her hands on her jeans.

"You can play double agent all you want, but Jane is a dangerous person to toy with. This is a bad idea," Kyle said.

Rebecca walked over to Kyle, resting her head on his chest. His heart thumped like a kettledrum in a rainstorm, belying his outward calm. Mountain monks would envy his ability to control his emotions, compartmentalize, and forge ahead. His heart raced for good reason, as did hers. Without question, engaging Jane was a bad idea. Trouble was, it was the only idea they had.

Kyle tightened his hold on Rebecca's hand as they strolled home from the subway station at 14th Street. Their bubble of silence passed around revelers loitering outside bars, grabbing smokes, and hopping in and out of Ubers in small groups.

He lifted her hand to his lips for a soft kiss.

Rebecca looked over and smiled.

"Crazy day," Kyle said.

"Yeah. And it's about to get a boatload crazier."

"Are you up for that?"

"Guess I have to be, for both our sakes," Rebecca answered.

"I love you. I'll always love you. We'll get through this, but it'll likely get worse before it gets better."

"But we're together. That's what matters."

They stopped in the middle of the sidewalk, their lips met for a deep kiss, sending Kyle's longing ablaze. She unraveled him like no one else, and he wanted more. Always more. Her hands cupped his butt, drawing him closer while his lost their way in her ringlets. The pair churned mouths, dead center of the sidewalk, ignoring the flow of people now weaving around them. He released her head, panting.

"Guess we should get a room?"

"We already have one. And a snazzy bed." She beamed back, eyes twinkling in the neon signs of the bodega behind them.

They resumed walking, swaying their joined hands.

"What do you think Jane will do next?" Rebecca asked.

"Be careful. There's no telling."

She stopped walking. "Do you honestly think I'm in danger?"

"I can't say. You're diving into a piranha pool. Getting bit is a given; the only unknown is how deep."

"I hate to admit this out loud, but earlier today, it disappointed me to think my MOD project was over. Truly, disappointed. She's hurting me to get to you, I get that. But I'm not a toy. Jane can't steal what I won't relinquish, and I refuse to go scurrying away while she claims my work and life story."

Kyle dropped her hand.

Is that what Rebecca thought he did? That he ran scurrying away from Jane instead of standing his ground? Perhaps not. But did she have a point? Had Kyle run when he should have stood his ground? The hospital dump-off made closure impossible. He was in no position to champion himself when just starting out and spiraling. But he'd grown since then. Gone was the young kid on anxiety meds trying to cope with the pressures of fame.

And truth be told, he couldn't even remember what happened the night he woke up in the hospital. They'd said he'd taken too many pills with scotch, but he didn't even drink scotch back then. He couldn't afford the stuff, not any brand worth drinking, anyway. Nothing from that night made sense. Just like it made no sense for Rebecca to subject herself to Jane's clutches.

Rebecca took his hand. "You're worried about me, but I'll be fine. I've lived my whole life being careful. Being quiet. Weighing possibilities before following through. For once I want to follow my gut. And my gut says to take Jane on. Throw caution to the wind and see what that feels like."

"Tornadoes are wind too. Hurricanes. Not all wind is pleasant."

"Thanks for the analogy, Mr. Weather Channel." She yanked his hand.

Kyle opened his mouth, but she silenced him with her finger. "No more tonight."

Their cone of silence returned. Rebecca sank into her thoughts, lips moving in time with the argument raging across her mind. Quelling his powerful instinct to keep her safe would take unspeakable strength. But as much as he hated to admit it, the fight with Jane was happening. At least this time, he wasn't fighting alone.

20

As Rebecca waited with Leslie in Jane's office for Viraj to return with the editor-in-chief, the New York skyline stretched before them, bathed in the morning sun.

Welcoming her.

Her city.

Her story.

Rebecca's body surged with pride. She'd done good. Whatever craziness was in store with Jane, she needed to remember her story was helping women. Nothing would change that now. Her pulse quickened as the time to meet Jane in person approached. The woman who had abused Kyle. The woman who reduced the value of her personal story to a bargaining chip. For the first time Rebecca realized that a flesh and blood woman would enter, and not a slimy monster with fangs and a spiky exoskeleton.

Could Rebecca star as the heroine of her own monster flick? She was about to find out.

Jane swooped into the room, her ivory blouse fluttering behind her in a silky blur. "Brava to the women of the hour."

Butterflies fluttered in Rebecca's chest as she and Leslie both jumped to their feet.

Viraj gestured to them. "Jane, I'm pleased to introduce Leslie Allen and Rebecca Sloane."

"Ladies, I'm pleased to introduce Editor-in-Chief, and fashion legend, Jane Stuart."

Jane dropped a notebook on her desk, then rounded the table to shake hands. In her pumps, she was a smidge taller than Rebecca's five-six frame. Her blond, sharply angled bob had not a hair out of place. Jane's loose top and wide-legged black trousers flowed as she moved with effortless elegance.

How could she appear so normal? Jane presented as a high-powered woman who ran a fashion empire. Where was the shrew who blackmailed men for sexual favors? Rebecca's intense scrutiny drew a raised eyebrow from Jane, but she shifted her gaze.

"Ms. Allen. I've enjoyed the work you've done for us. You have a brass set on you."

"Thank you, thank you. This is a real honor," Leslie said.

Jane's soft hands grasped Rebecca's. Firm. Powerful. Her superior station evident.

"Lovely to meet you," Rebecca said.

"Lovely? Did you hear that? She must not know who I am," Jane said over her shoulder while holding onto Rebecca's hand longer than necessary.

When Rebecca looked up, she met a querying set of hazel eyes. Rebecca held her gaze.

"Well, all right." Jane smiled back with a note of respect, motioning the group to her seating area. Two sofas facing each other across a lacquer coffee table.

"Please help yourself to some water," Jane said, sitting back.

Leslie leaned forward and poured herself a glass from the pitcher and downed it. She wiped her mouth dry with a napkin. "I'm sorry, but I've never been this nervous, and I've slept in gangster dens."

Jane roared with laughter. "Scarier than the mob. If only that's the first time I've heard THAT comparison!"

The group chuckled in polite response.

"Well," Jane crossed her legs. "So much to discuss. The team has been up all night fielding inquiries about our anonymous author Bedroom Diary. What a brilliant stroke. Whose idea was that?"

"Mine." Rebecca raised her hand. Was she effing joking?

"Genius. Pure genius," Jane said.

"We got more play for the article. It added a dash of mystery that excites the masses," Viraj parroted from his seat beside Jane.

"Now for phase two." Jane clapped.

"What is that exactly?" Leslie asked.

"The response has been overwhelming. Emails. Texts. Form fills on our website. Letters dropped off downstairs. That hasn't happened since, when?" Jane looked at Viraj.

"It's been a while. This story resonated with women everywhere," Viraj said.

"Well, that's good then, yes?" Rebecca gazed at her friend who sat shell-shocked.

Yesterday's launch gauntlet took its toll on Leslie. I'll have to step up today.

"Our Japanese bureau is translating their onslaught for us as we speak. Women are pouring their hearts into stories. Stories and questions. It would be criminal to ignore them."

"What are you thinking?" Rebecca asked.

"We'd like to create a 'Dear Bedroom Diary' column where you work thorough the questions women are sending in. Our team can narrow down the ones worth using. We can do this every week, but we would like to turn around the first column by tomorrow. Could you manage that?" Jane asked.

"Tomorrow?" Leslie snapped to attention.

"Yes, we will run it on our website to start."

"No, that's not possible," Leslie said.

Rebecca urged Leslie on with her eyes. They needed to play along with Jane, as discussed the night before. What was she doing?

"We need to work out the terms of this new arrangement before we begin any work."

Jane leaned in, tapping her finger on her nose. The face-off with Leslie was on.

"Letter writing was in the original contract."

"I read the terms, and while letter writing was included, the cadence and volume weren't specified. We must first resolve that and a few other issues," Leslie said.

Jane's eyes flashed anger, darkening as the storm rolled in. And she was right: Leslie had a brass set.

"Viraj, can you get this going with Legal? Tell them it's a rush."

"Yes, of course," Viraj said, scribbling on a pad.

"How much time to you need?" Jane said.

"Rebecca and I need to speak first, review the offer, and then we'll let you know."

"Give me a ballpark time frame? We could easily hire someone and do this without you," Jane said, her gaze steeling.

"You could. But it'd be a shame if word got out that you were using a fake writer for 'Dear Bedroom Diary,'" Leslie said.

The two women exchanged silent volleys. The electricity passing between them could power a skyscraper. How lucky was Rebecca to have Leslie on her side?

"Well, let's not get ahead of ourselves," Jane warmed. "We can begin sorting letters in anticipation that we'll reach an amicable agreement by tomorrow. Sound good?"

"Yes. Absolutely," Rebecca said.

Leslie's cheeks blushed, likely in relief that her hard negotiations worked.

The duo rose to shake hands with Jane and Viraj before heading out. But not before Rebecca took a last glance back at Jane.

Out in the street, Rebecca hipped her fists. "What was that about?"

"That dumb clause couldn't go by uncontested. That would have been more suspicious than us just saying yes."

"But now, I might get locked into something longer."

"No. Now, you'll get a defined out clause. The last one was so vague she might have been able to dribble this work out indefinitely."

"Why didn't you say anything before the meeting?"

"I didn't know it then. But something Barbara said last night clicked for me once we began talking."

"Good. That's good to know. We'll need to examine the contract closer this time."

Rebecca shouldered her handbag. When she looked up, Leslie was watching her, and not in a good way.

"What?" Rebecca said.

"This is a terrible idea. Moving forward with MOD. We should both walk while we can."

Terrible was generous. The idea was atrocious, as monstrously bad as Jane herself. But Rebecca refused to walk away. Quitting was worse than staying. Both she and Kyle would be stuck wondering where and when Jane would pop up next. Their own personal troll. But in real life where she could cause unspeakable damage. And that didn't even begin to address Kyle's wounds or how Jane wronged Rebecca. The stakes were no longer exclusively Kyle's. Rebecca had a stake in the outcome as well. And she wasn't backing down.

Leslie moved in close. "We both have day jobs. You're already complaining about being overloaded. Why commit to this and be stuck with someone Kyle obviously thinks is bad news? Unless…"

Realization dawned on Leslie's face. "Unless… there's something you're not telling me."

Was Rebecca that transparent? That Leslie could read her mind without her permission? But of course she could sense it. Why wouldn't she? They'd been friends for so long, she knew when Rebecca was keeping a secret. She did it so seldom, mostly because it made her skin crawl and was way too exhausting to keep straight. But it didn't help that Rebecca couldn't pull it off even when she tried. The last time Leslie wormed the details out of her anyway, drawing them out against her will like lifting nails with a magnet. But there was zero chance of that happening this time. This secret was Kyle's to divulge.

Rebecca turned away to face the building they'd just exited.

Leslie circled around to read her expression. Like a book, apparently. "There is more. Becca, you've got to tell me."

"I wish I could, but I can't."

"I thought we were partners in this?"

"We are. We are partners."

"You've got to understand my situation. This is a side gig for you. You can walk away anytime, no harm, no foul—Jane notwithstanding. But this is what I do. I have a professional reputation to consider. I don't have a Kyle. I don't have family nearby. This is it. Writing is all I have."

Leslie stood on the brink of tears. Rebecca was so wrapped

up in the cat and mouse games with Jane that she completely lost sight of how this was all impacting Leslie. How selfish could she be? Of course Leslie wanted to get out. Any normal person with functioning instincts would run cartoon style through a wall and never look back. And Leslie had the best gangster-den instincts going. She knew this would likely end badly. Rebecca ignored those instincts at her peril—and yet she must. It was the only way.

Rebecca clasped Leslie's hands. "I need you to trust me that I have a good reason for all of this. I just can't tell you yet."

"Then I need to beg your forgiveness and drop out," Leslie said. "I know it sucks about the Bedroom Diary name and all, but I have an awful feeling about this."

Rebecca hugged her friend, whose arms hung limp at her sides.

"I hate myself right now. I feel like I'm abandoning you."

"You're not. I get it."

"I can't risk it. Who'd hire me as a writer if Jane stuck me with her evil voodoo pins? No one. I'd be ruined."

"Hey." Rebecca pulled away, squeezing Leslie's shoulders. "It's okay. Well, actually, it sucks. But I understand. I do."

Leslie looked up. "Really?"

"Yes. It'll be okay. I'll be okay."

Rebecca released her friend, who wiped her eyes dry with her sleeve. The glass exterior of MOD's building guided her eyes up to where Jane was likely enjoying the view.

Rebecca's gut churned, as well it should. But exhilaration flowed as well. Rebecca would meet this challenge square in the face. After all, if she was going to present herself as an empowered woman worthy of social media praise, then it was time she started acting like one.

21

Rebecca snatched a pop-up tissue from the box on Viraj's desk and wiped her eyes using his darkened office window as a mirror. She'd only been reading "Dear Bedroom Diary" letters for 20 minutes and was already making a fool of herself.

Contract terms were reworked and clarified in 24 hours, so she could begin work. Though Leslie dropped out, Rebecca would forever be grateful to her for helping her navigate the new terms. Those included a clause specifying that Rebecca's name would stay anonymous when answering "Dear Bedroom Diary" letters. The established delivery timelines were neither the fire hose MOD wanted nor the trickle Rebecca preferred. All she needed now was to find time to complete the work.

She pocketed her tissue and stole a peek at Viraj. Back erect, his lean limbs typed with an energy and focus Rebecca lacked when fresh in the morning. He must have felt Rebecca's attention.

"Everything all right?" Viraj asked.

"Yes, just a little overwhelmed. I hoped the article would strike a chord, but 1,700 letters? From 15 countries? This is nuts."

Rebecca scrolled thorough the reader letter portal MOD created for their articles. Getting so many, it was an efficient way to track them all. Rebecca couldn't imagine if she had to sift through wads of letters on her own.

Viraj rotated his chair to face Rebecca. "Remember, our charge is only the top 100. We need to cull that back to three and formulate answers to each in the 150-200-word neighborhood. That will ensure our copy fits into the web page template."

"Why so short when we have ample material to work with?"

"Our web analytics show readers will only scroll so far, especially on mobile. Too long, and they'll bounce, missing the advertisements bankrolling this whole effort."

"I forgot about the business side of things," Rebecca said.

"Yes, and we must leave space for photography and graphics."

Viraj had a lot to juggle. He not only supported Jane, but edited multiple writers simultaneously.

"How long have you worked in publishing?" Rebecca asked.

"Almost six years, but I've moved around in a variety of roles. Every time I poked my nose into another area of the business, someone suggested I try it. So I always do. I envision it as gathering skills in a quiver. You never know when they'll come in handy," Viraj said.

"Makes sense."

Viraj refocused on his computer screen. "The more useful you can be, the more valuable you are to the business."

"And to Jane. How did you come to work for her?"

He darted a worried glance her way before refocusing on his screen. "Why do you ask?"

"No reason in particular. Wandering the halls here, I haven't seen many men. What drew you to fashion?"

"I always loved it, but it wasn't something my family encouraged."

Handsome, smart, and a skilled communicator, Viraj likely could have been anything he wanted. Rebecca wondered whether he came to Jane via the modeling or business route. The picture facing Viraj on his desk showed a woman in a sari with a pageant sash holding a bouquet. A winning bouquet.

"Is that a family picture?" Rebecca asked.

"It's my mother. She was Miss Mumbai when she was 20. I love that picture. The utter shock on her face is priceless. She's what drew me to fashion. All those pageant gowns were irresistible. My sister competed too. They'd make them at home, shooing me away from the stones and sequins until they finally let me help make them. The hand beading took hours, but she and my sister were living proof…" He looked at Rebecca.

"Proof of what?"

"That our dreams can come true despite our own doubts."

Rebecca broke eye contact. It was sweet of Viraj to pep her up. Her editor was turning out to be more relaxed and charming than the stiff persona he displayed around Jane.

He nodded his head towards Rebecca's laptop. "Do any of the letters excite you?"

"I've only read ten but, yes. Number 664 from Alexandra in Ohio. She's so overwhelmingly shameful about trying and failing to o—"

"You can say it," Viraj smiled.

"It's weird discussing this with a man, that's all."

"Isn't that the point of the article? That we should break the taboo of discussing women's pleasure needs?"

Touché. How provincial of her to feel uncomfortable discussing this with him. After everything Rebecca lived through, not to mention drafting the article, saying "orgasm" in front of Viraj was the least of her worries.

Rebecca refocused. "You're right. Number 664's inability to orgasm speaks directly to the original article. She's older than I am, too. She's in her forties."

"That is something."

"Yeah. I can't imagine being in the spot I was in for that long. Harboring shame for decades will be a hard habit to break."

"Perfect. That's the angle for Alexandra," Viraj said.

Rebecca checked 664 in the MOD dashboard. "At least she'll soon have some information to help her get started."

"Yes. When you write your drafts, always end on an optimistic note that sends them on a positive path."

"I like that."

"Anyone else?"

"Well, I could choose any of these." Rebecca scrolled down the screen. "Number 29 Elaine from Missouri. She has been having great orgasms with a partner, but doesn't know how to have them on her own now that her husband is deployed overseas."

Rebecca sighed. "I wish Heidi was here to help. She's the expert."

"Tap into your lived experience, you know way more than you think. What you've already shared has definitely inspired some interesting conversations with me and my girlfriend."

"Is that so?" Rebecca smiled so wide she felt her cheeks crease. The thought of Viraj and his lady having frank conversations about their love life was stunningly amazing.

"Who's next?" Viraj said.

"Number 894. Kika. But I can only read the first sentence.

Then the transcript is all jumbled."

He leaned over to view Rebecca's screen. "Interns scan them into the portal. We have transcribing software, but if the handwriting is unintelligible, the software can't read it."

Viraj clicked through the portal to open the PDF scan. "Looks like she's a virgin getting married and has been faking it for years. I can't read it all, but it says something about her wedding night."

"Oh, that's too bad. I'd love to help her. Is there any contact information? I could email her to get the full story?"

"We have two already. Let's get you started with those while I find a third." He flipped his wrist to check the time.

"I'm going to order out for some dinner. Vegan Chinese?"

"First time for everything. You order for me," Rebecca said.

"You can work in the next office writing your responses. I'll need all three before you leave tonight."

"I'll do my best." Rebecca stood up to head next door.

Viraj knew his stuff and was totally sensitive about the delicate topic. Working with Leslie was a whirlwind collaboration between friends, leaving Leslie too often playing therapist when they should have been writing. That was unfair to her, Rebecca realized now. Leslie was an award-winning professional who probably did their friendship a favor by stepping back. She'd have to thank her again for her wise counsel that got her this far. But first she had to write.

Rebecca settled into an empty desk and began typing. But not as Rebecca, as the wise mind behind "Dear Bedroom Diary."

22

Murmurs from the next door filtered through Rebecca's apartment wall as she walked to the window to look for Kyle's motorcycle. Kyle's reassuring anchor in a sea of madness, but it too was gone. An icy drift of late February snow in its place. A blizzard rolling in meant Kyle had to shelve his winter riding. He was on his way back from his motorcycle storage unit in Brooklyn.

Pools of streetlight bathed the snowy sidewalks, streets as empty as her insides. The last few weeks had been rough. Their busy schedules mixed with tussles over MOD and the wedding left Rebecca and Kyle orbiting different planets. They were so afraid of Jane coming between them that, in a way, she already had.

A cab pulled up to the curb in front of the building. The driver cruised his hand along the car to avoid slipping as he made his way around to the popped trunk to retrieve the passenger's suitcase.

Hmmm.

Maybe all they needed was a getaway? Some alone time would help them reconnect and remember why they were a couple in the first place. Some of the spark had fled their relationship in recent weeks. With Kyle's therapy progressing, she didn't want to push it. But she missed the confident man who made her heart flutter.

But where to go within a blizzard? A spa? Flights to anywhere warm were grounded. She grabbed her phone to thumb through options. If they could get someplace warmer... Hard to have mad sex when they were never in the same room, and when they were, Jane's phantom peeked over their shoulders.

Kyle's key slid the door. She looked back outside, but all was still empty.

Back entrance.

"Holy shit, it's freezing." He stomped clumps of snow off his boots. "Remind me to find a closer garage. I've been in the Uber for half an hour and am still frozen."

Kyle's normally olive skin tinged blue as he shrugged off his jacket. Rebecca rubbed her hands up and down his arms to create warming friction. "Your furnace needs a boost."

He pecked her forehead. "Maybe a hot shower will help."

Chill vented off his clothes as he passed, sending a shiver through her as she stood, anchored in place, staring at the closed bathroom door.

A shiver. A shiver where a tingle should be.

Perhaps that was harsh, but compared to when they were first dating, there was a definite drop in the excitement department. Back then, every Kyle entrance was an event. He'd double-ring the doorbell, then swoop in, embracing Rebecca before tipping her back into a dramatic dip.

Kissing her.

Wiggling his eyebrows.

Either that or pop over from his apartment across the hall to steal a kiss while throwing out the trash.

Or leave notes on her door.

Or summon her over to his apartment simply to hand her a single rose. He'd flash an impish smile before playfully closing the door in her face, only to watch her reaction through the peephole.

That was then.

Now, she got a forehead peck.

Yeah, they definitely needed a getaway. It'd do them both good.

Light glowed from under the bathroom door.

She strode down the hall. A wall of warm steam greeted her, fogging the mirror and hanging in a thick cloud at the ceiling. She turned the damp knob to close the door.

"Hey, Ky?"

"Yeah?"

"Can we talk?"

"Sure. I can feel my arms again. Thought I was going to remain a snowman forever," he laughed.

"You looked chilly, for sure."

Rebecca bit her lip. "Are we okay?"

"What do you mean?"

"I mean you and me. I feel like it's been chilly between us lately. With everything going on, there hasn't been a lot of 'us' time."

He popped his face out of the curtain. "Come here."

She pouted her two steps over. He leaned out, his wet lips meeting hers, before gently parting for more.

Her friend down below said hello.

"We're more than okay." He popped back into the shower and turned off the water. "But you're right, we should make some time for us."

Rebecca lifted a fluffy towel out of the rack and had her arm outstretched before he swept the curtain aside.

"Thanks." He grabbed the towel and blotted his face, then did a quick sweep around his body before rubbing his head dry. "I guess we jumped into playing house pretty fast, and haven't kept up with the dating part."

"Kinda, yeah." She shrugged.

"I'm sorry for that."

"Me too."

He stepped out of the tub, wiping the fog off the mirror to comb his hair.

"I have an idea. With all this snow, we can head up north and go skiing."

"I've never skied in my life."

"But you could!"

"Me? On skis? Sounds like a disaster waiting to happen."

"I could teach you. It'd be fun, and we'd swing by and see my parents."

"Can't we do something else?"

"Come here." Kyle grabbed her hand and led her out of the mist and into their comparably chilly bedroom before stopping at the window to point.

Blowing snow stuck to the glass like a holiday spray-on display.

"This is a sign. We should embrace winter and make peace with the snow gods."

"Can't we get cozy with a different god? Like a sun one?"

"There's sun in skiing."

"Is it wise for you to drag me into the wild unknown?"

"No wild and no unknown. One day. One passionate

night." He wrapped her in his arms. "What do you say?"

"I don't know. Where will we stay?"

"At my parents'. They've been dying for us to come up."

"A passionate night at your parents'?"

"Sure." He slid his hands until each had a handful of her bottom. "You'll just have to keep your climax screams down a little."

Her head snapped up. "What climax screams?"

"Your moans of ecstasy can be a little loud, but we'll take the guest room and that'll give us plenty of space. It's on the other side of the house."

"Way to make me self-conscious!"

"No worries. It'll be great. You'll see." He squeezed her butt firmly, before letting go to retrieve flannel lounge pants and a waffle-ribbed long-sleeved T-shirt.

Rebecca crossed her arms. "What'll be great? The sex or the skiing?"

"Both! It's a win-win?"

"I don't know."

Quick as lightning, he swept her in his arms into one of his patented dips. "Say yes. Yes, to an adventure."

"An adventure?"

Did he have to dip her? She was powerless against it.

"Oh, all right. But take it easy on me."

"Perfect," he said, righting her. "I'll take care of everything. You can probably borrow Libby's skis and outerwear."

"You're such a guy! These hips in Libby's snow pants?"

"I love these hips. Don't talk smack about these hips," he leaped to their defense with a caress.

She giggled. "You can like them fine, but if they don't fit into those skinny girl pants of hers, I won't be skiing very long."

"Okay, you buy pants, and the clothes you need. I'll take

care of everything else. Deal?"

"Deal." Rebecca kissed him.

By the time she opened her eyes, Kyle was already on the phone calling his dad. She hadn't seen him this excited in a while. The fire was burning for them again.

Here's hoping a trip to the snowy north wouldn't snuff it out.

23

Two days later they were out on the mountain. Sunshine glimmered off the icicles in the trees as Rebecca and Kyle rumbled uphill on the ski lift chair. Smooth mounds of snow-covered trees sparkled like tufts of whipped cream. Pristine. White. Untouched. A stillness Rebecca hadn't experienced in ages, if ever.

The mechanical whine of the lift tower was the only sound, save skis scraping on the surface below. Each skier carving downhill, leaning to one side, then the other, leaving the same trail of interconnected "Ss" she'd been unable to master.

They made skiing look so easy.

Rebecca hung her head, her booted feet clamped into her skis. Such odd contraptions. Who would invent doing something so uncomfortable on purpose?

Boots so tight you could barely wiggle toes?

Helmets, goggles, and poles?

Layers of long underwear, fleeces, and coats?

Out in freezing 20-degree weather?

And for what? It was a hell of a way to spend a Saturday.

Rebecca adjusted her mitten while wiggling her numb fingers within to get the blood flowing. You'd think she'd be warmer after her tragically acrobatic morning.

Kyle rubbed her thigh. "Hey, you're doing fine."

"I'm a lot of things, but fine isn't one of them."

"It's your first day."

"Did you plow over ski racks on your first day?"

"No, but—"

"It took three people to rescue me from under that jumble."

"You were following me fine until then."

"Little kids looked at me like I'm a bumbling mess."

"It's easier for them. They're lower to the ground and pop back up after falling. Plus, they're surprisingly fearless."

"I'll say."

The whole mountain conspired against the city interloper. Meanwhile, Kyle never lost patience, always giving her encouragement.

Rebecca sighed. If she kept complaining, she'd ruin the day for both of them.

"Why isn't the 'pizza' thing working for me?"

"I think I figured it out. Your tips are together in a triangle, but you need to cut your edges. The angle is what plows the snow and makes you slow down."

"How do I do that?"

"When we get off the lift, angle your knees together toward touching. Because your boots are connected, your legs will angle your skis. That's why it's all so stiff. You move your legs to move your skis. Make sense? Try it now. While we're sitting."

Rebecca moved her knees together, and sure enough, the

full length of her shin, boot, and skis moved as one.

"Interesting. Edging. Is that what makes the scraping sound?"

"Yes. Ski bottoms are waxed to slide; the edges are metal and can cut through. We have a nice corduroy snow today, but it can get icy. That's when sharp edges save your neck."

"I'm not ready for neck saving. It's more my butt I'm worried about."

"Yeah, you'll be sore, but you are doing great. Most people would have given up by now." He chuckled.

"Aha! I knew it! I'm not going great!"

He nudged her shoulder. "Yeah, shockingly bad. But, but! You're getting better with every run. You're applying that same can-do spirit you apply to everything."

"Aww, Kyle! You think I have can-do spirit?"

"Of course. The real Rebecca is a fiery tiger who doesn't quit. That's what I love about you."

Tears escaped her eyes, their warmth fogging the interior of her goggles. "I so needed that. Thank you, sweetie." Rebecca leaned in to kiss him, but they clunked helmets.

Kyle roared with laughter.

"Damn it, Kyle! For once, can we do an activity that doesn't require protective clothing?"

"Next time, I promise," he laughed, unable to stop. "No helmets."

"Thank you."

The chair ahead of them lifted its safety bar.

"Okay. Time to get off. Ready to edge?"

Rebecca slid her skis off the footrest. "Ready as I'll ever be."

"Can I help, Mom?" Kyle said as they stood in his parents' kitchen.

The centerpiece of their one-story, sprawling colonial, their open-concept kitchen had a speckled quartz island that separated the work area from the family room and dining areas beyond. Traditional furniture grouped into sitting areas defined by neutral rugs rested on dark walnut floors. The effect created a homey-elegance Kyle hoped to emulate with Rebecca one day.

"Carry the mashed potatoes?" Kyle's mom handed him a bowl.

"Can I take this?" Rebecca lifted a covered tureen of veggies.

"Sure, then have a seat," Sharon said.

"Standing is better right now, if you get my drift."

Sharon smiled. "Sore?"

"Very."

"What did you do to this poor girl?" Kyle's dad, Michael, hollered from his seat at the head of the table.

"She's fine, Dad." He put his bowl down and took a seat. "Rebecca never skied before today, but did great by the end, didn't you?"

"The day is a black and blue blur. Did I ever get to the bottom of a run without falling?"

"Yes, you did. Made it down without falling once."

"Well, I guess that's progress." Rebecca sat across from Kyle.

She shifted her weight in her chair, likely onto her less battered butt cheek, wincing as their eyes met.

"You okay?" Kyle mouthed.

Rebecca nodded and tried to look comfortable.

What a trooper.

His mom joined the group with a platter of roasted chicken, golden with skin crisped to perfection.

Rosemary evenly distributed.

Steam floating skyward.

Platter mouthwatering.

"Wait, wait." Kyle popped up to grab his camera from the counter. "A few shots."

"Now?"

"Yes, now."

"Can I at least put it down?" his mom asked.

"No, I want your arms with the apron behind. It's perfect."

His dad leaned over to Rebecca. "Does he do this every night?"

"Only if our takeout is especially tempting."

"Do you eat takeout every night?" his mom asked.

"We do, unless Kyle whips something up. I'm rather hopeless, I'm afraid. My family ate out most nights growing up, so I never learned to cook."

Kyle took a few shots of the chicken. "Everyone lean in and I'll get the table."

His dad grumbled, but joined the shot. "Humans. That's different."

"Food's easier," Kyle said between shutter clicks.

"Why?"

"No complaints," he joked, earning an eye roll from his dad.

"That's enough. The food's getting cold," Sharon said.

She put the platter down and sat, but Kyle couldn't resist scanning through his digital shots.

Pretty good. The family pic was a keeper.

Kyle put the camera aside to join the others in scooping

portions onto their plates. They liked Rebecca, he could tell. The way his dad talked to her. The way his mom let Rebecca help. Too bad their last dinner hadn't gone as well. The day Libby's drama exploded before they'd even finished appetizers.

On cue, his mom popped the bubble.

"Did I mention Libby is coming to town for her dress fitting next month?"

"Which town is that?" Rebecca asked.

"Oh yes, sometimes I forget where we are. New York. She bought her dress at the bridal building, but we're doing the alterations at a special boutique they recommended."

"How did you get her to go to the bridal building?" Kyle asked.

The 23-story building featured showrooms for everything a bride could want. Only open to the trade weekdays, the building opened Saturday mornings to the public for designer gowns at wholesale prices. Since the showrooms doubled as offices, brides had to change into gowns together in random spaces among desks. Not likely the shopping experience his sister envisioned.

"With what I'm spending on this wedding, I'll be damned if I'll spend ten grand on a dress she'd only wear once," his dad said.

"She really got a beautiful gown," his mom said to Rebecca. "A Dana Harel trunk show. Even Libby couldn't complain. We're doing some minor alterations at a divine place she'll love. The boutique is girl heaven. She'll get her bridal moment."

"That sounds lovely," Rebecca said, cutting her food.

"I hope so. I wish a few friends could join her. She has so much trouble maintaining relationships."

"I wonder why," Kyle snorted.

"Behave, you," his mom said.

"All I'm saying is that if she could blunt that edge of hers, she'd have more friends."

"Kyle's right. More wine, Rebecca?" Michael lifted the bottle.

"Yes, please," she held her glass, smiling.

"Our girl needs to be more like Rebecca," his dad said.

"That's sweet of you to say, but she's her own person. The girls had fun in Texas."

"It's okay, Rebecca. I heard what happened," Sharon said.

Rebecca crinkled her nose. "I'm sure she didn't mean it."

"I'm afraid we put you in a difficult position."

"Libby never wanted me in the bridal party. You know that," Rebecca said.

"Yes, but Libby has some growing up to do. You can help her, Rebecca."

"Dad, it's not Rebecca's responsibility to tame Libby."

"No, but we'd consider it a favor if she coached her in the right direction," his dad said.

Why were his parents doing this? They expected Rebecca to be the clean-up crew for their indulgent parenting. And why now with the wedding? Their behavior made no sense.

"I have an idea," his mom said. "Why don't you join us for the fitting? It'll be the three of us: you, me, and Libby. If you spend more time together, I'm sure she'll come around."

"Sharon, that's nice of you, but don't you and Libby want some mother-daughter time alone?" Rebecca asked.

"Weddings are festive. Shopping will be more festive if you're with us. I'm afraid she'll be disappointed if she steps out of the dressing room wearing her gown for the first time to an audience of one."

Rebecca searched Kyle's face for a rescue. She was in a lose-lose situation. If she said no, his parents would be disappointed. If she said yes, Libby would throw a fit.

"It's up to you. I'll support whatever decision you make. And so will my parents. Won't you?" Kyle aimed his best intimidating stare at each end of the table.

"Yes, of course," his mom leaned back.

"Dad?"

"Yes, yes," he grumbled.

"How about this? I'll text Libby and ask. If she says okay, I'll come."

"You see?" Michael chimed in. "Considerate. That's more of what Libby needs. Thank you, Rebecca."

Forks went back to work. Kyle traced his around a mound of mashed potatoes with his fork. Rebecca displayed saint-worthy patience this weekend. Tumbling down the mountain all day, only to be rewarded with an ambush at dinner? The Dillons were pushing their luck. But Kyle had an inkling of how to make it up to her.

24

Kyle's phone buzzed right as he was slipping on socks in his parents' guest room. Jane's face filled the screen. He silenced it, peering toward Rebecca who was toweling off across the room.

What the hell was Jane doing? She had balls calling him, especially when he made it plain he wasn't interested. Whatever neediness had suddenly blossomed in her would need to find an outlet somewhere else.

He pocketed the phone. "Did the shower help your soreness?"

"Not too much, I'm afraid. Parts of my body hurt that I never knew existed." Rebecca flexed her nude torso to the side, reaching an arm overhead before switching sides. "I guess all that winter treadmill running only goes so far."

"Yeah, you use muscles skiing not flexed in other sports, unless you work those muscle groups."

Rebecca slinked her voluptuous body across the room, landing between his arms. She epitomized the ideal woman. Curves for days. Silky skin and alluring dark eyes that penetrated the deep recesses of his soul and squeezed tight. The last flutters of sleepiness fled his aroused brain just watching her.

She grabbed his hands and plopped each on her perfectly shaped butt. "You'll need to massage me."

"Is that so? Are you sure you're up to it? Being all creaky and all?"

"You'll have to be gentle. You were a little rough on me yesterday—and last night."

He cupped her roundness, massaging gently. "How's that?"

"Mmmm. Lovely. Oh, right there. Stay there," she said as his fingers made their way north to the nape of her back.

"If I knew you'd be so amorous after skiing, I'd have taken you sooner."

"Well, this is our first winter together. It couldn't have been too much sooner."

"I forget," he pulled back to gaze into her eyes. "I can't remember me before you. And I don't want to."

Kyle's lips found hers, tongues exploring as his hands traversed her smooth skin. She arched into him, cupping his head in that way that drove him nuts.

Then his back pocket buzzed. Kyle went stone stiff.

Rebecca jumped back. "What? What is it?"

"Jane called while you were in the shower."

Now it was Rebecca's turn to freeze. "What should we do? Should you answer?"

"If I don't, she'll probably keep calling."

Rebecca retreated, looking back as she opened her overnight bag to get her clothes out.

The relentless buzz returned. "Jesus, that woman is relentless."

"Want me to take it here?"

"No. Please. I'm afraid I'll jump through the phone and strangle that lollypop head of hers clear off."

"Ahh, feisty and amorous..." Kyle said as his phone buzzed again.

"I'll take it in my dad's office." Kyle made his way over, sliding the pocket doors shut. Rich wood shelving walled the room, each full of business books, pictures, and awards his dad earned over the years. Evidence of the dedication that so often kept him away from the family. Kyle understood, of course, but it left a chilly distance between them. Hopefully, one day, they'd get past it.

His phone vibrated, but this time, he answered.

"Seriously? On a Sunday?"

"What's the matter? Still in bed with Rebecca?" Jane purred.

Kyle swallowed. "Who?"

"Let's not play coy, dear. I'm quite sure you heard me."

It was the moment he'd been dreading and failed to prevent. From her tone, she planned to milk it for everything it was worth.

"Well," she said. "We do have ourselves a pickle here, don't we?"

"We don't have to."

"Oh, but I love pickles. They're delicious. I LIVE for pickles."

"Why start something now?"

"You're the one who let your little Latina walk through my door."

"Don't call her that! Have some respect."

"Have respect!" she blasted. "How dare you say that to me? After the stunt you pulled?"

"What?"

"Endearing her to me. Having me invest in her, all the while you're pulling the strings in the background."

"What are you talking about?"

As much as he wanted to ream Jane, it wasn't yet time for them to come clean about all they knew.

"You planted that picture with Marco for me to find. What are you playing at?"

"That was a mistake. Marco snapped it."

"Why were you there?"

"I wanted to find out if you knew about Rebecca."

"Marco wouldn't know that. Dumb move."

"Oh, and tanking my modeling career? That wasn't a dumb move?"

"I thought that was rather masterful."

"I knew it was you."

"Of course it was."

"Why?"

"Insurance."

"I never wanted what happened and you know it."

"We're both adults. Let's not make it a federal case."

"So, what? You wanted to paint me as someone who slept around to advance professionally?"

"Stop acting so shocked. It happens every day."

"What's sad is that so many casting people believed you."

"Did you ever expect to get hired again and have those pictures in my pages? Or anywhere in Valis Publishing?"

"It was cruel. Cruel and unnecessary. Do you do this to everyone?"

Jane dropped her voice to a purr. "No. Not everyone. Only the select few."

Silence hung between them. She was either hatching a plan or looking for an escape route out of her cesspool of dirty work.

"I see you found a new profession," Jane said. "Fruit, I hear? How quaint."

Kyle's eyes darted to a high school picture of cherries on his dad's desk. It was the first color picture he'd ever developed. It wasn't a new career. Photography was the career he was meant to have all along.

"Whatever," she huffed.

"Why are you even calling?"

"Ah, yes. Thank you. I had almost forgotten. You need to accompany me to an event."

"Why would I do that?"

"Well, I just happen to have the identity of one young woman in the palm of my hands. It'd be a shame if it—got public..."

Kyle fingered his temples, elbows on the desk. Any proximity to Jane was poisonous. He tried to warn Rebecca. Tried, but failed. It was his own fault for not sharing the extent of the danger earlier on. What he didn't expect was to land smack back in the viper's den.

"I'll take your silence as assent. If you think about it, it's a win-win. You get to go with me to the MOD Gala, then go back to bed and fuck Rebecca."

"Watch it!" he blasted.

"Oh, my. Romeo, you do like this one. Maybe even love?"

"Why are you doing this?"

"Because no one fucks with me and gets away with it."

The call disconnected.

Maybe no one had gotten away with tussling with Jane to date. But there was a first time for everything. And the hands of her countdown clock were now ticking.

Rebecca slipped into Kyle's dad's office, closing the door behind her. Kyle paced the room like a caged tiger. He looked up when he saw her.

"That good, huh?" she said.

"Worse. It's worse. She wants me to escort her to the MOD Gala."

"You're serious."

"It gets better. If I don't, she'll expose your identity as Bedroom Diary."

It was worse. Rebecca walked into the blast zone wearing only a foolish air of invincibility. Shrapnel flying everywhere meant they were bound to get nicked. Instead of patiently snooping, gathering intel, and formulating an escape plan, the endgame had begun. The clock was ticking on their move.

Rebecca sighed. "Say you go—"

"No, Becca—"

"Listen. Just listen for a minute. Say you go. You take her and do everything she asks. Play the doting boyfriend for a night. Then what? Where does this end? Are we to become the emotional piggy bank she smashes for withdrawals whenever she wants? When does this end? How will this ever end?"

"It won't, unless we do something."

"Do what? Just tell me. I'll do anything," Rebecca said.

"The only way I see out of this is to out her as the sexual predator she is."

"Predator? There are others?"

"One, yes. At least I have a good inkling Jane was his abuser. I'd need to follow up and determine if he'd be willing to talk."

Others?

Viraj.

The idea of Viraj going through the same torture Kyle did churned her stomach. Rebecca sank down on an ottoman, hugging herself.

"You thought of someone else?"

"Her current assistant, Viraj. He's very handsome and the only male on Jane's team. Dark skin, light eyes, wavy hair. Ky, he looks like you."

"Shit."

"Viraj is by her side, always at her beck and call. Christ, Ky. He's got to be her latest victim."

The two of them sat in stunned silence. The snowy world out the window looked as pristine and pure as the day before. Icicles dripping, snow drifting. Inside, an unspeakable truth settled over them, weighing heavy like an ominous cloak. Rebecca covered her face as tears slid down her cheeks. How could such a beautiful world produce a monster like Jane?

Why had Rebecca never considered Jane would dare repeat her crimes with others? Violating young men unabated for years cast her in an entirely new league of evil. Her behavior more befit the underworld Leslie chronicled than the shiny corporate offices of a fashion superpower. Knowing, or at least suspecting, others fell prey to Jane's advances changed everything.

Kyle wiped away tears of his own. "If the pattern holds, then yes. Viraj is likely her latest victim, or soon will be."

"We've got to do something. We have to stop her."

"We will. I have an idea. But for it to work, we'll need back up. Others willing to come forward. Without corroboration, it'll be my word against hers. That won't be enough to topple Jane."

"But you're willing? To come forward, publicly?"

Kyle traversed the room, kneeling in front of her. "Yes. I'm ready. As long as you're by my side, I can do it."

They clutched each other, each squeezing life energy into the other. Sustaining energy. Kyle's fire burned hot. The weekend away restored them both. And not a moment too soon. It would require every spark of energy they had to take down the most powerful woman in fashion.

25

The happy hour contingent thinned while Kyle waited at the bar for Greg to arrive. It took a several rounds of phone tag over two weeks to get through since Kyle's calls and texts were screened into Greg's junk folder. But with Jane ever-present on his mind, Kyle needed to know if he'd have a reliable ally in the face-off to come.

Greg strolled in, pausing by the door to survey the room. Kyle waved. Greg answered with a head flip. He slipped off his scarf, balling it on the bar top before taking the stool next to Kyle.

"Thanks for coming," Kyle said.

"Never thought I'd hear from you." Greg hoisted two fingers to attract the bartender's attention. The young man with a bouncy mop of curls abandoned his chitchat at the other end of the bar.

"What can I get you?" the bartender asked.

"Guinness for me. You?" Greg said to Kyle.

"I'll have another scotch," Kyle said.

The bartender turned away to his work, while Greg eyed Kyle's glass.

"Haven't touched the stuff in years," Greg said.

"Any reason?" Kyle asked.

"Yes." Greg shifted his gaze to the mirror opposite the bar. Kyle caught him for an instant before he averted again.

Such intimacy could only happen between people who shared the same intense life experiences. Alone but together. Brothers in arms, joined by fate—not choice. Kyle cleared the lump in his throat.

"Something you said in that last session stuck with me. It's haunted me ever since."

Greg laughed. "Don't leave me hanging. What did I say?"

"There's no justice for us."

So simple, but so true. At least it had been up to now.

"I was in rare form that day." Greg sipped his beer, licking his creamy foam mustache off his upper lip. "Please excuse my explosion. The anger gets to be too much sometimes. I want to ease off the pressure valve, but that takes sharing, letting people in. I'm not in a position to do that."

"Where has doing nothing gotten us? Crying into our beers? You said she's right where she has always been, up in that glass tower of hers, clanking around in her dumb bracelets that she refuses to take off."

"Cuffs. They're cuffs. She doesn't like it when people call them bracel—" Significance dawned on Greg mid-word.

Chatter from restaurant patrons replaced theirs.

Kyle leaned in close, low talking. "It was Jane. It had to be," Kyle asked.

Greg slow-sipped, taking a moment.

"Jane has all the power," Kyle said. "She floats around,

untouchable, while we're twisted in knots years later. It's been eleven years for me, and every time I smell coconut, I'm back on her couch. I'm stuck. You're stuck. Doesn't that make you want to hold her accountable?"

"Of course I want to hold Jane accountable," Greg barked, before lowering his voice to a whisper. "But what are we supposed to do? I have responsibilities now. I'm the president of a company that depends on Valis Publishing for a huge chunk of revenue. Ironic, right? My family expects me to lead Bailey Cameras into the future. I won't go down in flames because of her. It's twisted as fuck, but there's no way out."

"There is a way out. Together. There's safety in numbers. From the sounds of it, you came before me. Don't you think there were others after us? Right now, she has an attractive male assistant. He is at risk if we do nothing to stop her."

Greg rubbed his beard. The struggle was real, and Kyle's ask could very well be too great. Kyle sipped his scotch as Greg's inner war telegraphed across his reflection in the mirror.

"I'd love to help," Greg said. "But I got out. You got out—"

"Got dumped, at a hospital. Is that what you want for this man?"

"A hospital?"

"Yeah, I can't remember exactly, but somehow I must have taken too many pills and ended up in the hospital."

"Pills?"

"Yes and—"

"Scotch." Greg eyed Kyle's glass.

"Yes," Kyle followed Greg's eyes. The golden liquid in front of him glowed with the clarity he'd sought for years. Never in all the time since that night did he doubt he self-medicated to end it all. Jane made it perfectly clear there was no quitting her. But the longer he stayed, the higher dirt mounded until the weight grew unbearable. There would be no freedom from Jane. Without freedom, only bleakness remained. When his anxiety swelled, she pushed Kyle to take medication. She said they'd help suppress the conflict he failed to wrangle on his own.

But she lied.

She set him up, then left him believing he attempted to end his own life.

He sought Greg's attention and had it.

"I woke up at Bellevue Hospital on suicide watch," Greg said. "I was so doped up it took three days for me to remember my own name. My family filed a missing person's report with the police and that's how they found me."

The parallels were uncanny. Waking up in the hospital, not knowing where you are or how you got there? In Kyle's case, Jane's driver dumped him in the ER along with his name. Guess she'd learned from Greg's incident and perfected her sick tactics. How much more formidable must she be now?

Greg continued. "I was home for a couple months, didn't go back to college, then went right into the family business. I've been there ever since. But now I run a historic company, so it's not all bad."

Kyle nodded as Greg sipped his beer. But as much as they both pretended to be fine, neither was, nor would be, until Jane wore an orange suit and leg irons.

He twisted to face Greg. "We can ignore the facts, but Jane is a monster, and she's still on the loose. If we don't stop her, who will? The empty chairs need us to step up. Let's be their voice. Let's do this, make her pay, and be done with it, once and for all."

Greg looked unconvinced. "This is ancient history—"

"Not for me, it isn't. She's blackmailing me, forcing me to escort her to the MOD Gala. I'm at risk, and now, the woman I love is at risk, too."

"That's rough for you, but…"

"She will not stop. She's not. Going. To stop. This will go on forever, and that doesn't even factor the other young men she's already hurt. How many more must suffer?"

Kyle tightened his fist on the bar's brass railing. Solid. He needed strength to convince Greg. Without him, their effort to topple Jane would be over before it began.

Greg caught Kyle's eye in the mirror. Kyle didn't have to guess the thoughts traversing Greg's mind because the same quarrel streamed live in his own.

What's the point?

No one will believe us.

It doesn't matter.

We have to try.

We must bring her to justice.

We deserve justice.

"Say I do it. What then?" Greg asked.

"We make this right. We make it so the world can't ignore us."

"We seek justice?" Greg asked.

"We do."

"How?"

"I've got some ideas brewing. You in?" Kyle asked.

Just then, the bartender ambled over. He removed their empty glasses and wiped the counter dry. The duo watched him work, welcoming the moment of normalcy before their world changed forever.

"Another round? Scotch and Guinness?" the bartender

asked.

Greg looked at Kyle. "No. Skip the Guinness. I'll have what he's having."

The boutique for Libby's fitting was the New York equivalent of the wedding explosion they experienced in Texas. This time, it was all white, sparkly, and floral. Monochrome, but with a dazzling array of textures, objects, surfaces—all girlie to the nines. Somehow when Rebecca texted about attending the appointment, Libby said yes. But a month hence, Libby's pained expression made it clear she'd forgotten. Hopefully wearing her own wedding gown would lighten the mood.

In the showroom area, single dresses hung at intervals on white linen walls, textured into a lattice design with opalescent beads at every intersection. Veils, top hats, and tiaras strategically placed on shelves above each dress transformed them into phantom brides missing heads.

Rebecca walked over to a rack of dresses. Clean lines. No appliques, beading, or bows. She picked up one reminiscent of a calla lily and held the hanger to her chest.

Did her heart flutter?

Rebecca turned to the mirror and a wedding popped to mind. Her wedding. The details were murky, with no destination, place, or size. But one thing was increasingly clear. She wanted her groom to be Kyle. She loved him. Their life together was everything she ever wanted, and she wanted it to last. Forever.

Did he feel the same way? Did he want Rebecca to be his forever girl? She thought so. They talked about the future like it was a certainty.

"Next year, let's go to Madrid for vacation."

"In three years when my parents have their 35th anniversary, we'll have to throw them a party."

The examples were endless. Moments of their lives weaving together like a tapestry. She smiled.

Sharon Dillon appeared behind her in the mirror. "Thinking of anyone I know?"

"Maybe," Rebecca said, unable to suppress her smile.

"You'll make a lovely bride one day. But let's get one Dillon married before we worry about the next one, yes?"

Rebecca hung up the dress. "Got carried away."

"Hard not to in a girlie wonderland. But I think Libby's about to come out. Let's go see."

Sharon and Rebecca returned to the dressing area where Libby would wear her own gown for the very first time.

"Ready?" Libby called through the door.

"One sec." Sharon fumbled with her iPhone. "I want to get this on video."

"No video, Mom. No video. I don't want Evan to see."

"Evan won't see. It's for me. I'm doing video."

Libby stepped out into the room, beaming. Her raven hair swept into an elegant French twist with smooth bangs across her forehead. Her strapless, sweetheart bodice gown hugged her slim frame, then flared out into silky perfection at her waist. No appliques. No beading. Simple elegance.

"How do I look?" she asked.

"Wow, Libby. Just, wow," Rebecca said.

Sharon tried to speak, tears flowing where words failed. She smiled and nodded.

Rebecca moved in to give Sharon a shoulder hug as they both faced the bride. She patted Rebecca's hand, grateful, as they took in the bridal view.

"Mom, you like?"

"Breathtaking. You're an angel," Sharon said.

Libby lifted her skirt so she could safely step up on the low box pedestal in front of the three-way mirror.

The seamstress entered with a pin cushion strapped around her wrist, a tape measure dangled around her neck. She spoke to Libby's reflection in the mirror.

"You, young lady, are the loveliest bride I've seen in this shop in a very long time. This dress was made for you. Your groom is a lucky man."

"Thank you." Libby beamed. "This dress. This dress makes everything feel right. I'm so ready to marry Evan."

"He's lucky to have you, Kika."

Libby pounced. "Mom! Don't call me that. Not in public."

Sharon looked around. "There's no one here."

"What's that name? Kika?" Rebecca asked.

"It's a funny story," Sharon began. "When she was little, we used to call her monkey sometimes. Not being able to pronounce it, she'd say 'KeyKey.' That evolved into Kika. And it just stuck."

"Don't call me that anymore, please. I'm an adult."

"Sorry, sweetie. It just slipped out. It's hard not to think of you as my little princess in that dress."

Libby kissed her mom's forehead. "It's okay—this time."

"Kika, it's unusual, but I feel like I've heard it before..."

"Maybe from Kyle?" Sharon suggested.

"If you don't mind, Rebecca, only family calls me Kika. And not anymore."

Way to make me feel welcome.

"Apologies."

Anger flashed behind Libby's eyes, but Rebecca stared back.

No way she's going to let some spoiled brat treat her like crap indefinitely. One of these days, they were going to have words, and it wouldn't be Rebecca suffering. That much she was sure.

The seamstress got them back on track. "So we'll take the dress in here on the waist and adjust the slit so it falls properly. But it looks well. Perhaps take up the length so you can move freely?

"Yes, I don't want to trip. Will you be adding the cups in the bodice?" Libby asked.

"Yes. We'll sew them in so you don't need to wear a brassiere that day," the seamstress said.

Libby clapped. "This is better looking than I expected. I'm shocked. I thought I was going to need a new dress. So glad!"

"Since we're done with the dress, let's think about undergarments. And perhaps some lacy lingerie? You'll want that for your wedding night," Sharon said.

"Mom, ewww. I'm not discussing that with you."

"I know, but you'll want to be prepared. They must have the lingerie you'll need. Maybe garters? It can't hurt to peek."

"Can you change the subject, please? I don't want to talk about my wedding night."

Libby swished her dress aside and stormed into the dressing room, slamming the door.

Sharon looked as confused as Rebecca felt. "I'm sorry. I don't know what got into her."

Her mom knocked on the door. "Libby?"

Sharon slipped inside and closed the door behind her.

Oh, my God.

Wedding night?

Kika?

Libby was Kika, the bride who wrote to "Dear Bedroom Diary."

Rebecca's eyes widened as she looked at her closed dressing room door.

For the first time since Rebecca met Libby, she finally understood her.

That's why she was always so mad.

That's why she closed herself off.

That's why she tossed off her boyfriends. Not, as her girlfriends said, because they were bad in bed, but because she didn't want to bed them at all.

Libby might even be a virgin. That added an extra layer of stress to her impending wedding night. Likely, one Libby didn't want to think about, let alone experience. If she did, she wouldn't have been writing to a complete stranger for help.

And if Libby wanted help, she'd get it. Whether she knew it or not, Libby, a.k.a. Kika, was about to get a new best friend.

Rebecca stacked empty plates and followed Barbara into the tiny galley kitchen of her brownstone apartment.

"How do you cook so well in a space the size of a closet?" Rebecca said.

"It's not the size, it's what you do with it that matters," Barbara chuckled.

"Whoa, now." Joe popped his head through the doorway. "So you know, she's not referencing the private parts of any particular man in this apartment."

"Of course not, my stallion," Barbara said, puckering for a kiss, which Joe gladly provided before retreating to the living room.

Barbara glanced back after him before whispering, "Might have well been a closet. The first time I used the oven, it smoked up because of a sock. In the oven."

"Oh, my God." Rebecca slapped a hand over her mouth.

"He said he used it as a dryer in a pinch."

"He so needed you."

"Did he ever!"

"Any space for this?" Leslie walked in carrying an empty glass bowl. "Barbara's house is the only place I go where salad is the most anticipated course."

"You should bottle that dressing, you know," Rebecca said.

"I'll add that to the list. After I go into the frozen food business and save the world from dumb-ass lawyers and their stupid clients."

"You set a high bar. We can't all measure up," Leslie said.

That reminds me.

"Hey, ladies, I can use your advice on something?" Rebecca asked.

"Is it about *MOD*?" Leslie asked, leaning in the doorway.

"Yes, and no. It's about Libby, Kyle's sister," Rebecca walked deeper into the kitchen for privacy.

Barbara nodded. "Hey, Joe, why don't you show Kyle those cigars you got on your trip? Out on the stoop, though. With the smokeless ashtray?"

"Good idea," Joe replied.

Kyle popped his head in the kitchen doorway. "We'll be back," he said with a smile.

A moment later, the door slammed shut after them.

"Way to clear a room, Washington!" Leslie said.

"Okay. Spill it. What does Libby have to do with *MOD*?"

"So we're doing these letters now, answering reader questions—"

"Stop it!" Leslie said. "She wrote in?"

"Yes."

"You can't make this stuff up. Unbelievable," Barbara said.

"She used a fake name, but I heard her mother use it with her today at the dress fitting."

"What are you going to do?" Barbara asked.

"That probably depends on the letter," Leslie said.

"What did she ask?"

"That's the problem. It wasn't entirely legible, and I hate for her to never get an answer."

"And?" Leslie asked.

"I was thinking of emailing her on the side; to keep it out of the *MOD* ecosystem."

"You might want to check your contract," Barbara said, her yellow gloved hands slick with floral-scented suds. "Take that towel and dry, would you?"

Rebecca grasped the wet plate and wiped it dry with a red-and-white checked dish towel. "I can't leave her hanging with no answer. It's about her wedding night. She's a bundle of nerves about it."

"Hard to blame her this time. She's scared and flips out at anyone who nudges too close to learning her secret." Rebecca handed the dry plate to Leslie and took a wet one from the dish rack.

"Definitely tragic. You think you can help her?" Leslie stacked the plate back in the cupboard.

"I have to try. She obviously has no one she feels comfortable talking to, or she wouldn't have written in."

"Didn't you say she's always rude to you?" Barbara asked.

"Yes, but now I know why. She's lashing out because she's insecure."

"And if she finds out it's you? What then?" Leslie asked.

"Hopefully, she'll be so relieved she won't care. Libby was totally obsessed with the *MOD* article on the bridal text thread. Now I know why. She'd be thrilled to hear directly from 'Dear Bedroom Diary.'"

"I love your big heart here, Becca. But it may very well backfire if she finds out."

"It could, but we're talking about something that will never happen. I'm not telling and *MOD* contractually can't.

Besides, they've created a sensation with 'Dear Bedroom Diary.' The account has 80,000 Twitter followers."

"That was fast," Leslie said.

"Exactly. They lose all that if they spill the beans about me. You were probably right about letting them handle it all. But I'm all-in until we figure out the Jane situation. And I want to see this through, even with Libby. Responding as Bedroom Diary could be the only way to help her."

"That bad?" Leslie said.

"Yeah, it is. I want her to enjoy her wedding, not panic all day about her wedding night."

"When you put it that way, maybe you have a point." Barbara handed her a dripping glass.

"I know I do. Leslie, you know how many women are out there wanting help? Libby's one of them. And I can make a difference."

"You've won me over. Hopefully, you'll do the same for Libby."

"Fingers crossed," Barbara said, draping her soggy dish gloves over the edge of the sink.

Rebecca handed the last plate to Leslie, then wiped her damp hands on her jeans.

If all went well, she'd have Libby purring on her wedding night. Being anonymous had some advantages. Rebecca just had to be sure she stayed that way.

26

The following Monday, Kyle rose early, dressed, and was out before Rebecca woke. He made his way outside, his breath puffing into white clouds in the chilly March air.

Instinctively, he turned to look for his bike, but a heaping pile of black trash bags mounded in his vacant spot. Soon. While spring had arrived, it didn't feel like it yet.

What he wouldn't give for a head-clearing motorcycle ride. Instead, he'd train it downtown to the MOD offices. Jane's texts nagging him to come in for a tux fitting arrived incessantly for days. After telling her to go stuff it, he relented. There was no telling how he'd react to being in Jane's presence for the first time after a decade. Best that not happen with so much at stake the night of the Gala. With his luck, he'd fall headfirst into one of his runway blackouts. Too much riding on his flawless Gala performance to risk screwing it up. As much as he hated to admit it, the smart play was to get performance jitters out of the way now. If Kyle could get through measurements unscathed, it'd give him the confidence boost he needed to survive one last evening on Jane's arm.

Was he a sap for resuming the role of Jane's boy-toy? How often had he held her elbow on the red carpet? Walked a half step behind like a servant? Acted the empty brain to accompany her master one? How did she put it? *"I think enough for the both of us. Don't bother."* How degrading.

But after hearing it so often, he couldn't avoid believing it himself. That he wasn't good enough and would crumble without her iron will propelling his career. She was brilliant. There was no doubting that. All the more reason to mind himself when in her presence. When agreeing to go, he'd suppressed the reality of standing in the same room with her.

Seeing her cold eyes up close.

Smelling that gag-worthy fruity perfume.

Hearing the flutter of silk streaming behind her like Old Glory snapping in the breeze. The sound sent staffers scurrying to clear her path, holding breaths until the danger passed.

But the worst was her self-taught high-society lilt.

Fakery. All of it.

And he was about to get a double helping.

Kyle pushed through the revolving doors of MOD's office building, the whoosh of the pink marble floor being buffed greeted him. The expectant ping of elevators arriving followed close behind. He flashed the pass Jane messengered over and strode past security, pressing 16 to visit the wardrobe floor. She hadn't even told him where to go. She knew he'd know. Only the date and ungodly time chosen to avoid staff scrutiny. She probably picked a new seamstress, one who wouldn't know him. Who wasn't working there back when…

Stillness wrapped the tailor zone, sewing machines standing idle like a pack of tiny elephants. All tidy, with not a single pin out of place.

Jane wouldn't have it any other way. *No loose threads.*

He walked past a pegboard stocked with a full color spectrum of thread cones. He pulled one out, and sure enough, the thread color and make was imprinted on the wall behind so each could find its way back home.

But where was his home? When he returned to New York, he wasn't sure. Now, home was Rebecca. His bones ached when they were apart. It took all his strength to crawl out of their warm bed to go meet Jane, the last person on earth he wanted to see. He had to keep reminding himself that their stealth operation had a purpose: to free them both. To protect their future. To keep Rebecca's name secret and to liberate themselves from Jane—forever.

But first, he had a few more performances to nail. *Rebecca's counting on you. Don't blow it.*

He replaced the thread and kept searching vacant rooms for signs of life. At the end of a dim corridor, the fitting room glowed brightly, illuminating a three-way mirror. As he entered, the full room came into view. It spanned the width of the building, with at least 20 identical styling stations awaiting orders. Outside the expansive floor-to-ceiling windows, dawn's crimson glow blushed Manhattan's tapestry of buildings awake from a bluish sleep. Among them, Jane's reflection sat at a table behind him, sipping coffee out of a huge white mug.

"Drinking in the fitting room?" Kyle's cocky voice emerged without consent.

"I've broken so many of my own rules with you, I figured what's one more?" Jane toasted him with the mug before taking another sip.

"Well, here you are. In the flesh. I must say, Mr. Dillon,

you never disappoint."

"It's been a while."

"Too long."

"That's one perspective," Kyle said.

Jane feigned an arrow piercing her chest. "You wound me so. Why must you do that? We're just two old friends talking. What's the harm in that?"

"Let's get this over with." Kyle slid out of his jacket and tossed it on an empty stylist chair.

She set her coffee aside.

"Do you even remember how to do a fitting?" Kyle asked.

"Of course I do," Jane snapped. "How can I keep my team on point if I couldn't do every job in this building myself?"

"Watch the tone. I'm not one of your minions."

She rose with a tape measure, pacing close. "Aren't you, though? Isn't everyone? After all, you are here. Caught in my web."

"Keep spinning. You're bound to get caught in it yourself."

"I sincerely doubt that."

He walked over to where she stood, looking down into her icy eyes. "Don't."

She flinched imperceptibly, then looked away.

Kyle walked behind a changing screen, the corner of his mouth creaking into a smile.

He donned the tux awaiting him on a hanger, his hands instinctively finding the zippers, buttons, and clasps without looking. How often had he been in and out of clothing in a cloud of backstage chaos? Too many. Enough for a lifetime.

"I'd forgotten." Her voice drifted over.

"Forgot what?"

"How you make me feel like a schoolgirl."

"Jane, don't—"

"Let me finish. I know you think I'm a monster, but

I'm not."

"Whatever, Jane…"

Jane appeared behind the screen. "Don't. Not you. You know the real me. This… this is a facade."

What a psychopath. Did she actually expect him to buy her wounded damsel routine? After the trail of bodies she'd left littered in her wake, his included?

"This is who you are. You crave power above all else. Sacrifice anyone to keep it. The only thing you love more than this magazine is yourself."

She shrugged. "Sue me."

Facing each other, Kyle flexed his hands open and closed. *Easy now. Don't take the bait.*

"Tragic, isn't it?" he said.

Her chin rose.

"You rule atop a tower of glass and stone, yet here I am at six o'clock in the morning getting fitted for a Gala you couldn't bear to attend alone." Kyle turned to retrieve his cummerbund.

Jane walked away. He followed, stepping onto the illuminated pedestal.

"You ought to be nicer to me. I hold all the cards." She began her measuring work, a pin cushion clasped to her wrist on a silver cuff, marking chalk in her hand.

"I'll vogue for the Gala, but I'll be damned if you get anything else."

You're not getting Rebecca.

"We'll see about that." Jane marked the trousers with chalk, feeling his leg more than necessary.

Uninvited touching.

A cold chill fluttered up his back as he looked at her reflection in the mirror. She was attractive enough. Powerful. She could have normal relationships. Consensual relationships. Yet, she took what was not hers to have.

"You didn't have to do it."

She glanced up. "You'll have to be more specific. I've done a great many things."

"Yes, you have. How can you stand yourself?"

She sat back, her ivory skin flushing pink. "I don't know what you're talking about."

"Don't you?"

"Certainly not. And you won't either if you know what's good for you."

"Okay. Play it like that."

She stood and walked across the room, hugging herself.

"I'm done here." Kyle stepped down and behind the changing booth walls. Once more. Only one more costume change, and he'd be rid of Jane forever. He only had to make sure no one replaced him.

27

Back at her desk, Rebecca tilted her screen to be less visible to passersby in the aisle behind her desk and logged into the MOD interface. Scrolling through the thousands of messages pouring in since the first article went live, she found the folder where she and Viraj put their top picks.

Searching for "Kika" the letter immediately loaded. Unlike the other night, she searched the contact information fields. Sure the name was Kika Montgomery, but the email address was ldillon@--.com.

How had she not noticed that before?

Through the platform, she clicked on the contact envelope and a composition box opened. The note would come from dearbedroomdiary@mod.com. Not the most stealth move, but it was the only way for her to communicate with the girl and be viewed as authentic.

It had to come from MOD.

And after all, she was the author. The originator. She should have the right to answer reader mail. There wasn't anything in her contract saying she couldn't, so she should be in a safe gray area. Should be.

Fingers poised over the keyboard, she let them fly.

Dear Kika,

Thank you for writing to us at MOD. Unfortunately, the upload of your letter was not legible. I would love to answer your question if you wouldn't mind sharing it again. I see you mentioned something about your wedding night, and I certainly don't want to leave you hanging.

Of course, letters to me are very personal, so I promise to handle it with the utmost discretion.

Warm regards,

Bedroom Diary

Rebecca tracked the line on screen with her finger to be sure every word was as intended. It sounded right. Struck the proper tone of professionalism and care. Then panic pulsed through her.

Who else would see the reply? Where did it go? There had to be some kind of distribution list.

After clicking "save draft," she entered the post's settings, and sure enough it was slated to go to their intern, Viraj, and one other person she didn't recognize.

There had to be a better way. She couldn't use her personal or work emails, but she could make a new email address for the reply. Libby wouldn't likely notice their conversation switched email threads any more than Rebecca noticed Libby's address to begin with.

New browser window open, she created a free email

account for DearBedroomDiary@--.com, using her personal email as the subscriber. Once validated, she recreated the message on her new account, copying the subject line from the original in the MOD system, adding an "RE:" to the beginning. If all went well, Libby wouldn't notice and Rebecca would be the only one to know about the correspondence. They could have an open exchange, without the MOD team's prying eyes. It was a chance worth taking to help Libby. After all, they might be sisters one day.

She went rigid in her chair. What am I saying?

All the wedding talk must have infected her synapses. Sure she loved Kyle, but the "M" word had never been close to being uttered by either of them. They were just getting used to being a couple, let alone being a forever one. At almost 30, she'd yet to remove the training wheels on her life. Marriage was the epitome of being an adult. It meant shoulders back, chest out, let's kick this life-thing into another gear. Was she ready for that? Wasn't there some initiation she had to pass to prove herself worthy? Then again, sometimes you just know. You find a perfect match and before you know it, life becomes a shared endeavor.

She took a deep cleansing breath. "Stop thinking about it," she said aloud.

"Thinking about what?" her desk neighbor, Paul, asked over the wall.

"Nothing. Just muttering."

She refocused on the screen, double-checking her draft and the other input fields. Her hand trembled on the mouse.

Was she really doing this?

Impersonating a corporate notification system to give sex advice?

Yes. Yes she was.

Click.

Done.

She sat back in her chair, her mouth creeping into a smile. She was doing good. And it felt good to do good. The closest thing at work she had to it was running the onboarding program. Helping new hires learn the tasks that would make them successful. Being Bedroom Diary took that do-gooder energy and amped it up nine-million-percent.

But it didn't pay the rent.

She turned her attention to the manager training that kept getting lost in the shuffle. She owed a proposed plan to Harry. One that would turn heads and boost performance. She pulled in her chair and got to it.

By the time she checked her fake email account later in the day, Libby's response was waiting.

Wow, a personal note from Dear Bedroom Diary! I'm so honored! Sorry about the written note, but it wasn't something I was comfortable creating a digital record of. I'm not comfortable even writing to you now, but how could I not? I'm the one who reached out for help!

Here's my sad tale. Please don't think I'm vain, because it all ties together, I promise. I'm pretty. I know I'm pretty and I have been since I was a kid. But even at nine years old, I started getting unwanted male attention. Comments, touching, hugs that went on too long, creepy stares, it was all so yucky that I did my best to keep them, and all people, away from me. It made it hard to make friends. Friends had older brothers, fathers... you know? And while no abuse ever happened, the lusty looks made me so uncomfortable. Do you know what it feels like to hate yourself for how you look?

As I got older, I got more and more lonely. My only friend was my brother, and he was off modeling. I even tried modeling to be able to tag along, but it didn't work out that way.

Anyway, if I wanted any attention at all, the male kind was all I had. Ironic, huh? So I dated. A lot. But never let anyone stay around long enough to be too intimate. Of course, the number of guys mounted, and they all told stories. I got a slutty reputation. Me!! I'd only kissed and petted a little. Not even taking shirts off. It was so unfair, but I was petrified for people to know the truth, so I let them think what they wanted.

Now that I'm getting married, and my fiancé has been such a gentleman and so patient, I'm petrified of my wedding night. Even with him, who I love so much, I don't know what to do. I don't want that night to be a disaster after making him wait until after we were married.

Please help!

Rebecca's mouth hung open. Reading Libby's story shocked the sensibilities, and yet, it totally made sense. The bratty girl routine felt false. Now Rebecca knew why. Libby's beauty arrived before she had the coping skills to deal with the attention she was getting. She grew angry and afraid and that's all the world could see. All she let them see. Wearing it like armor.

Libby had the same deep sensitivity as Kyle. But as a woman, she'd had a much bumpier path from a younger age, aside from Jane, of course. There was no getting around the pain Kyle was suffering through to this day. Thank goodness it didn't sound like Libby experienced any abusive behavior. At least not that she was willing to admit. Hating how you looked was bad enough.

Rebecca knew the feeling well. Since she was a kid, Rebecca was at odds with her body. Her curvy frame, big curly hair, and biracial ethnicity marked her squarely in between every checklist she'd ever encountered.

Other. Always the other.

Never had she considered the challenges of the those with greener grass. The good looks we all wish we had. Before meeting Kyle and Libby, Rebecca never would have suspected how heavy the burden of beauty placed on the people whose looks the world admired. It was far less rosy than she thought. In so many ways, Rebecca was better off.

She opened her fake email to answer, but then clicked it closed. Libby deserved a really good, helpful answer. Not a knee-jerk, seat of the pants missive. She'd think on it a while. For Libby's sake, she'd better think of something good and make it quick. The poor girl had waited long enough for someone to care.

The first round of "Dear Bedroom Diaries" reader responses finally dropped in the March edition of MOD. Rebecca should be used to the buzz by now given the answers she'd been submitting each week for the website. But 24 hours had passed since Libby's question, and she'd yet to formulate an insightful answer. Rebecca sat at her work desk, fidgeting with her hair. Before she knew it, her hoop earring was hopelessly ensnared in her curls to the point she couldn't unsnap the hoop and take it off.

Wonderful.

En route to the bathroom for a mirror, she passed coworkers clicking keyboards and talking on the phones. The social media notifications pinging wildly in her pocket turned a few curious heads.

Why hadn't she silenced her phone? Probably because she

still wasn't used to having anything to silence. But between midnight wedding chatter and MOD's social media frenzy, her world had gone from humdrum to click bait in a New York minute.

What were people saying?

Positive or negative?

Or did they ridicule?

Were trolls at it?

Approval from the faceless masses had become more important to her than she was willing to admit. Her digital feeds were a measuring stick for her self-worth, a drug, and a slot machine, all rolled up into one. Silicon Valley geniuses had crafted the ideal neurological fodder, specifically designed with lights, sounds, vibrations, and the promise of instant validation to entice you further into its depths. Rebecca was doing her best to avoid it for the moment, but her resolve was fading fast.

She pushed open the door to the empty bathroom and went to work on her web of hair. No wonder Darcy had stared at her like she was crazy. But maybe she was. Going crazy that is. The media-by-day, MOD-by-night lifestyle left Rebecca frazzled in the middle. How long could she keep it up? Waiting for Jane to pounce frayed her nerves beyond recognition, and it was starting to take a demonstrable toll.

She removed the tangle of hair from the now-independent earring and slipped it back on. Nature beckoned, so she headed over to a stall and closed the door as two people entered, mid-conversation.

"...what would make someone think that?"

"I don't know. Poor girl. To hate yourself?"

"Right?!?"

"She must miss her husband when he was deployed. At least now, she can get busy."

Elaine.

From Missouri.

The pair giggled as one hit the sinks, the other the bathroom stall next to Rebecca who stood absorbing every word.

Who needed social media when the real thing was right in front of her?

"And the other one? Alex?"

"Alexandra?"

"Yeah, Alexandra. I'd kill myself if I couldn't orgasm into my forties. I'd totally die."

"What would they have done without Bedroom Diary to save them?"

"They'd still be waiting. Alone and hurting, that's what."

"Whoever wrote that article is a godsend."

They finished and left the bathroom.

They got it. Women were getting it. She'd worked in offices for years, and had never once heard women so openly discussing orgasms. Maybe if they had, she and the others wouldn't have felt so alone. So freakish and broken.

Tears welled in her eyes as she stepped out of the stall, her butt buzzing incessantly.

Screw it. She grabbed her phone and opened Twitter, tapping her home screen and the trending hashtags.

"No way. No effing way," Rebecca said to no one.

#DearBedroomDiary was trending as was #DBD.

An abbreviation? Rebecca had arrived. Just like Kentucky Fried Chicken became KFC and Dunkin' Donuts became Dunkin or Dunks, now she was DBD. The MOD team definitely knew its stuff. The global head start on the Eastern time zone didn't hurt either.

The first few tweets she read were encouraging.

You're not alone, ladies! #Hope #DBD can help!

OMG! I'm totally going to try the #DBD remedy
#orgasms #bettersex

Come join us! Get it? Good luck and see you on the
other side! #DearBedroomDiary #YesYesYes

Someone entered, but she didn't look up.

"Shame on you, Rebecca," Darcy said.

"For what this time?" Rebecca said, eyes trained on her
Twitter feed.

"Playing on your phone? You're coming in late, missing
deadlines, and now you're standing here during work hours
playing on your phone?"

"What deadline did I miss?" Rebecca asked, genuinely
wanting to know.

Darcy snorted. "If you were on the ball, you'd know.
No matter, Evvy covered for you. At least there's someone
on the planning team willing to do your work. It certainly
isn't you."

She opened her mouth to answer, but shut it. No use.
Darcy was right. She had been distracted and letting her day
job suffer while she ran around playing ace reporter. But
she couldn't say she regretted it. Her words were having an
impact, more impact than she'd had in years at her desk job.

"Nothing to say for yourself? That's a welcome change.
I'll be talking to Harry about this. The bloom's off your rose,
my dear."

She entered a stall and closed the door. Not the grandest
of exits, but no way Rebecca was going to stay and pee
alongside her. She headed out to use the guest bathroom
near the boardroom.

But her pocket kept buzzing. Each one symbolizing

a person touched by her story. Her words. She was helping women and that felt really good. It was filling a void she never knew existed in her life. Being so broken herself for so long, it was a surprising twist.

The decor of the Executive hallway grew luxe. Different than the rest of the office, meant to impress visitors. But Rebecca was different as well. Changed. No longer the same person she was before her MOD experience. More confident. Less afraid of her shadow. More willing to take the risks in her life and aim high. Her only decision now: what to do about it?

Kyle was breathing easy as Rebecca left their dark bedroom, closing the door while sliding an oversized sweatshirt over her naked body. For the first time in forever, sex with Kyle was meh. They were together, but their minds were elsewhere. Not sure where he was, but her mind immediately flooded with guilt as she realized she'd never answered Libby's note. The moment that happened, her own romantic mojo fled out the door.

She crept down the hall and flipped on the light switch, dimming it to a tolerable level. Resuming her position on the couch, she covered her bare legs with a throw blanket before snagging her laptop off the coffee table and waking it out of sleep mode.

After typing in her PIN, the same blank page from earlier in the night greeted her. The cursor blinking. Rudely.

"What am I supposed to say?" she whispered to it.

The cursor blinked back. With attitude.

"Write it yourself if it's so easy."

Libby had likely been waiting on pins and needles these 36 hours for the great and wise sage from Bedroom Diary to answer. What a joke. She was a fraud like the Mighty Oz, only without the glitzy city and Technicolor flowers.

What should she tell a young woman petrified of having

sex for the first time?

What would she have wanted someone to tell her?

She tapped her chin.

Yes.

That was it.

The buildup.

Pop the buildup balloon, so she could relax and enjoy the moment.

Feel whatever came naturally. Without shame or inhibition.

He loves you.

He wants to please you.

Let him. Let him please you.

No right, no wrong. Only you.

Fantasize about whatever you want. People. Clouds. Horses. Colors.

Breathe.

Always Breathe.

Then please him as he pleased you.

She composed the answer her younger self would have wanted to receive. The specifics. The details. The emotions and the permission to just feel and not think so much. She gave permission to let go.

Rebecca reread her note, checking for typos as best she could through her bleary eyes. Then cut and pasted it into the reply note into her new email account. When all looked right, she clicked send.

Done.

All she could do now was wait.

Thinking through the note, guilt flooded her psyche. All those instructions could apply to her and Kyle this very night. Let go. No distractions. How could she give someone rules she wasn't following herself?

The digital clock on their never-used DVR blinked 2:58 a.m.

Why not be spontaneous?

She retraced her steps to the bedroom, ready to shed her hypocrisy. With a little assistance from Kyle.

28

The takeout food Rebecca ordered for herself and Viraj arrived at their apartment faster than expected. Having Viraj over was Kyle's idea, but would it backfire? If they were wrong about his loyalty to Jane, he could ruin their one chance to catch her by surprise. But confirming his safety outweighed the risk.

Rebecca opened the rarely used oven door, readjusted the shelf lower, and folded the takeout bag to fit in.

"That'll be a little better than you sitting on the drafty counter."

"What are you talking to this time? The toaster?" Kyle said, entering the kitchen.

"No, wise guy. The takeout."

Kyle turned away to open the fridge. "You up for this?"

"Yeah, you really think he'll recognize you?"

"I was a two-page spread in a recent issue. Yeah, there's a good chance he will. We only need a conversation starter."

The doorbell chimed, sending a chill down Rebecca's back.

"Showtime." Kyle popped a kiss on her cheek. "I'll be back when it's time to eat."

Rebecca exhaled, shaking tension out of her arms. You can do this. She grabbed the knob and swung the door open.

"Hi, welcome! Come in," Rebecca said.

"Hey," Viraj said. "My walk was only ten minutes. We may want to meet here Thursday evenings instead of at the office. Good idea."

She took Viraj's coat, the most stylish garment in their entire apartment. A floor-length black wool number that weighed half a ton. A little heavy for early April, but it was so gorgeous Rebecca couldn't blame him for stretching the season.

"I bought dinner," Viraj raised a white plastic bag.

"Oh, me too. I hope you don't mind. My boyfriend will join us when we eat."

"Love to meet him. It is your apartment, after all."

They made their way to the living room, where they sprawled out on the coffee table.

"'Dear Bedroom Diary' is going very well. Ad dollars are flowing in so fast, Jane actually said 'good job' to me in the hallway."

"Is the compliment unusual?" Rebecca asked.

"Yeah, impossible is more like it. But that's why she's been on top for so long. You have a good streak going so far. You've made an immediate impact on the two things Jane cares about most."

"What are those?"

"The magazine and herself," Viraj said with an impish grin.

"I can't believe you said that!" Rebecca giggled.

"It's okay. Take it as a compliment."

"I'm glad it's going well. I'd been wondering how I was doing," Rebecca said.

"The numbers don't lie. This feature is getting the second most clicks on the site, and the social posts are garnering amazing engagement. Our audience is thirsting for this content."

"It kind of seemed that way, but I'm a newbie. I don't know what I don't know when it comes to publishing."

"That's why I'm here." Viraj smiled. "But you should be proud. If you play your cards right, this could turn into something much bigger."

Rebecca stiffened. "How do you mean?"

"A job. Jane has big plans for 'Dear Bedroom Diary.'"

"You're serious."

Viraj paused. "I shouldn't have said anything. But yes. This kind of opportunity doesn't fall in your lap every day. We'd be crazy not to make the most of it."

A job. What was Jane playing at? She had no intentions of keeping Rebecca around. That would only prolong the twisted game of playing footsie with the woman who replaced her. If anything, Rebecca would be out sooner than expected. If the topic lit up their web metrics, like Viraj said, it's no wonder Valis Publishing consumed Rebecca's Bedroom Diary "brand" without a trace.

Rebecca's whiteboard of a face betrayed her.

"Did I say something wrong? The popularity is good news, isn't it?" Viraj said.

"It's bittersweet, if I have to be honest. I worked hard to build Bedroom Diary into something worth talking about. I'm a little surprised at how fast the company absorbed my ideas and brand. They are pretending Bedroom Diary was their idea from the start."

Viraj furrowed his brow. "How do you mean?"

Outrage boiled in her chest. With everything going on between Kyle and Jane, it almost felt like the thievery of Bedroom Diary got swept under the carpet. Yes, Kyle and Rebecca had a firm plan for tonight's visit, but she couldn't contain her frustration.

"That night you called? Was it a coincidence my domain expired while we talked on the phone? And—surprise—by the next morning Valis owned it?"

"Valis stole your domain?"

"The next morning, I awoke to see my domain redirecting here. To MOD." Rebecca shifted her computer to her lap to launch the browser window.

The screen hiccupped a moment, before redirecting to MOD's "Dear Bedroom Diary" page. The new destination a shift after the letters launched and their popularity supplanted the original Bedroom Diary article. More indisputable proof that their thievery was both deliberate and continually managed.

Viraj pinged his attention between Rebecca's face and her screen. His frantic fingers retyped the domain on his own computer, only to yield duplicate results. Defeated, his shoulders slumped. "I had nothing to do with this."

"Didn't you, though?"

"No. I would never condone these tactics."

"But you do by working for Jane. You see her up close every day. Can't you see it? The damage left in her wake?"

Viraj regained his composure. "If Jane were a man, she would be considered a bold visionary honored on the cover of Forbes. Instead, people say she's ruthless…"

"Because she is," Kyle said.

The duo looked up from the couch to find Kyle standing over them. "Jane makes everything personal. Whether the attention is welcome or not. Am I right?"

Viraj looked from Kyle to Rebecca and back, no doubt trying to make sense of the conversation's turn. "I'm sorry, you are?"

"Kyle Dillon. Rebecca's boyfriend."

Rebecca leaned in. "He modeled for MOD in the past. You might recognize him from the 'Our Favorites' issue?"

Viraj took Kyle in, scanning his face as he took a seat in the armchair. Thirty-year-old Kyle was no longer the lean teen who originally graced the pages of MOD. But his distinctive look was a favorite for a reason.

Realization dawned. "Jane has pictures of you in her apartment. Together. You dated?"

Rebecca and Kyle exchanged stares. That Viraj was in Jane's apartment long enough to notice pictures didn't bode well for his personal safety. But they had to tread lightly. Bringing Jane down required a masterstroke. But if they upset Viraj, their plan could unravel. Kyle broke the awkward silence.

"I know Jane better than most."

"I see. Jane has her enemies, but she gave me a chance when no one else would hire a brown guy who loved fashion. Everything else I've achieved has been hard earned. I've sacrificed a lot to work for her, but I've gained a lot too. I'd be lying if I said otherwise."

"But at what cost? What have you sacrificed?" Kyle leaned forward, the two passing silent understandings between them.

Viraj opened his mouth to speak, but pressed his lips together.

Watching him struggle to answer spoke volumes. Rebecca hugged herself to occupy the arms wanting to wrap Viraj in a bear hug. But they didn't have that kind of relationship.

Unlike Jane, she would never dream of invading his personal space. A pang of guilt rippled through her. Despite their good intentions, he probably felt ambushed. Rebecca shrugged at Kyle, but he sat unmoving, waiting for Viraj to speak first.

"We have work to do tonight," Viraj said at last. "If we won't be accomplishing that, I should head out."

"No. Please stay." Rebecca reached out to touch his knee, but retracted her hand in time. "You're right, we should get back to work, but let's eat first? We have enough food for an army." Rebecca's smile invited one from their guest, which he reluctantly surrendered.

The tense moment past, Viraj excused himself to use the bathroom while his hosts hurried to regroup in the kitchen.

"I'm sorry," Rebecca whispered. "I got so angry about my website."

Kyle wrapped his arms around her tight. "It's okay. We got the information we needed. We know he's been in her apartment. That looks pretty damn bad from where I'm sitting."

"You really think the night of the Gala is soon enough?" Rebecca said. "That's still two weeks off. What happens to him between now and then?"

"It sucks, I know. But he's worked for her for years. He'll have to last a couple more weeks."

"Ky, he's…"

"I know. I know, believe me." Kyle held her shoulders. "But if we do this right, it'll be over for all of us. Two weeks."

Rebecca sighed in futility. "Two weeks. Okay."

"We have to play our parts a little longer, then we can be free of her."

Kyle was right, but that did nothing to quell Rebecca's protective instincts. Every fiber of her being wanted to usher Viraj into witness protection. Or stand guard like his own Secret

Service detail, ready to repel Jane's sickening advances. The thought of him alone with her for a second longer made her head explode.

But facts were facts. Kyle and Rebecca were two people up against a powerful foe. To make this idea of Kyle's work, they needed every moment they could get to plan. Down to the tiniest detail. Meanwhile, they'd have to maintain appearances without raising suspicion. That would take effort, patience, and sustenance.

The smell from their takeout meals brought Rebecca back just as Viraj appeared in the kitchen doorway. Rebecca opened the oven to remove the take-out bags, filling their small galley with scents of garlicky goodness. Best they eat. They'd need all the strength they could get for the work ahead.

She unrolled the first bag. "Who's hungry?"

29

After their tense conversation, Viraj and Rebecca
knocked out the next set of "Dear Bedroom Diary" letters, working late into the evening. That made his name
lighting up her phone at 10:00 a.m. the next morning curious
at best. What could he want after seeing her hours earlier? Did
he tip their hand to Jane? Only one way to find out.

Rebecca answered, leaning into the corner of her desk at
work, and low talking for privacy. "Good morning. This is
unexpected. Everything okay?"

"Yes, good morning," Viraj said. "Well, no, actually. I've
been haunted by what Valis did to your website. You've been
working in good faith, and that's something I can't abide."

"I appreciate that. It seems a petty move for a huge
publisher like Valis."

"While I can't return the domain, I'd like to extend a
gesture of goodwill. The MOD Gala is coming up. I have an

extra ticket. Say the word, and it's yours."

Rebecca's stomach dropped. Her? At the MOD Gala? In all her conversations with Kyle about that night, never did they discuss her going. It was harder to get into the MOD Gala than the White House. The prospect of her attending, being present to support Kyle and back him up as needed, was an unforeseen gift.

"You there?" Viraj said.

"Yes, yes. Are you sure you want to give me your extra ticket? Don't you have a special someone to ask?"

"It may sound awful, but my girlfriend prefers watching it on television. I work the event, so she's left wandering alone in a crowd of famous faces she can't address. She dreads going and, I can honestly say, is relieved to sit home in pajamas. Are you interested?"

"I'm in. I'm so in," Rebecca said.

"It's only one ticket. Will Kyle understand?"

The ticket was the least of her worries, but Viraj didn't know that. Would Kyle care if she went? Rebecca certainly hoped not because she wanted to go more than anything. How many hours had she spent watching the red-carpet entrances on TV? The glitter, the gowns, the famous people from all walks of life? Unlike the Academy Awards, the crowd at the MOD Gala was an eclectic mix of fashion royalty, sports stars, actresses, politicians, and mega-rich entrepreneurs. Basically, anyone who was anyone, which would leave her the ultimate square peg. But for this chance of a lifetime, she'd deal.

Kyle hadn't yet mentioned many details of how things would shake down that night, so it was hard to say whether having her present would be a risky complication. She certainly hoped not. She wanted this. Bad.

She needed to respond to Viraj without revealing their plan for that evening. "Kyle's more of a T-shirt and jeans guy, these days. I'm sure he'll be okay."

After they hung up, Rebecca buzzed clear out of her skull. Her? At the MOD Gala? It would be her very own Cinderella moment. What would she wear? How would she get ready? Her heart raced a million miles a minute with the possibilities. She left her desk to splash her face in the bathroom. When the icy water connected, she knew she wasn't dreaming.

"You can't be serious?" Jane stormed into Viraj's office and slammed the door. Her chat reply became woefully insufficient to communicate the depth of her rage.

"It's my ticket. I can invite who I want." Viraj continued working on his computer, failing to afford her the courtesy of eye contact.

"Explain yourself." Fists flexing, Jane paced the tiny office.

How could he meddle in her affairs this way? No, he didn't know all the details at play, but he should. Why couldn't he read her mind as she could read his? She wanted no part of Kyle's fly buzzing about, distracting his attentions from where they should be.

"I thought it was a gracious gesture given how hard Rebecca has worked and the tremendous success she's brought to our doorstep." Viraj fingers clicked casually on his keyboard, but his tense posture spoke otherwise.

"How gallant of you?" Jane's voice dripped with skepticism.

"Yes," Viraj looked up. "It is."

"You expect me to believe that?"

"You have no reason not to." Viraj sat, eying the exit over her shoulder.

Jane glanced at the closed door, then strode into his line

of sight, challenging him with a mere head tilt of inquiry. But instead of looking at her square and true as he always did, he returned focus to his computer screen.

Curious.

Jane circled behind Viraj's desk, rolling his chair back so she could stand between his legs. "Is there anything you need to tell me?"

"No. Nothing." Viraj rolled his chair back to distance himself from Jane, averting his attention to his computer screen with the "Dear Bedroom Diary" letters dashboard open.

To an untrained eye, Viraj would present as relaxed. Committed to meeting his deadlines. They would be wrong. She knew this man and men like him. Each exhibited identical signs once they started to turn. When the walls went up. When their priorities shifted away from her and towards their selfish selves. His ease rang false. He reeked of tension. Conflict. Indecision. His wounded state was a mild turn-on, but she blinked the thought away. He was hiding something, something he didn't want Jane to know.

But why?

"Viraj, you might as well tell me what it is. You know I'll find out, eventually."

"Jane, we're on a deadline. Why don't you go back to your office and let me get back to work?" he said.

His stiff frame rolled back to the desk, dismissing her and her concerns as petty trifles.

After everything she'd done for Viraj, he rejected her. Who else but Jane would have picked a man, of Indian descent no less, for the coveted position she gave him at her side? It was a dream job anyone in their right mind would kill to have. Yet, here she sat, his office reeking with the unmistakable stench of defiance when she should have been enjoying another fragrance entirely.

Grabbing both arms of his chair, Jane leaned her nose into the crook of his neck, flaring her nostrils to fill every centimeter of her lungs with scent.

"Jane, please." Viraj craned his head away.

As if someone was going to see.

As if someone would dare tell her to stop.

"Be still." Jane closed her eyes to concentrate while he sat gripping the armrests like he was about to lie on the witness stand.

The fragrance was unfamiliar. The musky scent of Viraj was present, but an earthliness mingled too. A woody fragrance. Sweet? Creamy? Warm? Sandalwood. Yes. Yes, it was Sandalwood. Did he honestly think she wouldn't notice?

She bolted upright, rubbing her temples as she paced away, heavy breathing getting the better of her. Calm down. You need your faculties about you.

She turned to find Viraj's jaw locked in intractability. "Isn't it enough that I wear it at your apartment? Must I wear it here too? Must you mark me with scent like a skunk?"

"Oh, I'm a skunk, am I? A loathsome creature of the night that everyone can't wait to wash off? What's happened to you? Where is this coming from?"

Viraj stood to walk to the far corner of his office, the contours of his lean, muscular back visible through his fitted dress shirt, stretched tight where his arms crossed in front of him, holding himself for comfort. Soothing. There he stood, but all Jane could see was the richness of the skin beneath. Calling her. Begging to be touched.

Neither spoke.

His controlled panting the only music in the room.

Her slacks swiped gently as she crossed to him, his dark hair still glistening from a morning shower. It took hours to dry. For the little curls to form, then find their place amongst the others.

They'd find their place, and he'd find his.

Her hand found its home on his back, the weave of his crisp white shirt stiff beneath her fingers. His heaving back flinched at her touch, but settled, as always. His warmth radiating into her hand, inviting it forward. He wordlessly bid its partner to join, so Jane complied, exploring her way up his flexing biceps.

Always so tense.

But then, it took Viraj time to relax.

Neither moved, and slowly his breathing settled. Settled into compliance. Resignation. Submission.

That's it. Much better. This one might be saved yet.

She rose on her toes to whisper into the nape of his neck. "You forgot yourself. Forgot how much this job means to you. How much I mean to you. But I understand. After all, you've never felt the icy pinch of iron handcuffs snapping around your wrists. You've never seen your colleagues' faces twist in disgust as you're escorted from the building, whispering how they never suspected what a brute you are. I had no chance against your insatiable sexual needs. Your strength over-whelmed me; I had no choice but to comply. Yes, prison will be a new, exciting, and life-changing experience for you…"

Jane withdrew. His pools of fear tracked her brisk move-ments across the room to the door she flung open, his fate hanging on the precipice.

"Or," she stopped, turning back. "You could remember to wear the fucking coconut oil tomorrow."

30

A flurry of preparations kept Kyle distracted for the next two weeks, making time both fly by and crawl. But the day finally arrived. The MOD Gala was hours away and everything he'd worked to put in place would either come together or fall flat completely. By the end of the night, he'd know whose shocked face would land behind bars: his or Jane's.

Kyle paced Vivian's studio. "You know the plan, right?"

"Yes, we've been over it a thousand times," Vivian said. "Ritchie will have the AV system squared away. Marco came through. Relax."

"Who did Ritchie know on the event team?" Rebecca asked.

"Frankly, it's probably better if we don't know," Vivian said. "I don't want to be banned for life from the Metropolitan Museum of Art. My nephew likes the armor."

Kyle grabbed his head with both hands. "Yeah. Yeah, that's probably right."

"Shit, Ky, do you need a shower?" Vivian asked.

He stopped pacing. "Do I?"

Rebecca and Vivian exchanged glances before Rebecca answered. "It couldn't hurt. You don't want Jane getting suspicious."

Vivian handed Kyle a towel, and he entered the bathroom, leaving the door ajar so Vivian could relay instructions.

"After you dry off, I'll tape the microphone on you. It's a digital recorder, so be sure to login to the Wi-Fi when you get there. If the green light is blinking on the controller, you'll be all set."

Kyle turned the water off. "Green light. Got it."

"As long as it's blinking, it should automatically sync to the cloud. The battery is fully charged, so you shouldn't have any trouble."

"It's not the equipment I'm worried about," Kyle said.

"Think positive. You're in the right here. This is long overdue," Rebecca said.

Rebecca was right, of course. But he wasn't a super-spy and had no way of practicing what they dreamed up. As much as they tried to anticipate every conceivable angle, their success depended on threading a microscopic needle.

Pants on, he opened the door to supporting glances from two of the women he cared about most.

"You'll be fine," Vivian said. "That slick character you played when modeling always comes out when you're with Jane. Lean into that."

"One last performance?"

"It'll be epic," Vivian said.

"Greg knows?" Rebecca asked.

"Yeah. I have his blessing."

"Good man. He's brave. You both are," Vivian said.

"It'll take more than the two of us to bring her down, but it's a start. I'll be floored if there aren't others."

"She is a creature of habit," Rebecca said.

Kyle smirked. "Or a creature."

"Lift your arms," Vivian said. "Too bad you can't use a lapel mic."

"Not too incognito."

"It's not, but the sound is better."

"This will do," Kyle said.

Vivian ripped some cloth tape and affixed the mic to Kyle's chest, which he covered with a blue T-shirt and black leather jacket.

"Here's the earpiece. It's already tuned to the channel Ritchie programmed. You'll be able to hear him once you're on site at the Gala. He won't hear you until the end. When you give the signal."

"Then we'll meet as soon as we can at the rendezvous point, right?" Rebecca asked.

"Rendezvous point. Right." Kyle blew out the tension clogging his chest.

Vivian grasped his shoulders. "I am proud of you. Really proud."

"Thanks." Kyle turned to Rebecca. "You sure you're up for this? The shit's about to hit the fan and there'll be no hiding from it. It's going to get ugly."

Rebecca popped up on her toes to cradle his head. Her usually tender eyes hardened for the battle to come. "We're in this together. Jane's the one who made it ugly. She started eleven years ago and hasn't let up since. Let's end this. Let's end it once and for all."

Their lips met for a last kiss before he walked out the door.

The next time they'd meet, he'd be on Jane's arm at the Gala. But Rebecca would be where it counted: in his corner.

Back at their apartment, Rebecca's mind floated to Kyle. Would the plan work? Would he be in any danger? Distracted, Rebecca didn't notice her phone ringing until Darcy's face made her stomach fall.

"Where are you?" Darcy blasted. "You're supposed to be presenting to me and Harry, and he has a hard stop."

Shit. Shit. Shit. With everything going on, she totally forgot about her slot to present her new manager training proposal.

"I'm sorry. I know we wanted to do this in person, but can I present via video conference?"

"Sloane, it's Harry. This is unacceptable. Darcy and I were counting on you to be here. Where the hell are you?"

Home in her bedroom in bra and panties was not likely the answer they wanted. Though the camera was off, she slipped on a robe, tying the sash around her waist.

"I had a personal commitment that came up, so I'm home. I can still do the presentation…"

"Forget it. I have someplace to be. We were counting on you, and you blew it. I'm very disappointed."

The conversation turned to muted mumbles, likely Darcy covering the mic with her hand.

"Let me talk to Harry," Rebecca said.

"No. He's gone and you'll be next."

"You're firing me?"

"We were discussing a performance improvement plan, yes."

"A PIP? You're putting me on a PIP?"

"What do you expect us to do? Keep paying you for work you're not doing? You've been coming and going at all hours, handing in assignments late, shifting work to Evvy. You had no business taking on these extra assignments when you can't even get your own work done. Skipping this meeting is the final straw. Honestly, it's like you don't even work here anymore."

Rebecca slid down her bedpost to the floor. Darcy was right. For once, she was unquestionably right. Work didn't just slip her mind; it fell off her radar entirely. Even when she was there, her mind was elsewhere. Answering reader letters, emailing "Kika," plus hatching plans to take down Jane had become a full-time emotional roller coaster for her and Kyle. She had no legs to stand on, and that was no way to enter a negotiation.

"So what now?" Rebecca asked.

"I'm drawing up the PIP, and we can review it once it's complete. We rarely tell employees about it in advance, but in your case, your fall from grace was especially egregious," Darcy said.

A Grinch to her core, Darcy's heart likely swelled to human size in celebration of her victory over Rebecca. But for the first time, Rebecca didn't care. While she sat on the floor talking to her boss, Kyle was on his way to Jane. He needed her. Darcy didn't.

"If there's nothing else, I'll see you tomorrow."

"Don't you hang up on me—"

Rebecca's doorbell chimed. Barbara was due to help her dress for the Gala. As much as Darcy wanted Rebecca to grovel, that wasn't happening. That might spell the end of her MediaNow career, but there wasn't anything she could do about that tonight.

"Go ahead and work on the PIP. I'll connect with you tomorrow."

Rebecca hung up and jogged to answer the door.

"Was I right, or was I right?" Barbara reclined on Rebecca's bed, a proud smile on her face from a transformation well done.

A smooth sweep of hair gathered into a loose bun of ringlets which dangled in attractive clusters at her back. Fully formed ringlets. No frizz. Beneath, her new dress dazzled: a black halter top gown with a blinged-out waistband. Stunning by any measure.

Rebecca turned to face her friend. "I don't know how to thank you and your Aunt Evelyn. She keeps saving my butt with her salon connections."

"Antonio lives for the MOD Gala. He heard where you were going, and of course he agreed to help. His team was already in full Gala mode, anyway."

"Funny to think that this is an ordinary thing for some people. That they go to these things regularly."

"I don't think anyone going to the MOD Gala thinks it's ordinary. Fashionistas plan a year out."

"Seriously? Then I'm totally an interloper."

"But you look like a million bucks."

Rebecca turned back to the mirror, a cloud sweeping across her face as she stared at her reflection.

"What's the matter?" Barbara said.

As much as Rebecca wanted to enjoy her glam moment, she kept picturing Kyle walking back into the scene of the crime. That had to be terrifying for him. She wished Barbara knew, so she could assure Rebecca that Kyle would be all right. In her heart, Rebecca hoped it would, but vibrations in the universe left her with an uncomfortable sense of foreboding.

She forced a closed-mouth smile. "Nothing, I'm fine."

"Liar."

"It's nothing." Rebecca closed her lipstick tube and tossed it in her evening bag to take along.

"Is that clutch what I think it is?" Barbara asked.

"Yes. That swan is a real Judith Leiber."

"How did you ever afford—"

"Evelyn loaned it to me. It's probably worth a half-year's rent."

"Please let me touch it. I didn't know she had one." Barbara fingered the bejeweled clutch. "Damn. I need to get me one of these."

"Where would you use it?"

"For this purse, I'd find a place."

The pair laughed.

"Before you go, let's get some pictures." Barbara drew her phone. "Twirl for me, nice and slow, so I can get all the angles."

"This is silly," Rebecca said with a broad smile.

"Shush. Turn."

"A few with the purse."

"For sure."

"Being all dressed up like this makes me better understand the whole dressing up for a wedding thing. All that shopping. It does make you feel special."

"Absolutely. I'll be wearing a big, poofy ballerina gown when I get married," Barbara said.

Rebecca nudged her friend with her shoulder. "Do you think Joe is 'the one'?"

"Maybe…" Barbara said with a broad smile of her own.

"I think that's a yes, Counselor."

"We'll see. It feels right. How about you? Is Kyle 'the one' for Ms. Rebecca Sloane?"

"We talk about our future as if it's a 'when' not an 'if,' so that feels… forever."

Barbara walked next to Rebecca, speaking to their reflection. "Aren't we two lucky girls?"

Rebecca's nerves tingled. The dress. The hair. The fancy bag. Kyle was the only part missing. Hopefully, when they got home, with the mess behind them, they'd be able to rekindle their romance and start a new Jane-less chapter.

31

Kyle accepted the garment bag Jane handed to him. He hadn't said a word since arriving at her apartment to dress for the Gala. Not much had changed in her penthouse from the looks of it. A new, but identical, white sectional sofa sat in the living room. Maybe a fresh coat of navy paint on the walls and some new photos, including the one of Kyle she used in "Our Favorites." But it was hard to register much with his stomach in knots and the fruity scent triggering every tragic apartment episode he longed to forget. Yeah, his stony silence benefitted them both.

He walked to the bathroom, closed the door. Head in hand, he sat on the toilet lid. He looked around, noting the interior. She'd redecorated this room since he was last there.

Tigers?

Who put tiger wallpaper up on purpose?

The same person who used her power to get whatever

she wanted. No matter who she left hurting. Even her fucking wallpaper was a power trip.

But it was time for him to turn the tables.

He stripped down, careful not to dislodge the microphone. Pulling on his undergarments, the device was flatter than expected. Invisible. He checked that the controller light was blinking green. It must have magically found Wi-Fi in a neighboring apartment. Small miracles.

Looking at his reflection, his past self loomed large.

How many young men were forced to wash clean in this bathroom?

Hiding away, terrified about their fates?

Weighing their options?

Seeing no other way out?

It had to stop.

It was up to him.

Here goes nothing.

Kyle fisted his hand. "What the fuck!" he yelled, his knuckles connecting with such force, drywall chips flew in every direction. His chest heaved as he stood admiring the ripped wallpaper surrounding a gaping hole.

"What the hell are you doing in there?" Jane yelled from hall.

"Nothing. Fuck off."

She pounded on the locked bathroom door. "Let me in. This instant."

Stinging pain finally made its way brainward. Kyle shook out his hand, his knuckles already voicing their objection.

"Go away." He turned the porcelain lever of the cold tap, slipping his hand under the chilly water.

Door pounding persisted. "Did you punch the wall?

Did you actually punch the wall of my custom wallpaper that's $500 a yard?"

"It's ugly as hell. You overpaid!" The water finally began numbing the capillaries in his swelling knuckles.

"You're not here for a design critique."

Kyle flung the door open, water running. He dried his hands with a black hand towel.

"Then why am I here? Why are you doing this?"

She looked past his rage and confusion, to the running faucet. "Don't waste water."

Kyle turned toward the sink.

"You're joking." He turned the faucet off. "Water? You are actually more concerned about the fucking water than about me or the others."

"Get dressed. We're going to be late. I mustn't be late for my own party."

"Go alone."

Her face flushed red as her finger dug into his chest. "Need I remind you about why you're here? I own you, Dillon. I have, and I always will."

"I'll go public about you assaulting me and the others."

"God, you're thick. I'll cry rape, and blah, blah, blah…" She talked with her hands. "Who do you think they'll believe? You? A washed-up model? C'mon," she dismissed him over her shoulder with a wave.

"We're not done here," Kyle followed.

"We've been done for years. You've been replaced."

"Remind me of the order. Was it Greg, me, then Viraj? You must have squeezed in a few others. You wanted to catch up, let's catch up."

She swiveled on her heel. "I forgot all about Greg. Now he was a cutie."

"Don't you have a conscience?"

"Yes, a clear one. I sleep like a baby."

"You're a psychopath."

Jane's face brightened as she huffed a smile. "I see what you're trying to do. You want to upset me, so I won't go. I'm onto you, Dillon."

She picked up her drink and walked away.

He had to know.

"You could take anyone. Why me? It's been years," Kyle yelled to her retreating form. "Jane, why? Why me?"

She turned. Fear flashed across her eyes, fast, but unmistakable.

Could it be?

She hid her face, swooping hair behind her ear like Rebecca did. A coquette move. Yet Jane was anything but. Unless…

Shit.

He'd always wondered if she thought of him as anything beyond a boy-toy. Sometimes she talked about the future as if Kyle would always be in it. A twisted fantasy given why they were together. But then, Jane was as twisted as they came.

"I can't believe it."

She pursed her lips. "Believe what?"

"What we had wasn't real. You know that."

"Didn't we have fun? We could again."

"No, Jane. We can't."

"One night, Kyle. For old times. I've picked up some new skills…"

"No. No to you. No to all this." Kyle turned back to the bathroom, waving his arms. "I'm not going."

"Oh. You ARE going."

"This is ridiculous. You can't just stomp people to get what you want."

"You're going, Dillon. That tux is worth $7,000 and photographs will be in the press."

"You got a fucking sponsor for my tux?"

"Why not? You didn't expect me to pay for it, did you?"

"Unbelievable."

"What?"

"You could have gotten a real date."

Jane's body trembled with fury. "No! Don't you remember!?! No one dates Jane Stuart! The great and mighty Jane Stuart."

Her eyes filled with tears that fell freely with Jane making no effort to wipe them away.

Instinctively, Kyle took a step forward, but stopped.

Jane clenched her jaw, snatching a tissue to dab her eyes, mumbling, mocking, as she wiped. "No one. No one talks to Jane Stuart. No one. Not a single fucking person."

Their gaze met. Hers softened enough for him to see the green flecks in her hazel eyes. Sympathetic Jane was back. The version of Jane who had manipulated him into thinking what they did was okay. That he cared for her. That he wanted it.

The illuminated bathroom behind him reflected in a mirror. A jungle. A fake jungle. Just as fake as her crocodile tears. She'd almost made him feel sorry for her.

Her face twisted in disgust. "Get dressed. Get dressed or your sweetie's name will trend on Twitter within an hour." She stomped past him and slammed her bedroom door.

Kyle hipped his hands, speaking to his reflection.

"For Rebecca."

32

Spotlights searched the sky in front of the Metropolitan Museum of Art. The famous stepped out of their limousines to camera flashes and yells from the press lining the red carpet, each photographer trying to get their attention for the perfect shot. Rebecca hopped out of her Uber across the street. Too insecure to attempt the red-carpet walk, she opted for the side pedestrian entrance instead.

Whispers followed as onlookers behind velvet ropes attempted to discern her identity. Everyone at the MOD Gala was somebody. Except her. Nonetheless, she laughed and waved to anyone who waved at her. Why not share the joy?

She showed her ticket to the bouncer and gave her name to an event planner with a headset. After checking the list, she promptly motioned her through so the guests behind her could approach. Once clear of the gate, Rebecca stepped aside to watch the proceedings from the top of the museum steps. How many times had she seen this on television? Or in the papers the next day? Best dress, worst dress, it was a New York spectacle—and they had many. But even among them, the MOD Gala stood apart. It was New York's version of the Oscars. And she was there. In person.

And so was Kyle. From what he said, they'd be driving under the museum to the VIP entrance, then making some kind of grand entrance. Until then, until their world went mad, she had a few moments of normalcy. She'd best enjoy them.

Rebecca aimed her phone for a selfie with the entry in the background, but the image in the photo looked almost like a stranger. Beautiful. Glowing. Ripples of guilt crossed her mind for looking so amazing without Kyle. But she pushed the thoughts away to join guests walking toward the main rotunda.

The event theme "Moonlight in Spring" hung from a banner at the ceiling. Suspended stars glowed white despite the blue lighting, shifting to tiny orbs that lit the way to the main Gala area. The darkness rendered everyone anonymous, and perhaps that was the idea.

Her swan vibrated with a text from Viraj. How his girlfriend could ever tire of this spectacle was unfathomable. Rebecca would have to show her thanks somehow. Maybe send her a gift.

Viraj:
"You here yet?"

Rebecca:
"Yes. Just. Where are you?"

Viraj:
By Temple of Dendur. Next to a huge floral arrangement of our logo.

Rebecca:
I'll be right there.

As guests proceeded to the Egyptian wing, Rebecca soaked in her surroundings. Intricate beading on the ball gowns collided as the ladies walked, making the hall echo like rain. She expected the sights, but not the sounds of the gowns. She closed her eyes and listened when a crowd halted her progress.

Murmurs.

Swooshes and swipes. Pants? Men in tuxedos. They always got overshadowed by the ladies commanding near infinite options for ball finery. Did the guys mind? There was an occasional bold male dress wearer. Though most men were likely more concerned with the quality of the scotch and cleavage.

Bet the scotch here was top-notch.

Were this a regular date, Kyle would have loved some. But he'd never drink scotch—or anything—in the presence of Jane ever again. Not after he learned Greg ended up hospitalized in a suspicious case of mixing pills and booze. That news made their evening's goal critical to achieve. Otherwise, Jane would be free to scout her next victim with impunity.

As the lighting improved, Rebecca searched the faces, wondering how many other men in the room fell prey to sexual violence. Before Kyle, the concept never crossed her mind. Men? They were the aggressors, no? Learning one in eight men experienced sexual violence in their lifetime ate away at her insides. Men in this room. Good men like Kyle and Greg and...

Viraj.

He stood like an Adonis. Hair slicked back, tux fitted to his frame like a glove. Strong jaw, bright eyes shining in the room's twinkling lights. Viraj looked closer to the men in MOD's pages than the ones on the editorial team.

Jane had a type. Rebecca didn't even need to see Greg to guess at his appearance. The realization made Jane's actions even sicker. As handsome as Viraj was, there was no way Jane would keep her hands off him. And maybe that's why his girlfriend hated the Gala: the pawing mitts of her boyfriend's boss.

Rebecca squeezed over to where Viraj stood overlooking the proceedings. "This is something else."

"It is," Viraj said, distracted.

Rebecca looked where he was gazing. The center of the room where a reflecting pool surrounded the temple ruins.

"Everything okay?" she asked.

"Yes." He turned to face Rebecca, his tentative smile growing. "You look lovely."

"Thanks. So do you. I can't thank you enough for this opportunity. I wish everyone could see this once in their lives."

"Once would be fantastic. But the event is stressful for staff. Jane wants everything perfect and holds each of us personally accountable for the slightest misstep. I'll be glad when the evening is over."

"Since this is my first, and likely only, Gala, I hope you don't mind if I soak it all in."

As if on cue, a star whose latest film Rebecca and Kyle had just seen at the movies glided by in a silver gown.

Unbelievable.

The concentration of the famous was staggering. Nearly every face in the room was familiar. Models. Designers. Actors. Athletes. Mega-billionaires. She squeezed the swan purse with both hands to keep from running over for an autograph.

As if reading her mind, Viraj popped her bubble. "MOD advises staff to avoid holding eye contact. A pleasant smile is fine, but never speak to guests unless they speak to us first."

"Be seen and not heard?" Rebecca joked.

"Be invisible. As much as possible. Jane says we're not here to gawk."

"Well, since I'm only part-time, I'm going to gawk a little."

Viraj nudged Rebecca's shoulder. "Don't gawk too much. You're on Jane's good side now. The bad side," Viraj shuddered. "You don't want to be there."

Viraj held her gaze overly long, to let his point sink in.

"Okay. I get it," Rebecca said.

"Good. It's important for you to know before you join us full-time. It'll be different then. The accountability. The pressure."

"How do you stand it?"

"Who says I do?" His dead eyes drifted back to the glittering assembly.

The music crescendoed, like an announcement was coming.

Viraj craned his neck. "This is Jane's introduction. She likes to make a big entrance. Let's stand where we'll have a clear view of everything."

The music built as they walked carefully around the back of the 15-foot-high floral arrangement of MOD's logo. Viraj nodded to a security man with an earpiece before leading Rebecca up the metal stairs to a ledge atop the massive floral structure.

Once on the platform, they could see the entire room of glittery gowns, dapper tuxedos, and an occasional tiara sparkle.

Kettle drums boomed as the PA announcer, a woman with an English accent, echoed across the room, whose lights had dimmed to blue with white spotlights scanning the crowd.

"Ladies and gentlemen. Welcome to the MOD Gala!"

The crowd clapped and cheered.

"We're pleased to present your host for the evening, MOD Editor-in-Chief Jane Stuart!"

The room erupted in cheers, and the searching spotlight fixed on the doorway to the temple. Jane emerged, waving her arms and blowing kisses to the crowd. Her date stood back, out of the limelight. It took a moment for Rebecca to remember it was Kyle.

Up on stage.

This is really happening.

There was no turning back now.

Rebecca eyed the stairs they'd just ascended and the security guy at the bottom.

What the hell was she thinking being up here? In heels?

Her breath came in fits, causing the room to spin. Suddenly, their platform perch seemed like a terrible idea.

Jane grasped the mic. "Thank you. Thank you for coming and supporting the talented artists of the fashion industry with your patronage! You all look fabulous!"

The crowd clapped and cheered. Jane pointed to a few people, smiled, and looked over her shoulder.

"In fact, we have one more extravagant item to share, the newest in the Armani spring collection that my date is wearing. It will be on sale exclusively at Neiman Marcus tomorrow. One day. With all proceeds going to the Fashion Fund to support up-and-coming designers. I expect all you fabulously wealthy people to open your wallets once more and purchase this wonderful garment that Kyle is wearing."

As Viraj's attention remained fixed on stage, Rebecca sidled backwards, pausing her clapping to slip off her slingbacks, which she then clutched firmly in her fingers.

"Is that your Kyle?" Viraj said. "What's Kyle doing up there with Ja—"

Rebecca blanched. She had no answer. No reason on God's green earth for Kyle to be up on stage with Jane. When planning the night with Kyle and Vivian, none of them bothered to factor in what to do about Viraj.

Jane grabbed Kyle's hand and yanked him into an embrace, kissing him on the lips. The crowd cheered its approval.

Viraj turned on Rebecca. "Is this some sort of game?"

Rebecca tried to push past Viraj, but he blocked her path. "What is this about?"

"Put it together," Rebecca said. "Why would any man be with Jane? You think I want him up there with that monster for one second?"

Viraj stood processing, clutching her arm while his mind was off who knows where.

On stage, Jane wrapped her arm around Kyle, planting a kiss on his cheek to a chorus of "oohs" and catcalls. She waved to the crowd.

"Let me go," Rebecca yelled just as the music stopped. All eyes turned to her and Viraj, as did a spotlight.

Rebeca froze in the attention, looking back at the stage, where Kyle had wiggled free from Jane's arm.

Kyle glanced at Jane before mouthing the word "run."

Kyle froze. Seeing Rebecca exposed spelled trouble, but quick as a fox, Jane recovered.

"I see we have our first patron for the tux! Well done! Looks like she can't wait to get there!" Jane said as the spotlight trained on Rebecca and Viraj who stood atop a floral display.

As the crowd laughed, Jane whispered to Kyle, "I knew your pest would irk me tonight." Jane then clicked a switch to talk to the control booth. "Fellas, kill the spot."

The spotlight trained on where Rebecca wrestled with Viraj extinguished.

It's now or never.

Kyle stepped forward, taking Jane's hand and lifting it like a champion. She tossed her head and laughed as he pulled her toward the mic stand.

"Hello, everyone, my name is Kyle Dillon, and Jane Stuart is a sexual predator."

Terror crossed her face before she recovered, attempting to wrestle the mic away from Kyle.

"Hit it, Ritchie." A split-second later, Jane's voice boomed over the Gala's PA system.

"I own you, Dillon. I have and I always will."

"I'll go public about you assaulting me and the others."

"God, you're thick. I'll cry rape and blah, blah, blah… Who do you think they'll believe? You? A washed-up model? C'mon."

The crowd gasped as the PA grew silent. Jane stood in the spotlight onstage, cornered like a tiger from her bathroom wallpaper.

Kyle yanked her close to whisper in her ear. "You left too many loose threads."

Murmurs of the room drew his attention.

Rebecca.

He dashed off the stage, but two beefy security guards grabbed him before he could get away.

"Ladies and gentlemen, dinner is served!" the announcer said, sending a sea of confused people moving in all directions.

Jane closed on him, her red face rivaling her ruby lipstick. "How could you? How could you betray me like this? Here? Of all places… On my night?"

Kyle wrestled with the men holding him, to no avail. She flicked her head, and Kyle was on the move.

He struggled to break free but the men held fast, zip-tying his hands in front, then walking him into a celebrity dressing room, where they shoved him into a chair and slammed the door. The bolt flipped closed with a thud. Kyle hopped up and rattled the doorknob.

"Hey! Hey, you can't keep be here!" He shouldered the door, but it was hopelessly locked from the other side.

"Damn it," Kyle said as he looked around. The only other door had the same keyless lock.

"Fuck!" he yelled, dropping back into the armchair to fiddle with the black cable ties. But the plastic strips held fast, chafing his wrists as he attempted to slip them off.

What now? Think.

He bent his arms so his fingers could loosen his bow tie and top button.

They can't hold me. He did nothing illegal. Since when is speaking on a microphone illegal? It's not. Nor was telling his truth to the world. It'd likely be all over social media by now.

There'd have to be an inquiry.

Others would come forward to join him and Greg.

It was the beginning of the end for the mighty Jane Stuart.

So why was he the one tied up?

33

A soundless sea of guests parted before Jane as she strode out of the temple zone. Chin high, mouth closed, her nostrils flared to draw in enough air to quicken her pace.

She had to get out.

Damn Kyle. And his fucking martyrdom. She'll see him behind bars and those inmates won't be as gentle as she used to be.

Jane darted into the ladies' room, squinting in the bright lights as her back rested against the cold metal door. A bevy of gowned starlets froze at the sight of her. Conversations stalled. Lipstick hovered mid-stain. A latecomer exited her stall, moving until her mascara-clumped lashes widened beyond measure.

Gone were their adoring smiles, hoping for a moment's favor. A touch. A nod that she held them in good graces. That she'd consider them for a spread to promote their latest movie. Exalt them as an icon of sophistication. No more. Those same faces twisted in a traitorous mix of curiosity and disgust.

Faint jazz music played over the speakers. God-awful, but better than speaking to these ninnies.

As if reading Jane's thoughts, one brazen actress stepped forward. "Is it true? Did you sexually assault that man?"

Jane's outrage boiled over. "Of course not, you dolt. No wonder your last movie tanked. You're a clueless boob and a dreadful actress."

Tears welled before the imbecile ran into a stall and slammed the door.

Jane's chest heaved despite her, anger mounting as she surveyed the room, nostrils flaring. "Anyone else? Hmmm? Mere hours ago, my team drowned in a tsunami of fashion emergencies from starlets, some in this very room. You know who you are. Calls. Texts. Emails. Each more pathetic than the next."

Jane's eyebrows arched as she mocked their fervent pleas.

"Jane, please! My zipper won't close! I need a dress!"

"It's a worst-dressed waiting to happen. Jane, help me."

"The Gucci earrings, please! The ones from February, 2017? Can I borrow them?"

Jane strode over to the fading A-lister and tugged off her borrowed clip-on earrings. "Gucci earrings my ass. You will never get on my pages again. NEVER!"

The guests stood mute, not fearing, not awestruck, but repulsed.

"How dare you look at me that way! You disgust me. Get out. Get out all of you!"

The ladies scattered in a frenzy to empty the lounge, shoving lipstick and mascara in clutches then giving her a wide berth as they scurried past. Like she was an Untouchable. She sensed no embarrassment about their disloyalty. None. The tidal shift would sweep her away in a heartbeat if she didn't begin damage control.

Jane panted, her back barring the closed bathroom door.

Her cell rang within her clutch.

She flung the jeweled clasp open to answer her security detail. "Where the fuck are you?"

"We've secured the assailant. Where are you?" he said.

"I'm in a ladies' lounge. The one opposite the mummy room. We've got to get to my underground car."

"Negative."

"What do you mean 'negative'?" Jane said.

"We're on the move to your location, but the car is out front."

"Well, move it back, you idiot! I can't walk past those hyenas in the press!"

"Traffic is jammed. If you want it, that's where it is."

"Fuck!" Jane yelled, banging her fists against the door. "Just hurry! I have to get out of here."

Jane clasped her phone to her chest, tears streaking down her face. It had to be a bad dream. The eyes of the world waited outside. And now, they would bear witness to her walk of shame. The clip would loop on every news outlet the world over. Moving her car was a dastardly act done intentionally. Someone wanted her to suffer the humiliation of press scrutiny. But who would dare?

Her mind returned to where the travesty began. With Kyle. She would make him pay for what he'd done. He'd rot in prison before she relinquished her throne. She kicked herself for letting her guard down, underestimating him as the naïve 19-year-old who stole her heart. Instead, he'd landed the first blow. It was masterful, no doubt about that. Wounded, Jane's proverbial blood gushed everywhere. But she was a survivor; and the fight was far from over.

The world loves a damsel. She'd give them one for the ages.

Someone pushed the bathroom door from the other side.

"Jane?" the man said.

She opened the door to peek, collapsing with relief to see the bulking form of her security chief, Chuck. His loyalty would be rewarded.

Chuck and his partner grabbed her shoulders and together parted the jeering crowd, awaiting her retreat. She marked their faces, the freckled skin, pockmarks, and Botoxed wrinkles hiding beneath their manicured exteriors. Fakes. Fakes and phonies every one of them. If the public only knew.

The public.

Yes. If Jane's secrets were to be public, theirs would be too. No sense going down alone. The whole lot should crash and burn with her. She'd start with the celebrities and build up her rampage, saving the worst for Kyle and Rebecca.

Moving as one, her team muscled through the front door, only to be assaulted by a blinding burst of camera flashes.

"Jane. Jane, did you rape that man?"

"Jane! How many more victims are there?"

"Jane, is it true? Did you do it?"

"Any comment, Jane? What's your side?"

"Jane! Will you apologize to your victims?"

"Jane, do you have a message for your victims?"

Chuck removed his jacket to cover her head as he guided her down the red-carpeted stone steps of the museum to her waiting car. The valet opened the limousine's door for Chuck to guide her head into the vehicle and slam the door.

Banging the roof, Chuck yelled, "Go, go!"

The driver accelerated down a clear lane marked off with cones.

No traffic.

Not a single car in their path.

They could have easily pulled around, unless…

Jane spun to look out the rear window. Bulbs flashed as photographers chased her retreating car. Their lights illuminating the chaotic scene and the most shocking sight of all: Viraj shaking the hand of the parking valet.

Rebecca shook her arm free of the dazed Viraj. "Where would they take Kyle?"

Viraj stood mesmerized by the swirling chaos of guests. The once elegant assembly now roamed aimlessly like a pasture of bedazzled cows. But if Rebecca had any chance of rescuing Kyle, she'd have to act quickly, before Jane regrouped.

She grabbed Viraj by both shoulders. "Hey, I've got to get to Kyle. Where would they take him?"

"I'm sorry, but…"

"Think. A security room, or holding place? A dressing room? Where? It must have been part of the event planning," Rebecca said.

"Stop. Stop. I'm not helping you," he said, shrugging out of her grip. "You've lied to me this whole time."

"You found me, remember? I didn't ask for any of this! But what matters now is getting Kyle away from Jane's goons. We can sort the rest out later."

Viraj grasped his head. "I don't know what to make of this. I don't even know if I can trust you."

Kyle's bombshell threw Viraj for a loop, likely shoving him off an emotional edge. But they didn't have time for Viraj to process. They had to get to Kyle before someone took him, God knows where, and they lost him completely. At least for the next few moments, they had a chance of catching up while guests and staff were still reeling.

"Can you point me in the right direction?" Rebecca

asked, but Viraj turned away. What they did was for him as well. He didn't know that yet, of course, but she had expected a more supportive Viraj to emerge. Guess that was wishful thinking.

"Fine. Forget it." Rebecca pushed past Viraj, down the stairs, and into the crowd.

She tried to remember which direction the men dragged him, but the current of bodies had her off track. Instead of getting closer to Kyle, she was getting dragged back toward the mummy galleries.

Struggle as she might, she couldn't get through the way she wanted. She felt her throat constrict as tears welled in her eyes. It was as if every celebrity in attendance conspired to keep her and Kyle apart.

"Excuse me. Let me through," Rebecca swam with wild arms, while celebrities shrank back to avoid getting smacked by her flailing strokes. And it worked. She got through to the temple steps and was hiking her dress to ascend when Viraj caught up.

"Wait, hold on." He blocked her path with his body. "You can't battle security alone. Jane will simply haul you away as well."

"I haven't done anything." Rebecca made her way onto the temple landing where the microphone stand stood abandoned.

"Come on." Viraj took Rebecca's hand and led her across the stage and down the Temple of Dendur's steps, turning toward the American Wing.

"There are limited places to take him. Most administrative spaces are closed to us, and the rest are exhibit galleries. We set up an area for trouble makers. My bet is that's where they've taken him."

Now clear of the crowds, Rebecca struggled to keep up with Viraj's long strides, stopping twice to untangle her dress from between her legs.

"What will we do once we get to him? What excuse will we give?"

"They know me. I'll try to get past, say I'm doing it on Jane's behalf. It'll all depend on what we find," Viraj said.

"What we find? Would they have beaten him up?"

"Doubtful. There was one incident with her security detail two years ago that got aggressive. But with all the eyes on this place, I'd expect they'd follow our Valis security protocols. Actually…"

Viraj pulled out his cell to send a text before shoving it back in his pocket.

Rebecca choked down her worry. Thinking of Kyle lying wounded and alone somewhere in the museum was horrific. They ran past a case with sabers, and she was half-tempted to grab one of the priceless weapons for defense.

They reached the top of a service stairs, exiting into a long hallway with doors on either side. The thick air was tomb silent. They stopped short to listen, but their own heavy breathing masked all other sounds. Viraj turned back to her, worry apparent on his face. It looked like a dead end.

Kyle, where are you?

Kyle pressed his ear against the door. Nothing. No sound. There were 5,000 people in this building; where did they all go? It'd been mere minutes since he was hauled off the stage.

He paced away, scanning the room yet again. Still the same. A dressing table and vanity, green sofa with coordinating armchair, and coffee table. Wall sconces and a small basket with MOD monogrammed treats. No emergency call button. No phone. No clue how long they intended to keep him in this prison of a room.

Did the guests hear what he said?

Had the AV system worked?

They'd gasped; he'd heard it.

Jane flushed beet red.

He sighed. They had to have heard. This couldn't have all been for nothing.

He paced, his heavy phone banging into his bound wrists. If he could only reach it, he could try to call for help.

Despite being joined, he was able to unbutton his tux. Bracing against the doorknob, he dipped down to lever the phone up through the pocket flap.

Yes, that's it…

A moment later, the phone cleared the top and dropped onto the floor. He kneeled beside the device, depressing the button to activate voice dialing.

"Call Rebecca," Kyle said.

"Calling Rebecca," the phone chirped.

It only rang once before she answered.

"Oh my God, Kyle! Where are you?"

"They have me locked in a dressing room somewhere. Are you safe?"

"Yes. I'm with Viraj searching for you."

He sank back on his haunches in relief. "I'm not sure that's wise. Jane's got two tons of muscle that wrestled me off the stage. They took me downstairs into an administrative area. White walls, gray carpeting."

"Hold on." Rebecca relayed their conversation to Viraj.

"He knows where you are. We're coming."

"No. Get to Barbara's. We'll need legal help, and she has the best connections of anyone we know. I'll just have to figure out a way out of here."

"Don't be foolish," her breathy voice said. From their echoing footsteps it sounded like they were running. "How exactly to you expect to get here? You're locked in a room…"

"And tied up."

"What?"

"My wrists are bound, so I can't use my hands."

"Oh, and you expect to pull a Mission Impossible escape and get yourself free? We're coming. We're in this together and I'm not leaving this museum without you."

He opened his mouth to protest, but clammed up. Rebecca had a point. The adrenaline tank fueling him for weeks leading up to the Gala was on empty. In retrospect, not having an exit strategy for their amateur psy-ops operation was a gaping hole in their plan. Making it happen took all the fortitude he could muster. Making Jane pay. There was nothing else. Now, he wished he'd planned a mere ten minutes further and included time for them both to get safely out of the building.

"Tell me what you see. A door? A window? An air vent?" Rebecca said.

Kyle's laughter erupted. "You're joking. Air vent?"

"I don't know. I'm just thinking…"

As Kyle roared with laughter, a full measure of stress went with it. Stress he'd been struggling to release since he's not sure when. It all vacated in one intense moment of bliss, rising above his captive circumstances.

"Are you done laughing? This is serious…" Rebecca said, sounding both out of breath and annoyed.

"Sure, I'll just shimmy under the door," he said, trying to swallow his chuckles. "Or, better yet, I'll call my extraction team waiting outside in an unmarked van…"

"What about a guy with a key?" a voice behind him said.

Kyle turned to see Viraj, who entered from the adjoining room.

Viraj disconnected the call before placing the device back into Kyle's pocket.

"You, my friend, were hard to find. But let's get you untied, yes?" Viraj said.

"Where's Rebecca? I thought you two were together?" Kyle asked.

"She'll be along. I ran ahead as her dress kept slowing her down."

Viraj opened and shut drawers in rapid succession. "Ah here they are."

He raised a pair of scissors.

"How did you find the right room?" Kyle asked.

"Your laughter." Viraj angled the scissors and cut the plastic ties free with two snips. Kyle rubbed the chafed skin they left behind.

"Thanks. I owe you one."

"What you said. Is it true?" Viraj asked.

"Every word."

Viraj extended his hand. "You're a brave man. Braver than me. My career... I have too much to lose. I wish I could help..."

Kyle pulled Viraj close, slapping his back with is free hand. "I understand. But know we will be heard. She's a criminal and now the world knows. The hard part is ahead, but I'm ready."

Viraj pulled back. "The hard part?"

"Charges. Pressing formal charges. Me and one other will be doing that. I've made my decision to come forward. I've had eleven years to consider this moment. I wanted you to know, but you need to do what's right for you. Okay?" Kyle said squeezing Viraj's hunched shoulders.

They barely knew each other, but shared a sad bond few men could understand.

Viraj nodded. "I need to think about my next steps. My girlfriend, she doesn't know. I didn't know how to tell her."

"There's no shame in this. You didn't do anything wrong. Neither did I or the others."

"Somewhere inside I know. It's just hard to emotionally accept."

"Viraj? Kyle!" Rebecca appeared in the doorway and slammed into Kyle so hard they both tumbled back onto the floor into a pile of limbs and kisses.

"If writing doesn't work out, Rebecca, you can always try out for rugby!" Viraj joked.

"Oh I'm so sorry, are you hurt?" Rebecca's warm hands flew over him in a visual inspection of limbs, hands, and face.

"I'm fine. But we should get out of here before someone comes back."

Kyle stepped toward the open door. "Shall we?"

The trio retraced Viraj's steps through the adjoining suite, returning to the hall. Kyle kept a firm grip on Rebecca's hand as they trailed Viraj through a maze of corridors, past the museum's many antiquities and up two flights of stairs. In a few moments they arrived back by the front entry hall.

A commotion drew their eyes outside.

Jane.

"You'll excuse me." In a blink, Viraj dashed though the open door and down the carpeted stairs towards a mob of reporters clustered by the curb. A black limo screeched away, triggering a chorus of camera flashes.

Paparazzi. Sometimes, you gotta love those guys.

"Let's get out of here," he said kissing her hand before they strode away from the melee, down the stone steps, and past a splashing fountain.

Rebecca stopped dead in her tracks. Not only because of the lively water, but because her favorite actress sat on its edge, thumbs a blaze of action on her smartphone.

"Unbelievable," she said with a smile spanning ear to ear. "She's right there. I could just reach out and…"

"Get arrested for assault? Very likely." Kyle yanked her away.

"Well someone should, but it isn't me!" Rebecca squeezed his hand. "You did good tonight. Really good."

What the evening lacked in elegance and dining finery, it made up for in adventure. After all, everyone present could say they were there the night the great Jane Stuart was outed as a sexual predator.

Before any further delays, Kyle hurried them down a cobblestone path leading into the leafy darkness of Central Park.

34

B y the time Rebecca and Kyle made it through the park, her pantyhose were in tatters and her psyche was worse. Somewhere along the way, her shoes came off, having worn out their welcome. Thank God her clutch had a chain strap, or she likely would have lost the precious loaner somewhere between her frenzied tour of the museum and Barbara's brownstone.

She sat on a park bench to replace her heels before crossing the four-lane avenue of Central Park West. "Remind me why I wore these shoes?"

"You said they were cute and worth the pain." Kyle lifted her back to her objecting feet.

"Not so much."

Rebecca dragged her body up the three flights of stairs to where Barbara's face hung over the railing.

"Oh my God! Are you guys okay?" Barbara enveloped Rebecca in her arms. "You're chilled to the bone."

"Joe! Joe, get a blanket, quick," Barbara said as they entered the apartment.

Joe hopped up from the sofa where he was reading a book and scampered down the hall. He returned with a wool blanket which Barbara draped around Rebecca's shoulders as she guided her stunned friend to the sofa to sit while Kyle locked the door.

Barbara sat on the floor in front of her, rubbing her legs to warm her up. "It's all over the news, but I don't know what to believe."

Rebecca noticed the muted TV hanging on the wall. News vans camped out in front of the museum, completely blocking Fifth Avenue. The red carpet made for striking TV. Enormous crowds still lined the barricades, hoping to get a glimpse of the famous. But one night of glamor and drama would suffice for a lifetime. Rebecca half wished she stayed home in pajamas like Viraj's girlfriend, but then Kyle would still be hogtied in a basement.

"Becca, what happened after I left you before the Gala?"

Dressing?

Her bedroom?

Had that been today?

"Becca?" Barbara pleaded.

Kyle took a seat next to her. "You do it. I'm all talked out."

It was time. They had to know the truth, so Rebecca filled them in about Kyle's nonconsensual relationship with Jane. How he hadn't heard from her in years, until she ran that magazine spread to get his attention. About blackmailing him to attend the MOD Gala and their plan to rid themselves of her once and for all. It all came tumbling out in a huge mash-up of word vomit, unstoppable until fully purged.

"I can't believe it," Barbara said.

"Believe it. And she's a serial offender. We know of at least one other man she assaulted in the same way, and there are likely more." Viraj flashed across Rebecca's mind, but she blinked the thought away. The concept of that lovely, vibrant man being victimized by Jane broke her heart.

The doorbell chimed and Barbara rose to her feet.

"It's probably Leslie. I texted her when I heard you were on your way over." Barbara opened the door.

Leslie's flustered body rushed in, wrapped in a belted knit sweater. "Is she okay? It's everywhere. Kyle? Is what they're saying true?"

"Unfortunately, yes. It's all true. Jane is a monster." Rebecca sat, hugging her knees.

"Look. The clip is on again." Joe pointed to the silent screen where someone's cellphone video captured Kyle's moment of glory. Rebecca missed Jane going limp and using the mic stand for support while the two security goons wrestled Kyle off the stage.

"Turn it off. I've seen enough of Jane for a lifetime," Kyle said.

Joe reached for the remote and clicked it off. "Anyone want tea?"

Leslie laughed. "What are you, British?"

"It's more for me than for them. Feeling a little useless right about now."

Rebecca snuck a peek at Kyle. She knew the sentiment well. "Thanks, Joe. Tea would be great."

Rebecca pulled the edges closed on the blanket wrapped around her, the mere thought of warmth a distant illusion. Kyle's skin looked clammy, but wet curls stuck to his temples, a sign of how much the night had physically exhausted him.

Joe returned carrying a tray.

"Tea for the lady, and something stronger for the hostage." Joe tabled the tray and reached out to shake Kyle's hand. "Glad you're free, my man. That's a heavy burden you've been carrying."

They clasped hands. "Thanks. It was such a rush to stick it to her for once."

Kyle snatched the brown beer bottle off the tray. "I never was much for tea."

"That's not just any tea," Barbara said, handing the mug over the coffee table to Rebecca, who short-armed her reach to stay under the blanket. "That's my homemade Orange Spice."

"Wow, this is an occasion," Rebecca said.

"It's not every day we play host to international sensations!" Barbara said.

Warmth penetrated Rebecca's hands as they circled the mug. Cinnamon, cloves, and a citrus tang of orange zest awaited from the recipe Barbara's mother handed down through the family. Rebecca had missed its soothing embrace after Barbara moved out. She settled back into the couch to savor her first sip.

Kyle hugged her close to whisper, "We were too late for Viraj."

Her heart sank.

"That sweet man? How could she?"

"What's that?" Barbara asked.

"Another victim," Kyle said.

"That makes three," Barbara said. "That's too consistent a pattern for her to quit. She must have assaulted others."

Rebecca spun her head toward Leslie. "It's just like those awful cases you write about. You'd look at her and never know."

"Kyle, did you share a secret recording? They said you played one on the news," Leslie asked.

"Yes. I recorded her earlier today." Kyle opened his shirt to reveal the mic's red light blinking. "Looks like your Wi-Fi is more secure than the one at Jane's house."

He stripped off the tape and tossed the wired remote pack on the table.

Rebecca patted his leg. "Vivian came through. We owe her."

"That's a lot of evidence to refute," Barbara said.

"It is. But we have to be ready. Jane won't relinquish power on her own. The board will have to take it from her, and she won't make that easy," Kyle said.

"Oh, come on!" Rebecca chortled. "Witnesses and a recording? Outing at the MOD Gala? What more do we have to do?"

"I'm just saying. You don't get to be in Jane's position without having a lot of friends in high places. I wouldn't put it past her to lick her wounds and come out swinging."

"You make her sound like the Terminator," Leslie said to Kyle.

"She is," he said.

Worry glazed Kyle's eyes. In her head, Rebecca wanted to believe Kyle was overreacting about Jane, but he'd been dead right about her the whole time. Jane wasn't going to just slink away never to be seen again. She'd lick her wounds and be back. She locked stares with Kyle and his eyes said it all: Jane would be back.

35

Rebecca jiggled her wrist to bring her mouse to life. She must have been staring off into space for a while since her monitor went dark. But then she hadn't slept a wink. She returned home after the Gala, only to blink at the ceiling wondering what came next. When would Jane resurface? How could Kyle have survived so many years with Jane's shadow following him everywhere? The more she learned about what happened, the more respect she had for his resilience. He was an amazing man and deserved so much better.

Her fake *MOD* email pinged a notification.

Rebecca emailed every few days with Libby, answering questions and giving support anonymously. For someone as fiercely independent as Libby, Kika was as needy as they came.

Rebecca clicked on the email to read in her preview pane:

Not sure if you have time for another question with

everything going on at MOD *right now. But if you do, can you share your thoughts about whether there are supplies I'll need to have ready for our wedding night? My bridesmaids bought so much stuff, I'm not sure what's practical to bring along.*

Thanks again,

Kika

Given the frequency of their emails, Rebecca dispensed with the formality of their first exchanges, replying more in her personal voice:

Hi Kika,

Your wedding night is only one of what will hopefully be a long and loving pleasure life. There's no need to empty the toy box on your first go. Some lubricants and massage oils are likely plenty for your first night, and over time, you can introduce more toys, positions to enhance what you and Evan achieve together.

Like I mentioned before, enter the evening planning to be a mutual partner. You should receive pleasure and give pleasure as well. Your needs matter and your new groom should be more than happy to see you satisfied.

Warm regards,

BD

Rebecca checked the spelling and pressed send, a warmth swirling in her insides. It felt good to help women. With all the craziness with Kyle and MOD, the real purpose for it all was easy to forget. She'd miss that the most. With no blog, no MOD, and a PIP looming at work, her epic fall from grace merited a case study.

Rebecca waited for emotion to well, but none came.

306

Her side work on her blog and MOD filled a void in her professional life that she hadn't recognized before. With them gone, the hollowness would return. Even without the PIP, could her work at MediaNow rise to the occasion? Could she feel fulfilled without knowing she was making a difference in people's lives?

The office was just as it always was. Gray cubes. Animated voices negotiating on behalf of clients, relishing the wins. That used to be her. She used to love her work, feel like she was making a big difference in the businesses of her clients. And she was. She was making it easier for their customers to find and appreciate what they brought to the table. But now? Compared to changing people's lives? People with pain? And names? Actual women she could impact and who said thank you? It made the rest feel like an empty waste of time. Shuffling papers until the next stack came. It had been her everything. But now it wasn't. Not anymore.

"Walk with me," a voice said.

Rebecca looked up to see all six feet of Harry standing before her, sporting his rare "pissed off agency owner" face. It was an expression he reserved for combat, and he aimed it at her.

She jumped to her feet. "I'm sorry for missing the meet—"

"Outside. Now," Harry said, taking off for the elevator at a brisk clip.

Rebecca looked around, but every desk neighbor was absorbed in their work. Was Harry kicking her out before she could even box her things? Her pictures, mementos, work awards? What about the PIP? Were they skipping that?

"Sloane. Now."

"Right," Rebecca whispered as she slipped an arm into her sweater and scurried to catch up.

"But you agreed. I don't understand." Kyle jumped to his feet from Greg's office couch. The view from Bailey Cameras' offices was impressive, and as CEO, Greg had the best one. Seeing him in his natural position of power made it hard to imagine him under Jane's thumb. But from the sounds of it, he was happy to remain there.

Greg sat in a black leather chair, legs crossed, arms relaxed. "I can't have this shitstorm you stirred up blow back on me and my company. It's not a risk I'm willing to entertain."

"Bullshit, you already entertained it. You said so, and now you're chucking me into a tornado to fend for myself?"

"I'm sorry."

"No, you're not." Kyle paced away, but whipped around. "Why did you even tell me? Why did you encourage me down this path, only to pull the rug out?"

"You don't even need me. The world knows and others will come forward. You'll see."

"Don't to this. Let's go to the station and press charges. Like we planned. If you drop out, it's just my word against hers. If the two of us go, that's a pattern. A credible pattern that will give others the courage to step forward."

His mind went to Viraj. As brave as he was to tell Kyle, he was only at the beginning of his journey. Plus, he depended on Jane for his income. No way he wanted to drop this at Viraj's doorstep. Greg had means and would be a powerful ally, not that he wanted to be.

Greg sighed. "You're brave because you can be. You only have yourself to think about. I have hundreds of employees depending on me. I do business with Valis Publishing. What if they pull my contract? That's a financial risk I can't take."

Kyle's heart squeezed like a fist. Something was off. "She got to you."

"Who?"

"Jane. She bought you off."

"Fuck you. I've thought it through and made my decision. I don't owe you or her anything." Greg bolted to the window, arms crossed, back to the room. Greg was right about one thing: He had a lot more to lose than Kyle. But if powerful people stayed silent in the face of wrongdoing, what chance did the rest of them have?

"I can't do it. I'm sorry. You are way braver. No way I could have stormed the MOD Gala and outed Jane on stage. Fucking brilliant. I'd have given anything to be there."

Kyle joined him where he stood. "Then be there. Be there now, when it matters. Together, we have power and our words can make the difference between Jane walking free to abuse others and finally bringing her to justice."

The words hung between them, resonating with an energy of their own. Justice. Something Greg wanted, or said he did. But saying it and actively working towards making it happen are two different things. His struggle was real. Kyle knew, because it mirrored his own. But he'd overcome his doubts and knew Greg would never heal until he conquered the demons shadowing his life. Starting with the blond one.

"You have the recording. Her own words. That's enough. If you can't nail her with that, what's my testimony going to do?"

A commotion in the other room got their attention, then someone knocked on Greg's door before opening.

"There's a press conference starting that you might want to see. Jane Stuart."

"Thank you." Greg strode to his office's sitting area in front of a wall-mounted TV and reached for the remote. "This won't be good."

Kyle moved closer to watch as the TV blinked to life.

Greg flipped channels until the news station covering the local press conference came on. Jane sat alone on a dais, covered in a white tablecloth. She was at a local hotel, and there was a noticeable absence of Valis Publishing branding.

"She's alone," Greg said. "That's significant."

"Maybe, maybe not. Turn it up."

Jane's voice filled the room. "…completely unfounded. I am the victim here, not Mr. Dillon, whom I barely know from many years before."

"But what about the recording?" a reporter yelled.

"Taken without my consent and out of context."

"Why are you the victim if you harassed him?"

"Because I did not harass him. He…" Jane paused, looking at the room.

She's about to lie.

"If you must know, Mr. Dillon and I were involved for a time. He rejected me, verbally abusing me because I didn't perform to his liking in the bedroom. His behavior was shameful."

"What!?" Kyle yelled at the screen.

"She's got balls, that one," Greg answered.

Kyle clenched his fists. "How can she say that after what she did to me? To you? To all of us?"

A reporter yelled. "Aren't you just making up this story to cover your tracks? It's sounds like the recent article you ran in MOD."

"You're right. The story is from MOD," Jane said.

Murmurs erupted in the room. Jane smiled, tilting her head up. "The story is from MOD, but the story is my own. It's a story I struggled with for years. Kept hidden from even my closest confidants. Being a powerful woman can be a lonely place. But I refuse to hide in the shadows any longer. Today, I'm proud to reveal that I am the author behind Bedroom Diary."

Bedlam. Every reporter in the room spoke at once, yelling questions, flashing pictures. Jane sat alone at the podium, smirking, hands folded innocently on the table for what seemed like forever, drinking in the chaos like wine.

"One at a time," someone yelled, likely a PR person on Jane's team.

"Ms. Stuart, why did you feel the need to hide your identity?"

"Sexual problems are not something one boasts about. It's shameful. Even someone in my position, with the power I have, did not feel comfortable coming forward."

"Why now? Isn't this only a distraction?" a reporter yelled.

"No. I'm deeply committed to helping women, which is why we pursued this story. Yes, I was too embarrassed to use my name, but the fact remains that we are helping women everywhere and will continue to do so as long as I'm the editor here at MOD."

"You honestly expect us to believe that you wrote DBD? C'mon. This is a ruse to cover your crimes."

"The only crimes here were committed by Mr. Dillon and his accomplice, a freelance writer I hired to work on the project. I trusted her, hired her to help me with the articles, but she was part of this extortion plan. Their effort to out me as Bedroom Diary has failed because I have bravely come forward myself."

The press conference continued, with reporters peppering Jane with inane questions about her victimhood, her intention to press charges and to continue her selfless work helping women.

Kyle shut his eyes to the spectacle. Her performance, every moment, was a pack of lies. Too many for even Jane to explain away.

Greg clicked off the television.

Kyle lifted his bent head. "I knew she'd deny it, but this... this shows what a psychopath she is."

They exchanged glum stares.

"She needs to be held accountable," Kyle said. "We can do this. It looks bad, but we have the truth on our side."

"Kyle, I…"

"Think about it. We can find a way. A way for you to come forward while protecting your identity. Courts do it all the time."

Greg sat staring at the darkened TV screen, Jane's lies looming large.

Kyle's heart was pounding so loud in his ears, he almost couldn't hear Greg's reply.

"Okay. Okay, I'll do it."

"You will?"

"Yes."

"For real this time? You're not changing your mind?"

"No. I'm in." Greg stood and walked over to the minibar behind his desk. "I'll even drink to it."

Kyle followed and Greg poured them each a chunky crystal tumbler of scotch. He handed the heavy glass to Kyle and raised his own.

"To justice," Kyle said.

They clinked glasses and drank.

"You've not been yourself lately," Harry set out toward Union Square Park, one block away. "Missing deadlines, and meetings? That's not the Sloane I know. Darcy's drawing up a performance improvement plan."

"Harry, I'm so sorry. There's been a lot going on in my personal life," Rebecca said, struggling to keep pace with his long strides.

"Care to explain what happened last night at the MOD Gala?"

Rebecca stopped dead in her tracks.

Harry smirked before walking back to face her. "Something tells me you weren't running out to buy a tux."

"You were there?"

Harry had always been the one person who'd believed in her, even when she didn't believe in herself. He'd given her opportunities and barred the door against Darcy when she was on Rebecca's case. She owed him the truth.

"Please tell me what's going on. You've been off your game for months, and I can't figure out why one of my star employees is tanking."

After a reluctant sigh, Rebecca spilled the beans about writing for MOD. About Kyle, Jane, and, by the end, that she was the elusive author known as Bedroom Diary. Not even Kyle knew how she was feeling inside about it all. There'd been too much on his plate to worry him about her career misgivings. The cathartic release was beyond welcome.

Harry listened, his gray curls bobbing as he nodded to himself, chuckling and even exclaiming a few "oohs" and "ahhs" at choice moments and in between bites of the hot dogs he bought them both for a snack.

"That's quite a tale, Sloane. You? MOD's 'Dear Bedroom Diary' right under our noses the whole time!"

"Yeah, well. It's not exactly something you talk about around the water cooler."

"Maybe it's time we change that. Hmmm?"

"Yes, that's exactly how I feel. And it's why I'm so disappointed that I can't continue this work."

Harry blinked. "Why can't you?"

"I explained, MOD—"

"Screw MOD. They obviously didn't care about you."

"I've never heard you use foul language." Rebecca chuckled.

"This calls for it, and I guarantee you: I use it."

"I'll get it on video next time."

"My point is that all you need is a computer and an internet connection. Your fans will find you again."

"You forget. MOD continued without me."

"Yes, but you're the real deal. The true and original Bedroom Diary. That has to count for something?"

"I'm not sure it does."

"It does. Believe me."

She stared into Harry's eyes. His genuine concern was so welcome after the craziness of the last several days.

"What if I fail?"

"If you fail, you fail. At least if you try, you've got a chance to succeed. You have zero chance to succeed if you don't try."

"I never thought about it that way," Rebecca said.

"It's still scary. No way around that. Do you think Mitch and I weren't scared when we started MediaNow? We were scared shitless. Now, we have an agency with 60 people that outperforms the big guys."

Rebecca smiled. "We do, don't we?"

"You're damn straight we do. Well, except for one distracted person who's been screwing up…"

"I have been bad."

"Lately? Yeah, pretty out to lunch." Harry popped his last bite of hot dog in his mouth and swiped his hands clean.

"So what about my PIP?"

"Oh, you're still getting that. It'd be unfair to your colleagues to let it slide, set a bad precedent. But something tells me your heart now lies elsewhere. It's up to you to see where it leads."

Just then, Rebecca's phone started buzzing like mad. As soon as she silenced it, another notification binged. She looked up.

"Something must be up. My phone is going nuts."

"Sure thing." Harry picked up his own phone to scroll.

Rebecca scanned her texts.

Leslie: Don't worry. We won't let her get away with this.

Barbara: I have your back. Don't worry. I'm already looking into legal options.

Kyle: Please call. I have a plan in the works.

"It looks like I'm in some sort of trouble, but have no clue what." Rebecca scrolled through texts from her mom, dad, and a few people she hadn't heard from in years.

"Jane Stuart has just accused 'a freelance writer' of extortion and claimed the mantle of Bedroom Diary for herself. That's you, right?" Harry said.

"You're joking."

"She said the freelance writer threatened to out Jane as the anonymous author, and she was forced to come forward," Harry summarized the article as he scrolled on his phone.

"She's accusing me of doing what she did to us? It's totally backwards."

"From what you shared earlier, it appears that way."

"It's not true, Harry. I promise I—"

"I believe you." Harry patted her shoulder, quelling her hyperventilating. "The Rebecca Sloane I know would never do what Stuart accused you of. Hell, you've only just begun sticking up for yourself with Darcy."

She shook her head. "My documented lack of confidence. I've never been so glad to have a lame work review in my life."

"Not completely lame. Just less than you were capable of."

"Thanks for the kick in the pants, by the way. I like the new, confident Rebecca better."

"Me too, except for the screwing up at work part." Harry nudged her with his elbow.

Rebecca's phone continued its chorus of notifications. The most powerful woman in fashion just accused her of extortion at a press conference. The entire world would think she was a criminal. It was a recipe designed to drive Rebecca into a dark pit never to return. So why wasn't she petrified?

Her steady hand turned off her phone.

She looked up at Harry.

He knew the truth, but more importantly, so did she. Jane manufactured a lie, sewing it from scraps of cloth littered on the MOD floor solely to distract from Kyle's accusations of sexual harassment. Even Rebecca had to admit it was genius. Too bad for Jane, it wasn't true.

Harry rose. "Take the rest of the day. Take what time you need. I'm here to support you."

"Thanks. Thanks so much. For believing in me, for everything. It means more than you know."

Harry started back across the park toward the office, whistling as he went. Restored to his usual self. Relaxed. Not a care in the world when she'd just dropped this shitstorm at his feet.

She had a lot to learn from Harry.

She'd need to summon a calm like his to clear her head and figure out how to restore her name.

A loud squeak got her attention.

A mom, pushing a little girl with golden pigtails on a swing. A 20-something guy with a beard sat drinking coffee while scrolling on his phone. Two power-walking women stormed by, swinging arms, wiggling butts, and having an animated conversation about the British royal family.

Rebecca closed her eyes and stretched her neck from side to side. If only she could be alone. Alone to think.

But she wasn't alone.

Her eyes popped open.

She wasn't alone.

And it wasn't Rebecca's word against Jane's.

She had proof she was Bedroom Diary. A team of people knew Rebecca was the true author. There was the original email invitation from MOD, and their follow-up correspondence. She was also the true client of the elusive Heidi Quinn, sex coach extraordinaire. She'd need more, though. Just in case people didn't want to rat out the boss, scummy as she was.

Yes, a plan was forming. There was no way Rebecca would let Jane parade around, claiming Rebecca's history as her own. But it was mildly hilarious that someone so famous thought her history of sexual dysfunction was worth stealing.

Rebecca rose, and with confidence mounting, prepared to reclaim her good name.

36

Rebecca's door slam reverberated through their silent apartment. "Ky?" Rebecca called, but no answer came.

Her heels clacked the parquet floor as she entered the living room.

Empty. That's right. He was meeting Greg today. Goodness knows how the press conference impacted their plans to come forward. Jane certainly knew how to tighten the screws on her adversaries. Kyle knew it was coming. But did Greg? And what about Viraj?

Viraj.

This must all be a nightmare for him, causing a whirlwind of impossible emotions. He had the most to lose. Not only would his trauma be exposed, but he would very likely lose his job. A career he worked hard to build, on his own terms by working late and having good ideas. His success came despite Jane, not because of her.

He needed support.

He must feel really alone right now.

Rebecca tapped Viraj's number in her favorites. He might be in meetings. He might see her name and refuse to answer.

She'd follow his lead, only mention what he was comfortable discussing.

God, please answer.

"I wasn't sure if I'd ever year from you again," Viraj said.

"Are you at work? Can you talk?"

"No. I'm home. I couldn't go into the office after last night."

"Are you okay? It must be a shock," Rebecca said.

The pause was as pregnant as they come. Rebecca could only imagine the conflicting thoughts racing through his mind. Could he tell? Should he tell? Did Rebecca already know? Could she be trusted? Was he ready to be that open about something so personal?

Viraj broke the impasse. "Not as much of a shock as you might think. But then, you probably know."

Her throat tightened, squeezing tears out that made their silent way down her cheeks. She wiped them away.

"I'm so sorry. We hoped we'd gotten to you in time."

"It started well before you ever knew me."

Words of comfort came to her lips, but that level of intimacy rang false. They were work acquaintances. And as much as she knew about Viraj, she didn't really know him, the man. She wished more than ever that was different.

"What have you heard from others in the office? Do they believe Kyle?"

"Everyone I spoke to after the Gala believes him. And they likely suspect he wasn't the only one. They've begun putting the pieces together, looking at me with questioning eyes, as they say."

"This has to be your decision. Don't let me, Kyle, or anyone else pressure you into coming forward before you're ready."

"That might not be an option. The Board of Directors has already taken steps to investigate the claim. I'm talking to them later today."

"Wow, that was fast."

"That dog and pony show earlier might have worked for the press, but no one at Valis is buying it. People admire Kyle's bravery and want to support him. And you."

Rebecca perked up. "Me?"

"Yes, we don't take kindly to stolen valor around here. Jane taking credit for your work and the tireless work of others around the world has rubbed staffers the wrong way."

How amazing was that? People Rebecca barely knew willing to stick up for her. But were they riled enough to advocate for Rebecca against the woman who signs their paychecks? Even wounded, Jane was a powerful enemy. Her team would likely think twice before crossing her, no matter how noble their intentions.

"You think I have a shot at anyone helping me clear my name?" Rebecca said, plopping on the sofa.

"You can count on me. I'll ask around about others and let you know."

"Thanks, and thanks for helping Kyle last night. Locking him up was almost worse than blackmailing him to go in the first place."

"Blackmailing him?" Now it was Viraj's turn to be surprised.

"She threatened to expose my identity as Bedroom Diary. That's the reason he was there. But then we realized she'd never stop harassing Kyle unless we did something to stop her."

"Now it makes sense," Viraj whispered. "I didn't understand what he was doing there as her date. Especially given his history with her."

"She's a monster," Rebecca said, hugging herself.

Viraj sighed. "That she is."

"What will you do now? Are you going to keep working at Valis?"

"I don't know."

The silent apartment with its photos, knickknacks and memories suddenly felt like a museum of someone else's life. They'd forever mark time designating before MOD and after MOD. Before, when everything seemed normal but wasn't. Secrets casting a shadow over Kyle. After MOD was still unfolding, but there was a surprising lightness to having all their darkest secrets out in the bright light of day. All that remained was to disinfect themselves of Jane.

Kyle entered their bedroom, mind a whirl after doom scrolling for way too long. Posts by online "experts" claimed Kyle's allegations against Jane were ridiculous or impossible. He looked up and saw Rebecca's overstuffed suitcase lying open like a wounded elephant. His heart plummeted through the floor.

"Are you leaving?"

Even if shocked by the press conference, running away in the middle of the madness was not the answer. Rebecca looked at the suitcase, then back to him, her face softening into a wide smile.

"Sweetie, I'm not leaving. I'm packing for the wedding." She held up a hangar holding the god-awful bridesmaid dress Libby chose. "Libby texted asking what time our flight landed tomorrow. I'd completely forgotten with everything... Jane..." Rebecca swirled her arms before letting them drop at her sides.

The wedding. Libby's nuptials slipped his mind, understandable given everything going on. And the media hounding him by phone, text, and email clamoring for a scoop. Rebecca's family's name on the lease was the only thing preventing reporters from camping outside their apartment as well.

Rebecca tossed yet another garment on her haystack.

Her mind had to be as tormented as his. With all the chaos between him and Jane, Kyle lost sight of the toll it took on Rebecca. He vowed to do better.

She scratched her head like she'd forgotten something. "I didn't want to bother Viraj again, so I left a message with the admin that I'd be unavailable for a few days."

"Good idea," Kyle muttered. As much as he wanted to celebrate his sister's nuptials, leaving the next day complicated matters. He'd have to delay filing charges against Jane as he'd arranged with Greg. That'd give Greg more time to change his mind and bail. It'd also give Jane's lies free reign to take root in the public consciousness, worming their way into something the average person might accept as true.

After shirking the limelight for so long, Kyle's body ached for more. He envisioned himself marching into a newsroom to proclaim themselves ready to press charges. That would keep Jane busy for a few days. But he promised Greg to be discrete, and poking a hive of reporters would only send Greg running for the hills. Fantasies aside, nothing could proceed until they returned from Texas. Guests were flying in, and they were expected to be among them.

"By the way," Rebecca said. "Furious doesn't begin to describe your beloved sister."

"What about now?"

"That we 'launched a media circus days before her wedding,'" Rebecca air-quoted. "You need to call. She must have been desperate to lower herself to calling me: her least-favorite bridesmaid."

Kyle ignored every call pinging his phone, even those from his parents and Libby. After keeping the secret for over a decade, having strangers and family all discussing the most traumatic period of his life bubbled shame to the surface in a way that left his nerve endings raw. They all meant well, calling to pledge support. But talking was the last item on his agenda. He didn't even return Dr. Kaplan's call, though the good doctor was probably the one person he needed most.

"I can't deal with her right now. She'll have to wait."

"She's worried. I'm sure your folks are too," Rebecca said.

"I'll compromise and listen to her message."

Kyle strolled down the hall, but his sister's recorded tirade blasted from his speaker off the walls creating an echo chamber of rage:

"What the hell, Kyle? You detonate a fucking Atom Bomb before my wedding then don't give me the courtesy of a call back? One week. You couldn't at least put this off until—"

He hung up. "I'm fine, Libby. Thanks for asking."

After that reaction from his sister, dancing on hot stones for his parents was a no-go. He'd seen that movie before. Why didn't he tell them? Why hadn't he gone to the police? No, he didn't blame them for letting him model in the first place. No, he didn't yet grasp how the case would go, if the police would take him seriously, or whether the statute of limitations ran out. All he could do was to take life one day at a time.

Yeah, that conversation could wait.

Kyle sat at the table, drumming his fingers. The public reaction was worse than expected. Instead of sympathetic onlookers running to his rescue, they pelted him with rotten produce. He swiped his shirt, half expecting decaying tomatoes and cabbage to fall away. But his shirt was clean. The emotional blows landed where no one would see.

And the worst part: he'd invited the scrutiny. Live on stage, he thrust himself back into the spotlight unbidden. Unasked. Before, no one knew or cared about him or what he did with his life. Now? They craved every tawdry detail. Who was he? Where did he work? Did he have a record? Who are his close associates? Everyone wanted a piece of the man who dared cross Jane Stuart.

Rather than focusing on the woman at the center of the abuse, the dogs hunted him. No wonder women survivors feared coming forward. Why should they? If assaulted, it must be their fault. They asked for it, no? Look what they were wearing. They must have wanted it and changed their minds later. Lies, every one, yet the stereotypes persisted. In his case, sick conversations swirled about the mechanics of the deed and how it was physically impossible for his claims to be true. And who blamed them? He'd only discovered the truth himself a few months ago.

Public understanding would take time.

Kyle waited an eternity to feel whole, move on, and escape Jane's memory. This tsunami made screaming a logical next step. He'd done everything else, why not scream? But didn't he launch a primal scream for the ages at the Gala? Why didn't that wash the shame away? Why couldn't he let it go, be happy, and leave the ugliness behind?

In two days, his bratty sister would be married. His younger sister. The sister that always followed in his footsteps—into life, into modeling—yet, she'd skipped the line and got engaged first. She loved someone and did something to honor it, preserve it, and make it last. What had he done to build a happy future with Rebecca? For the two of them? Not nearly enough. That had to change. The future he wanted was within reach; he need only commit to making it happen. Jane would soon fade into history. Rebecca represented his present and future.

Kyle bolted out of his chair. Six o'clock? The shops might still be open. He laced his boots and snatched his motorcycle jacket from the closet.

"I'll be back in a few hours," he called down the hall.

He was about to embrace the life he wanted. Hopefully, Rebecca would see it the same way.

37

Jane sat at her desk, pinging staffer after staffer. None bothered to show up for work. She arrived after the press conference, to a smattering of junior employees who knew better than to attempt eye contact. Still, hours later, those she depended on failed to materialize.

"Elaine! Elaine, get in here!" she yelled to her admin.

"Yes, Jane?" the woman said.

"Is today a holiday or am I the only one who cares about this issue getting out on time?"

"Um... it's seven o'clock. I was about to head home for the day myself..." Elaine stood dumb, blinking with those wet blue eyes of hers that always looked on the brink of crying. The girl held out a slip of paper.

"What's that? Is that for me?" Jane snapped.

"It's a message from earlier for Viraj, but he didn't make it in today."

"Well, leave the message on his desk."

"I—I wasn't sure if it was important because it was about this weekend."

"Give it here. Come on, come on." Jane extended her hand and snatched the paper from Elaine's quivering fingers.

Who was she? Viraj's secretary? The Judas who sent her to the wolves at her most urgent hour? The vision of him shaking hands with the valet was only outmatched by the video footage of him releasing Kyle from the security holding room. She trusted her protégé, but in the end, he betrayed her.

Elaine remained at attention in front of her desk.

"And you're still here because?" Jane asked. Must she dismiss everyone, or was the girl gawking? She hated gawkers...

"She said she'd be out of town for a few days, unreachable."

"Who?"

"Miss Sloane. She said something about attending a family wedding in Texas."

Did she now? How sweet. They ruin her career, then escape their crimes into the warm bosom of family and friends. A regular Bonnie and Clyde those two. They deserved each other. They also deserved the same public flogging they gave her.

"Before you go, get my stylist on the line. I need her assistance with a last-minute event I'll be planning," Jane said.

As Elaine turned to leave, Jane reviewed the message in full. One look sent tingles of pleasure racing to her extremities. This is too delicious. Rebecca wasn't just heading to a family wedding. She was heading to the wedding of... Kyle's sister!

Her stylist's face lit up Jane's cell.

"Meet me downstairs," Jane said. "I need your help and want to look my best."

38

Relief washed over Kyle the moment their hotel room door slammed closed. It was all he could do to avoid Libby and his parents at check-in. He caught a glimpse of them in the lobby, but skirted through unobserved, dipping his head as he pushed their luggage trolley to the elevator. For once he was glad for Rebecca's overpacking. But his bliss would end momentarily. Once dressed, they'd head back down for the rehearsal dinner. A stream of Libby's texts arrived all afternoon, yet one rang warning bells too loud to ignore.

"Becca?"

"Hmm?" she answered, unpacking garments into assorted dresser drawers.

"What's this about Libby writing to 'Dear Bedroom Diary'?" Kyle asked.

The color drained from Rebecca's face, leaving it the color of the white shirt she clutched in her fingers. She swallowed hard.

"Libby keeps texting me about writing into 'Dear Bedroom Diary.' Is there something you need to share?"

Rebecca busied herself with unpacking, but her nervous energy prickled the hairs on his neck.

"Did Libby write to you?" Kyle asked.

"Yes, and no."

"Becca!"

She tossed a nightgown in a drawer and slammed it shut. "Okay, okay. Yes. She wrote in using a fake name, but I figured it out."

"With everything going on, shouldn't you have told me?"

"Not really."

"You're serious?"

"It was a private conversation. No one at MOD even knows. I set up a fake email and did it all on the side."

"No one knows?"

"Not even Viraj. It was a private exchange between me and Libby, or actually, between Bedroom Diary and Kika."

Kyle sauntered close, stopping his face an inch from hers. "Really?"

"Yes. I wanted to protect her privacy and didn't want her mixed up in any of the MOD nonsense."

Smart. Rebecca had the forethought to keep Libby safe. He popped a kiss on her forehead. "You're forgiven."

Rebecca cocked her head. "Wait. Keeping Libby's love life private from her brother doesn't warrant forgiveness. We're a couple, but each of us must be free to keep certain things to ourselves. To have agency, including over own lives, including our inner ones."

Rebecca had a point. Kyle was so new to sharing his secrets. Who was he to begrudge Rebecca the privacy and space she and

Libby deserved? He'd have to be mindful of that as they moved forward into the next phase of their relationship.

They continued unpacking, then dressed for the rehearsal dinner. But as they headed out, his cell buzzed with a call from Marco.

Rebecca stood with her hand on the doorknob.

"I've got to take this. I'll meet you downstairs," Kyle said.

"I can wait," Rebecca said.

"No, go ahead. I'll be along."

Rebecca paused for a skeptical moment, likely replaying their last conversation about personal privacy. Once the door closed, Kyle answered.

"This can't be good."

"You asked me to call if our mutual friend was up to anything," Marco said.

"And?"

"I saw her leave the wardrobe closet with her stylist. She's doing a sit-down interview with one of the networks."

Kyle sank onto the room's desk. Would that woman never give them a moment's peace?

"When?"

"This weekend sometime. You now know all I do. Were it more, it'd be better."

"Thanks for letting me know. Call back if you learn more?"

"I will," Marco said.

After hanging up, Kyle splashed his face. It was as if Jane knew when he was relaxing into a happy life without her. On cue, she'd reassert herself as a nagging reminder of his former self. But what to do with the little information he had? While glad to know, it wasn't enough intel to form a strategy or take any action.

For all he knew, the interview would happen next week and be unrelated to him and Rebecca. Though given Jane's track record, she likely planned to pad her coffers with more public sympathy at their expense. With such scant information, he couldn't see a reason to alarm Rebecca. Not yet anyway. Kyle opened his dresser drawer to remove his rolled-up duffel, which he refolded and locked in the room's safe before pocketing his key card.

Jane or no Jane, this weekend would be one he'd remember forever.

Rebecca hooked her handbag over her shoulder as she walked to the elevator, slipping the hotel room card into a convenient slot. Her cotton shawl tickled her shoulders as she maneuvered its netting to cover her back.

In the elevator, her phone buzzed.

Vivian:
I'm dying down here. You coming?

Rebecca:
On my way.

Vivian:
Hurry!

Rebecca:
What's up?

Vivian:
Meet me in the lobby in 2.

Rebecca's kitten mules clacked on the cream marble floors, drawing Vivian's attention. But then her head diverted to follow a chiseled man walking across the lobby wearing a navy linen shirt and black slacks.

"The men are so much hotter down here," Vivian said.

"Hadn't noticed," Rebecca said, a third wheel to Vivian's ogle exchange with the mystery man. He toasted Vivian with the glass in his hand and kept walking.

"Before your eyes bug clear out of your head, tell me what's up?"

"I need you to save me from the crazy people in that room." Vivian chugged her wine glass dry.

"What are you talking about? You're the one with the family history."

"Exactly. Hostile territory. Half the people in that room are acting like Kyle and I are still together. The other half know what I did and think I'm scum."

Rebecca creaked a smile. "I'm sure it's not as bad as that."

"Trust me. His mom's cousin, Alyssa, shot daggers through me the moment I arrived. Like, who is this woman? I didn't do anything to her! And his uncle Marvin, his dad's brother, thought Kyle and I were married. Wouldn't he have attended and remembered? How many weddings does this dude go to?"

Rebecca laughed. "Stop it. You seriously need to go to an open mic night."

"Comedians are too smelly and desperate."

"I mean on stage! Not to cruise for dates."

"Oh, yeah. Sorry." She smiled. "It's been a while, if you can't tell."

"Come on. I'll protect you." Rebecca linked arms with Vivian, yanking her through the threshold. But not before checking over her shoulder one last time, hoping Kyle would materialize. Mysterious calls amounted to bad omens in their world.

"Rebecca, dear, you look lovely," Sharon Dillon said, giving her cheek a kiss.

Sharon nodded, gesturing for Rebecca to follow. Vivian released her, but pointed sternly to return.

"I won't intrude to ask about what's happening with all that Stuart business, but our family is happy you're here."

"Thank you. That means a lot. It's been a rough few days."

"He'll need you by his side with all the world bearing down on him. Stay strong, yes?" Sharon squeezed her arm as Libby rushed over, Vivian in tow.

"Can you believe it? Tomorrow! Tomorrow I'm getting married! All the planning, all the work. I never thought this day would come."

"It'll be amazing. Your hard work shows," Vivian said.

"Awww! Viv! That's so sweet!" Libby kissed her on the cheek.

"Who are you and what did you do with Elizabeth Dillon?" Vivian teased.

"Nothing's going to get me down. Not this weekend. Not ever!"

Vivian and Rebecca exchanged glances.

"Hey, Melody! Wait up," Libby called to her bridesmaid and dashed off, but pivoted on her heels. "Come on, girls! We're doing the walk-through."

Rebecca followed the assembly into the reception room, stopping short at the doorway. "Wow."

Hundreds of chairs, each dressed in white satin bows, awaited guests in ruler-straight rows. A wide white runner led down the center aisle to the most stunning huppah she'd ever seen.

Lush greenery and white roses wove throughout the carved wooden trellis, its strong honey-stained lines a lovely contrast to the florals. White ceramic urns flanked the stage, each blooming up to eight-feet high with the same rose-greenery.

"Wow is right," Vivian said.

"Holy shit, Viv. How much money do the Dillons have?"

She leaned in to whisper, "Enough. That huppah probably cost a mint. You should have seen Libby's Bat Mitzvah."

"Welcome, welcome everyone! I'm Jerome, the Dillons' planner, and we're so happy to welcome you here tonight for our wedding rehearsal."

Jerome's cleanly shaved mahogany head framed a broad smile twinkling almost as brightly as his diamond-stud earrings.

Wrapped in a cranberry silk suit over a black shirt and bow tie, his fashion sense gave Barbara's a serious run for her money.

"Now, this is truly a rehearsal, people, so if you'll gather here up front, you'll see markers on the floor noting where you assemble after the processional."

They nudged forward and, sure enough, translucent stickers on the cream carpet displayed each bridal party member's name. Rebecca found hers at the end of the line behind Melody.

"Let's each come up and stand on your marker. That way, you'll know where you'll be walking to when we go back to reenter." Jerome's voice commanded attention. He'd transform them from wandering sheep into a fine wedding crew in no time.

As he described the entry, the empty spot behind Evan's best man screamed at her.

Kyle's place.

What was keeping him?

Jerome handed each of them a wooden dowel to hold vertically, practicing their posture as they headed back down the aisle. The groomsmen returned first, walking older female relatives down the aisle to their seats.

The flower girl practiced dropping imaginary petals, her excitement evident. The ring bearer followed, but Evan had to coax him up to the stage, where he got a high-five before being ushered away by his mom.

Trumpets blared, announcing the bride and jarring Rebecca's wits clear out of her head. As her pulse settled back down, Vivian craned her head around from the back of the line.

"Trumpets? When did you add those?"

"Shush!" Libby called from the rear, where she stood next to her dad.

But Libby didn't just smile back. She beamed, wearing a white lace cocktail dress, pearls, and a grin for the ages.

Being on site, all dressed up with guests in high spirits, made all the drama worthwhile. The wedding would be lovely, and far grander than she'd stage for herself. Her and Kyle's wedding would be modest. And definitely without a huppah costing $60,000.

What was she saying?

They hadn't even discussed marriage, let alone the right amount to spend on a wedding trellis.

Rebecca fisted her dowel for dear life, using its solidness to calm the nausea pulsing her body.

"Bad time to hurl, Sloane. Not your wedding," she thought as the bridesmaids made their way forward.

"Step, together. Step, together." Jerome called from the stage. "Use the music to guide your pace. Grace. Poise. That's it… You'll be fabulous tomorrow, ladies."

As the rabbi ran through the ceremony, Rebecca's focus drifted to the back of the room. Kyle leaned in the doorway watching the proceedings. He wiped a tear away, straightened his sports jacket, then plastered a smile on his face before jogging down the aisle to take his place with the groomsmen.

Rebecca sought his attention, shooting every bit of telepathic energy she could muster straight his way. But when he looked up, he feigned a smile and refocused on Libby and Evan, who stood under the huppah. Not an hour before, Rebecca admonished Kyle about the need for each of them to have space to hold private thoughts. She never expected to regret her words this quickly.

39

Forking her scrambled eggs the next morning in the dining room, Rebecca wondered what had altered Kyle's mood.

After the rehearsal, he'd mingled with relatives and family friends, introducing her around, but staying uncharacteristically quiet. She'd find him observing her as she spoke, wearing a shy grin—and more than once, misty eyes. The weight of the public drama might be catching up with him. How draining it must be to put on a brave face for people who believed themselves experts in your life because they read sensational articles online. Or worse, watched a grainy Gala video on the news. Meanwhile, Kyle stayed mum about his mysterious phone call.

Today, easy Kyle returned. He queued behind his mom for seconds at the breakfast buffet, whispering something in her ear that made her smile and kiss his cheek.

She lifted her coffee to her lips. "What are you up to?"

"Who's up to what, sunshine?" Vivian said, stopping at her table.

Rebecca shook the question off. "Nothing."

"Good. I'm going to grab coffee and we'd better head upstairs. Libby is about to fizz over with excitement."

"I forgot about the 'glamzone,'" Rebecca air-quoted.

"I've tried to forget, but Libby can't wait to launch our transformation into mounds of curls."

Rebecca grabbed a fist of ringlets. "As if I need to sit in a chair for an hour and a half to get curls?"

"Hey, those are the *wrong kind* of curls. We all need identical curls, and the rest of us are curl-challenged."

"So they're going to straighten my hair and add the curls back?"

"Exactly. They do it for photoshoots all the time."

"Those poor girls."

"And guys."

"And guys."

"Today is all about Libby and making Libby happy, so if she wants us looking like poodles, we'll look like poodles." Vivian sauntered towards the coffee urns.

As much as she wanted today to be about Libby, Kyle's odd behavior distracted her. To any onlooker, he looked relaxed. But something was brewing within the man she loved. Rebecca needed to decipher what.

"Ready to glamp?" Vivian said, returning with a lidded coffee cup.

"Do I have a choice?"

Libby's bridal suite could fit two of her apartments back in New York, with a bedroom, two bathrooms, and an enormous living room, half transformed into a beauty salon. The bride skipped over.

"Isn't this great? I swear, I booked this whole reception around this bridal suite. I mean, a salon right here? Tonight, those pocket walls close and we still have a sizable living room.

Genius, right?"

"A different word comes to mind." Vivian walked past to set her coffee down.

"Good morning, Rebecca!" Libby said.

"G'morning. Happy wedding day," Rebecca replied.

"EEEEE!" Libby clapped, prancing off.

Rebecca caught up to Vivian, who leered at the stylist chair. "Mine is not a face for curls."

"Come, come, girls! Time's a-wasting." Jerome clapped, whisking in with a trail of stylists, followed by a muscular woman in black holding a tray of makeup like a cigarette girl of old.

"Bridesmaids first. Bride, you can sit back and enjoy the transformation. We'll do you last like we talked about so you are fresh as a daisy for your day," Jerome said.

"Yes, sir."

Vivian called over. "She should marry you. I've never seen anyone get Libby to be so obedient."

"Sweetheart, I've had WAY worse than this one." Jerome hiked a thumb in Libby's direction. "I train them all."

"I'll take a bottle of your taming potion, Jerome," Vivian called from her chair, where her stylist was already parting her blond locks into sections.

"I'll add it to your room bill," he hollered over.

After a half hour, Libby calmed down, returning to the comfort of her cellphone. Rebecca's poked out of a side pocket in her bag across the room. But with her mind in a flurry, she wouldn't have registered anything popping across her screen anyway.

"Holy shit!" Libby yelled. "Turn on the TV! Turn on the TV! What time is it?"

Jerome checked his phone. "Nine thirty-seven, why? What's going on?"

"Just turn it on! I'm shaking too hard to try!"

"Yes, yes," Jerome searched for the remote on the coffee table.

"Libby, why the freak out?" Vivian called over.

"Jane Stuart is doing a sit-down interview to talk about Bedroom Diary." Libby clapped.

Rebecca's blood drained. It couldn't be. Not after everything Jane put her and Kyle through. Rebecca's heart raced, making the room spin. Her every instinct screamed to run and hide, but there'd be no escape from the maniac stylist yanking her hair. Rebecca clutched the armrests to steady herself. She could no more stop Jane from detonating her life on national television than she could escape the scalding curling iron searing her scalp.

Vivian shot Rebecca a glance. "Libby, let's not. Turn it off."

"No way. I have a personal stake in this. Jerome, what the fuck?" Libby yelled.

"Hold on, hold on. I can't get it off mute... the remote's not working..."

"Give me that." Libby grabbed the remote and aimed it at the cable box.

"I need to go... please..." Rebecca batted at her stylist over her shoulder, trying to stand, but the woman held firm.

"Don't move or you'll get burned. I'll only be a few more minutes."

She yanked a roll of hair tighter to prove her point, coiling down to the roots. Rebecca's scalp grazed the scorching metal, sending her nerve ending screaming, and her butt back into the chair.

Was Jane paying this woman?

"Shush, everyone!" Libby yelled. "How do I make this louder?"

"Libby, please. Don't do this," Rebecca said.

Libby's attention pinged between the stubborn remote and its TV accomplice. "Quiet. Everyone. Here, I got it."

Jane's voice filled the room, a soft voice she likely penned up in a basement well like Silence of the Lambs:

"…you're right. 'Dear Bedroom Diary' has been a wonderful opportunity for us to connect with women in a deeply personal way. So we were saddened to receive this threat to expose the identity.

"We didn't want to stand for that at MOD and felt obligated to come forward."

"Is that why you've joined us for your first sit-down since revealing your secret role in the breakthrough article and letter column?"

"Yes. I want what we've started to continue. We've brought in a whole new team to keep it going."

"Why'd the old team leave, Jane?" Rebecca yelled.

"Shut it!" Libby said from where she stood, swaying in front of the television.

"Explain the nature of the threat?"

"A former freelancer threatened to expose me as the woman behind the pen name Bedroom Diary and claim the title herself. That was a disgusting lie, so we felt obligated to come forward."

"You failed to mention the person's name at your press conference. Who is this freelance writer? Have you had any additional threats from her?"

"Her name is Rebecca Sloane. We received another threat just yesterday, and we are handling it with the proper authorities."

Rebecca hid behind her hands. Me? She's blaming me? Only a psychopath like Jane could spew such awful lies. Threatening to out her as Bedroom Diary paled in comparison. Now, the world would consider her a criminal, thieving a life story she'd lived herself with the battle scars to prove it. But Jane commanded what mattered: the media. No way Rebecca would keep her job now. The decision wasn't Harry's alone.

"Are you pursuing any legal action against Ms. Sloane?"

"We're considering our options, but expect by exposing the truth, we can end this and move ahead. The column will continue..."

Libby's trembling hand held the remote out to Jerome. "Shut it off. Shut it off now!"

Jerome fumbled, but found the off button, plunging the room into silence.

When Rebecca uncovered her face, every eye on the room trained on her, each pair sporting a mix of curiosity, wonder, and, in Libby's case, disgust.

"How could you? How could you do such a thing?" Libby yelled.

Numbness took hold. It now fell to her to explain away Jane's dumpster of lies. Rebecca threatening Jane? She the victim? The suggestion was beyond ludicrous, but there was nothing funny about Libby's reaction.

"I almost trusted you. That magazine column changed my life, SHE changed my life, and you wanted to take the credit? And threatening her at the same time Kyle is fighting for his dignity? How is that supposed to help him?"

"I didn't threaten anyone. Jane is lying."

"You're disgusting. How can Kyle have brought you into our lives?"

"That's enough!" Vivian hopped out of her chair. "You don't have all the facts, Rebecca—"

"Get out. Rebecca, get out. I want you out of here."

Vivian jumped in front of Rebecca, her palms pushing against Libby's advance.

Jerome pulled Rebecca to her feet, attempting to muscle her out the door while dangling metal clips and half-formed curls clanked against her head.

After everything Rebecca did for Libby, she'd toss her out without a word?

"Libby, please. I can explain!" Rebecca yelled, but Libby had already stormed to her bedroom and slammed the door so hard it rattled on its hinges.

Rebecca wriggled to get away from Jerome, but another assistant joined in, pinning her against the wall while Jerome struggled around her to reach the suite's door.

"Libby! Libby, open up," Vivian yelled, pounding on Libby's door. But Rebecca had more immediate concerns.

The formerly docile wedding planner was all business. His large, manicured fingers clamped into her arm so hard, resisting was futile.

"Time to go. I can't have my bride upset." He maneuvered her toward the door, trying to get it open, but Rebecca blocked his attempts with her body.

"I need a minute alone with Libby. Then I'll go."

"I know who butters my bread, and sweetheart, it ain't you."

With a mighty thrust, he flattened Rebecca against the wall while his professional wrestler of an assistant opened the door and shoved her out in one swift move. Rebecca turned back, but halted in time to avoid the door's room number imprinting on her forehead as it slammed shut.

"Shit." Rebecca grabbed the handle to wiggle in futility.

The carpeted hall stood empty. Just cream carpet and gold sconces casting cones of soft light upwards. No guests to raise eyebrows also meant no one to assist her. With no purse, no phone, and a half-curled head, Rebecca would've looked a fright to anyone watching.

Rebecca gulped air, her chest heaving. What to do now?

Kyle popped to mind. Please be in the room. Please. More than anything, she needed one person in her corner. Rebecca jogged to the stairwell and snapped the metal release bar.

40

Kyle sloshed water around his mouth, swallowed, then switched off the bathroom light. The glow of his phone went out.

Then it buzzed again.

And again.

What the...?

A series of texts flooded in from his mom, dad, and Vivian.

Mom:

What is this story about Rebecca threatening the publisher of *MOD*? Did you know about it?

Dad:

How could you bring this girl into our lives? Today of all days? Call that Jane woman and make her stop.

Vivian: Turn on Channel 10. Jane's on TV.

God bless Vivian.

Kyle clicked the remote and navigated the hotel menus to Channel 10, ignoring the text notifications pinging every second or two. Jane's face filled the screen.

"This can't be good," Kyle said.

He raised the volume.

"Her name is Rebecca Sloane. We received another threat just yesterday, and we are handling it with the proper authorities."

"What!? Jane, you fucking liar! FUCKING A!" Kyle yelled before kicking the trash bin across the room.

"Are you pursuing any legal action against Ms. Sloane?"

"We are considering our options, but by exposing the threat, we expect to end this and move ahead. The column will continue with the same nurturing advice we've been providing to date."

"I'm sure that will be a relief for readers."

"The column is extremely popular, and we encourage readers to continue sending in their letters. Now that you know about my personal involvement in the column, I hope readers will enjoy this extra insight into the mind of Jane Stuart."

Kyle turned off the television. Silence washed over him. All he'd done to protect Rebecca was for nothing. A waste. A total fucking waste. Jane used his protective instincts against him to secure everything she wanted: revenge, Bedroom Diary, and the world's sympathy. She added the extra knife stab for her own twisted pleasure.

He looked at his reflection. Alone in a room when the woman he loved needed him.

But would she still love him? He failed to prevent Jane's treachery and keep Rebecca safe. His heart sank.

He paced the room, fingers laced behind his head. "Fuck it."

Kyle grabbed his key card and raced out into the hall. Libby's suite was two floors up.

He looked in both directions, a red "EXIT" sign marking the stairwell opposite his room. He slammed the door open, then took the stairs two at a time until nearly colliding into Rebecca.

Wearing gray sweats and a mop of curls, her tear-streaked face spoke volumes.

Arms flew around each other, squeezing tight.

"Did you see? Jane said I…" Rebecca said.

"I heard. I'm so sorry. I never should have let you write that article—"

"Look at me." She pulled back. "There was no way to predict this. She's sick and should be in jail."

Kyle stroked her back. "The only factor in our favor is that she's lying."

"That's almost irrelevant. Who will believe us now?" Rebecca said.

Kyle cupped her head. "We'll make them see the truth. The facts are on our side, and soon the masses will be too."

"Do you think so?"

"Yes."

Kyle grabbed her hand and guided her downstairs to their room. Once alone, Rebecca flopped on the bed, hiding her face with her hands.

"How can I show my face at the wedding when Twitter is probably trending #ShameOnRebeccaSloane?"

"The Twitter mob will always bottom feed. Jane's team excels at fanning the flames. We'll set our own pace, regroup, then make some noise ourselves. I promise."

"How can you promise that?"

"Simple: you brought 'Bedroom Diary' to *MOD*. Leslie helped write the article, too. Jane already said you freelanced; she can't very well deny it now."

Rebecca raised onto her elbow. "Go on."

"The way I figure, we have Leslie, Viraj, and whoever Viraj can dig up at *MOD,* and we also have—"

"A contract. God bless Leslie, we have a contract!" Rebecca bounced to her knees on the bed.

"Yes, plus we can check the ownership history of your domain. That'll prove you owned it first."

Rebecca slapped her mouth. "Of course! There's a paper trail. A paper trail of premeditated treachery."

Kyle stroked his stubble. "This is good. A solid plan is forming. We'll fix this. But…"

"But what?" Rebecca asked.

He sat down on the bed next to her. "We're not solving this today."

"Ky, I can't pretend this disaster didn't happen."

"Then don't. You're free of Jane and Bedroom Diary for now. Hold your head high."

"But the rest of the wedding party? Your family? What must they think?"

"We'll tell them. Let's march right up to Libby's suite and come clean to everyone."

"Tell them Jane lied and I'm Bedroom Diary?"

"Yes."

"They'll accuse me of lying."

"I'll back you up. So will Vivian."

She sat, knees bent under. "I did nothing wrong. I keep forgetting that."

"Exactly."

To own her own history, Rebecca must first reclaim Bedroom Diary. Confessing to a hostile crowd wasn't on the wedding itinerary, but she had to start somewhere. Kyle squeezed encouragement into her hands.

"I'll do it."

"Good. I'll text my parents and ask them to join us in Libby's room."

"Your parents?"

"Yes. They're wondering what's going on and deserve to learn the truth from us. I'll be right by your side, today and always."

Rebecca smiled. "That sounds fantastic."

Kyle pulled her to standing and kissed her forehead, her warm head of curls tickling his nose. An odd realization triggered a laugh.

"What's so funny?" Rebecca said, tilting her head back.

"Jane wanted to drive us apart, but she's only brought us closer together."

And her timing couldn't be more perfect.

By the time Rebecca and Kyle arrived, at least 30 people attired in various states of wedding dress clustered around Libby's suite. Soft murmurs hummed in the room. A few guests shrugged or gestured in disbelief, tapping watches. Libby stood to the right, eyes rolled so far up in her head it looked painful. Evan's face filled the phone screen she extended in her hand, enabling him to bear witness without jinxing his bride-to-be by seeing her pre-ceremony. Rebecca owed Vivian major props for coaxing Libby out of the bedroom.

"Breathe," Kyle whispered in her ear.

"Right." She hiccupped an inhale. All her knotted chest would allow, given the nasty eyes glaring her way. Every gaze dripped with contempt or "this better be good" intensity. They'd love nothing better than for Rebecca to face-plant, providing more carnage for their social media feeds. They'd likely get their wish. How was she supposed to unravel the mess of the last eight months for a fuming mob of strangers?

Rebecca swallowed hard.

Kyle's hand squeezed energy into hers. "You've got this. Just tell them the truth."

Rebecca released a cleansing breath and began.

"Today belongs to Libby and Evan. And they deserve our full attention..."

Was that shaky voice hers?

Libby's scowl deepened, but Rebecca pressed on, the room's silence ringing in her ears.

"What Jane Stuart said this morning on TV was a lie. I never threatened to expose her identity as the author behind Bedroom Diary. That would be impossible because Jane is not the author. I am."

Skeptical murmurs erupted.

"I know what you must be thinking. Jane suggested I'd claim credit, but that's what makes her lie so cruel. *MOD* came to me after finding my blog, the original *Bedroom Diary*. They hired me to write an article on the same women's topic. Together with my girlfriend, Leslie Allen, we wrote the original article for the February issue of *MOD*. That article chronicled my personal journey, which I won't get into here.

"*MOD* turned my fear about writing under my name into a marketing gimmick. Their team hyped my work as Bedroom Diary around the globe, building the brand's tangible value. Jane is now trying to claim it for herself in a shameful act of stolen valor."

Power coursed through Rebecca. Rising to her full height, she released Kyle's hand.

"What's worse, it's likely Jane knew about Libby's wedding today..."

Commotion spread across the room.

"Yes, she is making these false accusations, today specifically, to disrupt this wedding and take credit for my life's story. Like I said, Libby and Evan deserve your full attention. It's their day, and they've worked so hard to plan a beautiful experience for us. All I ask is that you not let this slanderous TV stunt distract you from what we all came here to celebrate: Libby and Evan's wedding. I WILL clear my name. But today, we're celebrating. Let's get back to that. Let's focus on love and the future. I know I'm ready. Thanks for listening."

She reached back to touch Kyle. Not feeling him, she turned, but she'd moved out front. Alone. Stepping forward into whatever future presented itself.

Twisted faces in the room scanned her to assess credibility.

Was she fact or fiction?

Should they trust Rebecca, a nobody, or Jane?

One clap started, then others joined. The room thundered with cheers. She did it. She came clean. She stood tall and survived. Instead of scorn, they flocked to her side. The side of truth. With a deep inhale, she sprang her suffocating ties, inviting cleansing air into all the hollow places where shame clung with talons so sharp they pierced her insides. But no more. She blew it all away, and with it, all the fear that kept her watching life from behind laced fingers. For too long, Rebecca refused to let the world see who she really was inside. And by fearing judgment, rejection, and isolation, she suffered all three.

Rather than weakness, she radiated strength.

Her ideas deserved hearing.

Achievement beckoned with a curled finger and this time Rebecca would answer—but on her own terms.

Kyle's embrace squeezed tight. "Amazing."

Rebecca buried her face in Kyle's neck, inhaling the smell of safety. Of love. Unconditional love.

"Rebecca, how awful for you, dear," Sharon Dillon said from behind. She turned to find Kyle's mom standing with wide arms. "Come here."

Sharon wrapped Rebecca in a hug, her energy transferred something Rebecca craved more than anything: acceptance. Acceptance for who she was, faults and all. Kyle piled on from the back, losing Rebecca in a flood of happy tears. Front and back, Dillons wrapped her, just as she'd once been folded in her own parents' arms.

People mulled about the room talking, whispering:

"How awful of Stuart to do this."

"Today? How selfish to ruin a couple's wedding like this."

"This is so wrong. I'm posting to Twitter right away. Let's all do it. #StuartIsLying. #TeamRebecca."

"This is so unfair to Rebecca. People have a right to know Stuart is lying."

The only one avoiding her was Libby. Rebecca searched the crowd before spotting her suite door closed.

The twinge of unfinished business beckoned.

"Excuse me," Rebecca said to Kyle and Sharon. "I need a minute."

Chaos silenced with a door click. Sunlight flooded the white-and-gold wedding chamber with sunlight, complete with a huge canopy bed, towering floral arrangements, and a raven-haired bride sulking at the edge of her bed.

"Hey," Rebecca sat next to her, but Libby shifted her seat three inches away.

"I've never been so humiliated… Are you happy now?" Libby asked.

"Of course not. I only wanted to help."

"Who else has read those letters?"

"No one. Not even Kyle," Rebecca inched closer. "But even before your letter arrived, I guessed you had an issue."

Libby's face drained of all color. "How could you?"

"You dropped breadcrumbs. I only followed along behind and they led me to Kika."

"How could you lie to me? And let it go on for months?"

"Telling you would've accomplished nothing. You would've tossed me from the wedding and never spoken to me again. By keeping it between Bedroom Diary and Kika, you accepted help in a way you never would have accepted from me."

"That's not true…"

"C'mon. You've been bitchy to me from day one. Not once did you give me a chance. No, this was the only way to get through that prickly exterior of yours and get you ready for your wedding night."

Libby opened her mouth to speak, but stopped. Rebecca probably made too much sense to refute.

Truth washed over them as they sat, cleansing the negative energy crackling between them from the start. The sweet fragrance of gardenias registered. Fresh and clean, the flowers signaled everything would be okay. And while not out of the woods yet, Rebecca's soul lightened. But she still had to get Libby's there.

"How can I ever trust you?" Libby said.

"How can you not? I cared enough to get you ready for your wedding night, at risk to myself. I did it privately so no one else at the magazine would know about those email exchanges. They were completely off the MOD server. Look at the reply address, after the very first one. Go ahead."

Wary, Libby retrieved her cellphone from the night stand. Rebecca waited as she tapped through, glancing up intermittently.

"dearbedroomdiary@--.com. I never even noticed," Libby whispered.

Rebecca lay a hand over Libby's. "You can trust me. I only want the best for you, for your family, and for Kyle. I want this day to be the best day of your life. Don't let Jane ruin it."

Libby wrapped Rebecca in a hug. "I'm so sorry. I've been horrible to you."

"Yeah, you have." Rebecca hugged tight. She'd remember this moment for a long time. Their first warm embrace as possible future sisters. How could someone so slight cause so much trouble? But maybe Rebecca had a thing or two to learn from Libby's self-assured approach to life, at least outside of the bedroom.

"Thank you for helping me. I've been afraid for so long. Hiding it. Thinking I'd be found out, but you changed that for me."

Libby pulled back, holding Rebecca's shoulders. "I meant what I said before. 'Dear Bedroom Diary' changed my life, and to think it's been you all along? Crazy, right?"

"That gig is over for me now."

"I don't know what *MOD* will do without you. It won't be the same. I'm sure of it. You must have helped millions of women, couples too."

"Right now, we have a wedding to get ready for." Rebecca kissed Libby on the cheek and stood up.

Libby dabbed her eyes, then followed. "I'll get Jerome and the others. They must be wondering what happened to us."

The duo emerged into the living room where a pre-wedding party had kicked-in during their absence. Having helped themselves to the wet bar, guests stood chatting in small groups sipping from chiseled lead glasses.

Jerome put an end to the chaos with two loud claps. "People, people! We have a wedding today! Please exit the bridal suite and we'll see you in the reception hall promptly at three o'clock. Bridesmaids, you must stay to finish hair and makeup."

Kyle approached, cupping her face for a luscious kiss. "You are lovely without any makeup."

"Tell that to Ms. Sephora over there," Rebecca said, gesturing her head toward a woman slotting an array of makeup brushes into her black apron.

"Ky, get out! We're late as it is," Libby yelled.

"What? Don't I get makeup?"

"Out!!!" Libby pushed her brother out the door, but he got a few choice tickles in, sending his sister wiggling away. "God, you're such a pest."

Rebecca smiled. *Yeah, but he's my pest.*

41

A sea of faces smiled up at Kyle and the groomsmen as they stood on the dais. Strange faces. Among the 300-odd guests Libby invited, Kyle recognized their immediate family, first cousins and uncles, close family friends, and business acquaintances of his parents. The other 100 were mysteries. Perhaps new friends in Texas, or those from Evan's side?

Evan stood in his black tux awaiting his bride, whispering to his best man over his shoulder. The officiant wore a navy suit beneath his tallit and yarmulke, likely a rabbi from Libby's new synagogue. Funny to think of his untamed sister going to services and now becoming a wife. Somehow in all the wedding fuss, the true meaning of the ceremony—the life transition—was just sinking in.

Flashes of them playing on the beach with their Aunt Bessie rushed to mind. So many days of sand and surf, pails and shovels. His aunt sat in the front row, a place of honor given how much she meant to his family. Kyle would be forever grateful for his decision to move back from California to live with her. If not for that, he'd likely never have met Rebecca.

Flute music began, signaling the first member of the bridal procession. Flower girls dropped petals down the aisle to a chorus of oohs and ahhs. Flashes snapped, Kyle's fingers twitched seeking a camera he had to leave back in the dressing room. Later, he'd have a chance to capture the memories he'd want were it his own wedding.

His wedding.

One day.

Not too far off, he hoped.

Rebecca passed into view, pink gown, curls atop her head, her delicate fingers wrapped around a bouquet of cala lilies

Their eyes met, sending a wave of emotion through his body. More than anything, he wanted to knock the bridal party aside and claim the dais for his own. With Rebecca. Just the two of them and be married forever after.

Kyle slipped his hand into his pocket, fingering the velvet box he'd brought from New York.

He exhaled a shot of tension.

When he packed the box, he'd prayed that the right moment would arise to tell her how much she meant to him. How much she'd always mean.

Rebecca took her place behind Melody as Vivian followed close behind.

The trumpets signaled everyone to their feet, looking expectantly at the door, where Libby appeared in her silk gown.

What a beauty. Tears welled in Kyle's eyes as his sister glided down the aisle wearing a smile befitting an angel. Her white gloved hand squeezed their dad's arm as he looked down at Libby through tears of his own.

For all her craziness, she had a wonderful heart. Evan brought out the best in her. They had a bright future…

How many times had he been at weddings, scoffing at the weeping guests? He swallowed the lump in his throat and sniffed a smile as his dad handed Libby off to Evan. He shook Evan's hand, pulling him in for an embrace before taking his seat beside his mom.

As the rabbi began, Kyle breathed in the gardenias woven around the huppah. Stunning. Libby had really done a magnificent job. The affair was far more extravagant than he and Rebecca would want. She'd sooner get married in Central Park then go out for Chinese food.

He suppressed a laugh, drawing a curious glance from Rebecca.

Beneath all the curls and primping, his Rebecca lay underneath. Strong. Recovered from a day that would have sent anyone else hiding under a pile of blankets in a dark room. But she braved the spotlight, on stage in electric pink, giving him the stink eye to behave.

He mouthed, "I love you."

She flushed, then looked forward.

Vows and rings exchanged, but Kyle replaced theirs with the vow he longed to profess to Rebecca.

The glass shattered beneath Evan's heel.

"Mazel tov!" The room erupted, clapping and laughing as Libby and Evan kissed, guests whooping as he lifted her up.

The couple led them back up the aisle, followed by the rabbi and the bridal party two by two.

Rebecca grabbed his arm. "I love you too."

"I should hope so," Kyle teased, leading them up the

aisle and out into the foyer, where they would become part of the receiving line.

"I can't wait for us to be alone," Rebecca said.

He wrapped his arm around her waist. "Soon. Soon our jobs will be done and we can enjoy ourselves."

"The guests are coming," Vivian yelled down the line.

He held Rebeca close around her waist, their hips pressed together.

Her eyes darted up to his.

"Ky?"

He squeezed her tight, extending his free hand to shake the first guest's, his father's cousin, Elinor.

"Good to see you. Thanks for coming," Kyle said.

"Lovely ceremony!" Elinor said.

"Yes, yes, it was," Kyle answered. "This is my... girlfriend, Rebecca."

Something hard, small, and square, but not quite square, was in Kyle's pocket. It pressed into Rebecca's side. The shape was unmistakable. It took all her willpower not to stuff her hand in there to feel it herself.

Kyle sported a wide smile as he spoke to the guests. Turning to her, he smashed her hip into the bulge.

She wiggled to scope out the contours.

"This is Rebecca, my... girlfriend," he said.

Rebecca shook hands, the shape pressing into her left side, leaving her right free to shake the hands of stranger after stranger.

But why did he pause when introducing her? It was as if he struggled to remember their relationship to each other. To get the title right. Perhaps, he confused girlfriend with fiancée?

"Rebecca, this is my father's colleague, Frank."

She shook Frank's beefy fingers. "So glad you could make it."

The domed box shifted to its side. No way that wasn't a ring box in Kyle's pocket.

Only one question remained: was it Libby's empty box, or a shiny ring of her own?

"So glad you could come. I'm Libby's brother, Kyle, and this is Rebecca."

Kyle shifted his hand from around her waist to shake hands.

"Nice to meet you. Thank you for coming," Rebecca said, shaking the hands of who-knows-who.

Receiving lines? Why shake hands with every single person who schlepped to the wedding?

In between guests, Rebecca snuck a peek at Kyle's pocket. A bulge protruded beneath where his tux flap tucked inside the pocket. As if his hand fingered something.

There was no reason to toy with an empty box.

Kyle would only handle something valuable.

Something he didn't want to lose.

But maybe it folded in from earlier in the day? An empty box from Libby's rings would make more sense. Evan must have asked him to hold the rings. Or Kyle put them on the ring-bearer's pillow.

Of course. Of course it was Libby's empty box. With all the Jane nonsense swirling, when would Kyle have dashed out to buy a ring? No way he'd bring an engagement ring for Rebecca under circumstances like that. How much sense did that make?

Zero sense, that's how much.

Her legs buckled in disappointment, but she grabbed Kyle's arm for support.

But there it was again. Taunting her. Taunting her with a velvet-box future she hadn't yet earned.

When the next guest came by, she smiled and nodded without shaking hands.

While the bride and groom took photos alone and with their families, the bridesmaids returned to the dressing room. At her station, she reached for her clutch purse, a gift from Libby to all the bridesmaids. It vibrated. Or rather, the phone within did.

Twitter notifications arrived like a stock market ticker, one after the other. Dueling hashtags. For and against her.

She tapped and pressed the Twitter app, sending every app on her iPhone jiggling. She tapped the "X" to delete the app, confirmed, and the vibrations stopped until her phone rang with Barbara's picture.

"Where have you been?"

"In a wedding?"

"Forget that, Rebecca, this is blowing up. Jane making those claims? That woman is nuts."

"Clearly. I need your help. This has to be actionable."

"It's definitely actionable. It's slander. I've worked these cases before for our more high-profile executives. She had both forethought and malice. That won't go in her favor."

"Good. Can you start pulling our case together?"

"Yes, I'm on it," Barbara said.

"Oh, Viraj is ringing through."

"That conversation ought to be good. Go. We'll talk later."

Rebecca switched callers. "Hey, Viraj. Anything interesting happen today?"

"It's outrageous. Jane… we have to do something."

"I agree, but what?"

"You want a megaphone? I'll get you a megaphone. What can I do?"

"I'm at a wedding, so I've had no time to think. But I have to ask: Will this change your status at *MOD*?" Rebecca asked.

"I'm done with *MOD*. I'll quit next week."

"Good. That buys us a little time."

"Time for what?"

"You've worked in magazines your whole career. I'm a newbie. But I'm a newbie with a story that resonates. There's something here. You know it," Rebecca said.

"Yes. There is definitely something here. Readers are clamoring for these stories."

"Then let's give them what they want. You and me. Let's go out on our own. Let's give them the real Bedroom Diary, not the fake one. Jane stole my life story. I want it back."

Viraj grew quiet. Rebecca had nothing to lose, but Viraj did. Besides the same challenges Kyle struggled through, starting a new venture would be a lot to tackle at once. Not to mention the financial hardship they'd both bear until getting settled.

"A fresh start away from Jane?" Viraj said. "I like the sound of that. The letters will be a must. I have a few other ideas I've been tossing together. This isn't the first time I've considered branching out on my own."

"Oh, yeah?" Rebecca asked.

"You can't work at this as long as I have and not notice a few things you'd change if you were ever fortunate enough to be put in charge."

"Well, you're officially in charge. We both are."

"It'll be a lot of work. Are you ready for the commitment?" Viraj asked.

Kyle entered the suite and waved.

"Viraj, I've never been more ready for commitment in my life."

42

The smooth satin of Rebecca's gown slid beneath Kyle's hands as they twirled around the dance floor. Soft jazz filled the room, urging the dancing couples closer. He breathed her in, gliding his hand down the curve of her back to cup her bottom.

Rebecca's soft lips kissed his cheek. "Keep it PG, mister. There are still kids around."

"They've got to learn sometime," Kyle answered, squeezing to emphasize his point.

Her lips sought his, parting to welcome him home, their tongues dancing in time with the music. The night was theirs. No more pictures. No more events or interruptions.

Rebecca's hand stroked his back. "I could stay here forever."

"Right here? On the dance floor?"

"Sure."

"Let them mop around us?"

"Why not?"

"What a rebel you are," Kyle said.

"Only with you. When I'm with you, I feel invincible," Rebecca said.

"Is that so?"

"Absolutely." Kyle twirled Rebecca, fanning out the edge of her dress like a tulip.

"Well," she said, once back in his arms. "I've seen video of you on the catwalk and you can be a rebel yourself."

"Who… ugh, Vivian?"

"Yup."

"Figures. She always found the idea of me modeling clothing sidesplittingly hilarious."

"You look like you, but not. If that makes any sense? Did you ever watch yourself?"

"Had do. We got critiqued. A strut that perfect doesn't fall from heaven. It took effort."

"Well, you made it appear effortless." She smiled up at him.

The band finished their set, and the couples clapped before disbanding to tables to get their things.

He closed his hand around Rebecca's. "Let's go."

"Where?"

"Outside. I need some fresh air."

They walked across the lobby, down a carpeted hall, through the exit door to sneak outside. Thick, humid air greeted them, like it'd rained. But more likely, water vapor from the dripping tropical landscaping was heading skyward.

"It's beautiful out here," Rebecca said.

"I found the garden this morning."

Small lights built into the retaining walls lit their path. The unmistakable splashing sound of cascading water drifted over. Timed at regular intervals, jets of water shot skyward in a random sequence.

Rebecca inhaled sharply. "A fountain! I love fountains."

"I noticed. I've seen those pictures of your trip to Europe with Barbara and Leslie."

"I can't see one without wanting to jump in."

"Well, here's your chance."

"Now?!"

"Why not? No one else is here." He looked around the empty garden.

"My dress…"

"You mean the dress you hate and will never wear again?"

"Well, when you put it that way…" Rebecca said.

"Come on. We'll do it together." Kyle slipped off his shoes and socks.

"You're serious."

"Yes. Come on."

"I don't know…" Rebecca hesitated, spying the garden for witnesses.

Kyle stepped over the edge into the fountain. Inset lights warmed the slippery pavement which rumbled under foot as random jets sprang to life. Mist blew over, cooling his face.

"Oh my God, you really did it." She giggled from behind her hands.

He walked back, arms spread wide. "Don't make me jump into a fountain alone."

"Oh, all right. I can't believe I'm doing this." She slipped off her shoes, looking around.

"Who cares if someone's here? You're a rebel, remember?"

"Words I'll forever regret."

Rebecca sat on the fountain edge and swung her legs over and in. He took her hands in his, bringing his lips to her fingers.

"There's no one I'd rather be in a fountain with."

"There's no one else crazy enough to BE in a fountain with you!" Rebecca said.

He walked backwards toward the jets, water sloshing around their ankles until a powerful jet erupted from underfoot, soaking them instantly from head to toe.

"Ohhhh!" Rebecca screeched, slipping her hands away to clear her eyes. "This is nuts!"

Perfectly timed, Kyle splashed her just as a waist-high jet surfaced.

"Hey!" She splashed him back, laughing as she ran across the fountain to get away, only to get soaked by successive jets.

"I thought you loved fountains!" Kyle yelled, chasing her, but missing her as she dodged columns of water.

"I *think* of climbing in. I don't actually do it!" She laughed.

"You look right at home to me!"

Suddenly all the jets dropped, leaving them alone in a pool of shimmering water, rippling over white lights.

The ground rumbled. Kyle ran across and pulled Rebecca out of the way just as every jet launched skyward with an explosion of water.

Wrapped in each other's arms, Kyle watched the display as reflected in Rebecca's wide eyes. They clung together, drenched, motionless, water teeming around them.

His mouth sought hers, meeting a hungry partner, water dripping down their faces as they stood calf-deep in water.

Nothing existed but them.

They were together.

Sharing this moment.

Wet, but joyous.

Just as they were meant to be.

He pulled his lips away. "Marry me. Marry me and make me the happiest man in the world."

"What? Are you serious?" Rebecca said.

He fumbled in his tux pocket for the ring box. Opening it, he got on one knee, water rippling all around them.

"Rebecca Sloane, would you do me the honor of becoming my wife?"

Rebecca extended a trembling hand for Kyle, who slid the round diamond onto her slippery finger.

"Yes. Yes. Of course! Of course, I'll marry you!" She hopped up and down, holding her ringed hand aloft.

Kyle scooped her into his arms, spinning while kissing her smiling mouth.

"I can't believe it!"

"Believe it."

"Mrs. Dillon. I'll be Mrs. Dillon," she said.

"Yes, you will." She pulled his face to hers, pulling at the tux clinging to his torso.

Kyle carried her to the edge of the fountain and gently put her down, hopping over the edge himself.

He pulled her to her feet on the dry side. "Let's get you out of those wet clothes, shall we?"

Once out of the water, Rebecca's gown clung to her frame like a pair of soaked jeans. Socks stuffed in his pockets, Kyle slipped on his shoes while she bent to hook her sling-back heels around two fingers. She'd sooner throw them away than put them back on. No longer a bridesmaid,

Rebecca was now a bride-to-be.

She held her ringed hand out to Kyle, which he kissed before taking it.

"You have the right idea, the future Mrs. Dillon. My shoes are already full of water."

"I wish it were that perfectly planned!"

Water dripped from Kyle's hair and down his arms, pooling where their hands joined. He looked at her, lifting her hand to his soft lips for a squeaky kiss that sent chills down her arm. It was a sensation she craved and she'd have it whenever she wanted until the end of time.

Her finger wore a ring. Her. Rebecca Sloane. As if hearing her thoughts, the ring sparkled as they passed under the recessed lighting in the hotel lobby.

The few heads mulling about the reception area spun around as they squeaked across the polished floors. A blue-haired patron stood with her mouth agape.

Rebecca stood erect, muffling a laugh with her lips. "The fountain is lovely. You should give it a go."

A bark of a laugh escaped Kyle, but he sucked it back in. At least until they were alone, waiting for the elevator.

"Oh my God, did you catch her face?" Rebecca doubled over laughing.

"The fountain is lovely?" Kyle's warm, rolling laugh closed over her mouth as he smothered her in a kiss.

A chime pinged the elevator's arrival. She padded in behind Kyle, who pressed their floor, then yanked her tight while the doors closed. He pinned her hands over her head, leaning in for her lips.

She arched into him, want spreading from her mouth down her spine. Her shoes tumbled free from her fingers as he went to work on her neck.

"Mmmm…" she purred.

The elevator doors opened, but went ignored until they almost closed again. Kyle shot his foot out in time.

He unlocked their room, then Rebecca made a hasty shuffle to the bathroom, water collecting in sizable puddles on the white tile floor.

"Why didn't you tell me!?" Rebecca yelled after seeing her

reflection. A tuft of tangled hair hung limp as curls escaped their pinned confines to reclaim their natural helix. Mascara, and indeed, all her makeup, streaked down her face like the Joker after a bad acid trip.

"I didn't notice."

"Ky!" she smacked his shoulder.

"I swear, I didn't notice! All I saw was the beautiful woman I love. Here..." Kyle popped a makeup wipe out of the package on the bathroom counter.

"I look awful..." Rebecca pouted.

"Shhh," he said.

Gently, he went to work wiping her face from her eyes and forehead, down her cheeks and her lips, planting gentle kisses behind the trail. He unpinned her hair, running his fingers through to release her locks to the full length.

"This is making me so hot," she said.

"Keep your eyes closed."

Kyle ran the water and moments later a warm washcloth connected with her skin, the terrycloth soft as fleece.

"There. Open your eyes," he said.

Her reflection was back. The madwoman banished forever. She sighed with relief.

"This is who I saw. I saw you."

His fingers found her dress zipper, sliding it down to the nape. She shimmied out of the now damp dress, leaving her in a matching bra, panties, and garter with stockings.

"Fuck, Rebecca..." Kyle stood, mesmerized.

"Would you? Please?" She flung her arms over his shoulders to draw him down to her.

"Gladly." Kyle scooped her up in his arms and carried her to the bed.

He slipped out of his drenched clothes before crawling like a panther toward where she lay in the center of the bed. Her heart pounded so wildly she was sure he could hear it.

"Feel good?" he asked, nibbling her neck.

"You have no idea."

"How much?" He stroked her over her panties.

"Mmm-more than you can imagine."

Tension mounted as he pushed the cloth aside with his fingers.

"How about here?" He kissed her bra aside to nibble.

"Yes…" Rebecca said, breathless.

"And here?" His fingers went to work under her panties.

She inhaled sharply, arching into his breathy whisper on her skin.

"Ahh, you like that."

"Yes."

"I know you do. I know exactly what you like," he said, accelerating his hand.

"Oh my God, don't stop…"

He kept going until… Heat. Warmth. Tension and an unbelievable release radiated from her core, down her legs and out to the tips of her fingers. Everywhere, sending her to another dimension. Transforming their love into pure energy that consumed her in waves until it left her in a panting heap.

Kyle kissed her breathy mouth.

No words came as she lay with her hair tangled across her face. In Rebecca's limp state, she could barely assist Kyle as he slipped down her panties and stockings. He licked her spot, triggering a reflexive arch.

"I want you to wear me and the ring… nothing else."

He entered, exhaling a groan of his own while a pulse of pleasure shot up Rebecca's back.

"You feel so good…" she said.

His breath grew labored the faster they joined in a rhythm

they'd perfected, one giving each of them pleasure. Ecstasy mounted, building until…

Kyle moaned as intense waves pulsed across her own body, melting her brain in a climax far stronger than her first. For a moment, she forgot where she was. Who she was. Then Kyle collapsed on top of her.

Heavy.

Warm.

Hers.

Forever.

The last thing she remembered before sleep took her was twisting the diamond on her finger to be sure it was real.

43

Kyle maneuvered against the tide of reporters filing into the room for Rebecca's press conference. From the looks of it, every major outlet was represented, which boded well for Rebecca's effort to clear her name and put Jane in her rightful place. It took a few weeks to pull it all together, but their patience was about to pay off.

Kyle found a quiet corner in the hall to return Greg's call, the second in the last 20 minutes.

"What's up?" Kyle said, craning his neck to keep a watchful eye on the dais where Leslie, Barbara, and Rebecca would sit.

"Has it started?" Greg asked.

"Not yet, but it's about to. Everything okay?"

"Yes, I just wanted to apologize for not being there in person."

"No worries, I didn't expect you to be here."

Greg sighed. "Good. I wanted to be sure you didn't think I was backing out of the criminal case against Jane."

"You said you were moving ahead, and I trust you to keep your word."

"I will. They said I could come forward anonymously, and I'm comfortable being John Doe #2, at least for now."

Kyle creaked a smile. Rebecca was shedding her anonymous mantle, only to have Greg slip it on. But he had to do what felt right. The criminal case against Jane was growing by the week, with Viraj and two other men coming forward. Even if Greg didn't testify, they would have his deposition for the record. No way Jane was going to squirm her way out of accountability this time.

"You're brave to come forward at all," Kyle said.

"Doesn't feel that way sometimes."

"Because of you, more have come forward and Jane's reign of terror will be over."

"Maybe, but you're the face of this movement, like it or not."

"For the first time in a long time, I don't mind having my face out front. I forgot how much I used to like it. Before Jane took it all away."

"What now for you? Back to business?"

"That, plus Rebecca's new magazine venture. That will keep me busy. And there's a wedding to plan…"

"Must be nice to have that financial buffer with a wedding on the way?"

Kyle hadn't shared the terms of his financial settlement from Valis, but Greg knew enough about it to know it was generous. The offer came swiftly, and he accepted it after conferring with his dad about the terms. A master negotiator in his own right, their opening offer surprised even him. The sum would enable Kyle to grow his business and support Rebecca as she started hers. He tried not to consider the payment as blood money. More like overdue compensation for time served in Jane's pit of despair.

"It'll be a help, for sure."

Shutter clicks exploded as Rebecca and the others took the dais, each pulling out a chair to sit. Rebecca adjusted her microphone, and he saw her looking around and whispering something to Barbara.

"It's starting. Gotta go."

"Good luck. With everything. Don't be a stranger."

Kyle jogged to the front-row seat saved for him, directly opposite Rebecca—right where he belonged.

Jane threw her mouse across the room so hard it shattered her bedroom mirror. Why the hell was she working from her bed? She should be at her desk, making Valis millions of dollars just like she'd done for 33 years. Sacrificing her personal life and free time. Jane hadn't even attended a family funeral in ages. Not since... who? Her crazy aunt with the jet-black hair? What was her name? *Amelia? Agnes?*

She'd dedicated her life to building a publishing empire, only to be tossed aside at the first whiff of trouble. She'd proven her loyalty. Where was theirs?

No due process.

No opportunity to explain her side.

Instant suspension, with firing imminent once the paperwork routed for signatures.

She'd be damned if she'd let them kick her to the curb. But that might happen despite her best efforts. Valis had her dead to rights and would aggressively move in for the kill. That's what she'd do were the roles reversed. Were she in charge, she'd kick the offender to the curb without so much as a thank you.

Damn that harassment training. She'd taken the module annually for years, forced to take a test and sign at the end. That record could undermine her efforts to secure an equitable separation package.

Fired for "cause" my ass.

She shifted her computer onto her lap and woke it out of sleep mode, only to find a red error notice splashed on the screen:

Valis Publishing IT Notification

Your access to Valis Publishing hardware and software has been terminated. A return, postage paid, envelope will arrive in one to three days for you to return company property currently in your possession.

"Who the fuck do they think I am?"

She yanked the cord out and launched the device at her already shattered mirror. Plastic and glass exploded, littering her bedroom with debris.

Jane stormed to her living room bar, opening the crystal decanter of vodka. So what it if was barely ten in the morning? There wasn't anywhere she needed to be. Not anymore.

The phone on the bar lit up with her publicist's face.

"What?" she screamed, pouring her tall glass full to the rim with Stoli.

"Turn on the TV. There's a press conference you need to see."

Jane hung up without a word.

Turn on the TV. Return your computer. Suddenly everyone presumed to order her around.

Setting her glass on the coffee table, she clicked on her TV, surfing channels until a familiar face filled her screen. Jane collapsed to the floor, clutching her head, waling in disbelief.

"No. No, no, no, no no…"

The station's on-screen chyron said it all:

Disgraced editor, Jane Stuart, out at MOD. *Five victims come forward. Sloane to speak; clear name*

Rebecca sat at the long dais facing the room, heart thumping so hard, she expected cartoon imprints to pump out her blouse. Dread flowed through her in equal measure with excitement. After all, she worked like mad to make the press conference happen, with invaluable assistance from many—including Viraj. But the prospect of coming clean to the world terrified her nonetheless.

Leslie sat to her left, Barbara to her right, both emanating confidence and determination. There were no two women she'd rather have by her side as they brought this painful chapter to a close.

When all was ready, Leslie stood up.

"Thank you to everyone for joining us today. My name is Leslie Allen and I'm an award-winning journalist and coauthor of the 'Bedroom Diary' article that ran in the February issue of *MOD*. It was a deeply personal story about women who experience trouble climaxing in bed. We mixed reputable research on the topic with a distinctly personal journey to a more fulfilling existence, based on the life of my coauthor, Rebecca Sloane. She brought expertise to the story from her work with renown sex coach, Heidi Quinn."

Murmurs spread across the room at the mention of Heidi's name.

"Rebecca and I worked for months to craft an entertaining and informative piece that likewise conveyed the painful truths of her struggle. We collaborated on the article, honoring the terms of our contract with *MOD*. Jane Stuart had no involvement in drafting the article and was never its subject. That honor goes to Rebecca Sloane."

Rebecca leaned forward to her mic. She looked for Kyle's face in the front row as she twirled the now familiar ring around her finger under the table. After a deep breath, she began the commentary she'd practiced for two weeks.

"I wanted to share my story with the world, but feared using my name. I didn't know how the topic would be received and whether my frank account would create professional challenges for me at work. People don't talk about orgasms in public, and they certainly don't talk about NOT having orgasms in public…"

A chuckle waved the room, which Rebecca joined. The welcome tension release fueled her on.

"That's when we decided to use my personal blog of the same name, 'Bedroom Diary,' for the *MOD* article. *MOD* leveraged my fear of public exposure and used it as a marketing gimmick to fuel interest in the article. And it worked. Our article earned 120,000,000 hits worldwide, and a flood of reader letters followed.

"Given the response, I contracted to stay on and write a column answering select reader letters under the guidance of then *MOD* editor Viraj Gupta. This is the true origin of *MOD*'s 'Dear Bedroom Diary' column. I am the real and undisputed author known as Bedroom Diary, not Ms. Stuart, as she claims."

Murmurs returned.

"Our contracts prove it, and our notarized affidavits from MOD employees involved in the effort attest that I am the original author. We will now connect live to yet another witness who can further verify my account."

The monitor to Leslie's left blinked to life, and Heidi Quinn's tanned, freckled face filled the screen. More gray streaked her trademark red hair then when she left, but her insuppressible confidence beamed across the miles.

"Hello! This is Heidi Quinn speaking to you from my wildlife retreat in Maasai Mara National Reserve in Kenya, where I've been for over a year. I am here to set the record straight. I can 100 percent confirm that Rebecca Sloane is the genuine source of the content for *Bedroom Diary*. As a successful former client, she approached my office to find more voices willing to talk about their experiences for their *MOD* article. After we respectfully declined, Rebecca pressed forward on her own. Now I'll confess, I'm disappointed in Rebecca. Disappointed that she didn't feel comfortable using her own name. I've been in this business for decades, and there's no shame in having trouble achieving an orgasm. There's only shame in not seeking help when help is available.

"Rebecca could have avoided the whole mess if she'd just been honest about her experiences from the beginning and used her own name. But I'll be damned if I'll let a courageous woman like Rebecca be slandered. What I can tell you is that Rebecca was a star client of mine and I have never met Jane Stuart in my life."

The screen went silent and Barbara rose. "My name is Barbara Washington and I'm Ms. Sloane's attorney. We have sought and received a formal retraction and apology from *MOD*, which the board of directors of Valis Publishing has provided. They also provided compensation to Ms. Sloane, along with covering legal fees. Their statement reads in part, 'After an internal investigation into the matters at hand, we determined, conclusively, that Rebecca Sloane is, in fact, the original source for the "Bedroom Diary" article as featured in the pages of *MOD* and the "Dear Bedroom Diaries" letter column running on the MOD website. We extend our humblest apologies to Ms. Sloane for the shameful behavior of Ms. Stuart, who is now on unpaid suspension pending a formal separation agreement.'"

Murmurs threatened to drown Barbara's voice, so she raised hers until they quieted. "'Under the circumstances, we decided to cease publication of the "Dear Bedroom Diary" column and have reverted ownership of the domain and sizable social accounts to Ms. Sloane.'"

Barbara nodded to Rebecca, who leaned into her microphone, "And while what Jane Stuart did was a shameful lie, the authentic needs of women will not go unanswered. Today, we are also announcing the launch of a new online magazine we're calling *Dear Diary*. Women can direct letters to letters@deardiary and their questions will be answered. *Dear Diary* will grow over time to feature lifestyle articles and investigative journalism on topics of critical importance to women. We will now open the floor to questions."

Arms shot up, shouts ensued, but Barbara handled them one by one with grace. She called on a reporter in the front row.

"Is it true that others have come forward to file charges against Jane Stuart?"

"We won't be addressing the criminal case against Ms. Stuart or commenting on the five victims who have come forward. You can address those questions to the District Attorney of the Southern District of New York."

"One follow-up," the reporter yelled. "Can you comment on the financial settlement reached between Ms. Sloane's fiancé and Valis Publishing?"

"Sorry, no. The terms of the settlement are not public," Barbara added.

The frenzy continued, but Rebecca sat as Barbara fielded the questions. Rebecca only answered what she wanted to answer. She was now the master of her own life. Her voice, her choice. She had no idea what the future held, but was excited to embrace whatever came. Beginning with Kyle. Finding his supportive face in the chaos, she sat up tall, proud to no longer be anonymous.

Author's Note

What We Never Say brings the issue of male survivors of unwanted sexual experiences to the fore in a way we, as a society, rarely discuss. The US Centers for Disease Control (CDC) estimates between one in six to one in eight men fall victim to sexual abuse or assault in their lifetimes. Whether the abuse happens in childhood or as an adult, the scars are deep and slow to heal.

If a man in your life is in need of support, please connect with organizations like 1in6.org, who are dedicated to helping men who have had unwanted or abusive sexual experiences live healthier, happier lives.

Yet it's undeniable that the majority of domestic assault victims are women. One in four women experience domestic violence in their lifetime, often at the hands of someone they know or love. Such was the case for women I know, including a chilling incident I witnessed as a child that haunts me still.

If you are in need of help, organizations like the Rape, Abuse and Incest National Network (RAINN) offer a 24/7 hotline with trained staff to help survivors of domestic violence get the support they need.

We all deserve love, safety, and acceptance. Here's hoping you have all three in your life.

Paulette

Acknowledgements

The writer's journey is a lonely one, but I owe a world of thanks to the many people who supported me along the way.

To my editor, Miranda Darrow of Book MD Editing, whose skilled insight helped me transform the tangled cobwebs in my mind into a work I'm proud to call my own.

To my supremely talented cover designer and formatter, Rena Violet of Covers by Violet. Her instincts and market savvy create a depth and emotion to my covers that leaves me speechless.

She also made my three-character POV reading experience a seamless one. Thank you for saving the day—yet again.

To my proofreader, Diana Cox, of Novel Proofreading, for giving *What We Never Say* a professional finish.

To sensitivity readers Dr. Elena Mikalsen and Carolyn Imperato for your insights about mental health and therapy.

To Markus, my husband and partner in all things, thanks for braving my distraction, tortured musings, and face ever-aglow in screen light. I love you.

To my children, Max and Veronika, who are two of the finest and most loving people in the world. I am better because of you. Thank you for being so supportive of my bumpy writer journey.

To my parents, Martin Rosenblatt and Olga Tobin, for empowering me with the will to do anything.

To my critique partner, Kelly Ralston, who has become a true partner in all things literary. Thank you for being so invested in me, my words, and journey. Your confidence means more than you'll ever know and I can't wait to see your words in print.

To my dear friends Amy D'Alessio and Maureen Jones for helping me mold the story, fix what ailed, and calm frayed nerves.

To Laura Henry, Kate Imhoff, Sara Junghans, and Annemarie Stout for lending your insights and support during what can be a tortured, lonely journey.

To alpha readers Roxanne Media and Stephanie Tajima for giving me your frank ideas and counsel. I'm grateful for the time you spend with my unpolished words!

To the members of WFWA, the Women's Fiction Writers Association, who have welcomed me into the community and are committed to championing a genre that powers publishing, yet is too often ignored.

To the members of the Women's Fiction – Indie Author Support Group who provide invaluable, real-time support when I'm drowning under a pile of publishing tasks and don't know where to turn.

To the WFWA Indie Publishing Group and Every Damn Day Writers Group on Facebook, both wonderful supportive communities who uplift and propel writers forward.

Thank you all for supporting my author journey!

Post a Review

Your feedback helps other readers know my story
is worth reading!

Please take a moment to share your thoughts and leave a
review of *What We Never Say.*

paulettestout.com/review

Keep Reading

Read the novel that started it all:

LOVE, ONLY BETTER
BOLD JOURNEYS – REBECCA

paulettestout.com/buy-books

and the free prequel:

LOVE, ONLY BETTER: ALL ABOUT KYLE

paulettestout.com/free

CPSIA information can be obtained
at www.ICGtesting.com
Printed in the USA
BVHW071048110922
646361BV00003B/15

9 781736 637159